Femme Fatalité

A Lizzy Thorne Spy Novel

COPYRIGHT PAGE

Names: Moser, Edward P., author.
Title: Femme fatalité / Edward P. Moser.
Description: Seattle, Washington : Kindle Direct Publishing, 2025. | Summary: "Allied spies, famous authors, and pro-fascist operatives clash in Washington D.C.'s Georgetown and Embassy Row during the Second World War to control invaluable military codes."— Provided by author.

Identifiers: ISBN 979-8-9878077-2-9
Imprint: Moser Ink. Publications

Subjects: Fiction —Mystery. | Fiction—Crime. | Fiction —Thriller. | Fiction—History. | Fiction—Espionage. | Fiction —Romance. | Washington, D.C.—Travel. | Georgetown —Travel. | History —United States. | History — Second World War. | Politics —United States.

Also by Edward P. Moser

The Old Town Horror: Murder and Theft in America's Most Historic Locale

The Lost History of the Capitol: The Hidden and Tumultuous Saga of Congress and the Capitol Building

The White House's Unruly Neighborhood: Crime, Scandal and Intrigue in the History of Lafayette Square

The Two-Term Jinx!: Why Most Presidents Stumble in Their Second Terms, and How Some Succeed: Volume 1, George Washington–Theodore Roosevelt

Foundering Fathers: What Jefferson, Franklin, and Abigail Adams Saw in Modern D.C.! Second Edition

A to Z of America

Armchair Reader: World War II (contributing author)

The Politically Correct Guide to the Bible

The Politically Correct Guide to American History

Preface

Washington, D.C., and in particular Embassy Row and Georgetown, is the espionage center of the world. Some 175 embassies are in the U.S. capital, and many of their military, commercial, and diplomatic personnel are spies. America spies on them, and they spy on America, seeking to ferret out technological and military secrets, and to influence U.S. policymakers and special interests.

The District became the center of spying with the rise to prominence of the U.S. during the First World War. At that time, German diplomats conducted a wave of sabotage around America, and the U.S. Army set up the nation's first signals intelligence agency. Spy activity intensified during the Second World War, marked by FBI counter-intelligence operations against German operatives, Soviet penetration of the U.S. government, British agents placed in Washington to influence the Franklin Roosevelt Administration, Washington setting up the first U.S. intelligence agency, the OSS, and the U.S. Navy cracking the communications codes of the Imperial Japanese Navy. Another high point of espionage was the Cold War, with the Soviet Union replacing Nazi Germany and the Empire of Japan as the main adversaries. More recently, America has viewed Communist China, and Russia, as the main espionage threats.

This book presents a fictionalized account of one of these high points of spying in the American capital. Namely, the Second World War, in its early stages, and in the locus of espionage centering around Embassy Row. It focuses on a great point of competition among spies in that war: the attempt to decipher military and diplomatic communications codes. The British were successful in breaking the Nazi Enigma machine codes, and in obtaining the codes for the Italian and Vichy French navies, the fleets of two nations then allied with Hitler. Meanwhile the U.S. was able to break Japan's ultra-secret navy codes.

There was considerable fear at the time that Tokyo had learned of the latter exploit which, if that had been the case, might have prevented its great defeat at the Battle of Midway and other major fights. This novel revolves around the notion of an agent working for the German-Japanese Axis who learns of this successful U.S. operation, and the efforts of a daring female spy to thwart him.

A Word on Historical Accuracy

The book is based on actual exploits of a noted female spy of the Second World War. A woman who lived and worked in Georgetown during the time of the novel, in 1941-1942. The Spanish admiral character is also based on a real person. The Argentine character and his code theft scheme are fictional.

Roald Dahl, Ian Fleming, and C.S. Forester, all famous authors, did all work for British intelligence in Washington, D.C at this time. William "Wild Bill" Donovan was setting up the OCI, the future OSS (later the CIA) in spring 1942 as well. "Intrepid," the actual head of MI-6, was often in the U.S. during this period. The FBI's J. Edgar Hoover and Clyde Tolson were investigating a noted female American spy, as well as a suspected, female, Danish spy, and Lt. John F. Kennedy too. During this period, Cissy Patterson and Evalyn Walsh McLean were the doyennes of the capital's social scene, and Fiorella La Guardia did run the Office of Civilian Defense, which did have an office at the James G. Blaine House in Dupont Circle.

The American officials Alger Hiss, Harry Dexter White, and Duncan Lee were moles for Soviet intelligence during the war. Spanish intelligence worked with Imperial Japan out of the latter's shuttered embassy. Ranking State Department officer Sumner Welles had engaged in an illicit solicitation.

The Italian Embassy did order Italian ships in American harbors to be scuttled. The real-life character on which Liz Thorne is based did acquire the Italian Navy's codes, while she resided in Georgetown, and previously did have an important role in helping make sense of the Nazi Enigma coding machine. President Roosevelt did in fact admire the work of this femme fatale. With exceptions, the embassies and other buildings are described as they were. The Argentine Embassy does have a sterling ballroom, used today for flamenco lessons. Martin's Tavern, still a popular bistro, was a hotbed of espionage, foreign and domestic. The U.S. Navy did run a radio station in its temporary barracks on the National Mall to train its cryptanalysts in breaking the Japanese Navy codes. There has been speculation for almost a century about the purpose of the tunnels built near Dupont Circle (and the National Mall) by an eccentric entomologist, as well as suspicions that foreign agents made use of them.

The 14th St. Bridge reconstruction actually took place a year later than described, in mid-1942. Likewise, the OCI was formally set up in summer 1942, although it was informally operating that spring. The Belasco Theater canteen did not officially open until October 1942. Lastly, Harry Hopkins did live at the 34th St. house, but probably somewhat later than described.

Dedication Page

To "white hat" spies, whose exploits, because they are clever at their craft, and at covering their tracks, remain concealed.

Quotation Page

"Wars are not won by respectable methods." – Amy Elizabeth Thorpe, aka Betty Pack

"The exploits of the best spies are never found out." – Anonymous

PROLOGUE: A View to a Thrill

In the early spring of 1942, Aldiche Engardio wanted to get a view of it, and figured the highest point in the city would be best.

On that breezily cool day, the Monument itself, all 555-feet of looming granite and marble, seemed unchanged. Despite the ongoing emergency, the usual throng of tourists, clad in scarves, wool hats, and overcoats on that sunny afternoon, gathered outside in the line for the lift. Soldiers and sailors on leave—the enlisted men and officers, girlfriends and wives, the men in smart dress uniforms, a clutch of ladies in V-neck swing dresses—made up much of the assemblage. They were taking a break before heading back to their encampments, offices, homes. The flags with 48 stars flapping noisily at the base of the Monument, Aldiche thought to himself in his native Spanish, seemed redder, whiter, and bluer than normal.

Despite the declarations of war, the monuments and memorials had been kept open. Good for morale. Instilling a sense of continuity, and boosting the sense of patriotism at a time when everyone was on edge. From the fear of Nazi or Japanese bombings. From the sudden shortages of vegetables, gasoline, apartments—of everything.

Not Aldiche though. As usual during a crisis, he felt a thrill, felt more focused, was grateful for a mission and a renewed sense of purpose.

The elevator was crowded with sailors, jittery tourists, and lobbyists. *Señor* Aldiche Engardio's lean, muscular, 6-foot, 2-inch frame towered over them. The handsome Argentine, his thick, jet-black hair one of his striking features, found the ride to the top almost comically slow, as if people, not machines, were operating the pulleys. The front of the elevator was open to the shaft, so the riders, due to the light of the fluorescent bulbs, could clearly make out the words on the displays of the granite walls facing them. Explaining how the tribute to Washington had been the world's tallest manmade structure when completed 56 years before. How Monsieur Eiffel's construct in Paris had superseded it. How it had taken 100 years to build it, due to political disputes, including a riot over a papal donation of stones for the Monument. An anti-Catholic group back in 1854 had tossed the Pontiff's gifts into the Potomac.

The electric-powered lift, dating from 1901, continued its painfully slow ascent. Some riders wondered if they'd become stuck, and wondered further how they might be rescued. It was the only elevator in the Monument. Would officials have to mount the 900 steps to reach them?

9

They looked at screws fastened to the roof of the lift: Could they escape through an opening there?

All were suddenly jolted hard. Were they stuck? No, an open corridor with more historical displays was revealed before them. They had arrived at the top, at the viewing area.

Fingering the leather case of the Bausch and Lomb binoculars slung around his neck, Aldiche let everyone leave before him. He sauntered past the displays to the observation deck. He wanted to be alone for this. It was possible that someone in the diplomatic community might recognize him. If so, he would play the part of the tourist, of the foreigner curious about America's major memorials.

There were thick glass windows on all four sides. As L'Enfant had envisioned, the Monument gazed out to North, West, South, and East. About half the visitors were looking toward the Capitol Building two miles distant, with its majestic iron rotunda, and the magnificent Library of Congress to its right. The Smithsonian Castle, its reddish stone aglow, was about halfway down on the right, and seemed like a child's toy in comparison. A smaller group looked north at the city's rather pedestrian downtown, the height of its office buildings capped below the height of the Monument. Those onlookers were remarking on the traffic choking the downtown streets. Ever since Pear Harbor, the influx of soldiers, military administrators, and civilian helpers into the capital had brought on gridlock.

A somewhat larger group gazed westward toward the Lincoln Memorial, many with reverence, although some with roots in that Border South town had mixed feelings toward the 16th President. A young boy asked his mom about the buildings to the Memorial's right.

"That's the concert place," she explained in a soft Virginia drawl. "Such a nice place to hear music on a warm summer night. But them darn airplanes flying up from Hoover field make such a racket."

"What's that big building to its right?" asked the boy.

"That's a brewe—that's where they make the beer your father likes so much. The Heinrich Heurich brewing place. They take the water for the beer, I think, right from the river."

The boy held his nose in disgust.

Fewer looked southward. There was not much to see in the vast expanse of farmland that stretched from the river out to the Blue Ridge mountains. One could make out the little Washington National Airport, the new name for the Herbert Hoover aerodrome. And far beyond it, in Alexandria, Virginia, the 333-foot-high George Washington Masonic Temple, the region's other memorial to the first President. Directly across the river was Rosslyn, Virginia, a sad lump of parking lots and low-rise dwellings, rumored to host prostitutes frequented by sailors and Marines from the Washington Navy Yard and its nearby Barracks Row.

That direction did present one startling sight. A gigantic, five-sided construction. It was the new Pentagon, still taking shape. The *Evening-Star* said it would be the world's biggest office building when completed. It takes a lot of people to run a world war.

Aldiche walked slowly to the west windows. What he saw placed between the Washington Monument and the Lincoln Memorial was nothing like the pictures in the tourist brochures. Instead of the scrubby grass of the National Mall, he saw rows of low, cheaply made barracks, some complete, most under construction, that covered almost all the ground between the two famed edifices. Several dozens of these "tempos", or temporary buildings, had been built to house the offices of military personnel.

They were hardly temporary, some having been constructed in 1918, during the Great War, the earlier, global conflict, the one to end all wars. Although that bloodbath had ended 24 years prior, some of the tempos were still there and, after being empty in the interim, had filled again, and for the same purpose.

Their original construction had been supervised, fittingly, by the current Commander-in-Chief. During the Great War, he'd been the de facto Secretary of the Navy, surely a job after that old yachtsman's heart, with the actual Secretary too bored and lazy to fulfill his duties. So Assistant Secretary of the Navy Franklin Delano Roosevelt took control.

A pressing need then was to build offices for the Navy and Army administrators swarming into D.C. He originally thought of building temporary barracks on the ground just south of the White House's South Lawn, on an elliptically shaped patch of turf. But Commander-in-Chief Woodrow Wilson objected to the noise the construction crews would generate. So the barracks were plopped across B St., now named Constitution Avenue, and right onto the Mall. 25 years after their construction, the temporaries remained. Roosevelt had mused that, "I didn't think I would ever be let into the Gates of Heaven, because I had been responsible for desecrating the parks of Washington."

Now in the heat of another war, and another dire shortage of housing and offices, the tempos were being expanded, and would fill almost the entire Mall.

11

Aldiche took out his powerful binoculars, and stared at these structures. Directly below the Monument were two rows of ten, two-story barracks. Constructed of steel and concrete, they looked like the toy blocks of a new Danish company, named Lego. Beyond them was the straight line of the Reflecting Pool reaching to the Lincoln Memorial, and behind it the Memorial Bridge spanning the Potomac in route to Arlington National Cemetery. Between the Pool, a long and shallow artificial lake, and the thick woods of West Potomac Park were about 25 tempos. Aldiche imagined Pierre L'Enfant groaning in his tomb at these grotesque blots on a public green.

To the right of the Pool were more sets of tempos. Closer to the Lincoln were the seven barracks of the oddly named Munitions Buildings. They contained Army offices, not munitions; explosives would have been dangerous to store on the Mall. Aldiche trained his lenses on the roofs, and noticed dark blotches, stains from rain that had pooled there, causing some leaky workplaces within.

Across Constitution Avenue he spotted the new State Department building. It was supposed to have been the new War, Navy, and State Department Building but, as the tempos proved, the military agencies had grown too rapidly to be contained in that space. So it was left to the diplomats and their staff.

Nearer to the Washington Monument, he perceived, were the 10 barracks of the so-called Main Navy Building. Though much smaller than the Army, the Navy had gotten more of the tempos, perhaps due to the influence of the former Acting Navy Secretary-turned-President.

The Argentine eyed the strange little bridges connecting the barracks on either side of the Reflecting Pool, allowing administrators and enlisted personnel to travel back and forth without getting their shoes wet. In the far distance were forest and farmland, and to the right across the Francis Scott Key Bridge the densely populated village of Georgetown.

But it was the thrown-up Navy structures that most interested him. He noticed that five of these tempos appeared to have small constructions on their roofs. He focused the binoculars on these. Two were air vents, possible ducts for the new-fangled air conditioning units that government buildings and movie theaters were starting to install. It was said they might transform the work and living habits of the sweltering Southland town. A third was a construction of unknown purpose, perhaps a utility shed.

But two of the constructs were what Aldiche Engardio was looking for. 'They must be antennas,' he thought. He looked around the viewing area to make sure no one was paying him heed. He increased the magnification of the lenses. Antennas yes, he saw, and next to them, it was clear, a small radio tower. And on the roof of the same tempo. And an adjacent tempo had the same structures.

'Very significant,' he thought. 'Could they be transmitting and receiving? If so, could their purpose be to send and receive messages, not from afar, but to each other?'

If so, they hinted at a purpose which he was striving to confirm. 'The technicians might be sending coded messages to each other,' he reflected. He recalled the information his most valuable contact had provided him: 'So that they can practice *decoding* messages.'

'I wonder,' Aldiche mused, 'if I could get a better look from street level, from B St…No, I probably wouldn't be able to see them well from that angle.' He slipped out his chrome Leica IIIc camera, slipped on the telephoto lens and, after again looking about for anyone eyeing him, snapped pictures of the radio apparatus. He would have the images magnified, then he'd place them in a very safe place.

The tall Argentine put away the camera and binoculars, and headed to the elevator. It was enough surreptitious work for the day. He had seen what he wanted. His great mission was looming ever more important.

But for now, the athletic man longed for some of his favorite exercise—horseback riding.

SECTION 1

THE ENEMY CODES

From Country to City

A year before, in spring 1941, a hefty, 60-year-old, foreign naval officer was driving his Fiat 1500 Cabriolet up the newly built George Washington Parkway. His amber-haired mistress, her large green eyes glowing, leaned against his ribs. Lizzy Thorne cooed, as her long, soft, strong hands gripped the stick shift.

It had been quite the day, away from the bustle, and the possibility of being recognized together, of the congested District. They had driven out to the battlefields of Manassas, Virginia, at the national park established just the year before.

Admiral Ernesto Armando had been intrigued that the federally run park treated the soldiers of both sides as valiant, and that it took a subtly Southern view of the American Civil War. At the giant, equestrian statue of Stonewall Jackson, Liz revealed her upbringing as the daughter of a U.S. Marine officer. And she surprised her lover by speaking knowledgeably about military history. She talked about Jackson's tactic of falling upon an enemy unsuspectingly, from his rear or flank.

"Haha!" Armando exclaimed. "Like Hannibal crossing the Alps, then surprising the Romans on their own soil!" He was interested to learn that not one, but two, major battles had occurred on this turf, called Bull Run by some, and within 13 months of each other. "A most hotly contested place," he remarked to Liz in his moderately accented English. "Like Benghazi and Tobruk today, between the Italians, and Rommel, and the British." And he felt embarrassed, on realizing again that his English had a noticeable lilt, whereas Thorne, as with her French and Italian, spoke Spanish like a native.

After a hike along the twin battle sites, with Admiral Armando huffing and puffing, they climbed back into the red-colored Cabriolet, and drove along a dirt country road speckled with hickory and white ash trees. They stopped at one of the few wineries that had survived the shutdowns of Prohibition. "You Americans, *bien*, well, some of you," he told Liz, "have such a streak, such a puritanical streak!"

They bundled up against a chill wind on a picnic bench, scarves wrapped around their heads to help mask their identities. The Spaniard didn't mind the inferior quality of the American vintage. He stayed diplomatically mum about the hard, rather sour, local cheese. He was just thrilled to spend some hours off with his mistress in a lovely place.

15

In the vineyard's restaurant, he purchased a bottle of Marsala wine as a gift for his appreciative paramour. "As sweet as syrup," he told her, "just like yourself." And he took in her reddish-brown hair, with its unusual light tint, which reminded him of Galician beauties in the northwest vastness of his native land.

After their rustic idyl, the drive back through Alexandria, Virginia had been disappointing. The historic town hall quarter of the colonial and antebellum town had turned seedy, its centuries-old townhomes and brick businesses were faded. Further, its waterfront Torpedo Factory from the Great War, speckled with laborers transforming the installation into a working armaments plant again, was a sad intrusion of reality. And the narrow streets, laid out in 1749, and the many lorries carrying military material to the riverfront, made driving difficult.

But their mood lightened after turning onto the Parkway. Constructed by the Herbert Hoover Administration in the early 1930s, its engineers had carefully sculpted it to follow the lay of the land, namely, the tidal flats along the sparkling Potomac. The first speckling of spring flowers gave it a hopeful look. Sidling the road on their left was the long-abandoned canal, overgrown with vegetation, which had run down from Georgetown.

Despite the chill, Armando rolled down the windows of the scarlet-toned Fiat, a gift from his wealthy wife, who resided in their native land during his overseas postings. The duo sucked in the bracing air and cuddled closer. The admiral, Generalissimo Franco's naval attaché in Washington, let Lizzy shift the stick back and forth from third to second gear and back again, her green-tinted fingernails tapping on the instrument, her full lips quivering.

Elise "Lizzy" Amelia Thorne wondered if the time had come to make her special request. She almost had back at the vineyard. Armando had reminisced about his volunteering for Italy during the Great War, when he'd led a force of torpedo boats against an Austrian-Hungarian battleship in the Adriatic. "Mosquitoes against a bear," he recalled, "and the mosquitoes won!"

But a spattering of rain had ruined that moment. Then they'd been interrupted by a local matriarch, who couldn't stop talking about her long-ago trip through the Dolomites.

They approached Washington National Airport. Its tarmac appeared like a light-gray blanket thrown up against the river. The road congested from cars entering and leaving the aerodrome. Federal managers, contractors, foreign bigwigs, and Army officers were flying in and out of National in the newfangled Boeing Stratoliners. Their pressurized cabins were transforming air travel.

The busy highway, one of the region's laughably inadequate roads, congealed even more. They winded their way past buses full of female armament workers, taxies crammed with serious-looking colonels, vegetable trucks carrying their wares from Virginia farms, frustrated salesmen in their Chevrolet Coupes, a white-tired Packard hearse heading to the national cemetery, and troop trucks out of Fort Belvoir. Ernesto's face fell, Lizzy noted, and she knew the reason. He often reflected on the human cost of war, which in this case could mean the end of their relationship.

The gridlock was bad enough, but the stench made it nearly intolerable. The airport, stuck in a no man's land of slums and weathered warehouses between Alexandria and Washington, adjoined a town dump. Its emanations rolled over the vehicles, and mixed with the stale smell of the polluted Potomac at low tide.

The scent was worsened by a fire burning among the trash. A northwesterly breeze blew smoke over the runways, obscuring the view of take-offs and landings. Armando and his lady friend hurriedly rolled up the windows, but the odor still permeated their vehicle.

The Fiat 1500 edged past the center of the airfields. Ernesto Armando was astonished to see Negro children running across the tarmac, not far from the whirling propellers of passenger planes. Lizzy pointed to the kids' destination: "There's the amusement park, kitty-corner from the dump."

"Kitty Corn?" Ernesto asked. His peering eyes, deeply set, and framed by large, dark eyebrows, widened. "What a place for amusement!" he cried. The naval attaché wondered how many children had been maimed or killed there. They noticed two urchins, a brother and his little sister from the look of them, racing across the asphalt field, tripping and falling over a concrete block, then rising up to flee the approach of a small, single-engine plane.

The driver and his lover left behind the weird aerodrome and its adjacent, thrown-together facilities. Ahead of them was the Highway Bridge running across the river into downtown's 14th St. Thirty-six years before, it had replaced the bridge once ordered by President Jefferson to spur commerce between the capital and its adjoining state. Fittingly, the white marble dome of the Jefferson Memorial, just completed, gleamed at the bridge's terminus. Still, an ugly construction site yet surrounded its base. Ernesto momentarily thought of America's first foreign war, waged by Jefferson more than century before against the Barbary Pirates, off the Mediterranean shores of the admiral's homeland. 'Would American warships,' he wondered, 'soon be off the coast of Spain?

A convoy of vehicles coated in Army olive-green filled the span's two narrow lanes, which were grossly insufficient for the military buildup. With vigor, workmen and engineers were laying down several dozen pontoons, to support a new span alongside. Ernesto had learned from a contact inside the War Department that the Americans were building the bridge for troops to move rapidly about the capital region. The Great Depression was finally ending, as America geared up for another, seemingly inevitable, conflict.

The admiral's spirit sank from all the martial hubbub.

"What a blunder by Il Duce!' he exclaimed. "Why didn't he keep Italy neutral, as in the Great War, until it became clear which side offered his nation the greatest advantages! He should have stayed out of it like our Caudillo, Franco. The Generalissimo is playing the belligerents off against each other, letting us heal from our Civil War."

"Fighting in North Africa was one thing," he went on, turning to his amour, "to seize land from the arrogant English. But for Italy to soon wage war against our beloved America! The foolish Italians may drag us Spaniards into it!"

Liz patted the thick hairs on his right hand, and murmured, "Oh, for our nations to be on the same side! As *we are*, darling."

With a gesture of frustration he fingered his whisk-broom mustache, then placed both hands back on the wheel, while stealing a glance at Lizzy's peerless profile.

She was assured, as ever, confident yet understanding, and impossibly alluring. Thorne looked deeply into his eyes, and as ever the Spaniard felt that she was making him the center of her universe. Democratic America and Fascist Spain might be wary of each other, but he had this American angel in his possession, at least for these few stolen hours!

They looked out Liz's window at a dully-colored bus from D.C. that was disembarking its passengers. Actually, swapping its passengers, Ernesto saw. He had witnessed this maneuver before, but was always amazed at it. Some of the Caucasian passengers got out of the rear of the bus, walked to the entrance door in the front, and got back inside. At the same time, some of the Negro passengers, equally impassive, got out of the same front entrance and walked to the rear entrance, to get back inside. As soon as a bus left the District for Virginia, the Jim Crow laws on segregated transport kicked in, and the passengers had to obey them.

'Who was this Jim Crow fellow?' Ernesto wondered. He was reminded of the strict separation between peasants and his fellow aristocrats in his native province of Extremadura. But the strict separation of peons and gentry in the public places and transports of his home country was unimaginable.

The traffic picked up again briefly, and Ernesto relaxed. Liz stroked his right thigh, and heard him sigh with delight. But the traffic crawled to a standstill again, clogging up before the strange and mammoth edifice up ahead to their left. They saw the Army convoy arching toward it.

The duo could make out just one side of the low, concrete edifice, though they knew of course it had five sides. A whole neighborhood had been ruthlessly cleared away to provide the space for it. Even a single side of the structure was gigantic.

Lizzy told Engardio, "It'll replace what was once the world's most spacious structure—the Army, Navy, and State Department Building by the White House." Ernesto saddened at the thought, and at his growing fear his nation's allies would take on a sleeping giant, a foe far too large to defeat.

The pageant of vehicles rolling steadily off the Highway Bridge swung toward the behemoth. "Speaking of that," said Lizzy, in her soft and seductive voice, "*The Washington Times-Herald* had an article last week, on what's in those trucks. They're moving all the furniture and files in the War and Navy Department offices to this new residence."

Ernesto nodded, astonished at the speed with which the thing was being built. He could make out work crews hanging from ropes strung down the outside of the building. They were putting in windows for offices even as military brass began to occupy the rooms within. He had himself read in the *Times-Herald* that the man in charge of this dynamic project was a General Leslie Groves. At the height of the Depression, he had led the building of New York's huge LaGuardia airport. By working closely with the labor unions in that union town, he'd gotten it built in just two years. No doubt Groves would be put in command of another key military project when this Pentagon, as Washingtonians had taken to calling it, was finished.

Traffic eased somewhat as they left the edifice behind, and approached the stately Memorial Bridge. To their left were the long stone walls marking the edge of Arlington National Cemetery, with its several hundred thousand graves, dating from the American Revolution to the Great War. 'No doubt new graves will soon be dug,' Ernesto mused, while fingering the crucifix on his neck. 'For those to fall against the Japanese in the Pacific, perhaps, or the Italians or Germans in the Mediterranean and Europe. And maybe Spaniards as well.'

He was sincerely grieved, for America was practically his adopted country. His wife was from Italy, which the U.S. now considered a "neutral belligerent." She and he had initially seen Mussolini as a savior from the chaos following the Great War. Mrs. Engardio had relatives serving in Italy's armed forces. But she and he had soured on Il Duce, and deeply distrusted the Nazis. They were caught in a bind.

The pressure on Generalissimo Franco to choose one side or the other was immense, the admiral fretted. Spain, with its close military ties to Berlin, might have to take on Britain. Yet another possibility was a war with Germany, which was anxious to seize the key British base at Gibraltar, perhaps by first invading southern Spain with its mighty panzer divisions.

Ernesto thought of the war games in which he'd participated back home. One involved a land-and-sea counterstroke against a German armored thrust through Valencia. Another landed ships and troops against the German-allied, Vichy French colony in Morocco, with the French in turn invading Spanish Sahara. Then there were the exercises of fighting a British—and American—landing in northern Spain's Galicia province, and at the southern, port city of Cádiz.

The admiral knew his country was still weak from its horrific civil strife, which had only ended two years prior. Its army was feeble, its navy second-class, its economy in shambles, its people numb from the internecine slaughter. 'I pray to the Virgin that this dire situation,' he thought, 'never brings the dogs of war to us!'

The Fiat crept across the Memorial Bridge into D.C. The rectangular block of the Lincoln Memorial, a reminder of America's bloodiest conflict, rose before them. "So many echoes of war,' breathed Lizzy, breaking into his thoughts, "and all about us!"

"*Cierto*," nodded the admiral. He reflected on Madrid's intelligence sharing with Rome, especially on the joint effort to share the communication protocols and codes of the Italian and Spanish navies.

This cooperation would be critical if Madrid entered the war on the side of the Axis. It was a most sensitive initiative, one that he could never share with anyone, not even his beloved mistress. 'The electronic codes,' thought Admiral Ernesto Armando. 'Such a new, and strange, kind of war.' One in which radar, tanks with radios, sonar, and encrypted transmissions were critical to winning.

They crossed the west end of the National Mall and Constitution Avenue, and went up 23rd St. To their right was the National Academy of Sciences, set up by Commander-in-Chief Lincoln to develop the weaponry that helped crush the Confederacy. Ernesto pointed across the road and said, "Look, darling, another military outpost." Signs announced a small, U.S. Navy installation atop a hill. Construction workers and excavation machines could be seen at its periphery.

Lizzy smiled, for she knew better. The signs were a deception. In fact, the clump of college-style buildings on the hillock was part of the secretive, and awkwardly named, Office of the Coordinator of Information, or OCI. The fledging intelligence agency soon to recast as the Office of Strategic Services, the OSS, and morphing six years later into the CIA. Liz declined to share this nugget of information with her paramour. There was much else she hid from him.

They passed the non-descript lecture halls and dormitories of George Washington University, so urban compared to the leafy, Ivy League-like campus of Georgetown a mile and a half to the west. Although school was in session, the streets seemed quieter than normal. 'The calm before the storm,' thought Liz. Some in the student body had volunteered for the Army or Navy, and some of the professors were joining up with the military's intelligence or technical agencies.

It was mid-afternoon when they approached Washington Circle, and the equestrian statue of the first Commander-in-Chief. The roundabout there was as clogged as the other traffic roundabouts. The sun was bright, the temperature warmer, and Lizzy deemed this a good place to get out. She squeezed the naval attaché's right hand. "Darling, please let me off here."

"You don't want me to drop you off at O St?" he said in a disappointed tone, referring to her Georgetown address.

"Oh, I suspect," she answered coquettishly, "we'll be rendezvousing there again. Very soon." He blushed from the memory of their trysts.

"And the traffic there," Lizzy explained, "will be worse than anything we encountered today. All those colonels and captains taking up residence in my neighborhood." She kissed him on his cheek, then the lips, then the tongue. He momentarily felt like a teen again.

A blast from the angry driver of an Army truck shook Ernesto Armando from his reverie. Lizzy climbed out of the car with smooth alacrity. "I'll see you soon," she called out. "Contact me even sooner."

She stepped away quickly before the admiral could ask her to linger. He blew out a breath of longing as her form strode onto the lawn, and disappeared behind the giant block of the great general atop his rearing war horse.

Mission Mediterranean

Sometime before, her superiors at Britain's MI-6 had given Lizzy a difficult, even insurmountable, mission. To reacquaint herself with a man from her distant past, and obtain the most sensitive information from him. The man was Ernesto Armando, the naval attaché for Franco's Spanish Embassy.

London was then in a desperate struggle to stop Rommel's Afrika Korps, supplied across the Mediterranean by the Italian Navy, the fifth-largest in the world. It desperately needed the communication codes for Mussolini's fleet to enable the Royal Navy to defeat it.

Fortunately, MI-6 had had an intelligence coup, and it ordered Liz to take advantage of it. Britain's spy agency had learned that elements of Fascist Spain and Italy's intelligence services had been cooperating, and that through these interactions Spain had acquired copies of the Italian Navy's codes. These were deemed vital in the event Madrid entered the war on the side of the Axis, perhaps after a possible British or Anglo-American invasion of Spain.

A set of these codes was kept locked up in the opulent Spanish Embassy a mile north of the White House, on the sprawling grounds of a mansion designed by the architect of New York's Grand Central Station. Liz's task was to somehow convince Armando to turn over these communication ciphers. Thorne had been directed to persuade a man, a military man, decorated in the Great War, and a man whom she hadn't seen in years, to betray his country and his country's ally.

Their earlier, much earlier, relationship had been bizarre. When she was a pre-teen at a New England boarding school, Ernesto had been a diplomat stationed in D.C. He met Liz during a trip to New England, where the 40-year-old envoy became infatuated with the lovely, underage youth.

He arranged to have unusual meetings with her. He made special trips to her school's neighborhood, and they would have lunch together. Nothing overtly physical, mostly just conversation. But he was obviously smitten with her. It was like something out of Nabokov. It was an impossible relationship that was going nowhere, and it came to an end, never to be rekindled, or so it seemed.

Aware of this strange, prior relationship, MI-6—knowing that the war in North Africa, and perhaps the war itself, was at stake—gave Lizzy her marching orders.

As was her habit, she prepared thoroughly for the mission. She read up on everything she could about Admiral Ernesto Armando, in the years since their meetings, and about his decorated service in the Great War. She wracked her brains for memories of their assignations. She poured through dossiers that MI-6 provided her on the other major players at his embassy.

Superb at languages, she knew honing her Spanish would help. She listened to Spanish language records to perfect her pronunciation. She bought a Spanish translation of D.H. Lawrence's *Lady Chatterley's Lover*, and placed pages of it side by side with her own English version. She found this a quick and enjoyable way to better master the vocabulary of a foreign tongue. 'The trick,' she told an acquaintance, "is to get a book that keeps your attention, which makes you want to actually read what happens!" And surely romance of any kind got her attention. She also spent time walking near the embassy, to examine its layout and to observe the personnel and guests entering and leaving.

She determined to meet the admiral, and ascertain if the old magic still flared between them. She knew the aging process gave her an advantage. Elise was now a full-blown woman, stunning in appearance, and more youthful-looking than even her relatively young age. Yet from recent photographs of Armando it was clear he had visibly aged, and had put on considerable weight. Would such a man find such a woman particularly desirable? Quite possibly.

After puzzling over various schemes to meet him "by accident," she fell on the direct approach. With the help of her espionage colleagues, she learned his working routine: five or six days a week at the Spanish Embassy, staying late one or two of the nights. She herself had been posing as a reporter, and would use that as a cover.

One morning, at 11 am, when he was most likely to be at this desk, perhaps a bit weary and hungry, anticipating lunch, she dialed up the embassy. In her role as a journalist, she got the receptionist. Her guise of reporter, she estimated, would give both him and her a plausible cover if they did meet.

"*Buenos Dias*," she began. "My name is Elise Thorne. I'm a freelance correspondent, with *The Herald Tribune*, and I'm supposed to talk to the Ammiraglio di Squadra, the Admiral of the Squadron, *Señor* Armando, if I may. *Muchas gracias*."

Liz figured the young female receptionist might ask if she had an appointment, and was surprised when the clicking of the line indicated she was being put through.

She heard a familiar voice, albeit in a thicker tone than before.

24

"Eliz, Elise Thorne?" he said, in an accent that sounded like a cross between Spanish and English, as if he was struggling to sound like a fluent English speaker.

"Ernesto," cooed Liz. "It's been so long! I happen to have moved to Washington, and I saw you were working here. And—"

He cleared his throat, and cut her off. "—I cannot, talking to you is, quite impossible," he nearly yelled, sounding frustrated.

"But I'd so love to discuss old times," she replied. "And tell you about my career! I've never forgotten how we—"

"—I cannot talk. I must go."

Lizzy thought hard. "And I know you must be busy. Please reconsider," she said, speaking rapidly before he hung up. "My address is," and she gave her O St. address. She added, enunciating each digit, her phone number. She tried to continue, "And so—"

"—This is impossible," he interrupted, sounding angry. A pause. Then: "Don't call, here. Don't call!"

And the line went dead.

Lizzy put down the phone. "Well, that didn't go well," she muttered. She could call him again, in a day or so, but doubted she'd get through. She thought things over. She could go to the embassy and ask for an interview with him. Though that seemed unlikely to work. For now, she decided to look up the embassy's receptions, and try to meet the admiral at one of them. If he actually saw her, and in an attractive outfit, he might change his mind. She folded her hands in frustration. 'This will take time,' she fretted, 'and MI-6 wants the codes soon!'

The next evening, she was sitting in the living room, desultorily alternating between typing up a report on a suspected female spy she'd been tailing, and skimming through *Lady Chatterley's Lover*.

There came a knock on the door, and she grew worried. She wondered if the woman she'd been following had tracked her back to her home, to demand an explanation. Or was it "Intrepid," as the MI-6 boss in America was codenamed, and who actually had paid her a personal visit about the importance of the codes. Was he coming to pressure her, even to cashier her, about the lack of progress? 'Or,' she fretted, 'was it one General Franco's thugs, upset about my approaching their embassy?!'

Again a knock, a rapping on the door. She thought of the Beretta M1934 which a fellow spy had given her for protection, and which she had hidden in the kitchen. She took a deep breath, willed herself to be calm, walked to the door, and opened it a bit.

In the threshold was Ernesto.

He was wearing a business suit, not his admiral's uniform. He was heavyset, with jowls under his once-youthful chin. His expression was set, a little sad, his dark eyes flittering, examining her. Lizzy took this in and looked, as she always did in meeting a man, to see whether he was wearing a wedding ring. This married man was not.

Her reaction was not completely fake.

"I'm so glad you made it!" She stepped over, hugged him, and kissed him on the cheek.

Ernesto began to take her arms away from his upper back. He hesitated, looked embarrassed, looked sideways to see if anyone on the street had spotted him.

Lizzy understood. "Oh please, come inside!" And she tugged him within. "I'm all alone tonight."

He took her full measure, and said, in good, if accented, English: "You have matured from a beautiful girl into a lovely woman."

Liz took his full measure, and lied: "You haven't changed a bit!"

As Ernesto began to shake his head in disagreement, she stepped up, cupped her hands behind his head, and kissed him again. On the lips.

He didn't push her away this time. Her tongue licked at his teeth. He pushed his tongue to her teeth. She opened them, and he greedily licked her tongue.

The carnal relationship that followed for the next several weeks was not as intimate as its initial passion would suggest.

They would always meet—due to his concerns about being seen with a mistress, a foreigner, and a reporter to boot—at her house. They would have dinner, over fine Italian or Spanish wine that he brought, and an acceptable dinner that she prepared. The food in her home was ample, due to the extra ration cards her handlers had procured for her, to buy coffee, meat, fruit, sugar, and some hard-to-get delicacies. And the two would sip the excellent martinis she prided herself on making.

Then, typically, instead of making love, they would strip down and lay side by side, sometimes on her living room sofa, but more typically on her bed. Stroking and gently kissing and caressing each other, but without Ernesto penetrating her sexually.

The admiral, a worried man disappointed in his life, seemed to seek support and human contact more than physical conquest. Lizzy, who found him unappealing sexually, happily acceded to this.

As she stroked the hair on his chest, she'd let him drone on about his woes. About his failed, loveless marriage. About the pressures and tedium of his embassy work, compared to his prior life on the high seas. And about his sincere regard, love really, for the United States, and his dismay at Mussolini's decision to throw his lot in with Hitler. Now the Italian members of his extended family were intertwined with "the ambitions of that Bohemian, that mere corporal!" the admiral would rage. "Hitler is anti-Christian, he destroys hallowed traditions, he is unhinged!" He was also not pleased with Britain, due to its war with Italy. But also because many British, such as that "irritating scribbler" George Orwell, had fought on the side of the "godless communists" and the "disloyal republicans" during the Spanish Civil War.

Still, his complaints about Germany and his regard for America filled Lizzy with hope. While pretending to be sympathetic about the ongoing tensions between Spain and Britain, she encouraged his pro-American views and his antagonism toward Hitler. And mulled over her next move.

A possibility was to use their renewed friendship to gain access to his embassy. Perhaps under the guise of interviewing the other diplomatic and military personnel there. Could that give her entrée to the embassy's code room? That would entail a complex and risky operation, however. So again, she determined on a direct approach.

But first a startling incident arose.

One evening, Liz was at home, expecting the admiral to visit her after work. She was preparing a dinner of filet mignon, and had acquired a bottle of California sauvignon from a visiting friend. Europeans disdained American wine, but not Ernesto, who in this case, as ever, tolerated all things American. It had been a hectic week of dealing with sudden crises, and he wasn't sure if he could make it. But at a quarter after seven, he appeared on her steps.

He looked haggard, and even heavier than normal.

Liz ushered him inside, embraced him, and sat him down at her small but finely crafted dining table.

"What's the matter, Ernesto?" she soothed. "Let me know your mind. You know I'd help you any way I can."

The admiral refused to reveal his thoughts, only muttering, "I'm just glad to be here." He patted Liz's hands. "You are my refuge." His face grew sadder. "My refuge from this world."

Lizzy's curiosity was aroused. She had to find out what was bothering him. He hadn't mentioned anything about his wife in a while, so she imagined it had to do with work.

And with events in "the world". The Pearl Harbor assault was then still months away, but tensions between Nazi Germany and the U.S., in the Atlantic Ocean, were marked. American warships were protecting convoys to Britain, making them in effect an enemy of Berlin, and of its ally in Rome. U.S. ships had fired on German submarines, and Germany's U-boat commanders were itching for a green light from Hitler to retaliate. Yes, figured Liz, the chances of war breaking out between the U.S. and Germany, and possibly Italy and even Spain, was weighing on her lover's mind. She needed to find out the details.

Thorne knew well his weakness for wine and food. 'And women too,' Lizzy smiled. The food was already cared for. So she prepared a pitcher of her notorious martinis, with more gin than usual, and plied her visitor with them. And poured generous portions of the California wine. When she suggested they forego dessert for her boudoir, he gladly assented. And he was unusually aggressive in bed, releasing all the tensions of the week on her supple body.

They lay in the afterglow, the sheets covering the bottom of their legs and little else. Light from the moon filtered in through a window. Liz had brought the wine bottle in with her, and passed a glass of it to Ernesto. She stroked his chest and arms, but not the fatty girth of his stomach, about which he was sensitive, as the mark of age, of lost youth.

"I'm so glad to see you relax, Ernesto," she said softly. "You must have the weight of the world on you."

He suddenly tensed again. "You have no idea."

"I wish I had some idea," she replied. She paused. "I, I bet I could help."

"Well," he sighed, "there's no harm in telling you, as it's a—how do the French say it? It's an accomplished fact."

"A *fait accompli.*"

"*Si.* Yes. It's done. My contacts at the Italian Embassy have info—" and his voice, suddenly wary, trailed off.

He took a deep breath, as if deciding how to phrase things, and continued. "Tonight, all the Italian ships in your harbors will be scuttled."

Liz was startled, but said nothing. She had to know more.

As war between Italy and Germany and the U.S. approached, 28 Italian merchant ships had been moored in American harbors. Their captains feared capture or sinking by the Royal Navy if they attempted to break for home, so in port they'd remained. Liz knew that, as the U.S. edged closer to an all-out fight with the Axis allies, its War and Navy Departments had considered boarding the ships, as the properties of a belligerent power on American soil. She knew her British colleagues wanted the vessels seized, and turned over to the Royal Navy as supply ships.

"This week," said Ernesto, in a sad tone as he took Liz's hand, "Rome ordered its naval attaché here in Washington, a close friend and colleague of mine, to scuttle the ships. His nation's merchant marine! I feel terrible for him!"

Liz wondered if the attaché had told Armando personally, or if Armando had learned of it by reading Italy's codes.

"He was told," the admiral went on, "that Mussolini would rather destroy the fleet, than have the Americans, or the British, take control of them. My friend argued, if that is the decision, the final decision, then why not at least have them make—how do you say?—make a run for it, a run for the high seas?"

He sucked in his stomach, and for a moment looked like the warrior of old. "At least they would have a chance at escape and, if not, they could go down fighting, like valiant sailors."

Liz, while sipping her glass, tousled the hairs on his chest, and stated sympathetically. "But they refused your friend's advice? His sage advice."

Ernesto nodded quickly and said, "He thought of resigning. But how could he do that, in a crisis, what good would that do? So, he issued the orders two nights ago." He glanced at his watch, struggling to make out the time in the dim light of the room. "And within two hours, all those ships will at the bottom of your harbors."

Liz was stunned at the news. She wanted to race to a phone to tell MI-6, but needed to make a smooth exit. So she kept her breathing steady, and willed herself to maintain a false look of sympathy.

'Those ships must be saved, if possible,' she thought, 'and made part of the Allied merchant fleet!' But racing out of the room to make a call would obviously arouse too much suspicion. She needed to make a graceful exit, and thought of one.

Liz started by telling her lover, with much emotion: "That is so awful, Ernesto, my 'earnest one.' You know, my affection for you and Spain, and even its ally Italy, the Italian people I mean, it is almost, almost, as great as yours for my country.

"Such a terrible loss of ships!" she added. "And for what purpose?"

He patted her hand in silent accord.

"That's a terrible thing," she reiterated, moving her hand from his chest to his forehead, and patting it lightly. "No wonder you look so worried. I knew it, all this week, that something, something terrible, was bothering you. Oh, such loyalty to a friend, your colleague, your comrade in arms. It speaks well for you," she cooed.

She brought her hand back to her glass, and tapped it.

"Ah, this wine. *Le toilette* calls me." She stroked his arm. "But I'll be right back, *mon ami*."

As she left the room she brushed against the door, half-closing it. That would block the sound of her voice from the living room. She reached the table stand and, glancing at the bedroom door, her pulse racing, picked up the phone. She started to dial the number of her MI-6 handler. Then stopped. She remembered, had memorized, the number that Intrepid had given her. In case of an emergency.

This was surely one.

The head of Britain's foreign intelligence agency in America had a reputation he was omnipresent, never slept, and was available around the clock. He didn't disappoint. Liz got ahold of an assistant, an American in fact, in fact a Marine officer she had once flirted with. And within a minute he put her in touch with Intrepid. Glancing furtively over her shoulder at the door, she told him in rapid, whispered tones what she had just learned. Intrepid knew from her manner she was in a tense spot, and told her he understood and would take care of the matter. Then he hung up. They spoke for less than 90 seconds.

Relieved, Liz got up and went to the bathroom. She kept the door open wide, and flushed the toilet. She was supposed to have gone to the toilet, after all. Then she went to the kitchen and filled two glasses of wine. When she returned to the bed, Ernesto was lying down as before, awake and evidently unaware of her conversation.

As she sidled up to him with the wine, to further loosen his tongue and to calm her nerves, he said, "The wine is affecting me as well. I need to use your toilet."

He got up slowly, and wavered a bit walking to the bedroom door, then disappeared. Lizzy lay down, listening for a while, trying to hear the flush. There was none. 'Was it possible that—' She saw him appear at the door, face flushed, with a stricken look. For a moment she thought with panic he might have heard her make the phone call. Only her training and iron nerve kept the expression on her face calm.

"What is it, darling?" she asked in a forced, sympathetic tone.

He gulped, and looked down at the carpet.

"There are two men outside, watching the house!" he said with a note of despair.

Liz slipped out of the bed. She grabbed a sheet and draped it around her sleek form. She took her lover's hand, and she, and he, naked, stepped over toward the living room overlooking O St. Lizzy stood behind a beige drape covering part of the window.

"They're up the street, across the way," Ernesto whispered. "See them?"

Lizzy saw. It was dark out, illuminated just a bit by the streetlights, but it was obvious enough. One man was behind the driver's wheel of a 1938 Ford Standard, parked by the trolley tracks of the cobblestoned street. The lights were out, the engine was on. The other man was on the sidewalk, lounging behind the sedan, and leaning on a streetlamp. Both men wore off-the-rack business suits and ties. Both wore Fedoras.

Lizzy thought, 'G-Men.' Hoover's gumshoes, she strongly suspected, had been following her around for months.

Ernesto thought differently. There was fear in the voice of the old warrior. "I think they're Mussolini's men." He gulped. "They know I'm a friend of Italy's navy attaché. I bet they know I'm no friend of Il Duce. They tap phone lines. During a week like this, they're taking no chances.

"By following every Italian and Spanish diplomat with a military connection!"

He took Liz's hands, his voice desperate.

"If they see that I'm with an American, who they may think is an American spy…" His voice trailed off.

He didn't have to finish his remark. Lizzy knew the security men at Franco and Mussolini's embassies could be as ruthless as the Nazis, or MI-6 for that matter. Perhaps he was overwrought, but it was possible Ernesto might wind up in a shallow grave in Rock Creek or…

"They could toss me in the Potomac," Ernesto said, finishing his lover's thought.

Lizzy stared into the street, careful to keep everything but her green, iridescent eyes behind the drapery. She couldn't tell if the men looked like Spaniards or Italians. It was too dark. In any event they could be G-Men of Latin ancestry. Or somebody else. MI-6? The American OCI? German agents perhaps? Even Japanese agents.

She thought fast. One appeal of her spy house was a backroom entrance, which offered an escape route in a situation like this. A rear window faced a back yard, which in turn led to an alleyway. She turned to the admiral, and took his sweaty hands. "Darling, you can go out, slip out, the backway." He looked at her questioningly. He had always entered and left through the front door.

"Don't worry," she said. "Trust me. Quickly, get dressed."

Ernesto did so, and Lizzy led him to the back room.

Her heart was pounding now. What if these observers had the rear of the house covered? If they were pros, and they looked to be so, that would be an obvious move to make.

They walked to the window. Lizzy peeked through the slats of the blinds toward the yard and the alley fence. She saw no one.

She took her lover's hands again and smiled. Soothingly, like a mother to a young boy, she said, "You'll have to jump down to the yard. And then shimmy over the fence."

"Shim—shim, he?" he asked.

"Shimmy: Climb over. But it's not too far a jump. And the fence is not too high."

Ernesto looked dubious, but was desperate for a chance at escape.

"The alley leads down on the right down to Thirty-Third Street. Just two blocks from Wisconsin Avenue. From there you should be able to flag down a cab, and get back safely to your place."

Liz looked around outside again, saw nobody, and pulled up the blinds and the windowpane. Awkwardly, the admiral hoisted his thick legs onto the sill, and slowly dropped his legs down the outer wall, while nervously holding the sill. He lowered himself partly down the wall.

Thorne worriedly held onto his wrists. If he slipped and fell toward the ground, she didn't know if she could hold his weight. And she might get flipped out of the window herself!

Ernesto looked down anxiously at the dark ground, just eight feet away, but seeming a lot further. He looked up at Liz. He peered at her longingly. 'Like a lost puppy,' she thought. He extended his arms fully, making the drop smaller. He looked up again into her eyes, which glowed in the gloom, giving him strength. He pursed his lips in fearful determination, and let go.

Fortunately there was grass below him, and soft soil. He hit the earth, and fell onto his ample rump. He got to his feet with difficulty, but was unhurt.

Liz waved him to the alley fence. In the dim light, he heard her give instructions in a harsh-sounding whisper. He tried running across the yard, but stumbled in the darkness, fell, bruised a knee, got up, and plodded over to the barrier.

Now came the harder part. He jumped up, and his hands caught, then slipped, from the top of the wooden fence. He came down hard, slightly twisting an ankle. But he got a better idea of the height, and how hard he had to jump. He leapt again, and got a firm grip. But he couldn't pull himself up! And dropped again. He tried again, got a grip again, and relied on his still-strong shoulder muscles. He got to the top.

As Liz peered out anxiously, he nervously got both of his thick legs over to the far side. He cried out, as the points of the fence stuck into his rump.

After a long hesitation, he jumped. It was not a good landing. Liz could deduce that from the dull thump of him hitting the ground. 'Oh God,' she thought, 'What if he breaks a leg? What should I do?

'I know. I'll get to him the same way. Then help him down the alley to a cab!'

But then she heard, faintly, the sound of footsteps going rapidly down the alleyway. He had made it!

Liz felt much relieved, and suddenly felt very tired. Before collapsing on the bed, she took another peek onto O St. The two men were still there; both were now in the car. She waited to see if they took off, and was relieved when they stayed. Her getaway plan had worked. After downing a room-temperature martini, she collapsed onto the bed, and slept deeply until 10 a.m.

The Morning and the Evening After

By 11 a.m., Lizzy had walked the three blocks over to Martin's Tavern off Wisconsin Avenue. Hungry from the previous night's escapade, she lusted for an early lunch. The restaurant at the corner of N St. was dealing with a crush of military officers, support staff, locals, and politicians. Liz saw that, due to the lack of seating, three Army generals had to sit on produce crates before being called to their tables. They seemed like prisoners-of-war: unhappy with their condition, but unable to do anything about it.

Along with top brass, foreign spies frequented the place. Such as Elizabeth Bentley, not yet publicly renouncing her espionage work for Moscow. And Alger Hiss, the State Department officer not yet unmasked as an agent for Stalin. Of course, no one outside their secret circle knew of their actual work.

Liz went through the corner entrance, and a waiter began to greet her, then stuttered in astonishment at her beauty, saying, "Uh, a se—, at seat, ma'am. Ah, oh, our prr-prime, spot, open, is open, right here." And the sallow-faced young man, already on edge from expecting to be called up for the draft, nervously sat her at the first booth from the doorway. He realized he'd forgotten, distracted by the woman's looks, to give her a menu. He grabbed a greasy one, fidgeted while toweling it off, and placed it on the table. Then he ran off to have a busboy scrub her tabletop clean.

Lizzy blinked at the late-morning light filtering in through the street-facing window. An elderly woman was walking across the lane, carefully picking her way through the cobblestones. Winching from ankle pain, she picked up her pace as a trolley car turned the corner from Wisconsin Avenue. A U.S. Marine stepped in front of the electric car, and held up a hand to stop the trolley and let the woman pass safely. Liz smiled at the leatherneck's chivalrous deed.

The waiter returned, still nervous but now feigning confidence, and took her order. Glad that rationing had yet to be extended to champagne, though its price had soared, she asked for a champagne cocktail along with a Western omelet. She felt famished after the episode with the admiral, as well as hungover. The champagne would help with that. For now at least.

A busboy, shirt tail handing out from his starched white tunic, came over and asked, "Morning news, ma'am?" He placed the newspaper next to her fork and knife.

Lizzy was shaken by the headline. It was as if she had awakened from a nightmare, then plunged back into it.

"Italy Scuttles Ships in U.S. Harbor!; Coast Guard, Navy Seize Remnants; Congressman Condemns 'Act of War on Our Soil'…"

Thorne devoured the article, and asked her waiter to bring her another newspaper.

The admiral's narrative, and Intrepid's vow to act quickly, were borne out. Italian sea captains and crews had opened up the hulls of their ships, flooding and wrecking the machinery of the engines. Few if any explosives had been used, but the onrushing water had devastating effects. As the scuttling proceeded, an article stated, "quick-acting Coast Guard personnel who'd been alerted by alarmed locals and observant federal workers," Liz smirked at this, "arrived on the scene of many piers to stop the destruction on our shores. In almost every case, however, the damage had already been done…" The paper got that right. Most of the merchant ships had been badly damaged or rendered useless.

As she finished the articles, Liz downed her omelet, and champagne. Then, a little tipsy, she walked back home.

When an unscheduled knock came on her door early the next evening, Lizzy felt less tense than she normally would have. The thought crossed her mind the FBI, instead of arresting her, might be coming to congratulate her.

However, in the threshold she found a forlorn-looking Ernesto, and in his Navy uniform! He hadn't even bothered to change before coming over. His blue jacket was rumpled, his pale face whiter than usual, his gray hair rumbled and uncombed. His dress shoes were spattered with mud. 'Did he walk all the way over?' thought Lizzy, hiding her shock.

He made no movement toward her. He stood on the narrow front stoop, face down, woebegone. He opened his mouth to speak, then closed it.

Liz was unsure what to do. After hesitating, she stepped down to the admiral, then pulled him by his hands into her home. As she did so, she glanced anxiously up and down O St. for men who might be watching. She saw none.

Inside the doorway, Ernesto fell into her arms. His eyes were teary, his voice almost blubbering. "I had to come here," he said in anguish, sobbing a bit. "To my Golden Girl. The only one I can confide in."

Lizzy felt sympathy for the pathetic man, as well as elation he was about to let her in on some more secrets. She embraced him tightly, and started to lead him to the kitchen table. For one of her martinis. Then decided on a better place, her bedroom.

She took off his jacket, and unbuttoned the tight collar of his shirt, and the shirt buttons. She took off her blouse, while keeping on her brassiere.

She lay alongside him, stroking the gray hairs of his chest. "Tell me, 'Ernest'," she soothed, leaving off the final letter. He liked it when she anglicized his name. "Tell me everything."

The admiral visibly relaxed. He loosened his belt, his large tummy becoming more prominent. "Did you see the newspapers?" he said in a low, questioning tone.

"About the scuttling? And the Americans seizing a few of the ships?" she asked. And Liz ran her fingers down to stroke his stomach. "It was in all the morning editions."

"So you haven't read the afternoon papers." He sighed. "We, I—" He choked on the words, swallowed, and continued. "I fear our relationship, *mi carita*, my golden one, we, are coming, to an end."

"Have they found out about, us?" asked a worried Liz, while keeping her voice even.

"No. As far as I know, no, *carissima*. But your Finance Minister, the Treasury head, has, publicly, called my friend out. My fellow admiral. For scuttling Italy's ships in your harbors. Your official practically calls it an act of war. And calls my dear friend a war criminal. A criminal! And just for taking the right, the logical, actions, on his own ships!"

Liz nestled closer to Ernesto. "But surely any country would have done what, what *Italy* has done." She thought it wise to keep the conversation on Italy, and avoid Spain. "After all, those were, are, Italy's ships."

The admiral sharply nodded. "*Si*. Yes, yes! But that is not what is so bad. He did his duty, his patriotic duty, of course. But your government, your Ministry of State, uh, the State Department, is ordering him out of the country. My dear friend." He groaned. "He's called an 'enemy combatant'. An 'enemy', of the country he loves! He loves America as much as I do!" He swallowed hard.

"Can war with Italy be far off! With my own relatives drawn into it? And probably Spain as well!" he went on, almost whimpering. "After all, Generalissimo Franco is a man of honor! He can never forget how Mussolini, how Italy, firmly supported him when defeating the godless communists in our civil war!"

Liz listened with sympathy. She found his loyalty to his friend touching. Still, she thought the admiral was overreacting, exaggerating things. War with Spain was unlikely for now. As a student of history, Liz knew that Madrid, despite its current, fascist government, had had close trade relations with Britain since the Middle Ages. And feared the destruction a war would bring. London had made thinly veiled threats it would blockade and attack Spanish harbors if Madrid joined in with Hitler. So she strongly suspected Spain would remain a neutral party. So their relationship, and her access to information at the Spanish Embassy, would continue.

In all, she felt sad, for Armando. She felt no love for this faded man, but a certain sympathy. Liz went out to the kitchen, and returned with some drinks. Then she took off the rest of his clothes, and her own, and lay back down on the bed. They would share another encounter together, as physical as he wished. Another favor for a man who could help much with the Allied war effort, and her career.

A Direct Approach

As the British Army's situation in North Africa remained in peril from General Rommel, the MI-6 put heavy pressure on Liz to obtain the Italian Navy's codes. Previously, her handler had been content to Thorne "play out the string," as the Americans phrased it. But as the Afrika Korps threatened Egypt and the Suez Canal, it was time to act.

Time and again, Liz pondered where things stood. The Spanish admiral was firmly under her control. As a lover at least. As a target, she didn't yet know. He was very sympathetic to America. No, he loved it. But did he love it enough to betray his own country? Also, he despised the nation for whom Liz worked, Britain, for waging war near his homeland, in northern Africa and in the Mediterranean. It was an embarrassment the once-almighty Spanish Empire could not defend its own shores. Far worse, a cousin of his wife had been killed in fleet action against a British cruiser, and another relative horribly burned after his plane was shot down by English Spitfires over Tripoli.

Yes, Ernesto had Italian colleagues, and relatives and friends of him and his wife, who had been killed, maimed, or drowned in battles with the British. Oddly, even his Great War experiences as a volunteer for Italy had soured him on London, then Rome's ally. When he was winning his medals for military valor, he'd been dismayed the Royal Navy and British Army, instead of backing Italy in the Alps against Austrian troops, flung its forces into what he considered a fool's errand. Namely, an attack on Turkey and the approaches to Istanbul. A consideration of his that was proven correct, given the disastrous British landings at Gallipoli.

Worse were England's actions at the subsequent peace talks. It failed to back Italy's justifiable claims for the Tyrol region bordering Austria, as well as the Dalmatia coast in the Adriatic Sea. These had had been Italian, actually Roman, back to the time of the Emperors. But at the post-war conferences, London had given the east coast of the Adriatic Sea—Emperor Hadrian's sea!—to the new, jerry-rigged country of Yugoslavia. 'It can't be called a nation," Ernesto had angrily told Liz one evening over dinner and cocktails. "It is made up of at least seven different peoples," he snorted in disgust.

Liz had avoided an argument over Britain, for whom she had more than once risked her life, by never revealing her true feelings about it. While making clear her natural and fervent patriotism for the U.S., and sincere regard for Spain.

Their relationship had so proceeded, and Ernesto's affection and seeming dependence on her had so deepened, that she determined, pressed by her handlers, to try a direct approach to gain the vital codes.

She prepared things well that night. She made a dinner of Eastern Shore mussels, one of his favorite dishes. She selected a bottle of Chenin Blanc of rare vintage. She mixed cocktails that were stronger than usual. She was glad the night was cool and wet, to better encourage cuddling. Liz selected from her clothes closet a green cocktail dress with the hemline above her shapely knees, the top of it revealing a good amount of her bosom. The cologne she selected was Christian Dior white floral. She had first tried it, with romantic success, when she was a prep-school student for a semester in the French province of Champagne.

She had put Ernesto off for almost a week, aiming to stoke his fires of desire. And indeed, that evening, Ernesto was especially lively. At dinner, Lizzy steered the conversation to her father's military service, and how he had acted in effect to buttress Spanish culture against radical forces. How he had fought valorously in the Philippines against the Moro Muslim guerrillas, in tandem with native Catholics he had trained, Liz noted, "Catholics who had inherited their faith from the Spanish arriving in the 16th century." Further, how he had helped stave off a rebellion in Cuba, against extremists with atheist, communist ties, and had aided in putting down criminal gangs in "godless Haiti, the land of voodoo and Santería." Channeling Kipling, she stated, "I feel it is the responsibility of advanced nations like the United States, Spain, and Italy" to bring civilization to such benighted lands.

She then had Armando recount the battles off the Italian and Austrian coasts that had garnered him his military decorations years before.

"You should be serving with Italy's Ariete tank division in Africa," she laughed lightly.

"They're fighting alongside Rommel," he noted.

Her green eyes afforded him a piercing glare. "That overrated 'Desert Fox' would meet his match with you, I wager!"

The admiral replied in a heavy voice, "Well, our Blue Division of volunteers *is* fighting very well in Russia. I'm told German officers esteem those Spanish warriors as much as their own." His thoughts returned to the African theater just across from Spain and Gibraltar. His chunky face and neck looked like a worn statue atop his chest. "Though I am a sea fighter, not a land warrior," he sighed.

"Besides, I so dislike Hitler, his preening, how his propaganda plays up even his smallest success. As your wonderful King James Bible puts it," and he paused, tilting up his broad forehead at the ceiling, 'Pride goeth before the fall.' Liz, eyeing the crucifix half-buried in the hair of his chest, laughed and nodded approval. She rose, and went to the kitchen, and brought back a bottle of Amaretto, with a liquor content approaching 30 percent.

Later, in the bedroom, Ernesto was especially affectionate, and physical. Instead of lying on his back, he placed his amply belly onto her flat stomach, and parted her legs, while caressing her ears with eager lips. Liz felt like a heavy sack of wheat had been plopped atop her intestines, but was glad she had aroused him so. He entered her, and they were in coitus for minutes as he, and she, tried to prolong their communion. He had trouble finishing, but when his manhood softened Lizzy lied that she had never felt more satisfied.

They lay astride each other, the admiral dozing off, and when he awoke they took their customary positions, side by side, with Liz stroking his shoulders and chest.

She estimated the time was ripe for her entreaty.

"Ernest, darling," she began, "you are so good to me, so, so good for me."

"I would do anything for you, *carissima*, my golden one," he answered. It seemed a promising response.

She paused, kept her voice level. "There is one thing you could do for *moi*."

"And what is that?" he said, feeling the most relaxed he had in weeks. "I would do my best."

Liz tickled his stomach, then moved her manicured fingers up to caress the nipples of his chest. She lightly wiggled her feet, the polished toes glinting a bit even in the darkened room.

"I love how, well, I love you, and I love how you love America, my country." She paused, then began again quicky. "I have American friends, who love America, and Spain, and your cousin country Italy too."

Ernesto, though distracted by the massaging, became mildly interested.

"Spain?" he asked.

"Yes. And *Italia*. They want to help both countries."

"And how could they do this?" he queried, puzzled.

Liz wondered if her direct approach had led her directly into a trap. She hesitated, thought of changing the subject, then plunged ahead.

"By getting—codes. Mussolini's, Italian Navy codes."

Ernesto was quiet. He seemed to be thinking, processing her words.

"The communication codes," she added, feeling less confident.

The admiral slid a foot away from her. He propped himself up on his elbows, and said brusquely, "The Italian Navy, the codes, for it?"

Liz didn't like this reaction, but went ahead. "My colleagues, friends, in the American Navy, well, they see America and Italy as allies, natural allies, under different circumstances of course—"

Ernesto cut her off. "—Your friends? Agents for America?" His voice was cold, harsh.

"Well," Liz attempted, "Navy officers. In," she almost said "intelligence," then thought better. "In communications."

The admiral abruptly rose, and swiveled his legs off the bed, his belly bouncing above his thick, hairy thighs.

"Communications," he muttered. "Communications." He rose, walked over to his pants that Liz had pulled off and tossed to the carpet. She was worried what would come next. He was flabby, but still quite strong. She was all alone in an apartment with him.

She needn't have fretted about that, for now at least. After pulling on his trousers, he scooped up his shirt, and strode out of the room. He threw on his shirt and jacket, and walked to the exit. He was leaving, without saying another word.

Liz had to say something, try to make another rendezvous, before he left. She scrambled off the sheets, and ran into the living room, trying, and failing, to grab a robe on the way.

As her lover began to shut the front door behind him, she called out: "But let's try to meet again, here?" Even in the dark, she could see that the side of his face had reddened with anger. "In two days? In—"

And the door slammed shut.

Liz went to the dining table. A half-finished martini was there. She brought the glass to her lips, then put the glass back down, hard, almost cracking the stem.

She buried her face in her hands. She felt emotion welling up, and actual affection, for Ernesto. And shock at a botched operation. She cried like a child for a time. Then chastised herself for losing control of her emotions. She went back to her bed, but was unable to sleep.

After just one day, the waiting was too much. Liz broke a rule of spy craft by contacting a busted contact directly. He reached the Spanish embassy switchboard and, fearful of speaking to

Ernesto, left a message with his receptionist. She said, "Reporter Elise Thorne wanted to speak to him, at his convenience." She explained that a deadline made it impossible for her to speak now, but she could call back later.

He didn't return the call.

Two nights later, Liz had desultorily prepared a dinner, for two. Maybe he would come, as she had pleaded. Likely not. She didn't cook mussels this time, not seafood, but plain chicken. And rice, with mushrooms. *Pollo con arroz* with a few simple add-ons. Ernesto had previously praised her concoction of the standard Spanish dish.

A Spanish dish prepared by an American cook, for the two allies, now evidently estranged.

Liz dressed more conservatively that evening, wearing gray slacks and a long-sleeved cotton blouse. She felt cheap remembering what she had worn when meeting the admiral the last time. It had worked well though. Well, not really. She put out a small bottle of red wine, of middling alcoholic content, and sparkling water.

Thorne tried to figure out what she would do if Ernesto Armando didn't come that evening. He probably wouldn't. Probably never again. She couldn't bear to think of an alternate plan for now. Her head ached at the thought. She thought of going for a walk, up 34th St. to the Georgetown University campus. Its leafy beauty and neo-Gothic architecture usually had a calming effect. She was thinking of what to put on for the stroll when the door knocked. Three times. Like the other times. But lighter this time.

She went to the door thinking. Was it Intrepid? Had he found out somehow? Ernesto? The FBI? She shuddered.

'Maybe it's Mussolini's thugs. If the admiral has betrayed me to them…But he wouldn't, would he?'

Liz took a moment, blanked out the fear. If it were thugs, she would scream. The neighborhood was quiet, but densely populated. She'd draw someone's attention. Or go down fighting if need be.

She slowly opened the door.

Ernesto stood outside, cloaked in a raincoat on a clear evening. Looking sad, contrite, and worried.

Liz hesitated. He hesitated. She took a step forward. So did he. They clasped hands. His were clammy, but very warm. They stepped inside. Ernesto looked into her eyes. Green as ever, but teary, not iridescent. A few tears dripped from his own eyes.

He embraced her. His voice heavy, he said, "There is no way I could stay away from my Golden Girl."

He declined the wine, and the dinner. They went straight to the bedroom.

It was like prior times. He took off his pants and shirt, but kept on his underpants. She took off her slacks, but kept on her panties and bra, and rolled off the nylons she'd obtained on the black market.

After several hours of stroking and petting, and dozing on and off, Liz kept quiet. She thought it wise not to bring up the subject. It was enough, for now, that they had reestablished their relationship. But Ernesto brought it up.

Staring at the ceiling fan, he stated, matter-of-factly, "I cannot give you the codes directly, of course. The Navy codes."

'Directly,' thought Liz hopefully. She waited. He exhaled audibly.

"But I can give you the telephone numbers, the addresses, of the code clerks at the Spanish Embassy."

Liz's eyes brightened in the dark.

"Of the former code clerk, who just retired. But according to my acquaintances there, he would not reveal the codes." Liz's enthusiasm slackened a little.

"And his replacement, an official who's taken over that job for now. He—" the admiral's eyes narrowed. "—He has less, less character. You might *approach* him next." Liz's enthusiasm quickened, along with her surprise at the admiral's implication, by the way he said the word "approach," of her being a *femme fatale*.

Before leaving early that morning, he told her their names and contact information. And wrote them down.

He didn't have to. Liz, with her superb memory, had burned them into her mind, her thoughts already turning to her next move.

Romancing a Rough Romeo

While continuing her affair with the admiral, Liz turned her main attention to acquiring the codes. MI-6 was helpful there. As part of its intelligence research, it'd compiled dossiers of the major and minor players at the Spanish Embassy. As Spain was a potential belligerent, operatives were even tailing some of the embassy personnel.

One morning, an agent did a "brush pass" with Liz at the Peoples Drugs pharmacy on Wisconsin Avenue, a few blocks from her home. It was across from the Dumbarton Theater, which was playing a double feature, *Gone With the Wind* and *Citizen Kane*, both with themes, relevant in a time of war, that things once held dear were about to be swept away. In the cosmetics aisle of the drugstore, the MI-6 operative brushed against Liz, quietly handing her a thick Manila envelope containing documents on the embassy's coding experts.

Back home, she examined a file on the new coder, and the deputy chief of mission, Matías Barbiere, and a thinner set of papers on the recently retired coder, Luis Modesta. Sipping a Chardonnay, Liz poured over the photos, bios, and analyses of the two men. She easily determined whom she would target first.

Luis, age 57, was a short, dour, balding man. 'Ugly,' thought Liz. He was married, with two teenagers and an adult daughter. His wife lived with him and their teenage daughter in an Arlington, Virginia apartment; the adult and the teen boy were back home in Zaragoza, Spain. 'The hinterlands,' thought Liz. 'Who would ever want to live there?'

Luis had cousins, via a grandparent who had married a woman from Naples, who were serving in the Italian Navy and Air Force. Both were fighting, respectively, in the Mediterranean and North Africa.

Luis's life, Liz learned, followed a predictable pattern. A lunch prepared by his wife and consumed at the office almost each day until his retirement. He had taken the Columbia Railway Company trolley across the Potomac from Arlington every working day. He spends weekends with his spouse and daughter, at parks and at an occasional Washington Senators game.

Luis Modesta was apparently faithful to his wife, was not a heavy drinker, and had had a solid work record. His file supported the admiral's, and MI-6's, opinions, that he was loyal to, if not a fanatic about, his work and country. The conclusion was he couldn't be turned.

Yet Liz's emerald eyes glistened at a recent photo of Barbieri. 'Definitely my type,' she smiled.

Matías Barbieri seemed the epitome of a tall, dark, handsome, Latin lover. Lean and lanky, with wavy black hair combed back over his head, which had an eagle-like nose, prominent jaw, and thin cheek bones. A smile with teeth that gleamed like a photographic flashbulb. She checked his dimensions. 6-foot-two, 175 pounds or so. She checked his bio: 34 years old, divorced, no children. A short military record, during the Spanish Civil War, in the tank corps, and the diplomatic corps since. His military service seemed brief, given that four-year, fight-to-the-death melee of General Franco against the Republic. Liz wondered if he had been wounded. No, his dossier gave no indication of that. No known connection to the embassy's intelligence team. He might not even know about the navy codes.

Indeed, as she flicked through his dossier and the MI-6 commentaries, Liz tentatively concluded he might be conventionally patriotic, but was no true believer. He was not a member of Franco's Falange Party, though membership in such was known to aid a diplomat's career. She learned he had run up a modest amount of debt, but came from a Toledo family with money. They were international traders with connections to Peru.

He did have a reputation as a lady's man. 'What a surprise,' Liz smirked, running a hand along the edges of his photo. 'He probably couldn't wait to get out of uniform and into bed. No volunteering to fight in Russia for this *Guapo*.'

She continued reading through the thick file. A social drinker. Enjoys dancing, swimming. Liz found another photo, an attractive one of Barbieri, bare-chested, in swimming trunks.

'This lady for this lady's man,' concluded Liz. 'Matías first. Luis the backup, a distant second.' She mulled over the best ways to meet Barbieri. A typical ruse would be to "run into him" during a reception at his embassy, in her cover as a reporter. But the able researchers and field agents at MI-6 provided another approach.

Matías's life outside work was far more interesting than Luis. He attended concerts at Constitution Hall down from the White House, and at the Belasco Theater off Lafayette Square. He also enjoyed plays at the National Theater up Pennsylvania Avenue from the Treasury. Like Liz, he enjoyed swimming, but there are few lakes in the capital region, and few public pools, so not much swimming could be had. But like a good Spaniard, he loved to eat out late into the evening. His favorite bistros were the New Occidental Hotel restaurant near the National Theater and—Liz brightened at this—luncheons at Martin's Tavern, the restaurant near her house. An agent related he had meals at Martin's several times a week. Sometimes personnel from the embassy accompanied him to the place; more often he dined alone. On at least one occasion he had been seen leaving it with a woman he had met there.

'The most natural thing in the world,' figured Liz, 'to happen to meet 'an acquaintance' at a public house.'

At her behest, MI-6 set up an operation. Its contact within the Spanish embassy phoned her handler at MI-6 whenever Matías left for lunch. The handler contacted an agent waiting outside the embassy. The tail noted whether Matías walked away from the embassy, indicated he was going to a local restaurant, or got into a cab, which at that time of day he almost always took to Martin's. In that case, the tail followed in his own car. At the same time, MI-6 called up Liz, and told her to get ready.

The endeavor quickly hit paydirt. On the third day of surveillance, Matías got into a taxi and took it to Martin's. An MI-6 agent phoned a waiting Liz at her place. She was already "all dolled up." It took her five minutes, wearing a silky dress cut near the knees and Coach brand stiletto shoes, to get to the tavern.

As usual, the place was crowded. She managed to find a seat, and from it she glanced at the row of tables along the windows. There were contractors, engaged couples, military officers, several families, enlisted men, and some WAVES, members of a newly established Naval Reserve for women. But no Matías.

She glanced across the narrow room to the bar. It was crowded, two or three people deep by the rail, making it hard to spot her mark. No waiter asked if he could help her; the help was too busy. She looked up to the small backroom, also crowded. Then she noticed someone—was that the man she had seen at a British Embassy reception? She had been trained at recognizing and remembering faces, a skill with which she was naturally adept. Yes, she knew that aquiline face, and how it evoked quiet confidence. One Ian Fleming, a British naval officer. He was heading back there with some men in civilian clothes, and several American officers, and two British officers, one of them in a Royal Navy uniform, and one in a uniform that Liz didn't recognize. She had thought she knew the outfits of all the militaries. 'Some special branch, I suppose,' she thought. 'Very interesting. British-American military cooperation at a time of 'peace' for America?'

Three men in business suits put down their drinks and made their way to the rear space, evidently to take a booth for lunch. But they were stopped by the maître d, positioned there and not at the restaurant entrance. He sternly shooed them away.

'He's acting more like a military guard than a restaurant worker,' perceived Liz. 'A private room on a very busy day. Hmm. Must be some big shots. Fleming must have a friend or two high up in the pecking order.' She wondered what they were up to. 'A British-American task force of some kind,' she reasoned.

Various such committees had sprung up in the capital. Some believed they were informal discussion groups of British officials and pro-British American citizens. Others, especially on the isolationist side, believed they were a means for FDR to get around the Neutrality Acts forbidding U.S. involvement with the warring nations. 'I'll remember to ask my English colleagues about this,' Liz thought. 'Though I doubt any will tell me, assuming they *do* know.'

Thorne looked over to the bar, peered through the swirl of customers and soldiers—and spotted Matías. He had put an empty whiskey glass on the bar, and was pushing his way over to the tables fronting N St. This was the favored sitting area, with sunlight slipping through the smoky window glass, affording a view of passersby on Wisconsin Avenue.

She saw Matías grab a waiter and point to a table, the very first one by the entrance. The waiter made a negative gesture. The tavern was very noisy, but Liz had a close view of both faces, and put her lipreading skills in play. "I'm sorry, mister," said the server, a short, pale-faced man who could have been a student at Georgetown University, 'but that's reserved for VIPs."

"*I'm a V I P*,' said Matías sharply. He towered over the waiter. "Mexican Embassy," he lied. "I have an important meeting," and he glanced at his watch, "a meeting with your State Department within the hour, and I must eat now!"

The waiter, flustered, said he would check the schedule, then changed his mind and simply sat Matías at his desired place.

'He likes to bluster his way through things,' Liz saw. 'I'll remember that. Yet I wonder why he lied. Maybe because he knew he was being rude, and wanted to cover up his nationality.'

The lanky Spaniard's back was turned away from Liz, and the seat on the side of the booth opposite him was empty. 'An easy approach,' Thorne thought.

As he read the menu, she suddenly appeared above him, smiling her gleaming smile, teeth like white coral, opening and closing her emerald eyes more than usual, her eyelashes flashing.

"Excuse me, sir, I'm sorry, so sorry to interrupt, but are you *Señor* Barbiere?"

The diplomat looked up wide-eyed at the beautiful woman. "I am. But madame," he said, his eyes brightening, pupils dilating, "you have me at a disadvantage."

"I'm Elise, Lizzy, Thorne," she answered. She bent down and Matías reached over the table, and they shook hands. "I recognize you from a diplomatic reception."

"I see," he replied, in good, accented English. He thought a moment. "I have to say I don't remember when or where." He admired her fine clothes and lovingly formed face, which reminded him of a Greek goddess. "And if we did meet, surely I would remember you," he added, fawning. "And have tried to arrange a follow-up meeting."

"Oh, I would not forget you," she said, reading his immediate interest in her. "It was a brief," and she glanced up wistfully, "encounter."

"You were quite busy," she added. "It was very brief."

She hesitated, waiting for a response. And got it.

Matías put out his arm again and, palm up, pointed an outspread hand toward the empty seat. "Please. Miss?"

"Oh yes, thank you," said Lizzy, lightly rubbing her right hand over her ring finger, devoid of a ring, and gracefully sliding into the seat. Neither person could imagine that, 11 years later, in this same booth, Sen. John F. Kennedy would propose to Jacquelyn "Jackie" Bouvier. Still, both Lizzy and Matías had romance, of a sort, already on their minds.

"May I call you Matías?"

"*Cierto*," said Matías, "Well, you seem to know my work. Are you, are you working?" He imagined that a woman of such style and loveliness could be a kept woman, or on the verge of an engagement. On the other hand, many attractive single women were pouring into the bustling capital, in search of employment, or a husband.

"I'm a reporter," said Lizzy. "For the *Times-Herald*," she added quickly, namedropping the isolationist paper read avidly by the Spanish diplomatic corps. "And the *Business Journal* and others. Mosty free-lance work. I just had an article published," she stated truthfully, "on the munition plants that are starting up.

"With the war coming," she put on a look of gloom, "coming perhaps, some managers are finding it hard to find workers, so…" Her voice trailed off. Matías wasn't interested in this topic, so he maneuvered to one he was.

"Since I was apparently so rude to you last time, with us meeting, so briefly, and not remembering you, let me purchase—how do you Americans say—let me 'buy you lunch'."

Liz feigned embarrassment, and replied, "Oh, I don't know, I could put this on my expense account." And she tried, successfully, to look as though that would be a burden on a tight budget. The Spaniard held up his hand, caught the attention of a waiter, and said, "That won't be necessary. I could charge this to my embassy but," and he feigned a look as if money was nothing to him, "I'll pick simply up the charge."

Liz acceded, and Matías ordered for both and, despite her protestations, requested rich and expensive fare. Oysters, followed by an item new to Washington, antipasto, followed by lobster and steak. Washed down by robust Douro Valley wine.

The meal went well, mostly small talk about two persons from out of town, one who grew up in a distant state and the other in a distant country. At the end, Matías insisted on a dessert of ice cream custard, plus a bottle of champagne.

"You really have the advantage of *me* now," said Liz smiling, placing a napkin to her lips, which were painted with the Fleshpot brand of pink lipstick. "So I must treat you some time."

Matías expanded his chest, then exhaled, as if blowing out the smoke of a Cuban cigar. "That would be a pleasure."

He paused. Lunch time was over. But he had no pressing business back at the embassy. And if he had, he'd have cancelled it. What should he ask this woman to do now? Perhaps a walk around the beautiful side streets of Georgetown?

Liz read the mind of her man, and said, again smiling, "Shall we go a stroll? To walk off some of this fine but rather filling food?"

She steered him down Wisconsin Ave., and then over to O St., in the direction of her house, while letting him think he was doing the steering. Along the way she mouthed a few attitudes that would appeal to him. Of her admiration of Spain, of its Mannerist art, flamenco dancing, and imperial architecture. Of how she hoped Spain and the United States, and Spanish allies like Italy, would never go to war.

Matías listened genially. This was going well. He actually thought Americans brash and crude, and like this woman, very forward, but in this case he didn't mind.

He was beginning to think of hotels in the area when Liz, that clairvoyant, stated: "You know, my house is not far from here."

Matías felt desire welling up within him. But he managed a calm façade and said, "Oh, well, this *is* such a nice neighborhood." He noticed the trolley tracks running down the middle of the narrow street. "Do the, how do you say it, the electric carriages—do they keep you up at night?"

"Oh no, I sleep very, very soundly. Besides, early in the evening the conductors take the trolleys to the Car Barn."

Matías was confused. "They put these electric vehicles in a barn? Like cows?"

Lizzy read his face and, laughing, said, "Into a big garage, for the night, over by the Key, the Francis Scott Key, Bridge. They call it a 'car barn'."

Before the Spaniard could take this in, Liz said suddenly, "Why don't I show you my place? It's just half a block this way. After your treat, I should treat you to a liqueur. Or a martini."

Matías couldn't believe his luck. He lied, "Ah, I should return to my embassy soon." Then added, "Yet I think a small glass would be fine."

Soon Liz had him at her dining table, pouring a generous martini into his glass.

"Olive?" she asked, rolling an olive with the thumb and index finger of her right hand. "Some people don't like olives." He looked surprised. "But you're from the Mediterranean," she laughed, and plopped three olives in his glass. "So there." Some of the martini splashed over the brim of the glass.

While mixing more drinks in her kitchenette, Liz pondered tactics and strategy. This man seemed an easy mark, as she had expected. Should she seduce him here and now? It would be easy. But then the admonitions of her handler, and of Intrepid himself, came to mind. They had cautioned her to reel a man in slowly. Making him want you made him more likely to give you secret information. Make him think he played you, not the other way around. Playing hard to get might heighten his desire to please you in various ways, including committing treason.

Lizzy paused fixing the drinks. On the other hand, she thought, the same two men had told her that time was now critical, that the British needed the navy codes *now*. Just that morning, Liz had heard on the radio that Rommel seemed on the verge of moving through Egypt, and to the Suez Canal, England's vital lifeline to its India possession. That could bring on the death of the British Empire, a death blow to the Allies.

'I practically have him in my bed already,' Liz reasoned. 'So let me combine that with a direct approach. He doesn't seem loyal to Franco or to the Axis at all. No true believer, this fellow.

And my sources say he does need money.' She started stirring the potables again, her mind made up. She opened up a button on her blouse, and returned to the dining room with the drinks.

After Barbieri had drunk a large portion of a martini, she leaned forward, and offered, "Matías, I think I can speak to you directly."

'Oh,' thought the diplomat, surprised. 'Here it comes. She propositions me?'

"I am a 'reporter," Liz said with some hesitation. "But not only that."

'She's a prostitute?' thought Matías. 'Well, a very high-class one.' He looked at her in puzzlement. 'But do I have the money?'

"I am working for my country." She hesitated again. "And for yours."

'What?' thought Matías, more puzzled. 'Is she one of our spies? I didn't know…'

"I believe," said Liz with emotion, "that Spain and the U.S. should be allies. And what my country needs—" Liz hesitated. She was asking so much. She suddenly intuited she was asking too much. But impulsively she went ahead.

"—needs, is, are, the codes to, the Navy, to the Italian Navy."

Matías was stunned. Was this a joke?

"The Navy?" he asked, doubtfully.

"Yes," she said, hesitantly. "Italy's Navy."

'She is serious,' he thought, incredulously.

"You say we, we are all—allies," he sputtered, "but you want me to betray another country, a friendly country…" He stopped. He knew of the close relations between the Spanish and Italian diplomatic communities. And he had heard from a worker in the embassy's intelligence branch about the Italian Navy codes.

But of course he wouldn't betray such a secret. He didn't really care how the war turned out, as long as it improved his position. But to help this, this stranger, to acquire an ally's top-secret codes, possibly putting himself in mortal danger? From Franco's ruthless security men? Or Mussolini's? And for what? A roll in her bed?!

Liz could tell from his expression she had blundered. Badly. 'I should have 'let out the fishing line',' she told herself.

Stuttering now, and sensing it was no use, she went ahead anyway. "But you, you seem like reasona—, a good, a nice and reasonable man, uh, and—"

"What is you want?!" said Matías coldly, angry now at this brash American woman.

Liz fell silent. She became visibly embarrassed.

Matías suddenly realized he still had an opportunity at hand, if not the one this woman wanted. He forced himself to smile.

"Well, that is quite a demand." He smiled widened. "You took me by surprise, Miss Thorne. Elise.

"I need to think." He faked indecision. "How, how exactly would this work?"

Liz was surprised, and pleased, by this sudden change. Perhaps she should have been more diplomatic, but perhaps the direct approach was working.

"Well, in exchange for certain, valuable information, we would not lack, generosity." She drank some of her martini in relief. "Payments, sizeable payments, could be made, every month, or weekly, or—"

'She's treating me,' Matías thought, 'a man of class and distinction, like the whore I thought *she* was.'

He looked at her steadily, the brazenness of her approach still filtering through his mind.

'She is gorgeous,' thought the Spaniard. 'Though treacherous, and a liar. Thinking I could be had so easily!'

He stood up slowly, and stepped to the edge of the table. Emotions, the kind of emotions he had often found hard to control, were swirling up inside him. He took a step forward.

"Elise," he said softly, with feigned affection. "Elise, come here."

Thorne, surprised again, stared at him. 'He is very changeable, a mercurial man,' she figured. Then she rose slowly. 'And he is a handsome man,' she thought. She found herself taking a step toward him.

She *could* bed him. *Should* she bed him? Now? Before the negotiations on what he would get in exchange for the codes? Almost always in command of such situations, Liz felt confused, uncertain. She took another step forward.

He grabbed her by the waist, and hoisted her upward. Liz was surprised at how strong he was. He pressed his lips against hers, forcing her lips open, and her mouth. 'This is too fast,' she thought. She tried resisting the kiss. Then acceded, despite herself. Almost from habit, or desire. Then she resisted again.

He pressed himself against her harder. She resisted still. Then broke away.

He grabbed her, and again pressed his lips to hers. His lips felt hot, white-hot, against hers. She was unable to break from his iron grasp. She turned her head away sharply. At this, he raised his right hand, and brought the side of it down hard against her left cheek, like a Japanese karate chop. A modest blow, he thought. To get her attention. And her obedience.

To Liz, however, it felt like a heavyweight's punch. She was stunned. No man, even spies she'd betrayed, had ever hit her. Her gums felt sore; blood trickled onto her tongue.

"Name my price, eh?" Matías growled, his lust and anger growing in tandem. "*Tu putana Americana!*" (You American slut!)

Liz moved two short steps back to the table, but Matías, with sudden quickness, grabbed her by the wrists. Then pulled and pushed her toward the bedroom.

At the door he embraced her again, by the lower back, and tried kissing again. Liz resisted, then allowed the kiss. 'What am I doing?' she thought frantically. 'No!' She twisted her head away. Matías pressed his muscled chest to her neck, enveloping Liz in a bear hug. It knocked away her breath. It felt like she'd been hit again. He lifted her feet off the ground, and stared angrily, arrogantly, into her emerald eyes, which were filling with tears, and turning darker. He thought, 'I have her now. In my grasp, helpless!'

Her left high heel dropping off, he carried her, feet kicking wildly, into the bedroom. She caught his left shin with her right heel, which stung him badly. He lost his hold for an instant, and she moved toward the bedroom door.

He reached out, grabbed her, kicked off her remaining high heel, and brought his left elbow up, hard, to her jaw. It felt like a knockout punch. Liz thought dimly, 'That's what they mean by 'seeing stars.'" She felt groggy. Felt like she was sailing, slowly, through the air. She was being carried to the sheets. She felt the soft mattress, became more alert, than groggy again. She felt his weight upon her, felt naked. She tried resisting, but had no strength left.

Sometime later, she awoke. She felt pain in her jaw. And down below. She had been penetrated. Hard. She sensed what felt like blood on her thighs. Matías lay next to her, face down, breathing deeply, snoring lightly, his left arm over her left shoulder, a leg over her ankle. His shirt was on, but unbuttoned, she seemed to perceive in the gloom. His pants were down by his ankles. She could smell his liquor breath.

'I passed out,' she realized. She was very afraid, but even more angry at herself—for putting herself in this situation, for losing control—than she was at this pig by her side.

Liz willed herself to be calm. Her life might depend on what she did in the next minutes. And maybe her mission. Though that was likely in tatters.

'What time is it?' she asked herself. There was little light coming through the window shades. She couldn't have been out that long. 'Early morning,' she estimated.

She had to get away from this man. She had her loaded pistol hidden in the kitchen cupboard. Her mind was clearing. 'No. that would end his life, and my career. 'A diplomatic incident.'' Ruinous for her, and for her agency.

'But I must get away!'

He was asleep, a fairly deep sleep from the sound of it. His arm and leg were heavy on her, but nothing like the bear hug of before.

'What about clothes?' she thought. She was naked from the waist down, she knew. Her panties had been torn off. And her dress. No, she felt the fabric on her breasts. It had been pushed up on her chest. Good. If she managed to get to the street, at least she'd be somewhat clothed.

What would she do once she got there? 'Call my contact.' How? It was too late to ask a neighbor to use a phone. The police were out of the question. Oh wait. Weren't there emergency street phones up the block, with connections to the nearest fire department?

'Well, deal with that when I get there,' she decided. 'I must get out of here! This man is a rapist, a maniac!' She felt the panic returning. She knew it was possible he might kill her.

She slipped her leg out from under his. His breathing seemed to become still. Had he felt that? Then heavier breaths again.

She slipped her shoulder out from his arm. His head fell an inch or two. His breathing seemed to stop again. Then started up again.

She slid to the side of the bed, and saw stars once more. Her head ached terribly. As she got off the bed, he awoke, and reached for her. He missed.

She stood up, groggy, in pain, and rushed out to the living area. He got up, less groggy, in no pain, and started after her.

Liz rushed toward the door. 'God, did I lock it, push in the key chain?' She couldn't remember. Every instant mattered.

She reached the door, tried the knob. It opened! Matías was feet away, closing fast.

Liz stepped out onto the threshold. It was cold, but she didn't notice. Matías got to the doorway, and grabbed her left shoulder. She broke away and started quickly down the steps. As she

54

descended, he caught up and grabbed her neck and shoulders. She kept going down the steps, and he awkwardly stepped down right behind her. They looked like two drunken swing dancers slipping along face-to-back.

At the landing, Liz saw a man. A very tall man. Very nicely dressed. A handsome man. With a stunned expression. A knowing expression. Looking at her. Looking at him. Sizing things up, quickly.

He darted his head forward, as if to examine her face in the glare of a streetlight. He turned to Matías, the latter's bare chest showing through his unbuttoned shirt, and his hairy legs bare, a trouser leg still around an ankle.

It was an easy situation to size up.

Liz recognized the man. From a diplomatic reception. They had spoken for some time. She'd been impressed by his looks and intelligence. He'd said he was a British envoy, but he seemed something more.

Thorne saw the blur of his large, lanky form rushing past her. And the blur of what looked like a snake leaping past her eyes.

No, it was the man's left arm. Making a left hook. Connecting with the right jaw of a shocked Matías. Who crashed down onto the steps.

His shoes were off, she saw, his white feet glowing from the glare.

The other man's shoes were on. One of them kicked Matías in the jaw. His face bleeding on both sides, Matías passed out cold.

The man helped Lizzy inside her home.

Inside, Roald Dahl sat her down at the kitchen table.

He got a clean sponge, wet it, and wiped the blood and spittle from Liz's face. He found some bourbon and had her drink it.

Sobbing, Liz thanked him. She was very grateful, but her mind soon turned to her mission.

"What about him?" she asked. "Someone will see him, and…"

Dahl realized her embarrassment. Whatever had happened, she didn't want anyone to know. He said, "Don't worry about him. Let me get you to bed. Then I'll shake him awake, and send him on his way.

"Believe me, he won't come anywhere near here anytime soon."

He saw the worried look on her face. Sensed what she was afraid of.

"I doubt he'll want to make this a criminal case. After what happened in here." He paused, and smiled. "And out there.

"It might cause a diplomatic incident."

Pay for Play

Several days passed. Though still bruised and upset from the brutal assault, Liz vowed to get the codes. She had that other contact for the Spanish Embassy. She was pretty certain it wouldn't play out, but she would try, and then move on to another course of action.

Acting directly, Liz telephoned the retired coder, Luis Modesta. In her guise as a reporter, she told him she was interviewing Spanish nationals about the war. Somewhat to her surprise, he agreed to meet her at his Arlington apartment.

His was a ramshackle place on Wilson Boulevard, near the art-deco Navy League Building, a lobbying institution for expanding the rapidly expanding U.S. Navy. Across the street was the giant parking lot of a used car company. Down the way toward the Potomac were several weathered buildings that Liz heard were houses of ill repute.

The Modesta's single-floor apartment was small, even for a family that had only one of its children living with them. Its little kitchen was actually inside the modest-sized living room, which adjoined two tiny bedrooms.

At the appointed time, Luis Modesta, sour-looking and with graying hair fringing his pate, answered the door to the third-floor walkup. Thorne stood a good three inches taller than Luis. Knowing from the files that there was scant chance of a seduction, she had put on a brown, color-block collar dress, belted, and buttoned close to her neck, with the hem below her knees. Serious-looking and modest. She had also applied heavier-than-usual makeup to hide the traces of bruises on her face.

Modesta brought Liz to an upholstered chair in the living room, and took a wooden folding chair across from her. As she sat down, Thorne noticed the fabric of the upholstery had been repaired several times.

Luis called over to one of the bedroom doors. "Francesa! *Soy ocupado por algún tiempo. Por favor, déjame en paz. Gracias.*" ("Francesa, I will be busy for a while. Please leave me be. Thank you.") A muffled response came back, which Liz interpreted as an assent from his wife. She began by introducing herself in unaccented Spanish. Luis said he was pleased at "her attempt" to "speak in my own language." He then switched to English. "In my job," he explained, his expression still dour, his eyes heavy-lidded, "I have, had to, to know several languages."

Liz asked what his job had been, and was surprised again, as he readily admitted to having worked on encrypting and decrypting top-secret information. Without prompting, he went on at some length about the details of that job.

"Well," Liz attempted, "there are many countries who would pay a 'pretty penny' for information of that kind."

She was startled by Modesta's response.

"How much do you think the British, or the Americans, for example," and he looked at her sharply, "would pay?"

Liz paused, then answered with a four-figure amount that she thought might appeal to a man of Modesta's modest means.

As he slowly rubbed his thick tummy, he startled her again by asking, "And how would such payments be made? In cash, I imagine, and through an exchange between persons, and not through a bank?"

It was so obvious where Modesta was heading that Liz suspected she was being set up. She wondered if one or more of Generalissimo Franco's security goons were behind the bedroom door. She had no backup, and they could abduct her and carry her to one of their safe houses, or to her death, if they wanted. However, her feminine sense told her Luis was sincere. She decided to press ahead, hard, while giving herself an excuse for making a quick departure.

She stated, "I believe we are both on the same page, *Señor* Modesta. Let me be bold.

"Why don't we meet again, and soon, at a neutral place? Where certain interested parties would give proof, firm financial proof, of their sincerity in this matter."

Modesta's eyes flashed. After hesitating, he said, "Yes, I can see why this apartment might not be the best place for such arrangements. Or even for further conversation along these lines." And he agreed to a place and time of Liz's suggestion.

The very next day, at 15 minutes to three in the afternoon, Liz passed by the Italianate turrets of the administrator's building guarding Georgetown's venerable Oak Hill Cemetery. She walked inside the grounds, and past the Gothic Revival chapel designed by James Renwick, the architect of St. Patrick's Cathedral. She had once done a "dead-drop" of valuable information under the floorboards of the chapel, which had once been a temporary holding place for bodies before their formal burial.

In the spacious cemetery, Liz realized again how fitting it was for an espionage rendezvous. It was easy to hide oneself in its acres of rolling, thickly wooded hills. A bonus was the scent and tint of the forsythia, saucer magnolias, and daffodils in their springtime bloom.

Femme fatales, her sisters in derring-do, haunted the place. She passed the grave of young Lily Mackall, a courier for Rose Greenough, the Confederate spy who obtained Union Army plans for the war's first battle, Bull Run, leading to a Southern victory by Stonewall Jackson. Then on past the resting place of Gen. Joseph Willard, the Union officer smitten by another skillful Confederate spy, Antonia Ford. They both fell so in love she took an oath to the Union, while he resigned his commission for the same. The pair now lay side by side for eternity. Liz trod past the grave of Philip Barton Key, the uncle of the National Anthem's author, whose own son was murdered for his affair with the alluring wife of a jealous Congressman.

In the late afternoon, the cemetery was practically deserted, apart from its permanent residents, and Liz made sure no other mortal visitor was within a hundred yards. At length, she came to the tall, circular mausoleum of another noted, local femme, Marcia Burnes Van Ness. She lay buried next to her husband, General and Congressman Peter Van Ness.

Liz admired Marcia for her public service. Though wealthy, she had stayed in town during the region's first pandemic, cholera, to care for the sick. The "Florence Nightingale" of Washington had herself taken ill and died in 1832 from the deadly bacterial outbreak. In her honor, her spouse had built a resting place modeled on the Temple of Vesta in the Roman Forum.

It lay atop a knoll, and behind it was a steep decline that afforded a hiding spot. There, as Liz had directed him, Luis Modesta was waiting. Without saying a word, she walked past him, but not before handing over a small brown bag, containing $750 in cash. It was a classic brush contact. Mr. Modesta was very pleased with the money, and the prospect of many more payments.

By week's end, he had put Liz in possession of the Italian Navy's code book.

Words of Thanks

Some months later, Intrepid paid Lizzy one of his rare personal visits.

They sat at her kitchen table. He seemed more like the operator of a small business than a master spy. Five-foot, two inches, he was shorter than Liz. Always heavy in the belly, he was portly now, with thinning, graying hair. He was affable, but had penetrating eyes. She knew not to serve him a drink.

"I was in the neighborhood, so to speak," he said in an accent that seemed a mix of Canadian and British English. "So I thought I'd drop in, to let you know how valuable you were with the Italian code business." His voice dropped a register, making him seem conspiratorial.

Memories painful, and sweet, came back to Liz. Painful, concerning Matías's rape. Sweet, about how, after recovering from the assault, she had turned to the next target on her list. And had been able to easily bribe Luis Modesta with a modest monthly payment, and get a perfect copy of the codes. After being told he was likely incorruptible.

'If only I had gone after him first!' she had chided herself for weeks after.

Intrepid was businesslike and direct as always. "You have no doubt read," he began, "about the sea battle a little while ago, off Greece, off Cape Matapan.

Lizzy had. She eagerly followed the war news, especially in Europe and the Mediterranean. According to the press accounts, the Royal Navy had sent a significant chunk of the Italian fleet to the sea bottom.

"One always has to take," replied Liz, "any stories, especially about battles, with a big grain of salt. But it did seem like a significant victory."

"An overwhelming victory," answered Intrepid immediately. He leaned over the table, his forehead prominent, and looked up at Liz.

"I can't provide the details, of course. But instrumental in that victory was certain information provided by a certain one of our agents.

"One operating out of Georgetown."

He almost winked, and leaned back in his chair.

"The codes in question," he continued, "let us know the exact position of the Italian Navy leading up to the sea battle."

Liz understood. "A big advantage," she said, nodding.

"A very big advantage," answered William Stephenson, the man they called Intrepid. He took on a professorial air.

"Without that Navy, Hitler will be unlikely, very unlikely, to adequately supply Rommel's forces.

"His Afrika Korps should wither on the vine. And the conquest, the reconquest of Europe, should logically follow."

He got abruptly. He smiled a bit. And he walked out of her home.

Liz smiled herself. It was good to be appreciated. To know her work was making a difference. A big difference.

Lizzy's feelings were mixed. She had suffered through a physical and mental horror. Still, her affair with the Spanish admiral had led to astonishing success. Yielding a contact that led to the acquisition of the Italian codes. And their actual use in a critical battle.

The admiral himself had been recalled to Spain soon after the encounters with Luis and Matías. His transfer had nothing to do with the pilfered codes, as both Spain and Italy, as the Cape Matapan fight showed, were unaware of their theft. It was just that Madrid seemed closer to war than ever, and the admiral's services were deemed necessary to help defend his nation.

So Liz was completely free for the next mission that might involve a carnal relationship, at her "swallow's nest" on O. St.

'I would sleep with the Devil himself,' she thought, 'if it helped us win this damnable war.'

SECTION 2

THE FRIENDLY CODES

Prepping a Mayflower Meeting

The maître d was as finicky as anyone in his profession. He demanded things be just so. So naturally he was unhappy with the proposal to radically alter the city's finest hotel. So much had changed since the declaration of war the previous December.

Now, on this spring day in 1942, he and his head waiter stood at the Presidential Dining Room, the finest and most famous banquet room in the prestigious lodging. Its walls held framed portraits of early Presidents, as well as French and English royals.

The cavernous space had been the scene of presidential inauguration parties since Warren Harding. His crooked aides had reveled there before proceeding around the corner for gambling and cavorting with prostitutes. Harding's successor, in sharp contrast, was incorruptible, and reticent. At one banquet, a woman sitting next to that close-mouthed President, "Silent Cal" Coolidge, told him, "I bet I could get you to utter more than two words."

"You lose," came the response.

A place with such a notable past should be preserved as is, the maître d believed, but the hotel had come under the same pressures facing most hostelries and apartment buildings in the war-time city. There simply weren't enough residences for all the soldiers and workers pouring into the medium-sized town. Stenographers and couriers were doubling and tripling up in tiny apartments. Owners of small homes had taken to renting out their basements, and sometimes their living rooms. Even the slummy alley dwellings, the homes of fugitive slaves during the Civil War, and long afterwards the dispossessed, were being leased out to government clerks. The Mayflower's fellow five-star lodging, the Willard, had placed a limit on how long even admirals could stay in residence. The President's House itself wasn't exempt from the new imperatives. Instead of staying at the packed Blair-Lee House across from the Executive Mansion, visiting foreign dignitaries such as the exiled Queen of the Netherlands bedded down in the White House itself.

These lodging arrangements led to embarrassments. When, after Pearl Harbor, Winston Churchill visited his friend Franklin Roosevelt to plot military strategy, he took rooms in the President's House. Early one morning, when the restless Prime Minister had taken a warm bath, and stepped naked out of his tub, President Roosevelt barged in with important war news.

As FDR gazed, mouth agape, at the pudgy potentate, his visitor smiled, spread wide his arms, and stated: "You see, Mr. President, it is true what they say about me. I really have *nothing* hide from you!"

Now the Mayflower itself mulled turning some of its banquet rooms into residential suites. The maître d and the lead waiter were aghast. How were they supposed to put on large dinners, not to mention inaugural events, in the small spaces that would be left? The master of the house planned to raise his concerns again with the hotel's chief of operations. The latter knew how difficult it would be to install the required plumbing and wiring, given the growing shortages of laborers and materials. They might use that concern as a spanner to block the transformation. But early that afternoon, there was first a daily, pressing task to deal with.

He and the head waiter strode down the scarlet-toned Ottoman Court carpets, and reached the bustle of the main lobby. They pushed through a gaggle of contractors seeking federal funds to refurbish nearby Fort Washington and Fort Hunt. Those Potomac River installations south of the city had watched out for U-boats potentially coming upriver from the Atlantic during the Great War, or the First World War as some were now calling it. It was said General Brehon Somervell, the head of Army logistics, doubted the Nazis' large submarines could make it that far upriver, and had reservations about the price tag of the forts. But U-boats had sunk over a hundred merchant vessels off the Atlantic coast since Hitler's December 1941 declaration of war. The head waiter, in talking to the contractors at breakfast, had listened in on their sales pitch, which focused on that menace.

They approached the Connecticut Avenue entrance next to the front desk. It was clear from the pained expressions of the businessmen speaking to the harried concierge and receptionist that there were no rooms to be had. 'My goodness,' thought the maître d, 'that means more pressure to change over the banquet rooms.' On the other side of the jammed and deafening lobby was their destination, the hotel bar, back in business for nine years now, ever since the current President had lifted Prohibition.

The head waiter was sure things were ready, but with so important a visitor one had to make sure. The maître d' had taken to checking and setting his Geneve wristwatch every day at this, the lunch hour. It was so predictable; it had been going on almost every single workday for years. The two buttonholed their best server, Pablo Burgos, a hard-working fellow from the territory of Puerto Rico.

"Is the lunch ready?" they asked him.

"Oh yes," Burgos replied with a thick accent. "The usual." He smiled slightly. "It is not much to prepare.

"A grapefruit, sliced. Lettuce. *Café con no leche.* Bread. He has a most demanding job, and *el señor* does not like to be—what is the expression?—to be weighted down, by a heavy lunch. And—"

The head waiter broke in. "—It is iceberg lettuce, right?" He did not want to relive the embarrassment of the time romaine had been served.

"*Si,*" came the response. And for emphasis in French, "*Absolument!*

"And of course, I will not ask him, as I do with everyone else, whether he would like a cocktail, or some sparkling wine. A 'teetotaler,' *si,* that is the expression."

At that time, their expected guest and his top aide were still blocks away. The traffic on Pennsylvania Avenue—from their offices at the Justice Department on 9th St.—had been horrific, as it had for weeks. So on 13th St, they'd gotten out, and walked west, toward the Treasury and White House.

The man in charge smiled slightly at the flag-topped, 10-story building on his right, containing the offices of *The Baltimore Sun, The New York Tribune,* and many other papers. He had gotten plenty of favorable coverage, and in the news reels too, about rounding up Nazi spies.

The block was known as Newspaper Row, as well as Rum Row, due to the drinking habits of reporters, and its location in the city's entertainment district, or "red light" district, which stretched all the way to the foot of the Capitol Building. Leading to many jokes about the "prostitutes" in the halls of Congress. The top guy smiled a bit again, in recalling his busting up of bootleggers a decade and more before.

He and his Number Two reached the Willard Hotel, and its equally grand neighbor, the Hotel Washington. Yet the desolate little square across from the hotels was a reminder of another kind of war. A decade before, a battalion of an army had occupied that spot, recalled the assistant. That is, the Bonus Army, part of the tens of thousands of Great War veterans, many of them out of work during the Depression, who'd swarmed the capital to pressure Congress into granting their military bonuses in advance. They, and their wives and children, had camped out all over the city, including here. It seemed an ideal spot for pressure politics, as the Capitol dome was in sight just a mile-and-a-quarter down Pennsylvania Ave., and with the White House right around the corner. But the Senate had voted the bonus down.

While some of the veterans left for home, many stayed. Leading President Hoover to order some of the Army's leading lights to tear-gas and rifle-butt the former soldiers out of town. A handful of veterans and city police had died in violent brawls. The heads of the clearance operation— Douglas MacArthur, Dwight Eisenhower, and George Patton—were now rising far in the ranks as planners of the Pacific and Atlantic wars. The Number Two saddened at the memory of American against American, and kept striding ahead.

He didn't like this walk among the public. Not that he wasn't brave or out of shape. He had survived gun fights with the most dangerous outlaws, and was as fit as a college athlete. It was that, except for the President, and certainly more than the rather inconsequential Vice President, Henry Wallace, his boss was more of a target than any man in America. From the Nazis, for breaking up their main group of spies in America, the so-called Duquesne ring, in New York the previous year. From the former bootleggers, who still nursed grudges from the time of The Untouchables. And from the many Soviet agents in town who feared what he might know about their secret lives. Though not so much from the Mafioso families in New York and Chicago. He viewed their numbers rackets as "pennyante," not worth the trouble to pursue. Besides, in this new war against Germany and its ally Italy, their contacts could be useful among America's dockyard workers, and for possible future battle sites in Sicily and the Italian mainland.

The Number Two thought of a conversation with his agency's liaison to the War Department, and the paranoia about an air raid on D.C., resulting from Japan's attack on Hawaii the previous December. He swiveled his muscled neck to look back at the vast limestone, granite, and marble bulk of the Herbert Hoover Building, which stretched three football fields from Pennsylvania Avenue to the temporary barracks opposite Constitution Avenue. These Commerce Department offices named for the former Commerce Secretary had been finished ten years before, ironically during the paralysis of commerce in President Hoover's final year. It was a make-work program, and a beautification project, replacing part of old Murder Bay, aka "Hooker's Alley," the sleazy tenements and illicit businesses of the entertainment district. It was impressive in its monolithic way, with the orange, terra-cotta roofs breaking up some of the monumental monotony. When done, it became the world's largest office building, supplanting the old War, Navy, and State

Department Building, which was in turn being supplanted for that record by the Pentagon rising across the river.

The Number Two saw that war had indeed supplanted commerce, in the most literal way.

"Look," he cried, "atop the roof!"

His boss, without breaking his rolling gait, glanced quickly, then turned his steady gaze back up 15th St.

"I know.

Sandbags had appeared on the granite roof, along with three soldiers wearing the old-fashioned flat helmets of the Great War. And they were standing next to a rusty, 3-inch anti-aircraft gun.

"People got into a tizzy over the hysterical stories in the press, about the Japs or Huns bombing the District," the boss pronounced in a high, resonant, halting voice, which sounded rather like that of President Roosevelt. "As if they could fly, a thousand miles to here." He became silent, thoughtful. "Well, I suppose the Nazis"—he pronounced it as NAH-zees—"could put a small plane, atop one of their submarines. Though that would take one hel—" he stopped, careful not to curse in public—"a heck of a maintenance job, sailing through thousands of miles of salt water."

The Number Two nodded with approval. His superior continued.

"Not much of a defense though. That's an old gun. And it has no, no ammunition." He snorted. "Maybe if the Huns"—he again used the insulting term from the Great War for the Germans— "don't know that, they won't attack."

The Number Two knew that his boss, though a tough man ardent about protecting the country, was worried about overdoing things. Back on December 7, much of the Pacific fleet had been destroyed. The extent of the losses, in battleships and dead sailors, had been suppressed. Partly not to panic the public, but even more, thought the Number Two, to spare the President, that old Navy salt, political damage.

Due to the fallout from that debacle, the boss was now getting pressure to imprison, as potential foreign agents and saboteurs, the many Japanese-Americans in California. Yet the field agents there had reported few subversives among that group, and much patriotism. Further, his superior had, in the weeks after Pearl, rounded up thousands of the most likely troublemakers among persons of Japanese, and German and Italian, ancestry. He figured any remaining threat was minimal. His boss's boss, Attorney General Biddle, was known to be a civil libertarian. But whether the Justice Department could withstand political pressure from the White House and the voters was unknown.

The Number Two and his superior, often featured in the press, publicity hounds both, were recognizable to almost any Washingtonian, and most Americans. And the apparel of the two men also stood out.

Both were outfitted in identical gray, double-breasted, three-piece suits of fine material and finer tailoring. They sported fedora hats with wide black sashes encircling the brims. Their silk ties were pushed up tightly to the neck above starched white shirts. They strode atop highly polished Oxford shoes, brown and white for the boss, black and white for his aide. The only other difference in their apparel was the boss's tie was a bit darker, and the handkerchief in his jacket pocket was folded into two protruding tips, while his Number Two had just one.

Their physiques varied, however. Number One had a face that almost comically resembled a bulldog, a face that matched his squat figure. A face that matched a reputation for relentless pursuit of lawbreakers. His deputy in contrast was taller, noticeably leaner, lantern-jawed and, while younger by five years, seemed a decade more youthful.

Despite his aide Clyde Tolson's concern over safety, J. Edgar Hoover shrugged. He continued on with a short-legged but purposeful stride up the steep and busy street flanking the aircraft carrier-length of the Treasury. He smiled at the passersby who waved at him or called out, "Hello, Mr. Hoover." No one dared to engage with him further.

The two men, who were said to be inseparable, were already experienced in war. And both had gotten their big breaks due to one.

Tolson, now 41, had served as a key aide to Newton Baker, Wilson's Secretary of War in the Great War, and for two other War Secretaries after the armistice. Hoover, who was in charge of arresting German subversives in the war, had gotten his big chance in its aftermath, as the head of the Bureau of Intelligence, not yet called the FBI. He put the collar on many radicals, dissidents, and subversives, actual or alleged. By age 29, he was head of America's first nation-wide law enforcement bureau.

A key to his rise was organizational skills. He'd majored in records administration at George Washington University, and he kept careful files on thousands of suspected criminals, and on many politicians too. The latter knew about these dossiers on the skeletons in their closets, and thus were fearful of challenging him.

The duo passed the tinted plate glass of the Old Ebbitt Grill, now old indeed, 85 years in existence, and crammed like most restaurants in town. From the crush of new arrivals with government cash in their pockets, the Depression finally ending from the boom of war-time industry. Navy officers seemed to outnumber the ranks of their Army brethren there; fewer of them had yet to move out to the Pentagon from the old Navy Department building nearby. Intent on their luncheon place, and the important business to discuss there, the FBI duo barely glanced at the clientele within.

The Mole and the Embassy Agent

Yet if the FBI men had gone inside, they might have noticed a balding, mustachioed man of 49 years, the eyes of his owlish face peering from behind spectacles. This ranking Treasury official was attired in a business suit, his left hand tapping a copy of *The Atlantic* magazine.

His luncheon guest was just 28, and strikingly handsome, with a finely proportioned nose and eyes, and dirty-blond hair brushed up from a broad forehead, A long curl falling out of place suggested someone impatient and ever in a hurry. Yet Vitali Pavlov's light-gray pinstripe suit and knotted tie made him look himself like a U.S. official, not a visiting Russian. He noted the cover of the periodical, which by secret arrangement the man seated across from him was to display.

Because of the traffic, Pavlov had walked over from the Soviet embassy three blocks away. Actually a spy's nest as much as an embassy, with its 25 NKVD operatives working out of a suffocating, 40-by-20-foot space on an upper floor. The compound was the former mansion of the wife of a capitalist tycoon, George Pullman, of the railroad car conglomerate.

Pulsing with suppressed energy, Pavlov felt like kissing the older man, French style, on both cheeks, but was too professional to betray such emotion. His eyes, which fixed his subjects with a piercing, almost comical gaze, did not direct themselves at the guests down the aisle from them. That would have been too obvious; he had scanned the restaurant clientele as he had slowly paced to his contact. The Treasury official had reserved a seat in a quiet niche against a back wall, a perch that gave a clear view of the emporium, and hopefully any prying and unwanted eyes. Wanting to share that cautious view, he had taken a seat kitty-corner from Harry Dexter White, instead of directly across from him.

They quickly put in their orders. Confident they were unobserved, the handler said sotto voce to his mole, "It worked." His accented English had a happy tone. "It worked out!"

White, as the Assistant Secretary of the Treasury, under the President's confidante, Treasury Secretary Henry Morgenthau, Jr., was the critical player in his department's foreign affairs. At the advice of his handler, he'd pushed for the stiffest sanctions against Imperial Japan, sanctions that cut off most of the iron ore, copper, and oil fueling its military, at the same time it was in an all-out war with China. Japan's military junta, watching Hitler's legions gobble up western Russia that summer, had considered striking north, and gobbling up Siberia. But America, at

White's urging, had imposed its sanctions. With material for its war industries imperiled, Tokyo had decided to strike south, at the Dutch East Indies, for its oil, and at British Malaysia, for its raw materials. And at the east, Pearl Harbor, to thwart any intervention by the American fleet. White's gambit had succeeded.

To a Russian, a celebratory toast was in order. Pavlov ordered two shots of vodka. White declined a libation on a workday, but his handler happily toasted his mole.

"You did it. Of course it's impossible to know, how much influence you had on the decision-making. There were other things in play. But you, my friend, were a big part of it!"

Another Soviet agent, Richard Sorgie, based in Tokyo, had informed Moscow the Japanese would strike south and east. Thus Stalin was able to move over 12 divisions of troops from the Far East and Central Asia to the German front, as the Nazi panzers came close to taking Moscow. The Soviets' surprise counterattack in frigid conditions had bloodied the German legions, nearly collapsing them like Napoleon's a century before.

Pavlov picked up White's untouched shot glass, clinked his glass against it, and drained it too. "There'll be other missions," he told White. "But for now—how do you say? —stick to your bread and jam."

"You mean bread and butter," White corrected.

"Yes, yes. For now, then, no dangerous stuff. Just your basic chore, now that the United States and the Soviet Union are allies, of getting us as much food and as many weapons under your Lend-Lease plan as you can."

White had only picked at his food. Pavlov hadn't eaten at all, only drank, but he decided against another drink. There was more work to attend to. He thought of another ranking mole, a top official at the new State Department building. Also an authority on economic affairs. With a name that sounded, in English, like the sound of a snake. 'How fitting for a spy,' he reflected. "Hiss."

Pavlov congratulated White again, then got up and walked with deliberation out of the bistro, and up past the Treasury Building and toward the Soviet embassy. White stayed, and pretended to read his magazine. A slight smile of satisfaction marked his owlish face. Only a bit. He knew the dangers of overconfidence, a deadly attitude for a spy.

After a half hour, he got up and returned to his office, and his twin occupations.

The President's Park in Wartime

Meantime, Hoover and Tolson had turned onto the east side of busy Pennsylvania Avenue, and strode the short block up to Lafayette Square.

They approached the corner of Madison Place, and its two great buildings on opposite sides of the Avenue. On their left was the rear entrance of the Treasury. Although with its fine sculpture, and its location next to the White House entrance, many mistook it for the front. Just as many mistook the statue of the commanding, caped figure for Hamilton, the Treasury's founder. Actually, it was Hamilton's successor, Albert Gallatin. The figurine was crafted by the same artist who molded the Hamilton statue standing at the front entranceway. During the War of 1812, Gallatin had grappled with a bankrupt Treasury. Now his successors pondered how to finance the current and far more expensive conflict.

To their right was the granite walls and Iconic columns of the George Washington Riggs Bank, the District's largest. Its founder, named like so many Americans in the early days after a Founding Father, had made his fortune from a war. Namely, the Mexican-American, on loans to the War Department pegged to a hefty interest rate. Now there was a federal bank, the Federal Reserve, set up just before Mr. Wilson's war, to make loans during emergencies. For now, Morgenthau and White's Treasury men would rely on voluntary savings bonds to pay for weapons and troops. But most thought income taxes would come into play, as in the Civil War and the first global conflict.

Outside the Riggs Bank, a queue of customers waited impatiently to withdraw their cash. Hoover and Tolson overheard several complaining about the roaring inflation in goods. Tolson wondered when the rumored price and wage controls would come into effect. There were already shortages of tires, silk stockings, and items dealing with the housing crunch: beds and cots, dining tables, washing machines, even toilet paper and lightbulb sockets. On the day after Pearl Harbor, the shelves of many stores had been stripped clean. Some were still empty.

'Will our FBI go after the black marketeers, like we went after the bootleggers?' Tolson mused. He shifted his heavy briefcase from one hand to the other. 'Everyone expects rationing to begin soon.'

As they strode past the White House lawn, both men asked themselves how long the peaceful-seeming scene would last. As had been true since John and Abigail Adams resided within, government and business employees sat on the grass, enjoying their lunches, unblocked by any fence from busy Pennsylvania Avenue. The security seemed laughable. But that had long been deemed logical, for a republic oceans away from foreign broils.

Yet there were signs of change. In the narrow East Executive Avenue path between the Executive Mansion and the Treasury were excavation machines, operated by construction workers chatting away in Virginian and southern Maryland drawls.

"Maybe we're going overboard there too," remarked Hoover. As part of the post-Pearl Harbor panic, and the irrational fear of an air strike, the construction men were digging a bomb shelter under the White House, and a tunnel to another protective cocoon under Treasury. In the event of the Luftwaffe's appearance, the President and his aides were to hustle underground.

They passed the former Freeman's Bank for the slaves liberated by the Civil War. During a Grant Era scandal, the bank's director had shifted the deposits of thousands of those recently freed by Lincoln's emancipations into shady investments; when those went belly up, so did the Bank. Frederick Douglass had taken the place over in a final, futile effort to save it. The building later became the Belasco Theater, with its jetting cornice, arched windows, and ground-floor columns. In the wake of Pearl Harbor, work had begun to convert it into a Stage Door Canteen to entertain servicemen. Attached to its five stories of beige brickwork were wood scaffolds, giving it an ugly cast, contrasting with the green lawns and budding trees of Lafayette Square and the brightly painted White House.

Along with nightly theatrical performances, the emporium was slated to host a daytime restaurant and bar, with free food, cigarettes, and coffee for servicemen. A small canteen had already opened, and the FBI men eyed the unusual crowd lining up outside. There were Army soldiers, both whites and blacks, the latter from segregated units. Moreover, there were some dark-colored soldiers outfitted in the braided, colorful uniforms of foreign nations. Exotic places. A kind of English accent identified some from the British colonies of Africa. A patois marked others as Free French fighters from France's African possessions. A couple of others, their heads wrapped in red turbans, were evidently from British India, connected to the many Indians fighting for the Empire in North Africa.

These aspects and apparels were outlandish enough, but what struck Hoover, a native Washingtonian, was that the dark-skinned foreigners were standing cheek by jowl with white

Americans. In a District still covered by the segregation laws. Seeing his chief's expression, Tolson remarked, "War changes everything." Hoover nodded, but his face turned Sphinx-like. Just two years before, three blocks down 17th St., Constitution Hall had barred the black opera singer Marian Anderson from performing, due to, it claimed, 'the lack of separate bathroom facilities for the two races.' Anderson wound up performing to a far larger audience at the Lincoln Memorial. But the racial statutes were still on the books.

But not enforced at the theater, apparently. Perhaps the city magistrates did not want to pick a fight with battle-hardened veterans from overseas.

The G-Men cut through Lafayette Square, reminders of prior wars all around them. Past the memorial to the Marquis, with the Lafayette statue atop its pedestal, and a French general and admiral of the American Revolution at its base. Past the Thaddeus Kosciuszko statue, a hero from Poland, with its peasant gripping a scythe to hold off an invading army from Russia, now an ally. Or was it the Germans, now a foe? Past the Andrew Jackson statue at the Square's center, the general rearing on a high horse at the Battle of New Orleans. There the duo sidestepped a stream of military officers heading into the White House, to meet with the President's advisers, or with commanders in the adjacent War and Navy Departments. Everyone had a serious, determined air, a post-Peart Harbor, "they'll get theirs!" look. The pair reached the end of President's Park at the Decatur House, the home of the Navy Commodore who'd taken sailors and Marines "to the shores of Tripoli." Soon, aided by an exploit of Lizzy Thorne, American forces would return to North Africa.

The two waited at H St., clogged with taxis discharging Navy men, and waved away the black soot of exhaust fumes. Suddenly, pedestrians there were startled by a loud screeching sound, coming from where no one could tell. It was a noise that distorted into earsplitting, intermittent bursts, then stopped altogether.

"The latest, aborted air raid drill," remarked Tolson, as Hoover shook his jowls in mild derision. The city, going through the motions to prep for an unlikely air attack, had staged another drill, with equipment that worked poorly, to which few paid attention. Assuming they weren't close to the blasting alarms.

Shrugging off the alert, the pair walked up the short block to Farragut Square. In its center was its indomitable admiral, surrounded by bronze siege mortars green with oxidation. The papers were full of patriotic stories, and Tolson smiled in recalling one of them. How Admiral Farragut called out an aggressive order at the 1864 battle of Mobile Bay, Alabama. As a history buff, Tolson knew the exact, often misquoted, line. It went, "Damn the torpedoes, Jouette, full speed!" Jouette was Farragut's Lieutenant Commander, and they and their ships and crew captured the last Confederate port on the Gulf Coast. This blocked the rebels' export of their cash crop of cotton, collapsing the Confederacy's finances. Captain Jouette, Tolson had learned, was the grandson of a Revolutionary War hero. That earlier Jouett had saved Thomas Jefferson, Patrick Henry, and Benjamin Harrison—the latter the grandfather and great-father of two American Presidents—from being captured, and hanged, by the bloodthirsty British raider Banastre Tarleton.

Stomachs grumbling, fretful of lost time, the FBI men quickened their pace and neared their destination. On Connecticut Avenue they passed Harvey's restaurant, dating from the James Monroe Administration, and much remodeled since. Now it looked plain compared to the grand Mayflower Hotel next to it. But it was famous for its guests, who included every President from Ulysses S. Grant to FDR. As usual it was buzzing with clientele. The overgrown city had too few restaurants, and Harvey's was prized for its oysters and steaks.

Spy Scribes

Unknown to the FBI leaders, two men with a keen interest in literature were lunching inside. One was already famous, the other to become even more well-known.

The older man was 41 years old, bespectacled, and wearing a black, nicely tailored, double-breasted suit and striped tie. His dark, thinning air was neatly combed over. He had the lean look of a soldier on campaign, and the ascetic face of a serious scribe. His interlocutor, just 25, was tall, long-limbed, and strikingly handsome.

The first was named Cecil Scott, but he was better known as C.S.—C.S. Forester, famed throughout the English-speaking world. For his Horatio Hornblower series of novels about a Royal Navy officer of the Napoleonic Wars.

The two were astonished as ever at the abundance of victuals in America. Back home, they had adjusted to Britain's scarcities, with the U-boats cutting off much of the island's food supplies. Now, though they wanted to stay alert for their afternoon labors, it was hard to restrain themselves. The restaurant's fare was not exotic, but was very ample. They ordered grilled calf sweetbreads with mushrooms and roasted potatoes, and corned beef hash with fried eggs and coleslaw.

The younger man remarked, "We could order extra coffee, to keep us going later on today. I hear the Yanks will start rationing java soon. We might as well get our fill while we can."

Forester smiled approvingly, and continued their conversation dealing with the winter Britain had just suffered through.

"So, let's hope for a repeat of the Great War. The destroyers Roosevelt gave us are rust buckets, true, but they'll help. And the Americans, though preoccupied with the Japs now, have a large Atlantic fleet. With it and the Royal Navy, to protect the convoys, many more supply ships will get through to England. And many more Jerry submarines will go to the ocean bottom.

"This past winter may have been the one, the one to starve us out. But spring is here, and we can plant every acre in Britain, like last year. Victory gardens. And American corn and spam are starting to arrive—on the ships that aren't sunk."

"What is this spam again?" his interlocutor asked.

"It's essentially pork, with salt and potato mixed in."

"Sounds rather British. Or German."

Forester pointed his fork at the roasted mushrooms. "It cannot match the fare here, but it is filling. A cheap meat."

His angular face became tense. "Yes, *if* the pork and other foodstuffs arrive. The toll on the ocean has been horrible." He put down his utensil. "The Yanks were caught with their pants down. After Pearl Harbor, they might have known better."

"Keeping the lights of their coastal cities on at night!" exclaimed his companion in disbelief. "Instead of blackouts. Their oil trawlers are backlighted, an easy target for the U-boats."

"You're so right. They have blackouts, after a fashion, here, where there's no threat, but none off Charleston or Miami! The tonnage lost the other month was back up to half a million again. Almost a hundred merchant ships!"

"Still, things should get better." C.S. Forester's expression became more hopeful. "I've been learning about, as best I can, the tactics of the convoys, and their destroyer escorts. Hope to write a book about it. A morale booster now, or maybe a history after the war." The tense look came back. "What worries me is the margin for error. The U-boats are close to breaking us—they may break us before the Americans organize and come in full force.

"And it's not just the U-boats. One more Jerry battleship, unleashed in the Atlantic, could tip the balance."

He took on a mournful look. "We lost the *Princes of Wales* and *Repulse* to our Japanese 'friends.' And we have what's left of the Italian Navy to deal with in the Mediterranean."

"That's for certain," said his fellow secret agent. "When I flew in North Africa we didn't treat the Italians as a joke. They have some superb tank units, and daring pilots."

C.S. Forester looked about Harvey's conspiratorially, making sure no one was within earshot. The clatter of plates and the low roar of the guests helped ensure their privacy.

Still, he placed his right hand, half-cupped, over his lips, and whispered, "I'm hearing, as the Yanks say, 'scuttlebutt,' that the Jerries have readied the *Tirpitz*, for the high seas."

The latter's ears picked up. That "pocket battleship" was faster than any other ship of its class, and had greater firepower than anything in the Royal Navy.

"If it gets inside a few convoys, it's a wolf among sheep. It could push us to the breaking point. Hopefully it'll meet the same fate as the *Bismarck*," he stated, referencing the sinking of that Nazi battleship the previous spring.

The latter nodded in sympathy with his fellow agent's concern. He wished he was back flying again, taking on the Luftwaffe, perhaps on a carrier over the Atlantic this time, instead of flattering Yank officials at swank diplomatic functions. 'While our men are dying in the desert or over the ocean' he lamented to himself.

Forester lowered his hand and changed the subject. He had said enough of what perhaps he shouldn't reveal. The talk turned back to their writing.

The younger man praised the works of his elder. "I loved the one about the Kaiser's men in the 'Dark Continent,' and the missionary lady and the man who outwitted them. The, the *Africa Royal?*"

"*The African Queen,*" corrected Forester with a smile. He had been writing follow-ups to his best-selling Hornblower series, but enjoyed branching out to other places, other times. Maybe such works would be made into movies someday.

His ego was impervious to praise. As a world-famous author, he was used to plaudits, and knew how they could make a writer lazy. So he turned the subject, and praised the fledgling work of his companion. A valiant Royal Air Force pilot, who'd been injured flying in North Africa. Grievously wounded in the head, he'd been consigned to a desk job, and packed off to the British intelligence team in Washington. Bored to tears by the rounds of diplomatic receptions and cocktail parties required by his new work, he'd taken to writing up his war-time exploits.

"I love your own story of making it through the plane crash, in Libya," Forrester told his protégé of sorts, named Roald Dahl. "It is the work of a professional. As if you've been writing for years. I'm glad the magazine printed it as is, without any editing. It didn't need any."

Dahl, born in Wales of Norwegian parentage, smiled, his bright cheeks blushing just a bit. "If I can't go back to combat," he told Forrester, and he tapped his mended skull, "maybe this writing work will save me from going bonkers."

And he went on to talk about his latest creation, which he hoped might lead to a big success.

"Our Spitfires, our Hurricanes, going up against the Luftwaffe, they come down with plenty of mechanical problems. And lots of strange noises. Some of them unexplained."

"Pilots have a humorous explanation for those. We call them 'gremlins.'"

Forrester laughed. "I know the term. The Scottish engineers on our ships blame engine problems on those elfish creatures." He added, "We have to attribute unknown causes to something."

Roald Dahl smiled. "It lessens the stress, joking about dangers like that. But the thing is, well—you know about Walt Disney?"

"The chap who does those cartoon features, at the cinemas."

"Right, Mickey Mouse and that duck character. Well, he saw a little writeup I did about gremlins, describing them as forest fairies. With a quirky, childish way of speaking. He loved it, and wants me to visit his California studio, to talk it over for a cartoon film!"

"During the current emergency?" queried Forrester, looking pleased yet concerned.

"Well, yes, if I can get a little time off. I certainly don't have much to do right now."

Forrester looked furtively about the restaurant, and lowered his voice. He said, with some sarcasm, "Well, you are, as am I, a Very Important Person—a secret agent for MI-6."

Dahl frowned. "Oh, *really* important. I spend most of my time holding the hand of Yank officials. Telling them that they can rely on us as allies.

"If only I *could* work on a movie. Or if only I could get involved in some real espionage, some cloak and dagger!"

Forrester sipped his black coffee. "You have my sympathy, young man. Most of what I do is the same. Promoting 'King and Country' to the Americans." He smirked. "At least I have, like you, extra time for writing." He looked at his fellow agent with real admiration. "And I encourage you to keep at it. You must not waste talent like that!"

A Working Lunch

Hoover and Tolson left Harvey's restaurant behind them. They went through a wide revolving door into the lobby of the Mayflower. The main corridor was packed, but the maître d, standing outside the entrance to the bar, smiled and gestured them inside it. He took them to Mister Burgos. "Gentleman, he will be your waiter again, our best man at your service." The maître d bowed slightly, and went over to handle a contretemps in the kitchen. Due to a shortage of cooks, the chef was having another fit. Burgos took the two guests to a private table in the back. A partition climbing halfway up to a tall ceiling gave them privacy.

Tolson gave his order: pork chops and a salad with iced tea. And, as a concession to the Southern town, a side of grits. "With honey and butter, please." Otherwise it was just too plain.

Burgos nodded to the Director, "I assume the usual, sir?" Hoover didn't even nod. And the server went off to put in Tolson's order. Hoover's was already prepared.

Tolson loosened up the side straps of his briefcase, and placed half a dozen files on the table. For a man charged with protecting a continental-sized nation from aggressive foreign foes, the Director was calm, if intent. He ignored the files, and got straight to the main issues.

"Any follow-up to the Siebold arrests?" he asked, referring to the FBI's smashing of the Nazi spy ring in Manhattan. Meantime, Burgos placed the usual lunch next to him.

"Good follow-up," said Tolson, with measured enthusiasm. "A lot of them squealed; we've doublechecked their stories. We seem to have rolled up just about every Nazi agent in the U.S." His boss's face was impassive, except for his eyes, which glistened. He cut half of his grapefruit into four smaller pieces. Then his pupils narrowed. "Nothing about bombings, or poisoned cattle, or setting fire to ships?" Hoover was thinking of Imperial Germany's campaign of sabotage in America during the Great War. A shipyard of munitions across from Manhattan harbor had been blown up, damaging the Statue of Liberty. A weapons ship had been set afire in the Atlantic from a timed incendiary. In Maryland, German agents had manufactured vials of anthrax to poison U.S. Army horses. A German sympathizer had even set off a bomb in the Senate's telegraph office. German consulates had been behind much of the mayhem.

"Plenty of tips, but no evidence of that stuff," replied Tolson. "'Patriotic citizens' with overactive imaginations. And all the German diplomats are living the high life in their luxury hotel, in White Sulphur Springs," he added, noting the West Virginia resort hotel where they'd been consigned.

"They can't invade us, and they can't airdrop troops. So—"

"—So," added Hoover, finishing his thought, "we'll watch out for any saboteurs landing off from U-boats." His knife grabbed a shred of iceberg lettuce.

"The Coast Guard's already doing that."

Hoover shrugged in derision. He disdained any organization working in domestic security other than his own.

"OK. Now, what about Jap agents, in Hawaii?"

Tolson placed several more file folders on the table. "Nothing much. Of course we've detained thousands of Japanese-Americans, and the *Issei* born in Japan. No proven saboteurs yet, or spies. There's been no stirring of Americans of Japanese background against us. Mostly, they're fearful and angry, at Tokyo, and worried what will happen to them."

Hoover remarked, "And we figure that's the way it is on the West Coast. California, Washington, Oregon." He ground his teeth on a big leaf of lettuce. To Tolson, he appeared like a big bulldog eating a salad. But he knew not to smile, much less laugh at the sight.

"Like you ordered us," replied Tolson, "we have tails in L.A. and Frisco, and the airplane factories in Seattle, tracking possible agents and saboteurs."

"But the population's loyal," he went on, somewhat cautiously, thinking he knew, but wasn't sure, of his boss's view. "The young Japanese men want to volunteer for the Marines."

Hoover put down his fork, and pushed aside his abstemious meal of grapefruit and cottage cheese. "At the same time," the Director noted, "the War Department's pressuring Roosevelt to imprison, intern, the whole lot of them. Put them in jail for the duration, with the Army standing guard."

Hoover's broad cheeks reddened. "As if we don't have a handle on it!" he snarled. "Let them and the Navy fight the war overseas. And let us take care of things here!"

The Director eyed the bottle of salad dressing he had brought along. "I have to see the President on this again tomorrow. I'll recommend against internment. But the Army, and public opinion, may be hard to stop."

"Politics," muttered Tolson. The national unity after the declarations of war had worn off some, due to the vast losses from the U-boats in the Atlantic. Republicans had begun criticizing the war effort and, with the West Coast still worried about invasion, Roosevelt feared appearing weak against the Japanese threat.

Seeing his boss's anger, Tolson hesitated bringing up the next issue, which was sure to annoy him further. But it couldn't be avoided.

"I've been contacted by officials, of the OCI." Seeing Hoover redden, he quickly added, "They should be coming directly to you, of course. And it was really amateurish of them to send four people to us. A gaggle. Instead of just one person with authority. They don't seem to know what they're doing."

"It's the damn English," said Hoover. "They want to set up, *an American version* of their MI-6, here, on our turf! As if their own agents haven't been snooping around here enough!"

"It's bad enough," agreed the Number Two. "They want an American version of MI-6, or SIS, whatever they call it. Yes, their Secret Intelligence Service. Though I doubt our Army and Navy will stand for it. But it's really outrageous if they start interfering with our work." Tolson took a bite out of his pork chops.

Hoover tapped the side of his plate. "What do we have," and his tone shifted to one of mild derision, "on 'Wild Bill'?"

Tolson slipped out a folder on William Donovan, the President's newly appointed head of the awkwardly, and misleadingly, titled, Office of the Coordinator of Information, or OCI. This was the wartime intelligence agency Roosevelt was setting up, with the help of the British.

"Not much," Tolson answered, shaking his head, and flicking through the file. "No more than what you already know. Similar background to Joseph Kennedy," he said, mentioning the Ambassador to Great Britain.

"Wall Street, lawyer, may be worth millions. Irish. Not a philanderer like the elder Kennedy—"

"—Or the younger!" shot back Hoover.

Tolson continued. "He does keep his pants on. No skeletons in his closet. And he is courageous: There's no taking away his Medal of Honor from the Great War." He went on. "But he deserves his wild reputation. Unpredictable. We can't be sure he'll play ball with us."

Hoover patted the bottle of dressing. "There's no way, that his organization will play ball with us. A bunch of Ivy Leaguers, I gather. Dilletantes. Not lawmen, not soldiers. Except for him of course."

Hoover peeled off some grapefruit, then stopped. "I guess we should hurry up with lunch. We've got a pile of work back at Justice." He stopped, and grimaced. His face seemed like a guard dog sensing a threat. He asked suddenly: "What's the latest on that Elizabeth, Elise, Thorne, character? I smell a rat. A big one."

The bombings on U.S. soil by German agents during the Great War again flickered through his mind. He was determined to prevent any repeat, and it was possible that woman was a foreign spy.

"That thorn in our side?" replied Tolson with a small smile. "We're just not sure what to make of her." He put down his fork, and placed his palms on the tablecloth. "We know she's been 'seeing,' probably bedding down with, officials of the enemy and their allies. At the Spanish Embassy, for one. And probably the Italian diplomats." He reached for a folder, and pulled out several glossy photographs. He slid them across to his boss.

"And we know before this war she worked with the fascists in Spain. All this as the married wife of a Commonwealth diplomat!" Both of Tolson's hands tapped the table. "They're separated now. And I've been getting signals from Donovan's men that she's on our side. For now, at least. They won't give details, but they seem to think so."

Hoover's eyes were wide as he perused the pictures. He focused on a wedding picture from 1931 of a lovely woman, barely out of her teens, with piercing eyes that seemed those of an observant, and much wiser, adult. He added, almost absently, "Unless an amateur operation like theirs is getting hoodwinked."

"That could very well be," Tolson answered. "One of our tails reports she's made contact with a Brazilian official. We could check him out. Rio is filled with admirers of Hitler, after all."

The two men looked up suddenly. The waiter had padded over silently, and had seemingly appeared out of nowhere. Burgos knew Hoover never ordered dessert, and their lunch seemed over, but he stuck to his duty.

"Can I provide you gentlemen with anything else?"

Tolson nodded no. Hoover was silent and impassive. The helper left.

"I want *two* tails on her," said the Director. "Around the clock. And look into a tap on her phone." With FDR's approval, they had simply ignored the Supreme Court's ban on wiretapping. There was a war on, after all.

Hoover looked over the wedding photo of Thorne's. "She's a beauty all right.

"*Femme fatale*," he grumbled. Then he pushed the picture and her folder back to Tolson. "Let's go. We'll be working into the evening."

Dangerous Dalliance

The pretty lady had wanted to see it and, though it was a public place, fronting a major boulevard, he had agreed.

It was a Sunday, and that afternoon things were relatively quiet in the District, and especially so in the surrounding neighborhood. Occasionally a Chevy, an Oldsmobile, or a Navy lorry rumbled past on Massachusetts Avenue, then the quiet returned.

It was nothing like it had been just five months before, on the day of the dastardly attack, "the stab in the back."

Aldiche Engardio had rushed over like many others. A large crowd of Washingtonians and diplomats had gathered outside the iron fence, the locals more out of curiosity than from anger. People were still stunned; the news of the attack hadn't yet sunk in. And they had no idea of the fatalities or the number of ships that had been lost. If they had, they might have stormed the place, and lynched its residents.

Even so, a contingent of policemen and FBI agents had stood inside the enclosure to keep the crowd in check. There was diplomatic immunity after all, even in war, even after being rabbit-punched.

The reporters had been allowed to stand near the cops by the open gate. They noticed the smoke coming from behind the two stories of light-colored stone making up the Georgian Revival embassy. Unopposed, they strode up the pathway to the twin doors of the entrance. They went into a spacious reception room.

They saw Japanese staffers holding onto boxes, or bags crammed with documents, and rushing to the rear exit. No one stopped them, so the scribblers followed. On the lawn outside, the Nipponese were tossing the embassy's records onto bonfires. The smoke mixed with the scent of winter flowers, cyclamen, pansies, and hellebores. It was a truly sickly-sweet odor.

A strange scene. They were destroying papers that might have important military intel, and it was war, yet they also had diplomatic immunity. Should the American authorities stop them? The FBI men nervously talked about what to do. One of them ran inside the embassy to call Hoover's office.

Three months earlier than that December 7th, Aldiche remembered, a contact within the German Embassy near Logan Circle had confidentially given him explosive news. That his superior, the

German chargés d'affaires Hans Thomsen, had learned the American Navy had broken Japan's diplomatic codes. That revelation had set the Argentine on the path of his current espionage. Musing over that, Aldiche now stared with Adelia through the gate at the diplomatic compound. He told his American mistress that, after things had calmed down, the Japanese had become practical. The Americans instructed them not to leave the embassy, but didn't arrest them. Perhaps they wouldn't for a while. So embassy staffers telephoned stores at Dupont Circle and Georgetown, and placed orders that indicated they expected an extended, if pampered, stay. They requested oysters and whiskey, and mattresses and pillows. One might as well sleep comfortably, and eat and drink in style, reasoned the Japanese, while they waited. Some shops refused to take the orders, but most took a middle course. They would deliver the Japanese what they wanted, but only for hard cash.

But now the embassy, despite the spring weather, with cherry trees blossoming on the lawn, was mostly deserted. The diplomats had been detained, and sent via State Department trucks to the Homestead resort in Hot Springs, Virginia. They would be kept there like birds in a gilded cage until exchanged for their American counterparts stuck in Japan.

Adelia pointed to three smartly dressed man on the west side of the front lawn. "They don't look like Japanese," she told her companion. "They look like Europeans."

"You are correct, *carita*. They are Spaniards."

He took in her petite figure, and answered her questioning gaze. "As a neutral party, the Spanish Embassy is representing Japanese, interests, in America." Seeing Adelia's look of concern, he went on, "Rather like Switzerland is doing for American interests in German-occupied Europe. And they're not representing Japan's military interests, of course. But such things as the legal status of Japanese-American citizens, and the property of Japanese businesses affected by the war.

"Yes of course," he quickly added, "their government is evil, but some innocent people, betrayed by Tokyo's actions, have been caught up in the conflict." He smiled inwardly at the smoothness of his deceit.

Aldiche recognized one of the men on the lawn. In fact, he was an espionage contact.

For Spain, behind the cover of its neutrality, had set up a spy ring working on behalf of the Japanese. A ring that gleaned information about the convoys leaving U.S. port cities for Britain, or heading out to supply the U.S. Pacific fleet. Aldiche had used some of what these Spanish spies had learned for his own purposes.

In fact, when the Japanese vacated the embassy, they left a half a million dollars in cash for their fascist friends inside a dining room wall. The Spanish were using that money to finance their ring. There were seven agents in the operation, Aldiche had learned, including Spanish journalists, and an official of the Spanish Embassy in D.C. Namely, its army attaché, but not its naval attaché. Aldiche had been informed that that man, an Admiral Ernesto Armando, was lukewarm toward the Axis, and couldn't be trusted with such secrets.

An article of faith among spies was to shun a colleague when not on an actual mission with him. So Aldiche, ignoring his contact, persuaded Mrs. Adelia Baskin Callaway to leave the locale for the "quieter backstreets, *carissima*, where we can be alone together, just us two." Where it was less likely to be noticed. A sighting could prove embarrassing for either of them.

Despite the warm spring weather, they'd covered themselves up. Both had on thick scarfs as well as sunglasses. Aldiche wore a long leather jacket cut in the style of country residents on his native pampas. He pushed down on his head a black wool homburg. 'A pity,' he thought with rather humorous pride, 'my consort can't see me in all my glory, with all my fine set of hair.'

Adelia, almost a foot shorter than her companion, wore a pink linen women's coat over an angle-length, flower-print dress. The coat was sensibly priced, as befitting the wife of a mid-level officer, yet attractive and snug. And a sun hat, early for the season, over her lengthy blonde tresses. She fancied herself attractive-looking, despite the semi-disguise, and she was right.

Adelia Callaway, bored for so many months, desired to see some of the sights of Embassy Row. There was a lot to see. Dozens of Gilded-Age mansions, built for plutocrats in the days before the income tax, were all about. Aldiche steered her past the C.H. Harlow mansion, much later to become the home of CIA Director William Casey. Its limestone and stucco reminded him of the finest neighborhoods in Buenos Aires, or Madrid. Still, its heavy, overhanging cornice gave an impression of approaching menace.

They wended their way to a statue of the doomed Irish freedom fighter, Robert Emmet. The gleaming bronze statue of the 25-year-old revolutionary, depicted just before his hanging by the British, had been first commemorated in 1916, during Woodrow Wilson's presidency.

'Wilson's 'war to end all wars,' muttered Aldiche to himself sarcastically. Playing to his lover's pronounced romantic streak, he recited from memory, with his erudite, Spanish accent, Emmet's memorable last words, spoken from the scaffold:

"…I have but one request to ask at my departure from this world: THE CHARITY OF ITS SILENCE.

"When my country takes her place among the nations of the earth, then, and not till then, let my epitaph be written!"

Adelia's deep-blue eyes misted, as the wisps of golden hair pushing out from her scarf quivered in a slight breeze. She gazed up at the image of Emmet, who leaned back slightly, a pose that emphasized his visionary gaze, staring off, it seemed, toward the future freedom of his land.

"I so admire men of courage and adventure," she whispered to her consort, her voice catching. She took in the fine bronze work, then glanced about the pedestal. "Look! The four marks, the circles below the statue. They must represent four-leaf clovers!"

Aldiche was surprised at her insight. 'She can be perceptive,' he thought, as he adjusted his hat. 'I must take extra care not to give myself away, and to continue to throw out as many feints as I can." Then he glanced again at the tapered ankles peeking out from her dress, and the down visible amidst the freckles of her skin, and felt any caution weaken.

They mounted the steep hill of S St., passing the Czechoslovakia Embassy, a quiet and forlorn-seeming place. Aldiche took care to curse the occupiers of that land. "That's what started it, the Sudetenland, and Hitler breaking the Munich accord! The bastard!!" Again Adelila was surprised at the vitriol expressed by her companion, more like that of an official of a belligerent nation than the commercial attaché of a neutral land that he professed to be.

They soon passed the former residence of President Woodrow Wilson, with its arched, triple windows, and an American flag fluttering from the roof.

Aldiche hated Wilson for bringing America into the Great War against Germany, setting the precedent for the current intervention. But he was careful to seem the opposite to Adelia. "What an accomplished man!" he exclaimed. "The head of Princeton, and author of a dozen books." He paused, and pointed up at the Stars and Stripes. "Above all, the Commander-in-Chief who brought victory during the Great War!

"Let us hope Mr. Roosevelt does the same in our day!"

Adelia, who still felt tinges of guilt over their affair, was heartened by his exclamations. As much as she had come to dislike her husband, he was a patriot, and Aldiche seemed to exceed him in his pro-American sentiments. She felt like the bond between them was waxing stronger. They trod up the steep incline, Adelia breathing hard, while noticing the athletic Aldiche seemed to hardly breathe at all. They went on past the sumptuous townhomes of the uber-rich, some of them turned into embassies, fitting workplaces for the foreign elite.

The Argentine noticed a policeman in front of the next manse, and as a precaution steered his mistress to the other side of the street. Neither was under suspicion, but there was no need to take any chances with the authorities.

"Oh look, now I remember!" he said excitedly in a low voice, pointing at the mansion behind the officer. The Federal Era structure was a riot of open shutters and attic dormers. "That's the home of Herbert Hoover!"

"The homes of two Presidents on the same block?" wondered Adelia. And she admired not for the first time her lover's knowledge of the capital's history and culture. This was the kind of insightful outing she had expected from her husband, but never got.

"Yes, he's lived here since leaving office," Aldiche noted, while looking away from the cop. "With the war, he gets official protection again." He shook his head. "His reputation took quite a fall during the Depression. But at one time he was the most admired man in the world."

"You mean," noted Adelia with a warm smile, "his feeding of the children. In France, in Belgium?"

"Yes, leading the relief effort for all those starving during and after the Great War. Like Wilson, and like Mr. Roosevelt," and at this Aldiche nearly gagged despite himself, "he, he truly, is another great American humanitarian." He recovered himself, and continued the prevarication. "Your country produces so many men of distinction!

"Sometimes I wish," he continued, now sounding plaintive, "I was an American myself. Though of course I love my own country—"

"—Perhaps someday you will be an American," answered Adelia, with a trace of longing.

They reached the plateau of the hill. On their left was a block's-worth of green space. Aldiche, aware of its recent war-time dramas, became inwardly glum.

It is one of the oldest locales in the nation. In its earliest incarnation, in the 1660s, it was owned by Lord Baltimore, the first English ruler of Maryland. In the early 1800s, it was the property of a pamphleteer for Thomas Jefferson, a scribe who was jailed under the Sedition Act for criticizing the John Adams Administration. It was near one of the city's earliest graveyards, the Holmead, where gruesome grave robberies had occurred. And during the Civil War, Union troops had seized its venerable townhouse, and it had mysteriously burned to the ground. Aldiche took Adelia through some Newton apple trees to the porch of the original home. It was a humble frame house, long since abandoned. It seemed to call out to its long-gone occupants. "I so love these unexpected discoveries!" cooed Adelia.

The Argentine told her the place's recent history. Before the Great War, the German Embassy had purchased the surrounding property, but after war was declared the U.S. government had confiscated it. Following the armistice, the German foreign office had acquired the land again. And after the latest war erupted, the federal authorities had taken it back. "This place makes you feel you're in the middle of great events," remarked the woman.

They walked on to a charming spot, a small, balustraded water basin. Several dozen narrow granite steps went down to the street below. Adelia breathed in the scent of red cedars and magnolias flowering along the sides of the staircase. Looking downward, she remarked, "They remind me of the—what's the word?—the vertiginous, hills, in San Francisco, so steep that they end in stairways.

"I explored them with my husb—we explored them when stationed near the Presidio." Gazing down the steps over her supple shoulders, Aldiche remarked, "This is Decatur Terrace. After your great naval hero. The 'Don Juan' of your nation!"

She looked at him with surprise, and he realized she had mistaken his reference.

Taking her hands, he said, "Oh not the romantic side of Don Juan! But in his guise as a naval warrior, in defeating the Mohammedan Turks, in the great sea battle of Lepanto. As your Commodore Decatur vanquished Mohammed's Barbary Pirates centuries later."

He smiled devilishly. "Though of course Don Juan was a great lover too. One of those famed 'Latin lovers'." He laughed, and Adelia blushed, the scarlet of her face pulsing above her scarf. Yet she kept her hands in his, and gripped tighter.

He freed his left hand and pointed down the stairs. "The locals here call them the Spanish Steps. Like the famous ones in Rome, near the Spanish Embassy." Recalling his service at the Argentine Embassy in Rome, where he had forged military and intelligence links with Mussolini's government, he drew in his breath dramatically. "I would love to return there some time!" He paused deliberately, and stared into her azure eyes. "Although, as your Mr. Jefferson said, 'Foreign travel is best performed in the company of a delightful lady.'" Adelia blushed even more.

As they left the wooded, sweetly scented hillock, their eyes caught a four-story brick townhouse with a high, red-colored retaining wall.

"Its architect, Ogden Codman," said Aldiche with a knowing air, "also designed the Breakers mansion, for the Vanderbilts, in Newport Rhode Island." Adelia didn't recognize the term Breakers, but knew anyone employed by the Vanderbilts had to be choice. Certainly this Renaissance-like palace was remarkable. Aldiche, knowing his lover's Southern ancestry, went on: "Part of it is a home for retired, wealthy widows of ranking Confederate officers. Yes, some of them are still alive, and a few reside here." Adelia stared at the manse. The women mentioned were exactly the kind she most admired when growing up in Carolina.

Seeing her receptive look, Aldiche suddenly asked: "Would you like to see the site of an, a 'terrorist incident'? A bombing?" Adelia was surprised at the unusual question, but didn't say no, and indeed grew excited with anticipation of a new adventure, so they continued along.

They passed by a former residence of Charles Evans Hughes, who'd lost to Wilson in the close election of 1916. "He was the man most qualified to be President who never became so," Aldiche pronounced. "Governor of New York, and later the Chief Justice of your Supreme Court." He tried to sound like he admired the man, but in fact he disdained him for running as the "war candidate" against Wilson, the candidate who'd "kept us out of war." He had no love for Wilson, the defeater of Imperial Germany, but in his view the more hawkish Hughes was worse. 'These Americans,' he thought, 'are such an impediment to our fascist movements, while trying to control the world themselves!'

They reached the promised spot. Aldiche was pleased at one aspect of the startling event that had occurred there 23 years before, and undecided about the other.

2132 R St. was a sturdy townhouse of the type favored by the powerbrokers of a prestigious neighborhood. His eyes glowing, Aldiche pointed out the pitted stones near the basement windows and the facing of the front steps.

"This was the home of your Attorney General at the time, *Señor* Mitchell Palmer. In the spring of 1919, a man walked toward his door carrying a bomb, powerful enough to blow up the house, and the Attorney General with it." Adelia listened in wonder.

"But he proved unskilled at this craft: The bomb blew up as he approached, igniting prematurely, blowing him up, but not the house, and not *Señor* Palmer!" He paused for dramatic effect, then continued.

"The windows were blown out, and some of the exterior damaged, as you can still see." And he pointed once more at the basement foundation stones still marred by the blast.

Adelia placed her left hand to her mouth as she imagined the carnage. She looked down at the sidewalk, and realized she was standing on the place where remains of the man had been found. "Who was he?" she wondered aloud, her hands trembling slightly.

"A Galleanist." Seeing the blank look on her face, Aldiche explained, "Anarchists, socialists. From Italy, of the type that Mussolini put down." He stopped himself, having almost spoken approvingly of il Duce, now a fierce enemy of the U.S. He continued quickly, "They were right to oppose Mussolini, of course, but wrong to try to kill American officials. And to use such disgusting means!" As a younger man, Aldiche had been glad to read about the crackdown that followed, as Palmer led a series of raids around the country that arrested anarchists and suspected communists. It was what Mussolini, and the Führer, with harsher repression, had done upon seizing power.

Aldiche pointed with a flourish to the four-story townhome across the way. "The anarchist, yes, might have affected events if he had killed Palmer. But he might have changed the course of history if he had exploded the bomb just minutes before."

Adelia stared at him expectantly.

"For just before the explosion, two people had left that house. A powerful couple. But not as powerful as they would become.

"They were Franklin and Eleanor Roosevelt!"

Adelia was startled at the thought.

"Imagine if they had been killed by the explosion!" exclaimed her lover.

"America would have had a different President," he said in an excited, but rather neutral tone. "A different President during the Depression. A different Commander-in-Chief today." Adelia pondered the implications.

Aldiche had varying feelings about this. He disliked FDR because he had, he was convinced, steered the U.S. into war with Germany, Italy, and Japan. But, just five months after Pearl Harbor, he had yet to form an opinion of Roosevelt as a war leader. If he turned out to be a bad one, he would be glad he hadn't been killed 22 years before. Certainly the current American war effort wasn't impressive, with disasters in both the Pacific and the Atlantic. And Aldiche surely wasn't impressed with the security of its top-secret projects, or the discretion of those, like Adelia, who knew its secrets.

Sobered by the tale, the two moved down 21st St. to the Phillips Collection. Although the Smithsonian's National Gallery of Art had become a sensation since its grand opening weeks before, the Phillips, like the Corcoran Gallery of Art near the White House, remained popular. The Phillips made up a wing of the mansion of Duncan Phillips, a man grown wealthy from Pittsburgh steel. Over time, the collections were expanding, and Mr. Phillips determined that, on his death, his entire home would be incorporated into the art venue.

Aldiche would have loved to shepherd Adelia inside. The museum was the kind of place her husband would never take her. The sort of locale she'd imagined immersing herself in after her spouse's transfer to Washington. The impressionist paintings of Matisse and Monet would appeal to her romantic nature, and would no doubt strengthen her romantic feelings toward him. 'Renoir's *Luncheon on the Boating Party* alone would throw her into my arms,' he estimated. It would remind Adelia of their picnics along secluded nooks on the Potomac shore.

Yet he ran into a stroke of luck. Hanging above the entrance was a large-size, color reproduction of the Phillip's most famous acquisition, the *Boating Party* itself! He could tell from Adelia's reaction she loved that painting. She stood transfixed under it, taking in the fine reproduction. The Argentine joined her, and gently pushed his muscled torso up against her. They gazed up at the dreamy rendering of the young couples, in attractive, if informal, attire, savoring supper and wine during a halcyon day on the balcony of a rustic restaurant.

"I was at the that place in France," Aldiche lied, "with my former lady friend—how do you Americans say—my girlfriend. We shared a picnic not unlike the people in the painting. *!Que incredible'*" Out of the corner of his eye he saw Adelia's disappointed look on hearing him say "girlfriend."

"There was talk of us becoming engaged," he stated, with a wan expression. "But it did not come to pass. And there's been no serious one in my life since," he lied, as he was married. But his wife was in Buenos Aires, and he would never mention that.

He touched her hand lightly. "No one serious: Until recently."

In response, Adelia's cheeks burned like a conflagration.

"Oh, to return to such a place," he continued, "with someone who could appreciate it with me! Someone like *you*."

She turned to him, her heart swelling.

"Perhaps," she said, staring at him, then looking away into the distant sky, "perhaps someday, we could."

Aldiche had considered his scheme for some days and, given his lover's positive reaction, concluded it was a perfect time to put it into play. But first he had to maneuver Adelia to the far side of Dupont Circle.

Massachusetts Avenue Manses

At his suggestion, they walked down from the Phillips museum back to Massachusetts Avenue. Across the boulevard was a four-story, light-brown mansion, once occupied by a Wisconsin congressman. Its top had a French Empire mansard roof with dormers, befitting its French-born architect, Jules Henri de Sibour. It was a hive of activity, with roughly dressed construction workers, supervised by diplomats in tails and top hats, moving furniture and boxes into the residence.

"It is the new home of the royal lady of Luxembourg," explained Aldiche, hiding his distaste for the pro-Allies noble. "While in exile, she will reside here."

Adelia, wide-eyed, said admiringly, "The Grand Duchess?" Like the exiled monarchs of Holland and Norway, she had been much in the newspapers. All the royals were standing up for their occupied peoples. Adelia admired the lady's restrained elegance.

"Yes," replied her companion, tight-lipped. "Duchess Charlotte." He whipped off her full name: "Grand Dutchess Charlotte Adelgonde Elisabeth Marie Wilhelmine." He cleared his throat. "When the Germans annex—when they conquered Luxembourg, its royal family fled. Some of them will be staying here until the end, the conclusion, of the war."

'Her country is now part of the Third Reich,' thought Aldiche. 'As it should be. Absurd for such a small, German-speaking principality on Germany's very border to be independent!'

As they waited for a traffic light to turn, they eyed the mansion across the avenue. Outside it was a young man in the buttoned tunic and dark, visored cap of a chauffeur. He carried two stuffed, Louis Vuitton suitcases out to a Packard Super Eight sedan.

Adelia had seen many fine dwellings that day, but this was the grandest thus far. It was where Embassy Row formally ended, and the grand, still-residential homes of Dupont Circle began. The place looked like a hôtel de ville, not a mere mansion but a whole city hall that had been somehow transported from Lyons, or even Paris itself. Indeed the architects, Carrère and Hastings, had experience creating governmental structures: they'd designed the Russell Senate and Cannon House office buildings flanking the Capitol Building itself, as well as the august New York Public Library. This was a house fit for a king.

Indeed, Aldiche remarked, "The people living there are the closest to what you Americans have for royalty." Seeing her questioning look, he continued, "The lady of the house, Mathilde

Townsend, Mrs. Welles, was formerly wed to New England Senator Peter Gerry. His ancestor, Elbridge Gerry, was the Vice-President for the author of your esteemed Constitution, President Madison." Aldiche thought of the amusing American term gerrymandering, or the packing of a congressional district with one's supporters, and named after that Vice-President.

"In fact, your *Presidente*, Franklin Roosevelt, and Eleanor, lived there before moving into the White House.

"And the man of the house is *Señor* Sumner Welles, the head of the State Department for my part of the world, for Latin America, and for much else."

As if on cue, a tall man, his head held high over a pinstriped, dark-gray suit, his right hand fingering a cane, walked out of the front entrance and over to the Packard. He had a balding head that seemed to focus attention on his prominent nose and deep-set, dreamy-looking eyes. He gave some instructions to the driver, who went back inside the house.

"They say," Aldiche noted in a low tone, "that he is the real power at the Department of State. And that the Secretary of State, *Señor* Cordell Hull, is not too happy at that."

Adelia barely heard the comment about Secretary Hull, as she took in the block-size building and manicured lawn. It was actually three buildings, finished in 1900. A central, four-level home of Indiana limestone, with 11 front windows, and a mansard roof of dark slate, with a columned balcony in front. It was bracketed by light-hued walls holding four tall chimneys, plus another chimney piercing the roof proper. The smaller buildings on either side, also of limestone, had their own mansard toppings draped with copper supports.

In front of the stone rail and steps leading to the entrance were twin shrub gardens, blending into arboretums on either side that led to more lush greenery. Most of the acre of real estate had originally been laid out by Frederick Law Olmstead, the designer of Central Park and the Capitol Building grounds. The buildings were loosely based on a Versailles chateau of a king's mistress, Madame Pompadour, and a king's wife, Marie Antoinette.

Breaking in on her thoughts, Aldiche said, "Yes, fit for a monarch, no?"

They looked on as the current lady of the house, Mrs. Welles, came outside to join her husband. Wrapped in a fur coat, the 53-year-old madame still wore her hair piled up high, but its once vibrant, strawberry tint had darkened. And even from a distance, both she and Mr. Welles seemed forlorn.

Aldiche thought he knew why.

He had never liked Welles, "that hypocritical meddler," as he saw him. While pushing his "Good Neighbor Policy" in Latin America, and withdrawing U.S. troops from the Dominican Republic, he had made sure U.S. companies had gotten every dime owed them from local regimes. In his diplomatic excursions through Europe, Welles pursued bootless, Don Quixote-like quests. 'Trying to persuade the Führer from taking what was rightfully his, while standing for strict quotas on Jews allowed into America,' as Aldiche saw it. 'Trying to persuade the Russians from taking back a Poland that had been theirs for centuries, and trying to persuade both Moscow and Berlin from leaving the feeble Baltic States alone!'

The previous year, Aldiche's sources at the State Department had informed, Welles had been caught up in an almost unbelievable scandal. It was known that he drank, and it had been rumored he lusted for others other than Matilde—and that those others were of his own sex. In fact, a year-and-a-half prior, Welles had been on an interstate train returning from a funeral for Speaker of the House William Bankhead, the father of the glamorous actress Tallulah Bankhead. On route, a drunken and possibly drug-addled Welles had propositioned two black porters. They had reported the unwelcome advance to their superiors, who had reported it to federal authorities. Word had it that Secretary Hull and several Senators, none of whom were friends of Welles, had the goods to bring him down. But none other than J Edgar Hoover had sat on the scandal.

In this vein, Aldiche didn't believe the whispers about the close relationship between the FBI Director and his aide Tolson. He had, however, tried to corroborate the porter scandal, and so possibly blackmail the Assistant Secretary of State. So far, he hadn't succeeded. His next move would be to try to track down the two railway servants, and see if they would talk.

'If I could only blackmail President Roosevelt's chief foreign policy adviser,' thought Aldiche, 'and during a time of war! The influence I might wield, to cripple the U.S.!'

He and Adelia watched Welles and his wife enter the manse, and come back out with two liveried porters, who toted more leather luggage to the car.

"No doubt they're going to Oxon Hill," Aldiche stated.

"Oxes what?" she asked, puzzled.

"Ah, *cierto*, you're fairly new to this region. They have a grand estate in the Maryland county of Prince George, about fifteen kilometers south of here. Ten miles or so." He laughed. "The first President lived on that 'hill of the oxen'."

"I thought George Washington lived at Mount Vernon," replied Adelia, puzzled still.

Her lover smiled, somewhat arrogant about his great knowledge of the region. "The first President of your government *after* your Revolution, but before the presidency of *Señor* Washington. A man named John Hanson; he owned a large plantation there. Now *Señor y Señora* Welles occupy that space. They normally reside there, not here."

Adelia marveled at the wealth of a family that could afford two places of such distinction. And as ever at her consort's knowledge of the world.

As they strolled down the avenue, Aldiche glanced down 21st St., where a block away a Smithsonian entomologist, and suspected German agent from the Great War, had dug secret tunnels under his house. He claimed his children could play there, where he could conduct his own research on insects. Others believed it had been a nest for the Kaiser's agents, then conducting war-time sabotage throughout America.

Incredibly, Aldiche, with the help of German, Spanish, and Italian agents, had over a series of months turned the dark, abandoned warrens into a primitive safehouse for clandestine meetings. And a storehouse for sensitive documents they'd purloined. It was one of Aldiche's deepest secrets, and one he would never entrust to Adelia.

As they moved on, Aldiche chuckled to himself: 'For her, I'm saving the best for last.' He had shrewdly picked a block containing the most remarkable-looking private homes in the city. Guaranteed to impress.

So they walked up to another stunning place, the Walsh-McLean House. This mansion of one of Washington's society dames—though still owned by the lady in question, Evalyn Walsh—was now evidently part of the war effort.

Aldiche and Adelia watched women with eager expressions step quickly in and out of the house. At first look, their long white gowns, and black headdresses with white headbands, made them appear to be nuns. And they did have crosses stitched onto their gowns. But Adelia glimpsed a painted sign above the doorway that read, "District Chapter of the American Red Cross".

Her eyes darted up to examine the four grand stories of yellowish brick, crowned by a red-tiled roof, with seven arched windows on each end. Taking his lover by the elbow, Aldiche went along the circular carriage path under the columned portico, a shelter from rain, that jutted out from the entrance. The building's curved walls, which gave the impression the structure was wavering in place, hinted at Antoni Gaudí's hallucinogenic works that had taken shape some years before in Barcelona.

In truth, it had been owned by a couple bordering on the surreal, the city's most well-connected and scandal-ridden. As such, they had been a target of the cunning Aldiche, like a vulture waiting upon a dying beast.

The 60-room manse had been built in 1903, for the then-stratospheric price of $835,000. During a high point of the Gilded Age, for an Irish immigrant-turned-multimillionaire, Thomas Walsh, who'd struck it very rich with a Colorado gold mine. He and his family moved to the District's plushest neighborhood, and the *nouveau riches* proved their *bona fides* to their older-money neighbors with this lavish home, and its fully $2 million worth of furniture. "They even built a lavish stage for private theatrical performances!" Aldiche informed Adelia.

In 1886 the couple had produced a daughter, Evalyn Walsh. In 1908 she married a fellow trust fund kid, Edward Beale "Ned" McLean, the scion of a publishing clan who owned the *Cincinnati Enquirer* and *The Washington Post*. Ned McLean had the means, Aldiche told his lover, to purchase his bride the 45-carat Hope Diamond, for a mere $180,000. Adelia pursed her lips, imagining owning such a jewel.

"But the gem is said to be cursed," noted the Argentine. And the McLean-Walsh combo seemed intent on proving that. Evalyn and Ned entertained lavishly, with friends in the highest of places. Ned, a heavy drinker, Aldiche went on, had a fellow tippler friend in Warren Harding, elected President back in 1920.

The President's often sordid and crooked colleagues entertained ladies of the evening, and swilled bootleg gin during Prohibition, enforced on everyone else by the President's FBI. They partied at a townhouse of Ned's around the corner from the White House. Very late at night, the revelers would stumble two blocks to the "Little Green House," where one of Harding's most corrupt officials, Jesse Smith—a gofer for Attorney General Harry Micajah Daughtery, the nation's top law enforcement officer—hanged himself when a related scandal broke. And dragged Ned McLean into the mess.

"THE scandal of that era," Aldiche concluded. "'Teapot Dome,' where the President's aides took bribes from oil companies," in exchange for leasing them federal lands.

Adelia shook her head in disbelief. She knew she was no saint, having broken her marital vows, but surely her behavior was nothing like the McLeans.

"Do they still live here?" she wondered. "With the Red Cross workers?"

The Argentine shook his handsome head, and stared into the distance. "Ned McLean's bizarre behavior, his carousing and overspending, only got worse. Much worse. The couple divorced about a decade ago. Around then he was placed in an asylum for the insane. He died last year." His distant look became more focused. "But Evalyn Walsh," he added, "though given to drink and to profligate actions herself, has had an Epif, epifa—how do you say?

"An epiphany."

"*Preciso*. The *viuda*, the widow, has had an epiphany of late. Although *Señora* Evalyn still owns this place, she has rented it out to the Red Cross.

"No doubt Evalyn Walsh" added Aldiche, "remembers what her mother did here after the Great War. She and her friends knitted winter clothes for the poor children of Europe, during the terrible 'Spanish influenza'.

"Queen Eizabeth—not England's young queen—but Belgium's, presented her with a medal, in this very place, for her kind deeds. And now, due to her benevolence, the Red Cross itself is here."

Aldiche didn't mention he had dropped his hope of blackmailing Mrs. Walsh, for she was too evidently a patriot, and would have targeted Mr. McLean, but he had died.

Still, there was perhaps greater opportunity with the new generation. Namely in the lovely, blonde daughter of the Walshes, like her mother named Evalyn. She seemed to have as much sense as her parents. The previous October, though just 19, she'd married the choleric, four-time-married, 57-year-old Senator, Robert Rice Reynolds. Aldiche had heard rumors there was already trouble in paradise.

And to Aldiche, Reynolds was a natural political ally. Before the war a strict isolationist, the North Carolinian was an anti-Semite who'd argued for "playing ball" with the European dictators. He saw the New Deal programs such as the Work Projects Administration, which had been building the Blue Ridge Parkway in his state and in Virginia, as little different from Hitlerian creations like the Autobahn.

It was possible Aldiche could recruit the Senator to the cause. A plum target indeed, as he was next in line to chair the Senate's Committee on Military Affairs. He could become a conduit of America's most sensitive war-time information. Further, his obvious weakness for the ladies was a classic flaw of countless men who'd been gulled or blackmailed by female operatives. Aldiche had several femme fatales in mind who'd be up to the task. And if trouble developed in the

Reynolds's marriage, and trouble seemed inevitable, the young Evalyn might be worked on too. Aldiche would enjoy working on her himself.

As Adelia caught glimpses through a yellow-tinted window of the Walsh mansion's reception room, she imagined how grand it would be to reside within, or to be honored by a queen! She caught her breath when catching sight of the staircase. It was like the one on the *Titanic* she had read about. It rose up majestically for two floors lined by curved mahogany railings. The stairs were overlaid with red velvet, now worn away in spots, which only revealed something more opulent: white marble. Topping the cavernous space above the steps was a stained-glass window, light-brown in hue, which took up much of the roof, its natural light mixing with the glow from the ornate, ground-floor fixtures.

Aldiche peered easily over the soft, freckled shoulder of his mistress, and breathed in her fresh fragrance. He exhaled, and noted: "They say the elder Mr. Walsh buried a solid-gold bar within the house. *Por buena suerte*—for good luck.

"Perhaps in the foundation stone," he said, smiling, and reaching down and tapping the bottom of the wall. "Or perhaps inside that stairway."

They stepped out from the portico and back onto Massachusetts Avenue. The sun pushed through a scattering of clouds, and illuminated a four-story townhouse of attractive, beige-colored stone. Unusual for that busy, urban neighborhood, it had a small garden in front in place of the unusual sidewalk. An extra touch of class. Or vanity.

It was the home of another gossip legend, Alice Roosevelt Longworth. The uncontrollable, eldest child of Theodore Roosevelt.

She was now 57, and as wild and brutally honest as ever. She had married one Congressman, future Speaker of the House Nicholas Longworth, and had had an affair, and a love child, with another, Senator William Borah. That liaison was an open secret. Indeed, she had wanted to nickname the baby Deborah, in a play on "de Borah."

Aldiche was silent about this, but simply pointed out the imposing house, noting it was the home of the daughter of the first Roosevelt to reside at the White House. And that she "was wed to the late House Speaker, whom I have met," he lied, having arrived in Washington after Longworth's death 10 years before.

They next came to a towering, red-brick townhouse. It had a 15-foot-long, wrought-iron canopy that thrust out from the entrance like the prow of a ship. Employees were scampering in and out of this building too, not in uniforms, but in neat civilian dress.

"Speaking of Speakers of the House," said Aldiche, "this was the home of James 'G.' Blaine. Gillepsie Blaine."

"I think I remember that odd-sounding name," remarked Adelia, "from my school days."

Aldiche smiled. "This was once the embassy of my sister country, Columbia." He stopped, and forced his smile into a grimace about a nation whose stealth, cunning, and military ethic he much admired. "And, two decades ago, of that country who stabbed America in the back. Japan."

The wife of a Navy officer, however personally disloyal, had to share her lover's apparent disgust for the empire behind the Pearl Harbor attack. "To bomb us while they were negotiating peace!" she cried, echoing the sentiment of every American.

Yet neither, not even the seemingly all-knowing Argentine spy, was aware that when the Japanese occupied the mansion in the early 1920s, they were themselves victims of a subterfuge engineered by an operative more expert than Aldiche, and perhaps more than Lizzy Thorne. That was Herbert Yardley, who broke the encryption employed by Japanese diplomats, allowing the U.S. to read their coded instructions. Yardley, a brilliant mathematician and world-class poker player, had gotten his start in signals intelligence during the Great War, as a telegraph clerk for the White House. Bored, he'd spent his free time deciphering top-secret messages from President Wilson's aides in Europe. When he presented his unauthorized work to his boss, an Army major, he half-expected to be fired. Instead, he was hired—as the head of his nation's first signals intel outfit.

'If the Germans, Brits, and Russians read each other's messages,' he reasoned, 'why not us?'

In 1921, the major naval powers had met at D.C.'s Constitution Hall to work out an arms accord to limit their number of warships. Most negotiations centered on the capital ships for the three biggest navies: the U.S., Britain, and Japan. A kind of grand poker ensued in which the negotiating parties were coy about the restrictions to be placed on Tokyo. The Americans and the British were to have the same number of battleships, the Japanese somewhat less. But how much less would the Nipponese agree to? Perhaps a 5 to 4 ratio?

Enter Yardley and his team. By deciphering the instructions sent to Japan's delegation, they learned Tokyo would accept a 5 to 3 ratio. So that was what the Americans proposed, and the

Japanese accepted. The 5:5:3 ratio became the most noteworthy outcome of the Conference. Yardley later set up intel agencies for Canada and Nationalist China.

Adelia gazed up at Blaine's massive block of brick with its soaring chimneys. She felt intimidated. "It seems so official," she commented. "Like a schoolhouse. And a little bit like a haunted house."

"Well," said Aldiche, "James G. Blaine was an important official: Speaker of the House, Secretary of State, and the confidante to President Garfield who" and Aldiche lowered his voice, and feigned sadness, "who was tragically shot and killed by a crazy man."

"Actually, his doctors killed him," he added, twisting his lips and cheeks into a look of dismay. "You Americans, and we Argentines, did not yet believe in such things as germs and viruses. So the President's doctors, with unwashed hands, probed his wound to try to find the bullet. And merely spread the infection through the unfortunate man's body."

He saw that his lover cringed at this, and paused. He had thought of lying that he had met an elderly man who'd witnessed the shooting, but he couldn't quite remember when the assassination had occurred—1890? 1880? Before then? He didn't want an encounter with a witness to such a long-ago event sound implausible. And besides, he had been really laying it on thick, and his companion desired romance, not more tales of gore.

In fact, the Garfield tragedy made Adelia think of the current bloodshed. With America still revving up for offensives in the Pacific and in Europe, and with the war in Russia stalled by springtime mud, the newspapers and radio were centered on the fighting in North Africa.

"I wonder," she said absently, "when our boys will join the Brits in Libya."

Actually, Aldiche knew, from a press dispatch, that a small force of U.S. tanks and crewmen had been shipped via the Suez Canal to join the British, Australian, and East Indian troops faced off against the Italians and Germans of Rommel's *Afrika Korps*. The American contribution was small, but the U.S. Office of War Information had been eager to boast that U.S. soldiers were now engaged in that theater of operations. Aldiche had a contact in the Office, which was thought to be riddled with foreign, mostly Soviet, spies. Indeed it was a hive of Russian penetration. Yet American officials waved away concerns, saying "the Russians are now our allies."

The Argentine had learned that, remarkably, a former denizen of the Blaine mansion was leading that squadron of tanks. That was Major Henry Cabot Lodge, Jr., who'd lived in the manse the year after the naval conference.

Aldiche had a high regard for the Cabot Lodge family, a clan of Boston Brahmins. Not for their distinguished pedigree, but for their quasi-isolationist stance on foreign affairs. It was the Major's father, Henry Cabot Lodge, Sr., who had led the successful fight against President Wilson's Treaty of Versailles and League of Nations. Like many, Aldiche viewed the League as an impotent farce, yet the efforts of people like the elder Lodge had helped delay America's entry into the current conflict. And hopefully would allow the Axis powers to win before America got fully involved.

Champion of Civil Defense

He and his mistress were about to move on when a squat and very short man stepped briskly out of the Blaine House entrance. Almost 60, but with the vigor of a man 20 years younger, he had a round face with full cheeks, and spoke in a high, deliberate voice. Draped in a dark suit with broad lapels, he paused and, while spotting a taxicab pulling up, confidently chatted with seven young adults, evidently his employees, who had surrounded him.

Aldiche noticed that the four male workers were strikingly handsome, and the three female workers highly attractive and athletic-looking. The ladies, apparently in the Women's Army Corps, wore tailored, light-blue suits with wide jacket lapels, their heads topped by cadet caps. The men appeared to be Army Air Force pilots. But oddly, they were wearing their suede flight jackets and flight caps, not the light-green civilian dress one would expect of flyers off duty. But no, the spy perceived, these were not actual uniforms, but stylized versions.

Adelia recognized the man in charge. Her mood turned sunny at the sight of the nationally famous politico. Normally shy in public, her adventurous streak burst out.

"Mr. La Guardia!" she called, to the Mayor of New York, and the new head of the U.S. Office of Civilian Defense.

"My nephew loves Captain America! He even belongs to the Sentinels of Liberty!!"

The Mayor, grinning broadly, rushed over to shake the hand of his lovely admirer.

"Why, thank you, Miss?"

Adelia almost said "Mrs.," then caught herself, and simply uttered, with hesitation, her first name.

Fiorello La Guardia took this as shyness, which he found charming. "Any fan *of Marvel Comics*," he thundered, patting her hand, "is surely a friend of mine!"

Aldiche, fearful of being seen, stood back cautiously, while watching the two, and he recalled the cartoon drama of the previous spring.

The fledging comic strip, with war breaking out in Europe and with Superman-style comics all the rage, had put out a patriotic superhero, dubbed Captain America, who took on the world's real-life supervillain, one Adolf Hitler. Indeed, the cover of its first issue showed the red, white, and blue-garbed hero flooring *Der Führer* with a right cross to the chin.

Overnight, the 10-cent comic book, featuring top-flight writers like Stan Lee, became the country's most purchased publication. Fan clubs like the Sentinels sprung up nation-wide. However, the U.S. was a neutral country at that time. The pro-Nazi German-American Bund, which packed Madison Square Garden for a rally, howled in protest. Its would-be storm troopers stalked Marvel's 42nd St. Manhattan office, hinting at violence.

La Guardia had become the cartoonists' guardian, pledging protection from New York's Finest and personally visiting Captain America's creators.

Aldiche had little regard for La Guardia. For his openly anti-Axis stance. And for what he thought was his hypocrisy. Back in 1935, when Mussolini's Italy had invaded Ethiopia, La Guardia, of Italian descent, in a city with many Italian-Americans, attended a sold-out, pro-Mussolini Madison Square Garden rally. It raised hundreds of thousands of dollars for the Italian Red Cross, which used the funds for wounded Italian soldiers. A few years later, when the political winds shifted, Aldiche believed, the seemingly stalwart La Guardia had swerved like a sock puppet.

And Aldiche, a bon vivant who enjoyed receptions, horseback riding, and casinos, saw the Mayor as a stuffed-shirt moralizer. In New York he waged campaigns, in the spy's view futile and comic-opera, against minor vices like gambling and, of all things, the operation of pinball machines! They were linked to the slot machine and numbers rackets run by mobsters. And as a lover of music halls and show girls, Aldiche disdained the Mayor for shutting down the town's burlesque theaters. The man's socialist leanings also didn't endear themselves to a brownshirt-at-heart like the Argentine.

But the moralizer didn't seem at all like Billy Sunday now. He savored the attention he was getting from his admirers, especially the lovely ladies. One of them—with strands of her long, dirty-blonde hair pulled up above her forehead, and the rest in curled piles atop her shoulders, in the style of the Andrew Sisters ensemble—grasped La Guardia's hands.

"Mayor sir, we just recorded our ad for the war bond drive. Could we possibly perform it for you?" She puckered lipsticked lips and cast her sparkling brown eyes to the side. "It will only take a minute."

The diminutive La Guardia squeezed her hands and stared up at her rouged cheeks with delight. "How could I resist?!"

As if on cue, the three lasses stepped to the center of the portico, and the four men formed a semicircle behind them, a clam shell to pearls. The trio began dancing in place, moving their arms side to side, while the men broke out in perfect, four-part harmony:

. "He was a famous trumpet man from out Chicago way,

He had a boogie style that no one else could play;

He was the top man at his craft—

But then his number came up, and he was gone with the draft!

He's in the Army now, a blowin' reveille:

He's the boogie-woogie bugle boy of Company B!"

The men then pirouetted, while the women spread out their arms then brought them together. Next the women locked their arms and did a polka step, as the men reached out their left arms in a limp, spastic Hitler salute. Their voices rang out:

When der Führer says we is de master face:

We heil (spffft), we heil (spffft), right in der Furor's face!

Not to love der Führer is a great disgrace;

So we heil (spffft), heil (spffft), right in der Furor's face!

Are we not the supermen?

Aryan pure supermen?

Ja, we ist der supermen:

Super duper supermen!

A small crowd of passersby had gathered at the portico to watch the show. They shouted their delight. Adelia cried out with joy, and clapped until her hands ached.

Aldiche, displeased at what he took as a low-class dig at a historic figure, and nervous about being recognized, took a couple of steps back, and clapped perfunctorily.

The entertainment wing of the civil defense agency was controversial, he had read. Eleanor Roosevelt headed it. This drew criticism from Republicans who didn't like the activist First Lady, and from persons across the political divide who saw the song-and-dance routines as trivializing more important work.

Then the spy smiled, and clapped louder, despite himself, as lyrics from an American song that was a hit before Pearl Harbor, but after a controversial military draft had been imposed, popped into this mind. The words went:

"They now realize that skinny me

    Was the luckiest one of all:

    Who can stay at home with lovely Kate,

    While they face the cannon ball!"

Aldiche grinned, not at the entertainers, but at the lyrics, which he realized could apply to his war-time dalliances, a wolf among the lady sheep of Washington:

    "When the boys get back and see how I'm doin',

.   They'll be sorry that they left,

    'Cause one can't keep on wooin'

    And still be gone with the draft!"

He turned his attention back to the impromptu septet, which had launched into the final part of their medley. It was aimed at the Axis power Americans hated most, the one in Tokyo. Its arresting title was, "There's no Yellow, in the Red, White, and Blue".

Aldiche wondered what the Chinese, strong U.S. allies, thought of the slur. Like J. Edgar Hoover, he was aware some in the bureaucracy wanted to intern Japanese-Americans and, seeing the zest with which this song was performed, figured that desire would win out.

At the medley's end, Fiorello, "the Little Flower," shook the hand of each male performer and kissed both cheeks of every female. Waving at the pedestrians who'd gathered, he climbed into a taxi, calling out, "Well, I have my other job to do—in New York!" And off he went to Washington-National Airport.

Aldiche and Adelia walked on, the latter beaming, the former with curled lips, and they reached Dupont Circle. The spy told her that the First Lady has been put in charge of the entertainment part of La Guardia's agency.

"In fact, *carita*, her office is close by, right over there." And he pointed to a tall, very narrow, apartment and office building on Connecticut Avenue. Some likened the 12-story edifice to Manhattan's Flatiron Building, but others thought the brick-and-concrete pile lacked that structure's elegance. It seemed out of place with the elegant mansions in the neighborhood. But Dupont Circle was starting to transition from a neighborhood of the famously rich to one of small businesses and apartment complexes.

"Wouldn't it be something," asked Adelia, "if Mrs. Roosevelt made an appearance too?!" She continued: "Is it possible we could wait outside her office, and perhaps catch a glimpse?"

"Ah, I fear not, *mi hermanita*. For I have a special destination for you. And to get there, we must go past perhaps the grandest Dupont Circle mansions of them all. If only we could stop sightseeing, fascinating as this area is." He winked. "And if only I could stop talking!"

Adelia took his arm. "Oh never, never stop. You're the most fascinating man I've ever met." She winked. "Except for Mayor LaGuardia."

Aldiche had to laugh at that.

He and Adelia quickly strode through Dupont Circle. Its Beaux Arts fountain suggested the maritime work of the Union admiral for whom it's named. They stopped to let an ancient Ford Model TT junk truck roll by, and stepped onto a sidewalk arcing along one of L'Enfant's famous traffic circles.

Immediately to their right they viewed a mansion known around the country, indeed around the globe. Like that of the McLean family in earlier times, it belonged to another newspaper magnate: Cissy Patterson.

In 1927, the world's most famous man had appeared on its balcony to receive the thunderous applause of thousands. Not the President of the United States who appeared with him, "Silent Cal" Coolidge, who received respect but never acclaim. But Charles Lindbergh, returned from the first-ever solo flight across the Atlantic. He'd been mobbed by swirling crowds in Paris, led an exultant ticker-tape parade in New York, then became the District's toast of the town.

Aldiche had several soft spots in his heart for the master of *The Spirit of St. Louis*. He fancied himself as a man of machismo, and thus admired his courage. As an Axis operative, he admired even more his views. Before the war, the famed American's admiration for Nazi Germany and the German Army and Luftwaffe was well-known. And Lindbergh's powerful citizens organization had been a major brake on the U.S. getting into the war.

'Had the Führer,' Aldiche wondered, 'made a mistake by declaring war on the U.S. so soon after Pearl Harbor? Instead of tolerating its formal neutrality for a while longer? A neutrality egged on by Lindbergh's backers?' He rubbed the whiskers of his chin, and smirked.

'Doubtful, given the laughable performance of the American army and navy thus far.'

Still, he was sad that even Lindbergh had been caught up in the war fever. He was volunteering for the Army Air Force, perhaps to fight the Japanese. Assuming FDR, who despised him for his anti-interventionist views, allowed him to fight at all.

Adelia remembered when she was a girl reading about the meeting of Lindbergh with Coolidge at this place. Loosened her scarf a little, she asked, "I was wondering, dear. Have you ever met the President, or other Presidents?"

"Just Mr. Roosevelt, the current Roosevelt, at diplomatic receptions," he lied, ever eager to enhance his perceived importance in his lover's eyes.

Tracking a Prey to a Soiree

That every evening, Lizzy Thorne was intent on her own espionage, while eager for some festivities to begin. She half-hoped the focus of her assignment, a suspected female spy for the other side, did something out of the ordinary, yet half-hoped she didn't. In the former case, she'd be onto another important, exciting spy operation. One that might help clear her mind from the lingering memories of Matías. In the latter case, she'd enjoy a party of pulsating music, top-shelf liquor, and high-profile guests.

At first, she had found her current task mundane, even insulting. After all, hadn't she—when stationed in Eastern Europe with her estranged husband—helped procure a prototype of the Enigma machine? The very device the Nazis employed to encrypt most of their military and diplomatic messages! She dearly hoped British cipher experts were making good use of it. They certainly needed it, with the U-boats sinking much of the convoy traffic heading to Albion. 'Imagine if those codebreakers helped wreck some of those submarines, and staved off England's defeat,' she thought. 'How proud my Marine Corps father would be of me!

'Or would he think it weird, for a woman to follow in his martial footsteps?

'No, I knew him well enough before his untimely passing,' she reflected further. 'He'd admire my bravery, my patriotism. I'm a true daughter of my soldier-father, not my society-queen mother!'

For a week, Liz had been trailing her assignment, this mystery woman, trying to ferret out her contacts, and the men she had possibly seduced.

What struck Thorne first was this femme's attractiveness. Lizzy was not vainglorious, but she was quite conscious of her own beauty, evident from the instant effect it had on almost any man. But this target, she had to admit, probably matched her own pulchritude. As for personality and charm, she would have to wait until hearing her converse to judge.

At a Capitol Hill cocktail party for military officers a few days before, Liz, not to mention the officers, had been stunned by the woman's looks. This Inga character was the image of Nordic beauty. Very lean, yet somehow very curvaceous. Her platinum-blonde hair, slightly curled and frizzy, was brushed back behind her ears to reveal a perfect oval of a face. Lizzy had been trained to focus on an unusual feature of a target, to help in identification later. But in Inga's case her nose, eyes, eyebrows, and forehead were so perfectly proportioned that no one facial feature stood out. Further, her green-sheathed, V-neck, cocktail dress with flaring sleeves lent her a bracing, contemporary look.

The sight of this woman had triggered a memory. As a journalist, and secret agent, in Europe and South America and now the U.S., Lizzy obsessively followed the news. Where had she seen this pretty, no, this adorable, woman before?

She'd stared at the face; it was too perfect to place. But then she remembered the man she had been with, six years before, their image sprinkled in all the world's newspapers. It was at the Berlin Olympics. As a skilled rider, Lizzy had leafed through a publication to the pentathlon and equestrian events, when a photo had caught her eye. There was Inga, Inga Arvad, standing next to the most famous person in the world, at the Olympic Stadium in Munich. A personal guest of the Führer himself!

Hitler was quite taken with her, smiling, his hands folded below the belt of his white Party jacket, and the red armband, yet with a distant look in his eyes as Inga, lavishly adorned by a fur coat, stared up with happy concentration at something in the distance.

She radiated alertness and concentration. Like that of a spy, perhaps, zeroing in on an important sight, a piece of information, while maintaining a happy façade to the world, and to her all-powerful host.

That night, tracking her near Dupont Circle, Inga had on modest, yet stylish, attire. Liz observed she was wearing a patterned, black and white woolen jacket with plaited belt, and a scarf in the style of a men's tie. The outfit resembled a pinstripe suit, and lent her an aura of quiet authority. Lizzy followed her from the brewmaster Christian Heurich's Old World-style townhome, over to Connecticut Avenue, past the James G. Blaine House, and into Dupont Circle. The target stopped to look through her pocketbook and Thorne, careful to keep her distance, lingered at the fountain's 12 tons of white marble. Its streams of water had just been turned on for the spring. Thorne's iridescent eyes looked over the trio of statues meant to evoke the career of Rear Admiral Francis Du Pont.

The figurines, representing the Sea, the Wind, and the Stars, had been modeled by Daniel Chester French, the sculptor of the Lincoln Memorial. And carved by the Piccirilli Brothers of the Bronx, before they fashioned the Tomb of the Unknown Soldier at Arlington National Cemetery. The statues served as elegant supports for the fountain's base. Thorne knew the original statue, of Admiral Du Pont, had been removed two decades before, after the powerful

Dupont family judged it too ugly for a public place. Also, the neighborhood gentry had jibed that the statue, which was tilting on its base, seemed to represent more a drunken midshipman than an esteemed naval officer. So Congress had banished it to the little state of Delaware, home of the Duponts, and replaced it with one of the few *objects d'art* in the capitol's traffic circles that didn't represent a Man on Horseback.

Lizzy looked over the statues. "Wind" was a male, the type of man Thorne loved: strong, daring, alert, like the soldiers she'd bedded, like the Spanish baron during his nation's Civil War. The figure had the physique of a young warrior, his right hand and a sail barely covering the muscles of his lower abdomen, his left hand holding a conch through which Liz imagined a gale's gusts whistled. Inevitably, she thought of her warrior-dad, an officer once stationed in islands from the Caribbean to the Southeast Asian maritime.

Perhaps the most artistic of the three was Sea, its woman's diaphanous gown flowing down her leg like a waterfall to the little dolphin at her feet. Lizzy glanced at Inga, who stood still, pocketbook still open, as if undecided about her next destination. Then her gaze shot back at Sea, and she imagined the cascading cloth, stretching from breast to toe, taking on the shape of a large porpoise, or the body of a mermaid.

Her favorite was the other female figure, symbolizing the Stars. 'It is the loveliest of the three,' she laughed to herself, 'like me, or Inga.' The tall, lithe image was almost completely nude except for the tresses alighting on her shoulders, and the cloak covering a leg and the midsection. The woman depicted was holding a globe, and Lizzy reflected how her work on cracking the enemy's most sensitive codes might have placed the fate of the world in her own hands. The figure's eyes were closed, as though she were contemplating the universe, and Thorne realized she was becoming distracted. She looked over and saw Inga had begun to walk again.

Her target checked for motor cars, then strode across the roundabout's street. Inga approached a long, low, and lovely building, with a sliver of the moon rising behind it. Lizzy figured that was the destination for a woman so attractive, of the sort who would grace any society function.

The place was the prestigious Sulgrave Club, formerly the home, like so many in that neighborhood, of millionaires from up North. Originally the residence for one of those esteemed New Yorkers of Dutch ancestry, like the Roosevelts, and in this case Senator Charles Van Wyck. Over time, the Sulgrave Club had become a sort of a ladies' version of Manhattan's all-male, high-society clubs.

Inga walked back to the edge of the Circle, hesitated, and stared at a scrap of paper from her purse. 'She got the address wrong?' surmised Lizzy. 'Some spy!'

A man then walked quickly out of the Sulgrave Club. He was instantly recognizable, one of the most-read persons in America.

'I'd track him myself,' thought Liz, 'if I wasn't tracking her, and had a soiree to attend!'

Yet Inga, on glancing at him, looked away disinterested.

'Some spy indeed!', Lizzy's train of thought continued. 'Any agent worth her salt would start following him, given the government secrets he's privy to!'

That 45-year-old product of the news business appeared to be a stereotype of a working reporter. In fact, he had, along with journalist Walter Winchell, largely invented the stereotype. A broad-brimmed hat, not a fedora this time, was pushed down his head at a right angle. A trench coat covered the broad lapels of his dark-gray business suit. He scribbled on a notepad as he walked along, his fingers ink-stained. Though short, and of medium frame, he looked confident, ready for a fight. Not an academic author, but a street brawler of a reporter.

It was Drew Pearson, the influence maker of his day. The creator of "Washington Merry-Go-Round," a column featured in hundreds of newspapers. His intense, bright brown eyes and whisks of mustache framed a prominent nose above a broad forehead below his thinning hair.

'I can imagine why he was at the Sulgrave Club,' reasoned Lizzy. It was the rival to the Washington Club, at publisher Cissy Patterson's house across the way, the site of the party Lizzy was eager to attend. Pearson had long worked for Cissy, but then they'd feuded over the issue of isolationism, and U.S. recognition of the Soviet Union, and much else, and she'd fired him. Bruised but unbowed, he'd landed at the up-and-coming *Washington Post*, and remained the most syndicated columnist in the land.

'Though Cissy belongs to that Sulgrave club too,' reflected Liz. 'Everyone who's anyone does. 'What an incestuous world is Washington!'

Pearson was a multi-media personality: he appeared in movies, and had a radio show as well as his newspaper columns. He even wrote the dialog for a cartoon series, Hap Hooper, about an intrepid Washington correspondent, his fictionalized self. Lizzy found much of the humor juvenile, but deemed its sendup of the capital's women—gossipy and romance-obsessed—mostly on the mark. And sometimes Hooper was aided by brave, young female patriots who could have been modeled on herself.

114

The famed reporter walked briskly toward Dupont Circle. Lizzy wondered if he would head back to his humble home in east Georgetown, in the poorer, blacker neighborhood. She was stunned when he made a sharp right turn toward the lavish Patterson House, and stepped up through its grand front entrance.

Pearson had been close, very close, to the Pattersons, due to journalism, but even more to family ties. As a young and already-famous scribbler, Pearson had ardently pursued none other than Cissy Patterson's daughter. It seemed an odd match, but also logical. The son of an English professor, Pearson was hardly rich, while Cissy's daughter Ellen was the heiress of a wealthy clan that owned major newspapers in Chicago, New York, and Washington. Pearson was as well known in the newspaper trade as the Pattersons, and matched his love Ellen in restlessness and love of adventure.

Ellen Patterson was the result of one of the strangest unions of the early 20th century, and one of yellow journalism's biggest stories. In 1904, Cissy Patterson had been, at age 22, a fabulously wealthy and impetuous heiress. She fell for an unscrupulous Polish aristocrat, Count Josef Gizycki. To the horror of her parents, she agreed to marry him, and made off for his estate in what was then part of Russia. But his "castle" turned to be a dilapidated house, his income nil. He had married her for her money. A loveless marriage did produce a child, Felicia Leonora. But Cissy was miserable.

So, with the aid of her serfs, she grabbed the infant and fled to England. The enraged Count followed, and kidnapped the child! However, the Patterson family had friends in high places. It pleaded with President Howard Taft to intervene. As Poland was then Russian turf, Taft wrote the Tsar, requesting he act. He did, arresting the Count. Eventually, for a rumored ransom of a half a million bucks, Felicia was returned to Cissy. She then gave up the agonies of romance, and focused on managing newspapers and running Washington's social scene. Emotionally distant, she had her servants raise her daughter. Given such an upbringing, no wonder Felicia turned out wild.

In 1927, a 29-year-old Pearson persuaded the lovely Felicia, now 22, to marry him. The match of the volatile duo lasted but three years. But the ex-husband maintained acceptable relations with his erstwhile mother-in-law. Until they fell out over FDR's politics, as Pearson backed Sumner Welles's interventionism abroad, while Cissy and her editorial board were staunch isolationists. In Washington, politics and the personal ever interact.

Lizzy saw the door to Cissy's shut behind Pearson. 'He must be following up a very important story,' she thought, 'for him to go into that lion's den.' She grinned. 'The lioness's den.' Her eagerness to attend the party there only grew.

The Patterson House, she noted, was like a vast, unfolded accordion of stone. Three parts in one, with two four-story wings that turned on an angle of 90 degrees to the central entrance block. An alcove of a third-floor balcony was perched atop the sturdy columns of its second floor. Six windows framed by tympanums were arrayed along its sides, and a half dozen high chimneys crowned its dark slate roof. Its architect, the brilliant, combustible Stanford White, completed it just three years before a jealous husband took that Lothario's life.

It was another place fit for a prince, or in this case a princess of print.

From across Massachusetts Avenue, and partially shielded by a beech tree, Lizzy turned from the manse back to Inga. 'If she is a spy,' Thorne thought, 'she's a careless one—I haven't seen her look over her shoulder once.' She watched Inga step across the carriage path to the manse. 'All right, so that's where she's going. How fitting.' She chuckled. 'That place is about to get even more glamourous. Due to Inga, and to me.'

Two black valets, in red and white livery, and bowing slightly, opened the portal for Inga. Liz waited for the door to shut, then crossed the avenue, and entered herself. The two servants winked at each other, impressed at the incomparable beauties who'd just crossed their path.

Ambassadorial Assignation

Somewhat earlier, Aldiche and Adelia had crossed onto the roundabout of Dupont Circle Street, and paused at the sturdy walls of the long-closed Old Dutch Market grocery, its dark iron façade still gracing its first floor.

The Circle spread out before them, with its public park centered on the elegant fountain. Aldiche admired the artistry, while Adelia smiled sweetly at children, clad in plaid cotton dresses or wool knickers and tweed caps, playing hopscotch around the font.

Aldiche steered Adelia over to New Hampshire Avenue. Excited with anticipation, the stride of his long, muscular figure lengthened. His much shorter companion struggled to keep up. He slowed back down as two Negro shoeshine boys outside a corner market called out. "Mista, give ya a shine? Next to nothin'!" Aldiche heard them, and realized they presented an opportunity, to appear generous before his mistress. He strode over, pulled out a half dollar piece, bent over like a knight bowing before a king, and handed one of the boys the coin.

"Not today," he declared with a trace of sarcasm. "But thank you, gentlemen, for your kind offer." The boys' eyes widened, and they ran off to a candy shop across the Circle. "We can get a dozen Baby Ruths with this!" exclaimed one. "Let's sell 'em for ten cents each!" said the other. "Make a prof, uh, make some money!"

Adelia was indeed impressed by this sign of paternal-like affection. Then, a little nervous, but excited even more, she asked: "What do you have in store for me?"

"You shall see, *mi cara*, and you shall not meet disappointment."

As if to reinforce that thought, he theatrically swept his left hand up while staring at an edifice with an exaggerated look of astonishment.

Adelia gasped. The Dupont fountain was immediately erased from her mind. Could this place be grander than the Sumner Welles or James G. Blaine homes?

The Levi Leiter house looked like an ancient Roman temple, with an entrance side of a wide tympanum propped atop four, three-story-high columns, fused to a veritable emperor's residence, with 55 rooms, and huge bay windows crowned by a colonnaded porch.

Taking her hand, Aldiche lectured, "It was built by the founder of the Marshall Field department stores. Though given its, grandiosity, it has served as a consulate for Italy," Aldiche made himself grimace at this, "and for the Russ—for the Soviet government," he added, forcing a slight smile for the new American ally."

Wide-eyed, Adelia replied, "I think I heard of that. My hus—uh, attended a wedding, a wedding reception there soon after, I, moved to Washington. He, eh, I was told it was like a reception for Queen Elizabeth, the Second!"

They watched a gaggle of men in Army Air Force uniforms go in through the great entrance. The Argentine saw Adelia's questioning look, and explained, "They're your country's answer to the Luftwaffe. I've heard the heads of the flying force are taking offices within the mansion." And he made a note to pay the place a visit. 'Who knows what valuable intel I could glean from some naïve young pilot, more naïve perhaps than my lovely companion?'

Adelia had grown hungry from their lengthy stroll, and impulsively entered a French bistro on that block. "Let's have a quick snack, darling!" she called out. Aldiche reluctantly followed, wishing to move on to their final destination. 'These American women can be so unpredictable and headstrong,' he reflected. He arranged for a quiet table in the back where they wouldn't be noticed.

And by the time they left the restaurant on the narrow lane of 19th St., it was nearly dark outside. After the Blaine, Sulgrave, Patterson, and Leiter homes, Aldiche wondered if Adelia could be impressed by anything else. He needn't have fretted. His lover exhaled audibly after they passed up a short block and came to his Argentine Embassy, designed by the architect of Harvard's Widener Library.

It reminded her of photographs of the Hôtel de Ville, Paris's lavish city hall, which a wife of a Marine Corps officer had shown her. Indeed, the place was patterned after the country homes of King Louis XIV.

They stood in the carriage path of the entrance and Aldiche, acting as if he owned the place, took out a set of keys on a silver ring. He fingered one of them. It was a very large iron key, Adelia noticed, of the kind that might open the portcullis to a medieval keep. Smiling, her companion inserted it and turned it once, twice, three times. Then with both hands he pulled the heavy iron open.

They stepped into reception room with plush carpets and ornate wood paneling. Aldiche took off her coat, and ushered her onto to a Louis XV chair, next to a table with Tang dynasty vases, and asked her to wait. He disappeared up a grand staircase.

Adelia heard muffled voices above. One was Aldiche, the other a heavy male voice, and the third—was it?—yes, the bark of a dog. A large hound from the sound of it. The barking continued for some time; the dog sounded upset, perhaps at seeing Aldiche.

Her lover reappeared. He had taken off his hat and leather jacket, and came almost dancing down the stairs with excitement. He stated, "I had to explain to our security that I'm bringing a guest into the embassy.

"For a brief tour. Ah, perhaps a little longer than that."

Adelia, impressed by his mastery of the manse, willingly followed him up the steps, which in her excited state seemed twice as broad as the Blaine's grand staircase.

Up above, he showed off the embassy's magnificent ballroom, and wondered whether to show off his tango skills with the impressionable woman. 'No,' he concluded, 'we've spent enough time with our 'architectural tour,' and chatting with that hypocrite LaGuardia. It's time for the real purpose of our get-together.'

"Can I show you, *carissima*," he said, "the place we reserve for our most important visitors, such as the Queen of England?"

Aldiche took her hand and led Adelia down the hall to the "Queen's Bedroom." Lightheaded from expectation, she hardly noticed the portraits of Argentine potentates and Spanish monarchs framed about the long corridor.

At a threshold, Aldiche took out a small key with dramatic style. He turned to her, and said in a low voice, "Yes, we only allow the most esteemed visitors, *mi dulce*, to enter within."

He opened and pushed in the door to a room that looked like part of a royal museum. Dominated by a massive bed, its scarlet-tinged posts rising up, it seemed to Adelia, like the trunks of trees. The carpet, the wallpaper, and the blankets on the bed had a golden hue, set off by red-tinted sheets. The electric lights of the boudoir were out, but the place was illuminated, and scented strongly, by candles.

The Argentine stepped over to the window, closed the drapery, and stepped back, beckoning to Adelia. He pressed his hands on her cheeks, kissed her lightly on the forehead, and said, "Ah, the place for a queen, for my love, for you, *mi carita*." Next, he kissed her strongly on the lips. She did not resist, but pressed her hands hard on his hips, and lower back.

He thought of carrying her to, even tossing her onto, the majestic bed, but simply walked her over, and sat down on the sheets with her, the soft mattress giving way.

After several more embraces, he began to unbutton the front of her dress. But she surprised him by gripping the tails of his shirt, and with a single hoist lifting it over his head.

She tossed the shirt to the carpet, leapt onto his lap, and rolled him onto his back. He rolled her onto hers. Their emotions reached a fever pitch; the scent of the candles seemed like a powerful drug. They breathed that in greedily, as well as the smell of their own flesh. Aldiche found his pants ripped away from him, and he disposed of Adelia's clothing.

Though they became oblivious to anything else, if they had listened intently, they would have heard a large hound with keen hearing barking excitedly.

In the afterglow, Aldiche roused himself enough to ask, matter-of-factly, "What is new in your other life, *carissa*, your life at home?"

He was awarded with a lengthy revelation. It included the news that her husband's team believed it had begun, through its code breaking, to pinpoint the location of Japanese capital ships in the western Pacific. They were able to read the orders sent by Tokyo's high command to its admirals throughout the Pacific. Including the composition of fleets, and their direction and destination. Adelia spoke excitedly, happy she could impress someone who knew so much about military matters. Pleased she could share such secrets with someone she did implicitly trust.

Mulling over this information, the Argentine decided he would soon hand it over to the Axis. He would gather a bit more documentation, then his task would be done.

'I may be the most important spy in the world,' he congratulated himself. 'With this information, Hitler and Tojo, our side, will win!'

After some minutes of happy contemplation, he dozed off into post-coital bliss.

Milieu of the Millionaires and the Military

At Cissy Patterson's, the ground floor was crowded with guests chatting with one another before joining the festivities upstairs. Lizzy recognized several persons, but her attention became focused on the grand staircase leading to the gala above. A damask carpet of scarlet patterns draped the marble stairs. Yet more eye-catching were the black, wrought-iron railings, with their intricate grillwork, leading up to an intricate water fountain. This was made of two marble columns topped by a small arch, and a spigot in the form of an ancient Roman's mouth, like some art piece excavated from Pompeii. Below its basin stood a full-winged American eagle, also of marble. The new republic imitating the venerable one.

Thorne checked into the soiree, and decided to hold on to her purse. If Inga made a sudden departure, she'd have to exit fast herself. She mounted the regal staircase, which pivoted onto a corridor where stuffed animals were displayed ostentatiously: a cougar, a moose, and other big game. Decorations more befitting Teddy Roosevelt than the Pattersons. 'Who's the hunter in the family?' Liz wondered. 'Or is it just for show?'

A loud buzz down the hallway, plush with Persian rugs, heralded the party. Lizzy heard some tentative notes from three saxophones. 'Good, there'll be music, jazz music, and hopefully dancing,' she deduced. 'Why not have some fun while working?'

As Thorne had been a teenage debutante, shuttling from plush New England soirees to sumptuous District balls, she was accustomed to high-society functions. But she was stunned on entering the ballroom.

Some 120 persons, resplendent in formal attire or military uniforms, jostled and conversed. Yet they were dwarfed by the vast space and its ornamentation.

The rectangular room had oakwood floors that glared from the polish, with crimson-colored Turkish rugs covering the center. It had such a conglomeration of plated windows and French doors that it was hard to tell one from the other. Folded pink and lavender draperies adorned the apertures; light from streetlights and the evening's half-moon filtered through, as did the scent of early spring. Framed portraits and mirrors with golden brackets dotted the walls. Either side of the chamber had marble fireplaces, one of which was lit, the aroma of firewood mixing with the scent of sweat, breath, cigarettes, and hors d'oeuvres. The walls were lined with chairs and tables covered with ivory-tinted linen, porcelain, silver utensils, and tumblers from the Czechoslovakian Moser glassware firm.

Waiters in livery were bringing in pitchers of ice water, or starting to offer caviar and Chesapeake crab. On Liz's side was an area reserved for an 11-piece ensemble, a Negro outfit. 'I hope they're from U St.,' thought the spy. That entertainment district featured performers like Ella Fitzgerald, Cab Calloway, and the home-grown Duke Ellington, musicians among the nation's best who often performed locally. The outfit launched into a warmup tune, the nation's most popular dance number, Glenn Miller's *In the Mood*, beguiling listeners with its velvety riffs.

Left of the low bandstand and along a far wall were sets of covered tables, each sitting four and positioned close together. 'Reserved for the guests of honor,' surmised Lizzy. In the middle seat facing the banquet room was hostess Cissy. Liz also spotted Inga, standing at the far end of those tables, and anxiously looking about. 'Waiting for her date,' reasoned Lizzy, 'and worried he'll be late. With her looks, he must be something.' Lizzy fingered the card with her table number and seat, and slipped it into a pocket of her dress. The skilled operative planned to move freely about the room, talking to as many old friends and new contacts as possible while keeping an eye on her target.

Hostess Cissy Patterson looked tired, drawn and desiccated, yet intent, still possessing some of her nervous energy. She was 60 years old, her thinness accentuated by the giant bowtie slanting across her grey, silken jacket. Her hair was dark, possibly dyed, hair-sprayed back, and parted to a corner. Her right hand grasped a lit cigarette. Her expression was prim, penetrating, knowing, but occasionally lapsing into a vacant look.

She was standing next to a younger woman bearing a strong resemblance to her, no doubt her daughter. With a most aristocratic name: Countess Felicia Elenora Ludmilla Patterson Gizycka Magruder. The last, Magruder, the moniker of her second, divorced husband, of a clan that had been prominent Washington merchants since the American Revolution. The penultimate namesake, Gizycka, was the name of her father, the Polish aristocrat and child kidnapper. Surely ignoble, not noble, in his case.

Felicia, as everyone called her, was, like her mother, dark-haired, thin, and long-limbed. Also like Cissy, she'd been immersed in the publishing trade. In her case, novels that satirized wealthy and distant mothers like her own, a theme that contributed much to their troubled relationship.

122

She too wore gray, in her case a flannel dress stretching down to her ankles. Rather plainly attired for a countess, as if uncertain how much inheritance would be hers.

Despite the daughter's felicitous given name, neither woman was happy, Lizzy observed. Indeed, unaware they were being closely watched, they began to bicker. Thorne had heard of the intrafamily disputes over her will and testament. A special talent of Lizzy's soon confirmed this. A natural linguist and interlocutor, she had learned to lip-read at any early age. A special course of training with MI-6 at a secret Canadian base had honed her skill, so useful for a spy, particularly one who frequented large and noisy social gatherings. Liz concentrated hard, blocking out the brassy riffs of another Miller tune, *Chattanooga Choo Choo*.

Turning her head away from the Pattersons while fixing her gleaming green eyes on their mouths, she picked up pieces of their chatter. "The mansion…New York…horse stables…inherit…Virginia countryside…mansions…lawyers…legacy…north Georgetown…bonds, cash…this jewel here…" Thorne took the last fragment to mean the Patterson House, and not a gem, although, as guests were to discover, the greatest jewel of all was in this very place.

The family tiff ended with the approach of two middle-aged military officers. Lizzy recognized from their epaulets, and from her time in Kraków before the Nazi and Soviet invasions, that they were Polish. Their faces, worn and worried, gave them away too; no American, even a veteran commander, would have a gaze of such chronic disappointment. The hostess and daughter warmly greeted them, and they brightened somewhat. They were part of the exiled remnants of conquered militaries—Polish, Norwegian, French—that one encountered in London or Washington, trying to keep the flame of resistance alive on more secure shores. Lizzy did not recognize these two, but she had a special affection for the Poles, as they had helped her spirit the Enigma machine prototype to the math wizards of England's Bletchley Park.

She looked around the vast party space for Drew Pearson, but the hall was filling up too fast with revelers and dancers to spot him. She did recognize from newspaper articles the Assistant Secretary of Treasury, Harry Dexter White. The mustachioed moneyman looked unhappy, and it was clear why. He was arguing with one of the capital's best-known, and disliked, foreigners. Namely, the 39-year-old Soviet Ambassador to the U.S., Konstantin Umansky.

Square-bodied, with a solid jaw, pugnacious nose, and dark, frizzled hair, the aggressive diplomat was getting the better of the bookish, bespectacled American, a decade his senior. Liz caught enough of their conversation to realize it was about U.S. aid to the embattled Soviets, who thought the Americans weren't handing over nearly enough. White was mouthing something about gold, Liz saw from reading his lips, possibly a request for payment in bullion for foodstuffs and artillery. He was relieved to see another ranking U.S. official, Alger Hiss of the State Department, come over and take part in the discussion. Amidst the blaring of saxophones and trombones, Liz paused to get a better look at his lips. Hiss tried to appease the Ambassador with a promise of greater Soviet influence in the post-war period, along with greater aid in the present. Umansky remained bellicose, White was sheepish, and Hiss neutral-seeming. Liz figured the foreigner, despite being outnumbered now, would win this debate.

At a table separate from Cissy's, Thorne took in two Senators with whom she had a relationship, of starkly different kinds. She discreetly studied them. The congressional colleagues seemed estranged. Though just a few feet apart, they looked determinedly in different directions.

Thorne expected a cool reception from Senator Thomas Connally of Texas, so she approached him first, to save more time for Michigan Sen. Arthur Vandenburg. Connally, 64-years-old with thinning gray hair, noticed her approach with wide and knowing eyes, and looked askance. Liz's exceptional vision noticed his eyes did not dilate, as did almost every man's when she came by. He stared absently at her as she neared, nodded curtly, and shook her hand limply.

"Ah, the notorious Mrs. Thorne, or is it Miss, I forget," he said in his Southwestern drawl, his voice the rising and falling staccato-like. "Your charms, though some seem to believe are considerable, make no impression on a serious man." Sneering, he looked away toward an ash tray filled with cigar remnants.

The previous year, before Pearl Harbor, and while still working exclusively for MI-6, Connally had been "assigned" to her, along with Sen. Vandenburg. Her mission, which she chose to accept, was to charm the Senators out of their isolationist stance and bring them closer to Britain's views. That winter, London's Atlantic lifeline was nearly on the ropes from the German wolf packs. So it was vital to win American support for the transfer of old but serviceable destroyers to Britain.

She had tried the direct approach with Connally. It was at a cocktail party put on by the Canadian Embassy two blocks from the Patterson house. Her handlers figured the affair sponsored by a close ally of the U.S. might make a congenial setting for Liz's charms.

She found the Texas Senator sitting alone on a divan facing the courtyard. She pretended to be a journalist, her normal cover, and he feigned interest in the American reporter. She sat down close to him on the sofa, and they made small talk about the city's oppressive humidity. "The heat's worse here than in my own home state," drawled Connally wistfully, sounding lonely and sad, and perhaps vulnerable. Thorne waited until he had downed half of his second whiskey and soda, then "accidentally" placed her leg, the hem of a cotton dress wiggling just below her knee, on his ankle, before withdrawing it a tad more slowly than might have been expected.

She was surprised that he remained completely nonplused. Then he turned cold.

He looked her directly in the eyes and said, "I should put you over my lap, young lady—and give you a spanking.

"No, not that kind, though I suspect you've received a few. And given some."

Normally imperturbable, Thorne's jaw dropped.

"I know who you are, miss. Word has gotten around: Probably working for the British. Or an arms contractor. Trying to push us into a foreign war, instead of staying out. Another mess like the Great War. No thank you, young lady, we have enough problems here at home!"

Lizzy mouthed some more remarks about the weather, and crept out of the room.

She had had more success with Sen. Vandenburg of Michigan, just turned 58. He looked like a college dean with his bow tie and conservative dark suit. From the upper Midwest, he had been, like many from that region, such as Minnesota's Lindbergh, a fervent isolationist. His constituents dwelled near the middle of continent, far from Europe's broils, and many were of German or Swedish descent. If the Swedes could stay neutral, they figured, why not us? And there was that horrible specter of 1914-1918, and the arms "merchants of death" that many believed were the only ones to profit from the slaughter. Then there was the overt discrimination against German-Americans during that war.

Lizzy had employed a quieter tack with this congressman. Before the reception for diplomats, sponsored by the Washington Press Club just blocks from the White House, Lizzy had put on a dark-blue, open-sleeve cocktail dress. Just a hint of her Roja Haute perfume, with her hair pulled up and braided on top. She'd waited patiently for 70 minutes before the crowd around the Senator cleared, and made her introduction. Vandenburg's eyes had dilated, she immediately noticed, although he wasn't reduced to putty like so many others. After the usual banter, when talk turned to serious issues, Thorne stressed she understood why he wanted to stay out of another bloody mess, while adding she felt afraid of the growing power of the Nazis, and the Imperial Japanese. "My uncle was a missionary in Peking," she lied, "and we all feel so bad about what's happening to the poor peasants there." They'd parted amiably, and after some discreet prodding from Liz they'd arranged to meet for lunch, with some of the Senator' aides at the palm trees-and statuary-lined courtyard of the new National Gallery of Art. This was followed by a private dinner at her Georgetown home. Where she made a stronger pitch for backing Britain.

And then…well, Lizzy wasn't sure of her impact, but when the vital vote for "lending" London military supplies came up, a measure decried by the isolationists as a leap toward war, Vandenberg had surprised many by voting Yes. The measure passed, and London got some of its desperately needed war material.

At Cissy's, when Liz turned away from Connally for Vandenburg, the latter was amicable as before. But worried. Not that he regretted his vote: How could he after Pearl Harbor? But he informed Thorne that "I am concerned about those battleships at the bottom of the Hawaiian harbor, and just as much for the oil tankers at the bottom of the Atlantic." He looked away and added, "And at the slowness with which our leaders seem to be organizing the war effort." As his tongue lolled about the olive of a martini, he said, "I fear this will turn into a quagmire, like the previous war." He swallowed, and his cheeks took on a ruddier pallor. "I know one thing for certain, Elise. When this thing is over, and we've won, we must somehow stop a third war from happening!"

An aide came up to the Senator with a press clipping. His face turned pale as he scanned it. He excused himself, and walked rapidly away.

'More bad war news,' thought Lizzy. 'A Japanese thrust toward India? A German advance toward Cairo?" Remembering her mission, she glanced back where Inga had been. She was still there, and holding court with some American officers. So Liz looked across the room, and spotted another of Washington's grand dames.

Dodging officers in light-colored dress uniforms and waist-coated waiters, Liz nearly skipped across the parquet floor, and imagined herself for a moment swing-dancing. She glimpsed Inga outlined against a French window of the outer wall. 'Good, she hasn't escaped.'

As Thorne approached Evalyn Walsh McLean, she wondered how she might introduce herself. Along with Cissy, Eleanor Roosevelt, and Clare Booth Luce—the author and wife of the powerful *Time* magazine publisher—Evalyn McLean was the best-known woman in the capital. Evalyn was outfitted far more outlandishly than her hostess. Though now 54, she wore a black leather evening dress that would have better befitted a granddaughter. This was partly cloaked by a mammoth mink coat, open at the breast. Her fine ovaloid face had begun to soften and sag, yet this was partly masked by the dark, speckled veil hanging from a slanted, sashed silk hat. This was style, if too much of it.

But everyone greeting her was drawn to the parted fur, and her personal treasure chest. Namely, two gold necklaces, one short and tight about her neck, the other drooping down below her breast. From the former hung the Hope Diamond.

Liz eyed the 45-carat gem, as any onlooker must, and found it disappointing. She had seen rubies and inlaid pearls more spectacular, while possessing less of a curse.

Glancing back at Inga, Liz saw the beauty beaming like a Nordic goddess, seated facing the dancers, and three U.S. Navy officers competing for her favor. 'Very nice,' thought Liz, 'she'll settle down there for a while.'

Thorne was herself a top-shelf attention grabber, but her own eyes were taken by a 34-year-old man with jet-black, slicked-back hair, and striking facial features marked by an owlish expression. He was sitting in pricey civilian clothes with officers at a table down the dance floor from Inga. Thorne recognized him immediately, from a party she'd attended the previous week at his Georgetown townhouse. He and his fellow English housemates were residing in a modest rental on 34th St. Lizzy had stayed late that night, dancing slowly with the man to the torch songs of Billy Holiday, her lugubrious voice dripping out of an old Victrola. Thorne hadn't minded the record player's scratchy sound, which seemed to fit the singer's raspy vocals. A voice of woe for a world at war.

Sad-sounding yes, but Holiday seemed to embrace romance as the ultimate high, whatever heartaches followed. It had surely set a romantic mood, after a long evening of crisp conversation and expensive, Justino's Madeira which the young housemates had procured. They were well-educated, that was clear, and well-off. They were not in the service branches, which was odd, given the dire state of their nation. Perhaps they were in the secret-service branches?

127

The other two men had stayed, unfortunately, instead of acting as "good wing men" and diplomatically leaving the two alone. Lizzy had reluctantly left the place at 4 a.m.

Thorne walked slowly by these British men to get their attention. She needn't have bothered, as her would-be beau, Ivar Bryce, named after an ancient Viking warrior, smiled her a killer smile. He radiated wealth, confidence, and an Eton education. His tie was carefully knotted, his hair greased and combed back carefully over eyebrows that framed a knowing look. He had the impish smile of a wise-guy teen. He waved her over.

Ivar was sitting at the edge of a small table with a tall man, also in his 30s, with a handsome, rectangular face that seemed cut out of stone, and resembling an eagle, and possessing eyes that seemed both dreamy and penetrating at the same time. Liz recognized him from Martin's tavern. Ian Fleming was his name.

Next to him was a younger man, very tall and lean, his back turned to Liz. He turned around, and she saw his strikingly handsome face, and the wry gleam in his eyes. She smiled involuntarily. He may have saved her life, after all. It was Roald Dahl.

A fast-rising American Army captain, just 27, and husky enough to pass for a college lineman, sat opposite Ivar and with his back to the dance floor. He swiveled and smiled broadly at Lizzy. Ivar Bryce waved her into the empty chair next to the Yank.

Ivar reached over to lightly shake Lizzy's hand, then bent over to kiss it, smirking mischievously as he did.

"It's been a while, like a week since we last saw each other," he winked. "Though to me," and he feigned the role of a smitten lover, "it seems like only yesterday, and yet somehow 'forever'." Lizzy had to laugh at his cheek. This guy might be as much as lady killer as she was a man hunter.

Yet she found herself glancing at Dahl. He was exceedingly tall, 6-foot, 6-inches, with the lankly physique of the soccer and cricket player he had been. While he kept to a quiet smile, his penetrating eyes seemed to take her in completely. Lizzy felt naked, not physically, but mentally, as if he were mind-reading, piercing whatever facades and fakeries that femme fatale might employ. As she began to turn her gaze back to Ivar she noticed that Fleming had the same slight, graceful smile, and eyes as penetrating as an X-ray machine.

"I'm being impolite," said Ivar. "As perhaps I was on the night we, and my friend Roald here, encountered you at our little party." He smirked again, then turned on his million-dollar grin.

"First, let me pour you something. It's D'Oliveiras; I believe you enjoyed it at our get-together." Liz had. During her times in France, she had become expert in wines, and appreciated those with a knowledge of the subject. "And let me introduce you," Bryce added, "to my friends and our guest.

"You've already met Roald, Roald Dahl, he's our attaché to you Americans. He's seen a bit of combat. Got shot down after shooting down some of Adolf's and Benito's pilots in North Africa." Dahl shook his head in a gesture of modesty.

"He can't fly for a while," continued Ivar, "so they put him on the embassy circuit to babysit our grand ally. Or so I've heard. I can assure you he's bored out of his mind going to endless cocktail parties, so if you have any suggestions for having fun in this overgrown swamp of a capital, he'd be very interested." Ivar guffawed, and Roald smiled a little more.

Lizzy noticed Dahl had been doodling on a cocktail napkin. Was he sketching her? But Fleming—their superior perhaps?—hadn't laughed. Neither had the American captain.

Ivar said, "And this is, Ian Fleming, our commercial attaché. A lot of people think he's, a spy, but he's," and Bryce laughed again, "he's just trying to buy, well lease, more of those new Stuart tanks, as well as depth charges, from you Americans."

Ivar had hesitated before the word "spy," and the perceptive Thorne thought that might have been a giveaway. 'I'll have to look into Fleming,' thought Liz. 'He might prove useful down the way.'

"And this chap, our good ally, is Cap—"

"—Captain Creighton Abrams, ma'am," the officer said in a firm but soft-spoken voice, his broad American accent contrasting with the others. "Pleased to make your acquaintance."

Lizzy saw his initial look of admiration had swiftly turned to one that signaled, "Let's get back to business." Though young, he struck her as a hardened, serious military man, someone who had actually seen battle, like the many English and Scottish combat veterans she knew, even though this officer's compatriots had hardly taken the field.

"Like I was saying," he said more loudly, "and the lady here can rest easy we're not giving away any secrets—'Loose lips sink ships'—we should go for the jugular, right off the bat. Or the cricket bat, as you fellas might put it.

"Yes, invade northern France this year! Just like when we landed a million men there in 1918, just one year after we entered the fray."

The other Brits seemed to defer to Fleming, who answered in a refined, British public-school voice.

"But you declared war in the spring, of 1917, and didn't have many troops in theater until 14 months later. Assuming it takes as long to mobilize, and things are not proceeding rapidly right now, that would make it February, or the early spring of 1943, before you'd be ready."

"I bet," said Abrams, his thick jaw shaking with emphasis, "we could have half a million men ready by this summer. The Germans nearly collapsed outside Moscow last Christmas. There'll have their hands full with the Red—with the Soviets. They've got nothing stationed in western Europe. With your battle-hardened men, and the Canucks, we could roll up to the Rhine before Hitler realized he was in for a two-front brawl."

Ian Fleming shook his head. "You Yanks didn't go through what we went through during the Great War. Half a million dead in the trenches against the dug-in Jerries. It could happen again if we're not sufficiently prepared. Why, we were worried about a German invasion of *us* up until last summer."

Roald Dahl broke in. "You're a tanker, Captain, sir, and understandably see things from the view of a land fighter. But I assure you," and Dahl rubbed the portion of his skull that had been injured from his North African crash, "air power is as important as armies in this war." And glancing at Fleming, he added, "Though I hate to say it, as important as the Royal Navy. Look at what the Nip carrier planes did to your battleships at Pearl Harbor. And the Nazis have control of the skies over France."

Abrams almost added, "And look what they did to your battleship *Prince of Wales* off of British Malaya," but out of politeness to an ally he bit his tongue about Japan's sinking of that vessel. This gave Fleming a chance to add, "We barely fended off the Jerries from our own skies. And they're still bombing us." His lips touched his wine glass; he was savoring the Madeira as he spoke. Liz got a quick impression of a *bon vivant*, one knowledgeable about both war and on how to live the good life.

"We have our hands full in Africa," Ian Fleming went on. "We should start slow, and sure: Get Libya and Malta in order, then start pinpricking the—what's that wonderful phrase our Prime Minister has used—start pricking the 'Soft Underbelly of Europe': Greece, then Rumania. That's where all the German oil is. Take that, and none of the panzers can move. None of their Messerschmitts either. Checkmate."

'And he's not just a warrior,' thought Liz, 'but a strategist. Or maybe a spy. Maybe some combination of it.'

Abrams had heard about the British desire to protect their imperial interests in Egypt and the Suez Canal, and their longstanding interest in Greece and Turkey's Dardanelles. What they were saying made sense from their Empire's perspective, but not from that of the United States.

"That's just frittering away your forces," he answered. "That way, by the time we focus on the main theater, France, the Russians might have bled to death. Then we'd have to invade against the full force of the Wehrmacht."

"But that's exactly why," rejoindered Ian Fleming, "we have to carefully prepare for a cross-Channel invasion."

"There hasn't been a successful one since 1066," noted Dahl in support. "Napoleon couldn't do it; the Spanish Armada couldn't pull it off; Hitler had to call off his own plans for…"

Thorne was interested in this strategy session; someone, their tongues loosened by the wine, might let slip out some interesting intel. 'I don't' mind collecting it from Our Side as well as the enemy's,' she reasoned. Every scrap of information might help her in her work. But glancing over at Inga, she saw the blonde bombshell had gotten up from her table. Was she preparing to leave?

Lizzy rose, and stated, "For now, I'll leave you gentlemen to your 'men's talk.'" She gave all five a blast of her green gaze. "It has been a pleasure, and perhaps we can chat again, perhaps later in the evening."

As she moved away, she noticed Ivar and Roald gazed at her intently, from top to bottom as they say. Ian drained his wine glass first, then did the same.

She neared Inga's table, and nimbly dodged two dancers stepping woozily to the Tommy Dorsey and Frank Sinatra tune, "I'll Never Smile Again." Liz saw that a U.S. Navy officer was lighting the Danish beauty's cigarette.

He was a bit over six feet tall, slim yet athletic-looking, though he was holding his back in a gingerly fashion. He was ruggedly handsome, his face freckled, with reddish-brown hair cropped a little past regulation length. He looked startlingly young; in fact, he had recently turned 24. The two officers with him were higher in rank: a captain and a rear admiral. So what was a mere lieutenant, though sparkling in his Navy whites, doing with them? An assistant, an aide-de-camp? He didn't seem so.

As she moved past their table, careful to avoid her face from the glamourous Inga's, Liz got a good look at the lieutenant's. She immediately recognized him.

He was the son of the U.S. Ambassador to Great Britain, Joseph P. Kennedy. The second-oldest of the litter.

As part of her preparation for Senators Vandenberg and Connally, Liz had studied the other leaders of the isolationist movement. Ambassador Kennedy was one of the most prominent. Irish to the core, he loathed the British. He had even bootlegged liquor, like a true Celt, during Prohibition. And he believed, at least before Pearl Harbor, the Germans would bound to win. Putting him in charge of relations with America's closest ally seemed folly. Perhaps FDR thought the appointment would get Kennedy out of his hair. He needed, it was said, the billionaire's campaign contributions, and the support of Irish-American voters. A diplomatic posting was a typical reward for such a backer.

'Well,' thought Liz, "at least his sons Joseph Sr., an Army air flyer I think, and John F—what did that F stand for again? Francis?—at least they were serving in the military. The dad made sure the press covered that.'

'A Navy lieutenant,' she thought on. 'He'll probably wind up in the Pacific. And with his father's connections, he may get preferential treatment with these admirals and ship captains.' Then her keen mind turned to the subject in which she was expert: relationships. It was clear there was chemistry between Inga and Kennedy. Even with the two higher-ups in attendance, there was something going on. Inga licked her lips in between puffs of her Lucky Strike cigarette. Kennedy's greenish-gray eyes locked on hers in a kind of soothing, seductive way.

'Have they known each other for a while?' wondered Thorne. 'Could they actually be having an affair?' She drew on her prodigious memory. Where had Kennedy been assigned for now? It wasn't a ship. Some kind of desk or research work?

She remembered: Naval Intelligence! With its office in the old Navy Building next to the White House itself. What a mark he would make for a foreign spy!

Inga's cigarette went out, and John—was it Francis?—Kennedy stepped over briskly to light it again. As he did, the sleeve bars indicating his rank brushed against Inga's waist.

'Maybe young John should get a room at a hotel for himself and Arvad,' thought Lizzy, 'before he embarrasses himself before his superiors." The admiral turned away, but the captain looked at Kennedy wide-eyed, but more out of admiration, it seemed, than from anger at his ungentlemanly, wolfish behavior. Finally, as Inga sat down, the admiral pulled Kennedy and the captain away to discuss an official matter.

Lizzy's feminine instincts, which were close to infallible, screamed to her the two were lovers. The son of the U.S. envoy to the Court of St. James, in bed with a woman who was a favorite of, and possibly a spy for, Adolf Hitler!

What a scoop that might be for her. Liz promised herself to write up these suspicions in her morning report. Her handlers respected her enough to pour over every word of her missives, even the gossip and the suppositions. She suspected they'd quickly put a tail on Kennedy to find out the truth. Would she be the tail selected? Wouldn't that be something! A tail on the trail of two high-profile lovers! One thing for sure: if she were picked for such an unusual operation, she would not get involved with Kennedy. 'Though he is rich and darn handsome!' she reflected. 'But what a mess that would be!'

While getting some wine and keeping a wary eye on Inga, who was swarmed by officers from the military's newest wing, the Army Air Force, Liz was approached by another U.S. Navy lieutenant commander. He had none of the glamour-boy looks of Kennedy. In fact, this tall, gangling man, who seemed to be on a starvation diet, was downright ugly, with outsized ears and a craggy nose. And his accent was so Southern, in fact Southwestern, that Lizzy strained to understand his words.

He had a strange confidence, however, in his direct approach to women. And Lizzy vaguely recognized him. Before Pearl he was, what? A businessman? Too young. A politician? Seemed too young, and he was hardly photogenic. Yet before she could place him, he had asked, actually ordered her, to dance.

As they swayed to Jimmy Dorsey and Helen O'Connell's "Amapola," he got her name and her "occupation" of reporter, and his giant ears picked up at this. She wondered if he would use her to get his name in the papers somehow.

He got close, too close, his hands on the middle of her back, and stated, "Let me introduce myself," he said in a firm, resonant, yet oddly soft voice. "

I'm Congressman Lyndon, B., B. for Baines, Johnson, of Stonewall, Texas. Stonewall, like the soldier. Mighty pleased to make, make the acquaintance, of a darling like you." And the "you" came out as two, maybe three, syllables.

"I'm taking some time off from my public service, in Congress, to serve the people in another capacity, as one of our brave fighting men."

Lizzy was plotting how to extricate herself from this ambitious, lizard-like man when Inga supplied the excuse. The Dane had been glancing about the ballroom, looking for Kennedy no doubt, but he had been spirited away by an Army Air Force colonel to a table. Arvad rose suddenly and, excusing herself from the flyboy, grabbed her purse and wrap and strode in green-spangled heels out of the banquet room.

Lizzy clasped Lyndon Johnson's sweaty palms in hers, brought her feet to a halt, and said, "Sorry, but my girlfriend is leaving. And I have to accom—chaperone her tonight. Nice to meet you."

And leaving the Lone Star Congressman alone and disappointed, she strode down the stairs, and out of Cissy Patterson's soiree.

Secret Encounters

Liz followed Inga briskly through the darkened streets. Arvad's heels clacked through the night; her pursuer muffled her own footsteps. She stayed less than a block behind on the other side of the street. The cars parked along the street helped cloak her presence. The route was in gloom, her shadow a ghostly image under the few streetlights they passed. 'I must not lose sight of my prey,' Liz cautioned herself, 'if she turns suddenly at an intersection!' She hoped Inga wouldn't grab a taxi; there were few cabs about, and Liz herself might not be able to find one.

From Cissy's party, Inga followed the diagonal path of New Hampshire Avenue to the northeast. She passed the shingled Whittemore mansion, built by a railroad and insurance magnate, indeed the founder of the Fidelity and the Prudential companies. Now the home of the Women's National Democratic Club, sometimes visited by Mrs. Roosevelt on her walks about Dupont. Soon, they went by Aldiche's place of work, the Argentine embassy. Unusually, there were still a few lights on in it.

Their pace was fast, and Liz began to sweat despite the coolness of the night. She watched Inga pass the stunning Perry Belmont manse, built by Commodore Matthew Perry's grandson, its wrought-iron corner balcony looking like the booms of a Navy hero's ship. Across the street was a giant building block of molded stone, a temple for the Scottish Rite Masons.

As they neared the upper part of 16th St., a mile north of the White House and laden with hotels and embassies, Liz shortened the gap to her mark. She had an encyclopedic knowledge of the city's streets, and knew that, at the next intersection, Inga might move in any of five directions. Without stopping for the red light, the Dane went heels clicking straight across 16th to where New Hampshire Avenue morphs into Florida Avenue.

Liz thought of her favorite Negro restaurant a couple of miles up Florida. The place was an epitome of downhome Southern cooking, and her stomach growled. At Cissy's she had had wine, but nothing solid. But the thought of victuals vanished as Inga, the hem of her dress rippling in the night, abruptly turned about and went back toward the intersection, slipped into Meridian Hill Park, and disappeared from sight.

'Had she spotted me?! Did she give me the slip?!' thought Liz anxiously. 'Me, fooled by an amateur, by a beauty queen?!'

Caught on the far side of New Hampshire, Lizzy had to wait as five trucks, carrying building materials for the Washington Navy Yard, rumbled by. Silently cursing, fearful she'd lost Arvad, Liz raced across the street to the park entrance, and stopped. The illuminated gateway would highlight her form, and she didn't dare be spotted, if she hadn't been already.

She admired Meridian Hill Park for its beauty, and for the heroine, one of her idols, whose statue it contained.

Liz stepped slowly to the entrance, and stuck her head past the gateway's iron grill. She peered in at a long, rectangular reflecting pool, and saw the statue of a President, the hapless James Buchanan. Beyond the image of a Chief Executive who temporized while his country drifted into civil war was the upright image of a more formidable man. And there was Inga, walking away from it, about a quarter of the way up the park. She was going slower now, moving away from the statue of the poet Dante Alighieri.

'May she burn in the lowest circle of Hell indeed,' thought Liz, 'if she is an accomplice of the Führer!'

The Dane was heading to the park's distinctive core, a 90-foot series of descending granite steps, with arched, stone terraces on either side, and a colonnaded temple above a cascading waterfall. The light-colored stones were discernible in the dark. At its top was the figurine of Lizzy's heroine, Joan D'Arc, the only equestrian statue of a woman in the city. Behind it, light from a faraway church steeple twinkled in contradiction to the blackouts.

When she was barely a teen, Lizzy's family, during one of her mother's social reconnaissance trips down to the capital, had taken her to the bronze depiction of Joan during its 1922 unveiling. Liz remembered the event clearly. President and First Lady Warren and Florence Harding attended. Liz, already an avid lover of horses, had thought the statue, though honoring a great warrior, silly. St. Joan is presented with legs akimbo, though supposedly about to enter battle. 'Anyone riding like that would fall right off her mount,' young Liz had concluded. Still, she admired Joan's valor, patriotism, and eagerness to strike quick at a foe.

Liz crouched down, and started up the terraced slope. She eyed the triangular symmetry of the waterfall's main components, visible even at night. She heard the burble of the descending water, and saw Inga heading toward a tall shape at the waterfall's base.

Thorne blinked at the form Inga was nearing. She knew there was a third statue in the park, of a slouching female figure called "Serenity". But this figure was upright.

And it was a man! And not a statue at all.

Inga came up close to him. Very close. Were he and Inga embracing, or simply holding hands? Lizzy couldn't tell.

Then they walked off at a measured pace toward the west end of the park. Liz saw them turn down a path, and toward her!

She rushed over to the reflecting pool, and laid out prone, taking cover behind a short retaining wall. Inga and her companion walked over, shrouded by chest-high shrubbery. Thorne pressed her head to the ground as they came without yards of her. She heard some words of affection uttered by the Dane.

Too taken with each other to notice Liz, they walked up to a gate, and out of the park. Thorne jumped up and followed.

Outside, she saw them moving, quickly now, south on 16th St.

'Back to Dupont?' Liz wondered.

But as soon as they crossed the next street their destination became clear.

Five rectangular chunks, each eight stories high, of granite and fine light-brown brick, rose up before them. In the dark, Liz imagined them as giant horses. 'The Five of the Apocalypse, perhaps', she thought, smiling. 'Knute Rockne's Notre Dame linemen.'

It was the Roosevelt, perhaps the capital's most luxurious hotel. President Roosevelt himself gave speeches there, and it was believed a special elevator for the statesman stricken with polio had been installed to ease his entry and exit. Indeed, many newcomers to town assumed the place was named for him, as it seemed the three-term President had been in office forever. But it was in fact named for his fifth cousin, Theodore Roosevelt.

Liz watched the duo, slowing now, walk into the carriage circle in front of the hotel's main entrance. 'Do they still call these things 'carriage' circles?' she asked herself. The Roosevelt had been built in 1920, when cars had just about displaced the horse and carriage. Several taxis loitered in the street outside.

She strained to make out the two persons, who were cloaked in shadow, as the hotel lights were muted due to the blackout.

Suddenly, they separated. Inga walked back in Lizzy's direction—'Did she see me? Will she confront me?!,' Liz wondered, her nerves jangling—but Arvard made a sharp right toward the side of the center block of lodgings.

Thorne glanced at the man who, with his back to her, was walking up to the entrance, while Inga walked down a little alleyway to a side door.

Liz was torn. 'Who should I follow?!

'And is this glamourous Dane going in through the service entrance?!'

But Lizzy realized what was going on, and knew she had to identify the man. That wasn't her assignment for the night, but her superiors liked it, and she loved it, when she showed initiative. Also, her curiosity was aroused.

She quickly combed her auburn hair, straightened out her party dress, and applied some lipstick. She walked past a black doorman, his bright brown eyes gleaming at her beauty, as he held the door for her.

The finely appointed lobby was crowded, offering her cover. Inga's man stood at the reception desk, a cashmere coat covering his shoulders, his pants standing out brightly. The receptionist, a young, smartly dressed woman, smiled bright-eyed at him. And looked down at his white pants. The dress pants of a uniformed officer.

He took the key to his room from the receptionist and turned away.

Lizzy saw his profile.

As she half-expected, it was Lieutenant Kennedy.

No doubt here for Inga!

He walked somewhat awkwardly across the room to a wall telephone, put in some change, and dialed a number.

Liz looked over the lobby and realized its depth afforded her cover. She silently stepped the 40 yards to its far end, and lay out on a divan. She took out a silk scarf. She realized its dark-green color would blend in with the green wallpaper behind her. She wrapped the scarf around her head, and peeked over the top of the sofa toward the reception desk. She was practically invisible.

Kennedy took his time with the phone call. 'Is he calling his superior,' Liz wondered, 'to tell him he won't get back in time for 'lights out'? And where is Inga?'

Thorne remembered a previous visit to the hotel, with a Vichy French press attaché with whom she had a brief affair, that there were waiting rooms on the other side of the reception area.

'Waiting there for her lover without doubt,' Liz surmised.

After a minute or so, she watched a man enter the lobby. He looked young, and well-built, wore a fedora hat, and a business suit that looked like it came off the Sears and Roebuck rack.

'An FBI man if there ever was one,' estimated Liz. 'I bet Hoover's on to Inga and Kennedy too!' The man glanced at Kennedy, and strode quickly to the receptionist. He seemed to push something—his ID?—onto the desk. The receptionist called over a well-dressed, middle-aged man—the concierge? the hotel manager?—and he spoke to the newcomer for a minute. It was too far away to read his lips, but Liz made out a very serious expression on the older man's face.

'What is the G-Man doing?' wondered Thorne. 'Obviously it's too much of a coincidence for him not to know about Inga and Kennedy.'

The "G-Man" ended the conversation, and walked out of the hotel. A few minutes later, Kennedy finally got off the phone and went to the reception desk. A lengthy conversation with the well-attired man ensued. From the body language of both men, they seemed to converse angrily at first, then become relaxed.

Liz watched intently as Kennedy walked, with stiff stride, around past the desk toward the reception area. Thorne tried to figure out what the FBI man was up to. 'Could they be bugging Kennedy's room?' she estimated. 'To get the goods on a foreign spy?'

Ten minutes later, Kennedy came back, got something from the receptionist, undoubtedly the room key, then walked over to an elevator, and disappeared within.

About five minutes later Inga appeared from the direction of the reception area, and walked into the elevator.

Satisfied, Liz headed back slowly, trying not to bring attention to herself, through the lobby. At the carriage circle outside, shivering from the night's chill, she was partly elated, partly concerned.

'Well, this is another feather in my cap,' she figured. 'My surveillance may have uncovered a major scandal. But if this comes out, about the son of our ambassador to Britain, it could cripple the ties between the two nations.' On the other hand, Liz knew that Joseph P. Kennedy was notoriously anti-British, even pro-fascist. 'I wouldn't mind if the scandal triggers his withdrawal from London,' she went on thinking. 'It's ridiculous not to have a patriot in such a vital office!

'Then there's the surveillance, if my hunch is right, by the FBI! My handlers would love to know about that too.'

In fact, as Lizzy edged back to the 16th St. sidewalk, she looked over at the path to the service entrance, and noticed a blue, four-door Ford sedan parked in the alley. Its lights were dimmed, its engine running, but a streetlamp illuminated it, and its driver.

It was a man, in his thirties perhaps, dressed in a dark suit, and with a fedora pushed down on his head in a comical attempt to hide himself.

'He might as well have 'FBI' stamped on his forehead,' she figured. She couldn't tell if he was the man who'd been at the receptionist desk.

Suddenly, he looked up at Liz. She wondered if he was one of the agents who may have been tailing her as well.

If so, would the FBI surmise she was somehow mixed up with Inga?

The man got out of the car. Inga tensed. But he walked toward the hotel, not her. He went inside the lobby.

Liz watched him, wondering what he would do inside. Full of energy, she wanted to follow. That could be dangerous; she might be identified this time. A selfish alternative was to go back to Cissy Patterson's party. She could have some fun and make some more contacts. But her duty was to get the word back right away about Kennedy and Inga. The FBI might know, but the OCI, and MI-6, did not. The lovers' relationship could trigger a major scandal, damage the nation's security, and aid Hitler. The heads of the spy bureaus needed to know about this. And about the FBI's eavesdropping as well.

Still, Liz stayed for another 20 minutes or so, furtively watching the hotel entrance and the G-Men's car, hoping to glean more information. Then, with reluctance, wishing like any good spy she could be in multiple places at once, she climbed into a taxi, and sped back to her Georgetown apartment. She sat at her Underwood typewriter into the early morning, writing up a report on what she'd learned.

Hiring a Mount

The next morning, as she lay in bed at her Georgetown home, Liz was trying to shake off the weariness from attending Cissy's party, from following around Arvad and Kennedy, and from writing up and sending out her report in the early hours.

The sun was peeking through the window blinds. A trolley car clattered outside, the noise one of the few inconveniences from residing in that abode. She thumbed through the previous day's *Washington Times-Herald*, which had forecast cold, but clear, weather. An extremely active person, she found that exercise didn't tire her, but revived her.

She determined to undertake her favorite sport, horseback riding.

Liz often rode in Montgomery County, Maryland, and in Virginia's even more extensive network of trails. Even in colonial days, the Potomac basin had been "horse country." It's said George Washington was the region's finest equestrian.

Even with the city's ongoing expansion from the world wars, farm and horse country still predominated outside the District's limits. And there were many miles of trails within the city, especially in the 1,700 acres of Rock Creek Park. Liz often rode there, as the park started less than a mile from her house.

'That is it!' she determined, still feeling a bit groggy. 'No need to go out of town.'

She quickly dressed, and phoned the Yellow Cab Company, which was then starting its second decade of business. When the driver pulled up to her house, he was surprised to see a beautiful woman in riding regalia trot down the steps, her leather riding boots and black Hampton riding cap tucked away in a cloth bag. The cabbie was from southeast Washington, and like most of the native whites there spoke in the drawl of the sleepy Southern town of old.

"Where can ah take ya, ma'am?"

The morning traffic was light, and within ten minutes the driver approached Washington Circle. In its center the Clark Mills statue of General Washington sat on his war house. Near the University named for Washington, the taxi turned onto 26th St,, and then into a narrow, trash-strewn alley called Snows Court.

The cabbie looked into the rear seat. "Are ya sure ya want this place, ma'am?"

His and her eyes widened. They had turned into a section of the District's infamous "alley dwellings."

The short street was an amalgam of low brick buildings on one side of the narrow road, and wooden shacks on the other. There were about 40 structures in all. Many of the residents, most of them black, and many shabbily dressed, were sitting on the stoops of the two-story buildings, or leaning or sitting against the wooden walls of the shacks.

Down the dusty steps of a brick home came a black woman with a blonde wig and not much else on her person. She swayed, from her very high heels and too much liquor. Several men were lying on the littered street, passed out drunk. The taxi driver broke out into a sweat, and cautiously wheeled around them.

"Not exactly a Sunday church gatherin'," drawled the driver nervously.

This neighborhood had formed in the 1850s, for the waves of hardscrabble Irish and German immigrants flooding into Washington. Supplanted in the 1860s by a flood of newly freed blacks rushing into the federal capital and unable, like the Celts before them, to afford anything better. And like the Irish, many were stricken by disease, by ignorance, by vice.

For almost a century the city had been filled with such narrow, densely peopled byways and back alleys. A movement had sprung up to eliminate them; the first slum clearance laws had passed. A big proponent was President Woodrow Wilson and his wife Edith. Partly out of reform, and partly, perhaps, out of bigotry at the black denizens. In Lizzy's time, President Roosevelt and his wife Eleanor also wanted something done about these slums, which were seen as slurring the image of America. Some, like the current First Lady, felt sympathy for the dwellers. She had in fact come to this very block just two Christmases before to hand out food packages. Others, including many in her party, simply wanted the dwellers ousted. To clear the way for government workers and professionals to move into nicer residences that would replace the wood shanties and crumbling brick piles.

But the replacement was incomplete, and Liz and her driver were getting a full taste of the remnant.

The cabbie dodged two kids, brothers by the looks of them, who were throwing a baseball back and forth in the street. No gloves, just bare, blistered hands. They scurried over to his window to beg for some nickels, but he just kept going.

To his relief, they moved past the residences, and came up to a commercial building.

"This is it," said Liz in a low voice from behind. "Nine Two Oh, Snows Court."

The driver was surprised at the sight. Three stories of sturdy red brick, with many windows, some open, some clapboard-shut. He was very surprised that the rooms of the second floor were occupied—by horses.

Brown mares and black steeds stood in three open-air stalls, two of them looking down out onto the alley, one presenting its prominent hind quarters and a wagging tail.

The smell of hay and horse manure was marked, as well as the stench of liquor wafting from a first-floor office, its door pulled wide open.

The cabbie asked, "Should ah take ya back, ma'am?"

Lizzy laughed, and brushed a hand over her orange riding jacket. "Well, at least I seem dressed for this."

"You know this place?" he asked in wonderment.

"I've been here a few times. It's the closest place in town to rent a horse. Good horses, too." She climbed out and paid the driver. With a dubious look, he roared off to George Washington University, thankful to leave the alley.

Lizzy, grasping her bag of gear, walked past the second of two carriage entrances. Its door was propped open, and she glanced inside.

Sitting in a circle on a pile of straw were six men. Two whites, two blacks, and two of mixed ancestry, four dressed in overalls and two in dress shirts and trousers. None of their clothes were clean. Bottles of beer and liquor were tangled up in the stubble. The middle of the circle had been swept of straw, and had a scattering of coins and crumbles of green-colored bills. One of the white men in overalls was about to toss a pair of dice into the little clearing.

"This is it for me!" he cried. "I gotta get home before my gal wakes up. She'll probably kill me at any rate!"

"Come on, baby," he enthused, rolling the dies in his palms.

"Throw that dice already," said an older black man, also in workman's clothes. "We all gotta get back sooner or later. Cut the stalling!"

The other man took a breath. "Make it a six!" he yelled, and tossed the dice.

"A four!" screamed one of the professional-looking men. "You lose again, and I win!" And he grabbed at some of the bills.

'A lot of people', observed Liz as she walked on, 'were 'out on the town' last night.'

143

She came up to an open-air office. The smell of manure was less here, but the smell of liquor stronger.

Within was a battered rollup desk awash with strewn papers, an ancient telephone with a separate earpiece, a dirty coffee cup, a glass carafe of water, and a bottle of Green Hat gin. On a swivel chair of broken leather slouched a very old man, slat-thin, florid-faced, and wearing a brown cotton vest with a watch chain, but no watch, draped above brown, cotton-suit pants. At least Lizzy thought they were brown; perhaps they hadn't been cleaned in ages. This was possible, as the suit had the cut of Late-Victorian times.

"Ha, Mrs. Thorne, I see," he drawled in the local patois, "who ah'm always happy to see.

"And is it Mrs., or, can I hope, Miss?" he smiled slyly. "I forget."

Liz gave him her radiant smile. "Oh, I'm always happy to see you, Mr. Wormley."

Wormley tapped the gin bottle with his right hand and cupped the coffee mug with his left. "Can ah offer you something to take on the mornin'? Ah may have a clean glass somewhere."

Lizzy smiled benevolently. "Oh no, I had enough of that last night, I'm afraid."

She stared at the stable master. He never admitted to his age, which was a topic of speculation in the neighborhood. The best guess was somewhere above 85, as he had occasionally let it drop that he had served in the Civil War, though he didn't say which side nor in what role. As a drummer boy, perhaps?

Fixing her gleaming green eyes on him, she tried to discern Negroid features in his flush, Caucasian face. He had once told her, as had a stable hand, that he was a distant descendent of James Wormley, a legend in the "colored" world of the District. Wormley's enslaved father had been freed in a court case, with the help of a Georgetown lawyer, one Francis Scott Key. His son James had begun a career, as many antebellum blacks did in horse country, by working in stables, caring for and feeding horses.

Feeding horses led to work feeding men. He started a catering business and, with a loan from a helpful congressman, founded a restaurant. From it sprung a series of eateries and hotels just northeast of the White House. His customers included the man many in the 1850s considered most likely to become President: Mississippi Senator, Secretary of War, and Architect of the Capitol, one Jefferson Davis. Later a President, yes, but not of the U.S.

When the War Between the States erupted, Wormley's clientele shifted to people more to his liking politically: Lincoln's Cabinet. He supplied late-night strategy sessions at the Executive

Mansion with delectable treats. He grew wealthy from his trade, and became a philanthropist, building the Wormley School for grade-school blacks in the heart of white Georgetown, just a few blocks from Lizzy's lodging. James Wormley had been of mixed heritage, so it was just possible, thought Liz, that her Wormley could be his grandnephew or such.

The stable owner, whoever he was, poured a gush of gin into his cup. "Ah guess ah should start the day with java instead of this stuff," he ventured. "Or continue the day," he corrected, "as ah started it, in our nightly craps games."

He looked up smiling, his cheeks flushed. "But ah suppose ya'd like me to offer ya a horse."

"Surely you can," smiled Liz. "Is Tayloe available?"

Wormley got up from his desk with sudden speed, as if the name of the one-time racehorse inspired him. "We do indeed, indeed we do."

Liz had taken the 10-year-old stallion before, and admired both his stamina and enduring speed. As a four-year-old, Tayloe had won three races in Maryland, and had even been considered for The Preakness, before a back injury from a tumble ended that hope. He was named after a legendary horse breeder of yore, a Virginia planter who'd built an extant mansion, the Benjamin Tayloe Ogle House a half block from the White House. That home, Liz had learned from her superiors in the espionage trade, had been a Confederate "safe house" for Southern agents during the "Late Unpleasantness." Such a deep tradition of local subterfuge in which Liz was now herself ensconced!

The pair went outside onto Snows Court, and stepped over to the stable. Looking out from the second story was Tayloe, his nose bristling, sniffing, steam rising, all at the happy sight of Liz. A racehorse appreciates a skillful rider, and he'd enjoyed his prior outings with this adventurous woman. No dressage riding for her, but always a fast-paced adventure through the forest and fields.

Wormley made a gesture to a stable boy, one of the kids who'd approached the cab driver, and two minutes later Tayloe began to move. Downward, in the old grain elevator in which he'd been standing, a working relic from one of the building's former enterprises.

Lizzy winced at the grinding of ancient gears, and her eyes nearly bugged out when the elevator hit the ground hard. Bu the stable boy brought over the stallion, unfazed, and Liz gave him a handful of sugar cubes.

"I'm not sure where you get your energy," Liz cooed to the creature, patting his fine brown coat, but noticing again the ribs clearly visible on his torso. This made the retired racehorse look aged, though she knew Wormley fed and cared for him well.

The stable boy, himself quite thin, offered a helping hand to this glimmering white lady, who reminded him of the angels he'd seen sculpted on the sides of the National Cathedral. But she just shook her head, and rose up effortlessly into the saddle.

"So long, young man," she told him warmly, while giving him a half dollar. Liz called out to a watching Wormley, "I'll be back before dusk."

"No rush, Miss, Mrs. Thorne. But remember, cash only. Cash is king." Wormley had never grown accustomed to the I.R.S. set up 29 years before. He reported little of his equestrian enterprise, and none of his craps and numbers rackets.

Liz trotted up to M St., where the motor vehicle traffic was light, and headed west the short half mile to the start of Rock Creek Park.

Soon she was at one of her favorite haunts, one of America's largest urban parks, and its seemingly endless series of trails. She and Tayloe trotted up steep slopes rising from near the waterfront to the hills soaring high above Georgetown's harbor. It had turned into a lovely morning, cool but no longer cold, and sunny. A few other riders and hoofers had taken advantage of the mild spring weather to enjoy the park. She thought about heading to the riding academy near Dupont Circle. She had many friends among the wealthy and well-connected there, some of them contacts for her secret work. But on an impulse she determined to go into the heart of the park.

Heading northwest by north, she and her mount left behind some black locust trees and came upon a clearing of level ground. A few folks had put out blankets to lay in the sun. Before Liz was a gray stone construct from the 1820s, a shuttered mill, which had ground wheat through the force of the creek water coursing through its sluices. A park service sign announced its name, "Peirce Mill." Lizzy laughed at the name, pronounced "Pierce" by locals. 'Evidently those old-time millers were bad at spelling,' she figured.

Lizzy patted Tayloe, and he went into a quick trot up a hilly trail along Beach Drive. 'A silly name,' she thought. 'There are no beaches in Rock Creek! Plenty of streams though, and places to picnic.' In fact, Liz reflected sadly, there were no beaches at all in the District. The last one, in the Tidal Basin next to the new Jefferson Memorial, had been closed 17 years before. Due to congressional concerns over white folk and black folk "mixing" along the shore.

She and Tayloe arrived at another plateau, one of the horse's favorite spots. A flat and almost perfectly circular trail ran off to their right for about 425 yards. It was practically a quarter-mile racetrack.

Tayloe's broad nostrils quivered. He'd run this trace before. Lizzy gently spurred him, and they took off, bounding along the flat trail, the stallion undeterred by puddles and patches of mud. The remnants of Lizzy's weariness vanished with an adrenalin rush, her leg and stomach muscles taut as she directed her charge around the course. Halfway about, she noticed a fallen red ash tree blocking the circuit. Many would have slowed, and dismounted. She merely thought, 'A steeplechase!,' and urged Tayloe on. He took the tree in a graceful bound, soaring well above it, as Liz brought her chest down toward the saddle.

At the three-quarter mark came another obstacle, the low-hanging branches from a sycamore tree. Lizzy's reaction was the same. She urged the horse to go even faster, and leaned far down to the left side, keeping her head below the horse's mane, even as some yellowed leaves rustled by Tayloe's large, alert ears.

They neared the end of the circuit, slowed, and Liz patted his forehead, cooing, "What do you say, fella? A quarter mile is just a warmup for the likes of us, no?" She nudged him with her heels.

The racehorse understood, and without prompting took off into the start of the circuit again. They had encountered no one on the course. Liz, an expert rider, was gleeful at really cutting things loose.

Equestrian Encounter

At that same time, Aldiche Engardio, having left his lodging hours before, had come down Rock Creek from Maryland. He was a fine equestrian himself, schooled in the gaucho provinces of his native Argentina. He would often put his horse, a coal-black, five-year-old mare, through her paces in the farm and horse country of Montgomery County. An alternative route was to take her down the Rock Creek trails.

The day had waxed perfect for riding, so he'd gone down the main road farther than normal. He figured he'd head to Peirce Mill and then turn around—but then he'd caught sight of a woman. A striking woman, lean and athletic. And outfitted like a professional rider in her orange jacket, tight-fitting beige britches, dark cap, and sleek, black-leather, Marlborough riding boots. Her steed, although not young from the look of him, was strong in bone and sinew, and moved with a smooth, brisk gait. Aldiche was about to call out to the lady equestrian when she sped off, like one of Robert Goddard's rockets, into a forest trail.

Aldiche silently cursed. 'I'll never see her again!', and looked wistfully into the woods. But after just a few minutes he saw her again, trotting briskly at the end of the trail and back to the starting point again.

Her lithe, smartly attired image took his breath away. Her legs long, straddling the back of the veteran steed, her tawny curls sticking out from the tightly fastened helmet, her stomach firm as she bounced lightly on the saddle.

He opened his mouth to call out, but she quickly rode to the entrance of the circuit, and exploded into it again.

Aldiche acted, spurring his mare and bounding toward Liz.

Tayloe sensed the horse coming up from behind before Thorne did. He reacted as his rider would, instinctively, by quickening his pace against this challenger. Sensing this, Lizzy turned her head 90 degrees and saw the newcomer in her peripheral vision. She made her mount go even faster, not by spurring him, but by whistling, their signal to speed up.

Aldiche was surprised.

'This woman has spirit, as well as looks! Oh, to have her as my companion!' He spurred the mare to go faster.

148

They closed the gap, but more slowly than he expected. 'This lady is so fast!' he exclaimed to himself. 'Her steed is impressive.

'But my mare Tercia is younger, I think, and should be able to take her. And surely I'm a better horseman than this woman, however talented for her sex!'

They got within 15 yards, but then the right hoof of the mare slipped on a puddle, reared some, and fell back. Aldiche was so intent on watching Lizzy that he swayed in the saddle, and feared for an instant he'd fall off the horse, but recovered. Frustrated, he spurred his horse harder.

Both creatures were galloping now, keeping to the left on the counterclockwise course. They approached the fallen tree, and the Argentine relaxed some and slowed his mount. Surely the woman would pause here.

To his amazement, she went faster, and leapt over the tree with a single, graceful bound. Aldiche spurred, and brought Tercia to the thick limb, and held his breath as they jumped. Tercia was a fast mount, but steeple chasing was not her strength, and they hadn't made such an attempt before. But he couldn't concede to this impertinent lady.

With relief, he and his mare rushed through the air, just clearing the tree, Tercia stumbled a bit on touching the ground, but recovered, and returned to a sprint almost immediately. "That's a great girl!" Aldiche praised, "I'll get you a nice snack after this is over." But the mare was lathered in sweat, he noticed, more like at the end of a mile race than a mere quarter-mile workout. She was not used to this, and neither was he, but he couldn't stop.

They came to a blind bend in the trail. He stared ahead, intent on catching sight of Liz again on reaching the straightaway. Because of this, he noticed the low-hanging branches too late. So did Tercia. The horse felt a thorn prick her ear, while a tangle of tendrils smacked her rider as he tried belatedly to duck.

His hold on the reins loosened, the horse bucked, he lost his grip on the saddle horn, and his momentum carried him straight off the mount, tossing him toward a puddle as Tercia neighed loudly and swerved the opposite way.

In a crisis, Aldiche had nerve. Even as he sailed through the air, he calculated he could hit the ground in a way to avoid serious hurt. He pivoted his torso and legs, so that he landed, not head and hands first, but on his rear, and slid down on an angle, instead of with a thumping crash. He scooted along the mire and pebbles, ripping his pants, scraping his lower back and hamstrings, and came to a halt sitting up.

He was relieved at this, but chagrined. He looked over at Tercia, who had stopped, and was looking at him with concern.

'To be bested by a woman!'

He was feeling his back and shaking his hips to make sure he hadn't broken anything when he heard the slow but firm clop of the steed approach. He looked up and saw Tayloe, quite close, and sweating slightly. And looming above him, like a Diana of the forest, not sweating at all, was Liz. She looked down at him worriedly, mirroring Tercia's gaze.

Lizzy paused her mount above the Argentine. She switched to sidesaddle; her tapered legs dangled over him. While noticing his impressive physicality, she felt genuinely bad, remarking, "I'm so sorry, sir. Perhaps we shouldn't have turned our jaunt into a little race. And on such a fine day."

Her voice was confident, deep-toned, beguiling. Aldiche was impressed by her sang-froid, and concern for his health.

He got up suddenly, ignoring a sharp twitch in the lower back.

He was quite tall, Liz noticed; he stood not far below her despite her being mounted. He spoke, in an accent she immediately recognized.

"An error in judgement on my part, mada—is it Miss?," said Aldiche, apologetically yet firmly. "Like yourself, I perceive, I am an avid equestrian, and could not restrain myself on seeing a fellow rider."

He forced a rueful smile, and looked back down the trail at the branches. "Unfortunately, I am not familiar with this somewhat challenging course."

Liz slid smoothly off her mount and stood face to face to him. Aldiche loomed above her. His fall had pushed his shirt up his torso, revealing powerful stomach muscles.

She reached down and lightly brushed away some mud on his exposed left hamstring. "You're bleeding. You're hurt!"

"No, I'm fine. Miss..?

"Yes, miss, Miss Thorne. Elise, Lizzy, Thorne."

"I appreciate your stopping, Miss Thorne." He let her fingers continue wiping away the last bit of dirt. He took in her figure, her fine hair, her smart outfit. She stood up, and he stared into her glowing green eyes.

"Yes, I am unhurt. No broken bones, no muscle—how do you say?—no strain of the muscles."

"A muscle strain," she answered, looking up into his deep-brown eyes, "Your accent is Castilian, is it not?"

He could have passed for the brother of her lover during her MI-6 work in Spain during its Civil War. When she had a torrid affair with a man of aristocratic class and bearing, also an equestrian. He had been on Franco's pro-fascist side, she regretted, but their love, while it lasted, had trumped any politics.

Aldiche's deep-set eyes widened in surprise. "You recognize my accent?" He smiled, which seemed to highlight the bristles on his chin and lower cheeks. "Many take me for a Spaniard. But I merely did my graduate studies in La Universidad de Castille."

"*¿La Universidad La Mancha, si?*" answered Liz in unaccented Spanish.

"*¡Si, señorita!*" he blurted out, pleasantly surprised.

"However, I am a native of Belen de Escobar, not far from Buenos Aires."

"*Yo soy tan alegre,*" said Liz, "*que me encuentro a usted.*" ("I am so happy to meet you.")

"*Yo mas alegre,*" he rejoindered, '*que me encuentro a una señorita de tan talento y gracia.*" ("I am more happy that I met a young lady of such talent and grace.")

She smiled at that. To Aldiche, the gleam from her teeth seemed to merge with the beams emanating from her iridescent orbs.

"Will you allow me to mount, and to ride with you a while? More slowly this time." He bowed. "For I am with my superior as a rider."

Lizzy was charmed. 'Just my type,' she thought. 'Educated, classy, a sportsman.' She had had no real lover since her Spanish don. The relationship with Admiral Armando wasn't romantic, nor even deeply physical, but a means of obtaining information. Then there was that Matías. She occasionally had nightmares about him. Though lately, she had met Ivar, and Roald.

'At last, things are picking up!' she chuckled to herself.

"But of course, *señor*. And I'm certain, if we had a fair match, on ground familiar to both of us, you would be the one coming out on top!"

Aldiche thought that was true, that this lovely woman was merely being generous. But given her smooth, effortless riding form, he wasn't certain.

He watched Liz walk, with a ballerina's grace, over to Tercia, who was sad-looking and jittery. The mare's eyes widened and her demeanor softened, however, at the female equestrian's approach. And grew completely calm as she stroked his neck and chest.

151

"You have a sure way with horses," remarked Aldiche.

"And horseback riding," Liz called over, "is only my second-favorite equestrian sport."
Aldiche shoot her a quizzical look.

"Polo's my favorite. I often played it when stationed overseas. In Chili, for instance. Santiago has a fine polo community."

The Argentine brightened, his bruises almost forgotten. A South American connection with this beguiling woman?

"You were, stationed, in Latin America? Perhaps in my homeland too, Argentina?" He paused, calculating the possibility of a lucky break for his espionage. "A diplomatic posting?"

"Newspaper reporting," answered Liz. "Articles for the English-language press." She didn't mention her articles had often been opinion pieces, taking the side of Britain against Germany and Italy. This strapping fellow was from a country that, though officially on the side of the Allies, was filled with immigrants from central and southern Europe whose sympathies were with the Führer and Mussolini.

"Ah, a scribe," said Aldiche. "A woman of intellect as well as athleticism." He bowed slightly again, which again reminded Liz of her Spanish lover. "I myself am a diplomat, with the Argentine embassy." This rarely failed to impress a lady, and it did in Liz's case.

There was a pause. Aldiche stated, "So, shall we ride a bit? Together, and not as fast?"

They trotted the circuit, and then went down by Peirce Mill, with the "diplomat" insisting he accompany Lizzy back to Georgetown. On the way he spoke effusively, to impress, about his job of "commercial attaché." Liz mentioned several newspapers that had carried her work, both isolationist and interventionist. Aldiche figured this American was naturally opposed to the Axis. If so, that gave him an opening.

He nestled Tercia closer to Tayloe, put on a long face, and said, "Oh, I fear for democracy in my own country! So many supporters there of the fascists in Germany, in Spain, everywhere! I hope and pray your admirable nation, and its new ally of Britain, will soon put the Hitlerites back in their box!"

Liz completely agreed. And was glad this possible future lover would be, unlike her Spanish don, on the right side of politics.

Not far from where Rock Creek meets the Potomac, they bid adieu. But not before Aldiche obtained Liz's telephone number.

He reared his horse dramatically, like a nobleman in a Hollywood production.

"May I have the great pleasure of riding again with such an accomplished equestrian? And to explore together some of your capital city?"

Lizzy readily assented and, without hesitation, gave him her address as well. They agreed to meet soon.

Inga Investigations

J. Edgar Hoover sat kitty-corner from his Number Two in his well-appointed private office. They were ensconced on the fifth floor of the Justice Department, on Pennsylvania Ave and 9th St., placed strategically halfway between the White House and the Capitol Building.

For someone who had put so many hoodlums and Nazi spies in jail, the 47-year-old Director seemed almost imprisoned himself, behind all the bric-a-brac. Two tall, cylindrical brass desk lamps on either side of the desk came up to his prominent chin, invariably described as that of a bulldog. A statuette of a Greek demigod crushing a monster with a club rose even higher. Higher still was a bouquet of roses from an admirer. Behind him were two flagpoles spangled with stars representing the 48 states. Lower down and in front of him were the two speakers of the office intercom, and rising again was an inbox stacked with memos, books, reports. Little souvenirs and paperweights like a plastic ice cream cone were scattered about, along with small, framed photographs. The ink blotter directly before him, however, was punctiliously neat, with just a memo pad, a single report, and an ink stand. To Hoover's left was a window with partially opened blinds that afforded a blinkered view of the National Mall and the Smithsonian Castle. The behemoth J. Edgar Hoover FBI Building lay three decades in the future.

The window was partly open, and a slight, humid breeze blew into the office. Hoover scribbled a note to himself to ask building maintenance about the recently installed air-conditioning. It would be warm soon—Washington warm, and humid—and he wanted the newfangled thing to work properly, to permit his hardworking agents to work even harder at their desks.

His close friend and trusted aide Clyde Tolson, a taller and thinner man, sat facing the boss on a swivel chair a few feet from the window. He cranked the seat up a few inches; he was one of the few allowed to sit at nearly the same height of the Director, who preferred looking down at his visitors.

On a table next to Tolson was a stack of documents. The Number Two held a thick dossier, which he patted expectantly.

The Director, in his firm soprano, spoke into the intercom: "Hold any calls, except for the President or General Marshall, or the Attorney General."

He flicked off the device's switch, and turned to his aide.

"So it's quite the story, huh?"

"It is, and as we expected. And it could turn into a bigger scandal, a big-league scandal."

Hoover tapped the top of a pen. "I'm listening."

Tolson opened the dossier, spread several of the pages on his lap, and began talking.

"As you know, we've been staking out the Arvad woman for weeks. And, as you ordered, increased the surveillance.

"She's a real social butterfly. We've photographed her at Cissy Patterson's uptown home on Wisconsin Avenue—"

Hoover interjected, "—Her uptown place?"

"Yes, the one she's converted into a guest house for servicemen. In upper Georgetown."

"That's very patriotic of her," said Hoover evenly. He admired Patterson's nationalism, but was keenly aware his boss, Franklin Roosevelt, despised her, and pulled his opinion of her even in his confidante's presence.

"We got a recording of Inga Arvad at the National Press Club," continued Tolson, "and photos of her in the lobby of the Army-Navy Club over in Farragut Square."

"Any hard evidence yet, that she's a spy for Hitler?"

"Nothing hard, yet. But suspicions."

"Yes, lots of suspicions." Hoover thought of the many foreigners his Bureau were tracking, and thought of another.

"Has she separated, from her husband yet? The Hungarian, the movie director."

"Paul Fejos? No, but they might as well be divorced."

"No evidence has turned up that he's working for Hungary's fascists?"

"He's clear. An egghead, intellectual, yeah, but he hates the straight-jacket the Nazis put on creative types."

"All right. His wife: What was she doing at Army-Navy?"

"A reception. For officers, and 'invited guests.' A few press people, which she claims to be. But she didn't stay long, nor did she stay over, this time, at one of its guest rooms."

Hoover laughed. "I like the nickname our gumshoes have for her."

Tolson grinned broadly. "'Inga Binga'."

Tolson stopped smiling, and set his prominent jaw. He put the papers away. The event was burned in his mind.

"But last night was the doozy."

"Young Kennedy again?"

"Yes. He was in town, again, on leave from his Navy quarters in Carolina. As you know, one of his superiors alerted us with his suspicions. Two of our men photographed them leaving the party."

"Together, or separately?"

"Separately. So our guys improvised, split up, with one following Inga, and the other Jack, John Kennedy."

"I like to see initiative, on the part of our agents, by the way. Make sure you write down their names for me."

"I will. Officers Martin and Petersen. Officer Martin followed Kennedy, and Petersen followed Inga. In fact, Petersen shares the same last name, the maiden name of Inga. Anyway, after about twenty minutes of tracking, guess who they were surprised to find?

"Each other! Kennedy and Arvad both! Outside the Roosevelt Hotel."

"FDR's lodge?"

"Yes. Our men sauntered off to the side of the hotel, and got a driver they'd contacted to pull up, and they clicked photos of both of them, entering the Hotel from separate entrances."

Tolson paused. He figured the boss wouldn't like hearing of the agents' next move. In fact, he would likely explode. But he had just praised "initiative," so maybe not.

The Number Two puffed up the agents' reputation a bit more. "Petersen and Martin stayed outside the Hotel the whole night."

Hoover raised an eyebrow. "The whole night, eh?"

"And they took photos of the two leaving, leaving early in the morning."

Hoover started to say something, and Tolson quickly added, "Leaving separately. Though just minutes apart."

He cleared his throat, looked down at the government-issued carpet, and said, sotto voce, "The agents did something else on their own initiative." He paused. "And mine, with, mine, my backing."

The Director stared at his aide with complete focus.

"It wasn't hard for them to figure what young Kennedy and Inga were up to." Tolson exhaled. "So they contacted headquarters. They got me. I was here working late on the Jap internment matter."

"You know I don't want them interned," said Hoover, with some hardness.

"I know, and I made that clear to the President's man, Mr. Hopkins." He paused again, looked down at the carpet, then past his boss.

"The agents, on their initiative, requested permission, to bug Kennedy's room."

Hoover was surprised, wide-eyed.

"They took the initiative, quickly," said Tolson. "They had surveillance gear with them from their work on that Thorne woman, and—"

"—Oh yeah," said Hoover. "I want an update on her…But then?"

"Petersen went into the lobby, and saw that Kennedy had taken a seat on the sofas, then went into a phone booth to make a call. Kennedy took his time there.

"So Petersen acted fast, real fast. He identified himself to the concierge, said a security matter of importance was in play, having to do with the war, and got him and his boss to agree to, to let him bug Kennedy's room."

"What!?" exclaimed Hoover. Though more out of surprise than anger, Tolson noted.

"It seems the hotel manager fought in the Fighting 69th, in the Great War. He's a real American and likes the FBI, likes you, very much. Well, he immediately agreed with Petersen." Tolson shook his head in admiration, then caught himself from seeming too enthusiastic. He couldn't read Hoover's reaction yet.

"Our Petersen," he continued, "does seem to be one fast operator. He got McCarthy, the manager, to stall Kennedy when he asked for a room. Saying rooms were tight due to the war and all that. But that they had a special suite for an officer, but it would take time to get it thoroughly cleaned. But the wait would be worth it: the suite was a place fit for a President, he said, really laying it on, the digs were guaranteed to impress anyone.

"He cleaned it all right," added Tolson conspiratorially, "but he didn't *swipe it* for bugs."

Hoover didn't laugh, didn't look happy now. "Go on," he stated.

"Meantime Martin had come into the lobby, talked to Petersen, and rushed out to get their bag of tricks.

"In short order, they had Kennedy's bedroom and living room place bugged. And McCarthy got them the adjacent room, so they could record and listen in real close like."

Hoover's frown made him look more like an angry hound than ever.

Tolson sucked in air. "I take full responsibility. You were asleep. I was here. A decision had to be made one way or the other. I made the call, and gave him the green light."

Hoover placed both of his beefy hands on an ink blotter. "I care little," he said softly, "about you bending the law. We're at war, with Hitler and Tojo. FDR would okay a wiretap, or some inside job, or worse, in an instant. But I do care, that I wasn't alerted." Then he raised his voice, one of the few times he had with Tolson. "You should have called me! Woken me up, whatever the hour!"

He rubbed stubby fingers across his Vaseline-slicked hair. "We're playing with fire—the son of an ambassador! Whose father's a top donor to Roosevelt. Who's got kid gloves' views about Hitler! What if Drew Pearson got ahold of this story? The blowback could throw us both out of Washington!"

Hoover stopped talking, still steaming. Tolson exhaled. Maybe he would be the one fired. He had truly crossed a line. His hands nervously tapped the dossier, and the magnetic tape under the papers.

He attempted, "When they discovered Kennedy was back in town, and meeting this Inga, well, the agents assumed it was a spy op."

Hoover looked dubious. He wondered whether Tolson, who he trusted implicitly, could actually be trying to con him. He stared across the desk at him.

"O.K," he said, his voice calmer, but with an edge, "what does the transcript say? What did they hear?"

Tolson began to reach for the transcript, hurriedly typed up that morning, but figured he needed to make his case fast. He pulled out a reel of tape, and pointed to a cabinet where Hoover kept a reel-to-reel machine.

"The fastest thing," he stated, "is to play this. Just a couple of minutes, and one gets the idea." Hoover nodded impassively.

Tolson took out the machine and propped it on a table next to Hoover's desk. He inserted the reel, and forwarded the tape to the desire location. After pushing the start button, he sat down, while Hoover leaned back in his chair. The Director didn't say anything, but his canine expression read, 'Better make this good.'

The tape crackled and snapped, and a muffled female voice was heard. Tolson jumped up and turned up the volume, then raced back to his swivel chair.

"I have much to teach you," said the female voice, in a Danish accent, which sounded like German to Hoover's ear.

"I have much, much to learn," said the male voice, in a high, nasal, and distinctly Boston accent, stretching out the vowels in 'learn'.

Inga then laughed, loudly, for ten seconds or so.

Kennedy then moaned, and shouted, "Oh my God! Never, never have I had a woman like you!"

"I bet you've had many a woman," answered Inga, her voice deep, "but no, never anyone like me!"

Then came the unmistakable sounds of mattress springs rustling. Punctuated by loud moans and grunts, both Nordic- and New England-accented, for over a minute, before Tolson strode over to stop the tape.

"It went on like that for much of the evening," he explained. "Love talk."

Hoover's lips were as prim as a Puritan preacher's. He asked sharply, "Did they talk about military matters? Secrets?"

Tolson said, "Only briefly. That talk went like this." He pressed the Forward button for some time, then hit Play again.

"What's it like at your base in South Carolina?" asked Inga Binga.

After some heavy breathing, Kennedy said, "Boring. Some decent food, especially compared to Boston. But country bumpkins. And especially boring as you're five hundred miles away."

"Ha, ha. Is your work at least, interesting?"

Hoover's ears picked up, his hands tensed.

"No. Just a desk job. Routine matters. I'm like a million others. Waiting to be shipped overseas." Hoover's hands relaxed.

"That," said Inga, "I would find very boring. If you were a million miles away."

There was a pause. The breathing, Kennedy's apparently, became shallower.

"Well, there's that thing we've talked about. I resign from the Navy. You get your divorce. Then we head out West together. I'm a Harvard grad. I could get a teaching job out there."

Another long pause, with no audible breathing. Hoover was all concentration now. He placed his chin on his hand, listening intently.

Then Inga said, with a trace of anger, "And your father? How would he like that?"

"He wouldn't. But I could…" And Kennedy's voice trailed off indecisively.

Inga immediately said, "You have two backbones, Jack. Yours, and your father's."

After a long pause, the sound of smooching, followed by grunts and moans, came back again.

"And that," commented Tolson, "was it for the talk about his military work."

The Director blew out a deep breath, his anger subsided. "Well, that was a very, interesting, tape. Of course, it's hardly proof, that she's not a spy. Does she still have that job?"

"Yes, a reporter, a columnist, for the *Times-Herald*. She has some bylines."

"Terrific," said Hoover sarcastically. "Working for Cissy Patterson, an arch-isolationist. Though now 'a perfect patriot' like everyone else. A perfect perch for a foreign agent to collect intelligence."

Tolson, though somewhat relieved, was still nervous.

"So, what do we do with Kennedy now?"

Hoover looked worried. "At a minimum, he needs to be kept in Carolina. These occasional forays to Washington are a pain in the neck. Keep him, and her, under surveillance. And I want him wiretapped, wherever he goes."

Tolson nodded eagerly.

"And I'll have a chat with Kennedy, Kennedy Senior. He doesn't want a scandal. Especially after his friendship with Lindbergh's crowd, the isolationists. Having a son linked to a possible Nazi spy, that would completely wreck his high hopes for the future of his kids."

A slight smile came over the bulldog countenance. "All this might play out to our advantage, after all. Joseph P. Kennedy's a powerful man, and doing him a favor, alerting him of this, might put us in his good graces."

His left hand holding his prominent jaw, Hoover was thoughtful. "And so might telling the President of what we uncovered."

"Yes," Hoover nodded, "he would be glad to learn of a scandal averted. And maybe of a bargaining chip he could play on his Ambassador, who's been a burr in his side."

The Director thought of his busy schedule that day with higher-ups, and called an end to the meeting. He noted, "Maybe Petersen and Martin didn't do such a bad job after all."

"And let me have that reel," he instructed.

And, as Tolson left the office, Hoover locked the tape in the wall safe. There he kept the most sensitive materials, particularly those containing damaging personal information on Very Important Persons.

Undercover Operations

It had been quite the evening at the clubs of U St., famed for its jazz emporiums, its bistros with white and Negro guests, and for hometown hero Duke Ellington and visiting players like Tommy Dorsey. They had actually caught Billy Holiday at Bohemian Caverns on 11th St., a half dozen blocks east of the "color line" whose real estate covenants separated black neighborhoods from white.

Yet in the dim, smoke-filled underground club, Aldiche was actually bored by the siren's languid singing. His mind wandered off to his home country, and a skiing buddy of his, Major Juan Peron. They saw eye-to-eye on the fascist regimes in Spain and Italy, with Peron hoping, given the emergencies of the new world war, to help bring about the same in Argentina.

For her part, Liz found Holiday's blue-note vocals beguiling. And she was fascinated by the largely black audience, with its loud clothing and louder voices, so unlike the diplomatic receptions she frequented.

Thorne was somewhat annoyed when her companion yawned during the singing of "All of Me," with its clever lyrics. "You took the part, which once was my heart—so why not take all of me?" She thought of Roald Dahl, who had intrigued her at Ivar's place and at Cissy's party, and figured he'd appreciate such a lively, out-of-the-mainstream place.

Aldiche's behavior was puzzling. He had claimed to be a big fan of jazz, and very knowledgeable about it. Neither assertion seemed to be true. She wondered if he was fibbing about other things. For some reason, while Liz was thinking about this, she had a flashback about Matías, and his terrible assault upon her.

But she had forgotten that hours later. It had been a chilly eve, and early morning, but now they felt toasty-warm. They lay by the fireplace in Lizzy's living room, on a plush Afghan, the logs no longer burning, but still crackling, cackling, popping, smoldering. They were bereft of clothes, except for the gray woolen socks Aldiche had neglected to take off in the initial haste of lovemaking. Liz nestled fetus-like in the crook of his muscled side, cooing softly, as his right hand rubbed the soft, almost translucent skin of her upper back.

It was their third overnight there. Her place made more sense than his, a smallish apartment during the war-time housing shortage. And Liz's abode afforded more privacy than a hotel room.

The place was in fact a steal. It had a living room with street-facing windows, a kitchen, a cozy bedroom, a small den, and storage space in the basement. All for just one person, well, often two persons, in a town where generals and titans of commerce would pay premiums for a hotel suite or a rental home.

Lizzy had lucked out when the pervious occupant hurriedly left, to help run a munitions plant in Washington State. The landlady was clueless about the inflated prices of war-time residences, and had leased it to Liz, with MI-6 as the secret payer, for the pre-war rent. The contract read that no "single woman" was to have overnight visitors, but Liz was still technically married. In any event the landlady, whose own home was in southern Maryland, was seldom around. During the last time she had paid a call, she was impressed at how spotless Liz kept the place, and concluded she didn't need to check on her again.

Now, Lizzy squeezed Aldiche's waist, and breathed deeply, her nose nestling in his chest's mat of black hair. Her painted fingernails slid down and along his firm biceps, then down to his pronounced abdominal muscles. He was awake, but exhausted from their exertions, and smiled at the tickling.

'This is my kind of man after all,' thought Liz, relaxed and tired but not as sleepy. 'Athletic, strong.' And did he have combat experience, like her other favorite lovers? He hadn't mentioned it, but the way in which he spoke about military and diplomatic things made her think that he had. He had mentioned he was an excellent shot, and competed in biathlons, shooting at targets while skiing cross-county in the Argentine winters. Was that a fabrication of his? She was willing to give him the benefit of the doubt.

'Is he old enough to have fought in the Great War?' she wondered. He had the kind of look of a man, who hadn't done much manual labor, who could be anywhere from 30 to 50. About 40, she reasoned. 'It's possible he served in his late teens late in the Great War, the first war. But no,' she reflected. 'Argentina was neutral. Or did he volunteer for the Allies perhaps?' Adventurous young men from non-belligerents had willingly fought for one side or the other.

She heard her lover begin to snore, and was disappointed. She had hoped for a third bout of lovemaking, to follow the fast one in the bed when they had come back to her place, and a second round on the rug. But no, though in excellent shape, his stamina did not match hers. She hadn't encountered anyone who did.

But Liz had no real complaints. He was the first real lover she'd had since the married Spanish aristocrat during Spain's time of troubles. It was strange, she thought back, that she had been wildly in love in Madrid and Seville with an officer for the Franco regime, which Hitler's tanks and Stuka bombers and Mussolini's warships had helped put in power. But that was then, before this new war, back when it was possible to have friends on both sides. When the republicans, or was it the communists—the lines were so blurred in Civil War Spain—had imprisoned him, Liz had risked her life to help him escape from jail. Then he had fallen into the maelstrom of war again, and Liz and her diplomat husband had been assigned to Eastern Europe. That was the end of their relationship.

But she'd always look back on it fondly. From the time when they had first noticed each other, when she was just a teen, and he a Spanish official visiting America. They had run into each other on a golf course, and the admiration had been strongly mutual. Then years later, another chance encounter in Madrid, a romantic city she so loved, and their romance was immediate and electric. He was a soldier, an officer of the king's guard, and superb at polo and at tennis. Handsome, confident, aggressive, smart. 'Just like my father,' she mused. 'A lot of women marry a man who reminds them of their father,' her train of thought went on. 'Why shouldn't I go after the same? Someone who craves the same excitement, the same release from tedium, that I do!'

Aldiche stopped snoring, but was still asleep. Liz felt like stretching, but didn't want to disturb him. She recalled the last man she had willingly slept with in her home. How different the Spanish admiral had been! Not at all satisfying.

Then, unexpectedly, thoughts of Matías popped again into her mind. The horror! She tried, with limited success, to forget about him. Before finally falling back into sleep.

Defusing an International Incident

Clyde Tolson, sitting in the Director's office next to his boss, thought it would be an uncomfortable phone call. It was.

J. Edgar Hoover, his visage in a most serious cast, his head tilted down at a sharp angle, was speaking into the phone's mouthpiece.

"Oh, Mr. Ambassador, we think we have, a solid handle on any Japanese agents."

Tolson suspected the Ambassador, embarrassed by his past coddling of Nazi Germany, was urging the Director into a severe crackdown on Japanese-Americans.

"We all remember," the Ambassador said, "the fine job you did during, and after, the previous war, when you threw all those anarchists and Germans and, yes, even some disloyal Irish-Americans, into jail," he said. "After Pearl Harbor, millions of Americans are expecting the same for our little yellow friends."

Hoover diplomatically declined to state his opposition to internment of the Nisei, and didn't mention how his men had broken up the Duquesne spy ring of Nazis.

"I can assure you, Ambassador, we have that matter, firmly in hand." He paused, his jowls shaking some. "But what I needed to talk to you about is, somewhat, is a personal matter. Involv—"

"How so, Mr. Dir—"

"—Involving a Kennedy, sir."

A long pause.

"It involves your son."

"Joseph? Why he's a straight arr—"

"Your son John, Mr. Ambassador."

Another long pause.

Then Joseph P. Kennedy, Sr. said in a hard voice: "Has he not been keeping his pants on again?!"

Tolson watched the normally very serious Director suppress a laugh. 'Like father, like son,' Hoover thought. 'And it takes one to know one.'

"Well in fact, Mr. Ambassador, your son John has been involved in a, delicate matter, that could reflect, badly, on your family. And on the nation."

Hoover quickly added: "To save yourself embarrassment, I thought I'd call you directly, to address this."

Kennedy's voice became weak and hesitant. A call like this from the all-powerful Director could lead to terrible consequences.

"Well, I appreciate that, Mr. Hoover, I—"

"—Thank you, Mr. Ambassador. It's like this. Do you know who, Inga Arvad, is?"

There was another pause, shorter this time.

"Wasn't she that 'knockout' who was a, 'friend,' of Hitler, or something?"

"She was a reporter, from Denmark," said Hoover evenly, "who conducted some interviews with the German Chancellor."

Another pause. Tolson could imagine Kennedy, the accused Nazi sympathizer, breaking out in a sweat.

"She's in the United States now. Supposedly still with a Hungarian, a movie director, named Fejos. He's fruity, a Hollywood type, but anti-Nazi.

"She's been in Washington for some time." Hoover stopped for emphasis. "Our men have been following her, following her around. You can understand that, due to the Germany connections."

"Yes."

"And, well, my men have found that she and your son, John, have been seeing each other."

Ambassador Kennedy didn't pause.

"Seeing each other," he said in a flat tone.

"They are having," said Hoover directly, "an affair."

"Jesus Christ!" Kennedy almost shouted. Then in a lower, but still angry, voice: "Can't keep his pants on! Son of a bitch!

"Mr. Director, where have they been having, meeting each other?" Kennedy had no illusions that Hoover knew every detail of whatever was going on.

"In hotels about Washington, sir. And, this is a serious matter, so I wanted to tell you directly, and—"

"—I appreciate that. And?"

"Well, the Navy recently transferred him, to a base in South Carolina."

"I know that. That was a step prior to sending him overseas."

"Actually, Mr. Ambassador, his superiors sent him there, to get him away from this Arvad."

"The *Navy knows?*" wailed Kennedy.

"But no one else," Hoover jumped in. He nodded at Tolson. "Except me. But the press knows nothing."

The Director went on. "But the, this matter didn't stop there. Arvad has been traveling down to Carolina, to meet your son there.

"Meeting in hotels."

Tolson imagined he heard the gnashing of teeth and the tearing of clothes on the other line. He winced with the thought.

Hoover stated rapidly, "But I, we, the Navy, the FBI, have a solution."

"Yes, your son will be transferred overseas. But not right away. No need for that.

"Because we're sending Arvad out of the country."

After another pause, Kennedy said: "You can do that?"

"She's an alien, Mr. Ambassador. With some suspicious ties to the head of an enemy nation. We can do that. We will do that," said Hoover confidently. "And soon. That should end the prob—, end the matter."

"I appreciate that, so much, Mr. Director." Kennedy sounded relieved.

"It'll happen soon. We'll get her on a plane out of the country. If that doesn't end things, I'll be the first to tell you. But I don't think you'll need to hear from me about this again."

"Thank you, Mr. Director. You don't know how much I appreciate this." Hoover figured he knew.

"If you ever need a favor from me I—"

"—No, no, Mr. Ambassador, no thanks needed. Nobody wants an embarrassment to the country, during a time of war, especially."

"Yes, exactly."

"Well, I just wanted to let you know."

"Thank you so much. If you need to talk to me, about anything, just call directly."

"Thank you, Mr. Ambassador."

Hoover hung up. He looked at Tolson and said, "Just one more call, and that should be that."

Tolson looked at this wristwatch, the one the press called his "Dick Tracy" watch.

"Well, it's scheduled for a little later."

"I'll probably be put on hold for a while, so I might as well call now."

The Director dialed a number known to only a few. The voice of a middle-aged woman with a Mid-Atlantic accent answered.

"Good day. Office of the President."

"Hello. This is—"

"—Oh I know your voice, Mr. Hoover," Grace Tully said sweetly. "The President is expecting your call. I'll put you in."

There was a pause of five seconds or so, while static crackled on the phone line. Tolson leaned forward expectantly. Hoover sat with the receiver to his ear and his head cocked at an angle, his eyes gleaming.

"Well, Director Hoover," came the deliberate, patrician voice with a trace of irony, "do you have any more Nazi spies to turn over to me today?"

"Good day, Mr. President, thank you. I do have the very latest report on Nazi, and Japanese, and Italian, suspects, if you like. But there was another matter I wanted to bring up, first, if I may."

FDR became terse and attentive. "Go ahead."

"Well, Mr. President. It has to do with your Ambassador to England." Roosevelt was silent. Kennedy was a regular source of trouble for him.

"And his son."

The President replied, "His son," in the same flat tone the Ambassador had initially used.

And Hoover outlined the "Inga Binga" affair.

Roosevelt listened silently, and when Hoover had finished, the President said warily, "This is, interesting. But what does such an, indiscretion, have to do with me?"

"Well, Mr. President," answered Hoover in an earnest voice, "This could cause embarrassment to the Ambassador, to our new ally England—and to yourself. That's why I wanted to tell you about it directly."

"I see, Mr. Director. Thank you…So, what do you think should be done?"

And Hoover explained how he was already arranging to have Arvad sent out of the country, and against her will if necessary.

Roosevelt was a little disappointed at this. 'The scandal could be used against Kennedy,' he thought, against a man who had become a real pain in his craw.

'But it would be an embarrassment, or worse, to my Administration,' the President continued to reason. 'And to our nation at war. Yes, better to have no issue to deal with at all.'

FDR came to a rapid decision. "I give your plan my wholehearted approval," the President said in a deeply affectionate voice.

"And if other matters of this type emerge, why don't you call me about them directly?"

"Why of course, Mr. President," said Hoover, smiling, and nodding, "you can count on me to do so.

"And congratulations on your sons, and their service to the country. All four of them in the armed services! That is something every American can be proud of."

The President happily thanked him, and the Director, looking like the Chesire Cat, put the phone back on its receiver. Tolson watched him break into a broad smile.

Hoover had collected more favors for possible use in the future. One from an Ambassador, and one from a President.

And he made a mental note to place all the files on all the Kennedys into his safe.

Coded *Pantalones*

For days, Thorne's mood had taken a marked turn for the worse. She didn't feel like talking to anybody. Especially any man.

She wasn't herself. For three nights, she was plagued by recurrent nightmares, of Matías's violation of her. The dreams seemed to go for hours. Nightmares with her stuck in that terrible situation, imprisoned in her own house, her own bedroom, unable to escape from that horrific man. And this time, no Roald Dahl appeared as her savior knight, to impose a just punishment on the scoundrel. She had to endure the torture by herself, until finally waking up from a fevered dream.

She had heard that, if one thinks of the subject of a nightmare before going to sleep, that nightmare would not occur. But they did occur. And the memory of them haunted her throughout each succeeding day. It just wasn't like her, a woman of unusual courage, to be affected in this way. By the third night, she had almost gotten accustomed to waking up with her bedclothes soaked in sweat, her nerves all jangled.

And for three days, she let her phone ring without picking it up.

She realized that, as a spy, she might be missing out on valuable intel. From a call from her handler. Or Intrepid. Or Aldiche. They had been seeing each other for weeks now, sometimes winding up at her home, other times at the Argentine Embassy, at an ornate bedroom which he particularly liked.

But she dreaded it might be Matías calling, however unrealistic that might be. He hadn't been seen or heard from since Dahl had administered his beating. There was scant chance of his contacting Liz, much less approaching her, or her home. But that was reason and logic speaking. It was emotion, and the horror of memory, which gripped her at this time.

She shuddered at the memory of his voice. She winced at the memory of the pain in her jaw. In the half-sleep upon awakening, she wondered if Matías might bring charges against her, and against the man who had punched him out. 'Maybe I'll be dragged into a legal case!' she'd fret. That would end her career, her missions gone by the boards. It would greatly inconvenience Dahl. And his diplomatic, or espionage, career, whatever it was.

In fevered, restless sleeps, she even imagined returning the Italian Navy codes to the Spanish Embassy. Then she'd fully wake up, and feel the sweat sliding down her breasts, and realize with relief her mission had been successfully accomplished many months ago, a world of time ago, before Pearl Harbor.

On the afternoon of the second day of trauma, fate seemed to play a cruel trick. She had a waking flashback, a daydream, as she was leaving her house to pick up some groceries at a Wisconsin Avenue store. As she went down her front steps, the image of Matías's fist hitting her flashed in her brain. She stumbled, and hit her head on the steps' railing. Liz suffered a nasty bruise on the forehead, which she tried to cover with makeup. But in applying the cosmetics before her bathroom mirror, the dark blotch, a reminder of the hurt she'd suffered from the rapist flipped her back into a waking nightmare. She stumbled out of the bathroom, gasping, and sweating profusely, as she had the previous nights.

During the fourth evening, the nightmares thankfully ceased. She continued research on another espionage case she'd been assigned. However her waking mind still ached from the impact of the dreams. On the following morning, her phone rang. It was the fourth time it had rung while she was home and hadn't answered it. Wearily, she wondered if the time had come to pick up. Yes, duty called. Her work was so vital. Still, she hesitated. Her mind a blank, her emotions blanker, she held up the receiver.

It was Aldiche.

"*Carita*, I've been trying to reach you."

"Aldiche," she said, with little emotion. "I've, I've—been busy." She started to say, "How have you been?," but her lips wouldn't move.

He was a man. He wanted her for a reason, one reason probably. That reason no longer appealed to her.

The Argentine heard the flatness in her voice, and said, "Ah, are you tiring of me, Elise?" He feigned sincerity. "Did I do something to make you mad? I hope not."

"No," replied Liz.

She liked him, enjoyed him. But he was a man, as Matías was, and he was not a part of one of her missions. On that day, after the reoccurrence of the Matías experience, she felt numb toward him, as she would have toward any male.

"Are you sick?" asked Aldiche. "With that influenza, that's been going around? Oh, how I pray we never experience, how do you say it, the flux, the flu, of the Great War again."

"No, just a cold," she answered tepidly. "I'll be, better, in a few days."

Good to put him off, she thought.

"Ah, I understand," said Aldiche, though he figured something else was going on. She no longer liked him as much, perhaps, as in their initial encounters of passion. That was normal in a sexual relationship. But there was something else that had happened to her, he sensed. Yet he still admired her, lusted for her.

'*Mejor aflojar el carrete*,' he thought in his native tongue, 'best to let out the fishing line.' Let me loosen the reel a little. And this delectable fish will come back to me again.'

"Well, *carita*," he said soothingly, "if there's something I can do for you, perhaps pick up medicine or whatever thing you need, let me know." He laughed softly. "Maybe some soup? Some broth for you. No gazpacho, ha ha, but something hot, and good for a cold."

"Well, Aldo," her pet name for him popped out, but in a neutral tone, "you don't have to, I, ah. No, I prefer not at this time."

"Oh," he said in an understanding tone, "I should just let you rest. Let me call back in a few days when you're better."

There was no response.

Shrugging, he repeated, "I will contact you, if I may, in a few days. Get better, my sweet. I do wish you well." He added with emotion, "I want you better."

Putting the phone down, Aldiche figured, 'The ball is in her court.' He thought again: 'No, it is in mine. I do really like her.' He hadn't come upon a woman like this in years. Maybe it *was* just a bad cold, nothing more. He would call her in a couple of days. And tomorrow he'd have roses delivered to her home.

Two days later he phoned. Liz hadn't had any more nightmares, but was still very low emotionally. After some small talk, Aldiche asked if he could come to her house the next night. Liz felt too weak to reply. Her mind said, "No," but her mouth uttered the word, "Maybe." Aldiche seized on this, saying, "All right, I'll see you at seven. And don't bother to prepare anything. I'll bring food, and drink."

Liz tried to tell him no, but the weariness and lack of purpose that had consumed her that week kept her mum. She started to reply. But before she said anything, Aldiche had hung up.

In the intervening hours, she kept meaning to call him to cancel the engagement. But she couldn't bear to speak to any man, even to tell him not to come over. 'Maybe he won't come,' she lied to herself. 'And, I'm feeling better, after all, the nightmares have ended, things are picking up.'

That morning, she intended to call and cancel four times. And each time she procrastinated, her mind diverting itself to some other, inconsequential topic.

Promptly at seven that evening, she heard a knock on the door.

Unlike the other times, she was dressed modestly, in light-brown pants, loafers, and a white blouse. Her hair was pulled back, not hanging down seductively. That morning she'd put on the lightest of makeup, and a bit more on her forehead's bruise. No perfume.

She walked to the door in a daze, her mind mostly blank, but a part of it fearful. She slowly turned the knob.

Aldiche was there, smiling genially, carrying more flowers, roses, in one arm, and a bag of dinner and wine from Martin's in the other. He thought about kissing her, but something in her distant manner told him not to. He walked to the dining room and put down the victuals. The table was bare, unlike the other times, when Liz had carefully set it.

Liz slowly walked to the table, then stopped. Aldiche walked over to her, and took her face lightly in his hands. He kissed her forehead.

"*Carita*, I miss you. I hope you are well, are feeling better. If there's anything I can do…"

He stared at her. She gazed blankly at him. She looked like someone who had been through a heartbreak. Or a fight. Wait!

The bruise on her forehead was visible through the cosmetics.

Aldiche had been an amateur boxer in Argentina, and he figured he knew where such marks came from.

"*Cara*, did someone hit you?" He had been convinced, in his vanity, that there was no other man. That suddenly seemed foolish, with a woman so desirable.

"I, I fell," said Liz, with hesitation. "I, I was woozy from my cold, the flu maybe, and fell down the front steps, I—" But Aldiche's remark brought back stark memories of the rape, and the recent nightmares. She felt dizzy.

He lightly placed his hands on her cheeks and mouth, stopping her from talking. He ran his fingers over the marks. 'Surely these are bruises from a punch,' he thought.

He took a step back, anger overtaking him. A protective instinct.

"If you tell me who did this, I will make him pay."

This was hardly what Liz needed, another physical confrontation. Involving another diplomat. "No, don't, you can't do that." Confused, she blurted out some of what happened with Matías, without saying his name. "Yes, he hit me." Her head sunk. "A long time ago, it seems now. And it, it doesn't matter now.

"A misunderstanding. He is gone. Nothing more to do."

Aldiche cradled Thorne against his chest. The feelings Liz had suppressed about the beating came out, along with vivid images from the nightmares. Keeping her face against his neck, she began crying. Softly, then hard.

He let her cry from a long time. Then he led her to the table. He thought that, despite her protestations, the beating had occurred recently.

He took plates and utensils from the kitchen, and laid out the dinner and the wine for her. She, and he, ate without much appetite, but some color returned to the fine cheekbones of her face. Then Liz quietly told him about some of the assault, as much as she could without telling him anything of her mission.

Aldiche didn't dislike her for having had a fling, as he saw it, with this callow man, whenever it had occurred. Instead, he realized she was more like himself than he had imagined. 'A female Lothario,' he thought. 'I will not hold it against her.' Maybe he and Liz were truly meant for each other. And he did feel real anger about the callous beating of a woman.

For her part, Liz felt surprisingly relieved at talking about the matter, about having *someone* to talk to about it. Even if it was a man. 'Yes,' she reflected, 'I am feeling better, maybe this will get me over the nightmares completely.'

Some of her affection toward Aldiche returned to her. 'Not all men are horrible,' she told herself. Some, like her handlers, like this Argentine, are okay, are supportive.

When they finished eating, Aldiche got up to leave, and went to the door. She went halfway over to say goodbye. He walked halfway back, to kiss her goodnight.

She returned the kiss. He kissed back.

A strange feeling of loneliness overcame Liz. She did not want to be by herself again. She and he kissed again, and embraced. And more so, and more ardently.

Aldiche felt his desire inflamed, after the absence from his paramour. Lizzy was surprised at her own reaction. She felt a hot flush coursing through her face, felt the heat of her lover's own face. They gripped each other's hands, which were as warm as a stovetop.

The ardent Argentine loosened one of her blouse buttons. She stopped him. He unbuttoned another. She didn't stop him.

Acting quickly now, he took off the blouse, and pulled his own shirt off. Liz felt her resistance crumble. She waited, expectant. He unzipped his trousers and cast them aside.

Aldiche led her to the bedroom. She still felt numb, but very warm, like being in a sauna after a long, tiring horseback ride. Not unpleasant. 'Just relax,' she thought. 'Let it go.'

He placed her down on the bed. She lay there passively, in a trance. She felt so weary.

She offered no resistance, unlike the time with Matías. It was good not to have to fight. To let this man take complete control of her. But not in a negative way, like that other time, but in an affectionate way. And he was certainly tender toward her. And manly and viral, which is why she liked him.

Sometime later, Liz woke up, with a start. She had dreamed again that a man was assaulting her. A surreal dream, as earlier in the week. The man's body had been Aldiche's, and his face that of Matías. She raced about the living room, for hours it seemed, a man pursuing her, just a foot or two behind, as she stayed just out of his grasp. Then suddenly, she was on a horse, while still in the house, galloping about, a different man chasing her with his own horse. Bizarrely, he had the face and body of Admiral Armando. His bulk pressed down on the mount, which was Aldiche's horse Tercia, who neighed sorrowfully from the weight.

Awake, but still in terror, Liz glanced at the man lying beside her. She lay face up, sweating hard, her chest heaving, while Aldiche slept quietly on his side just inches away. She forced herself to think rationally about the startling images. She realized it had been simply a nightmare. Her heart rate started to slow, her breathing steadied. Then she felt a strong urge to relieve herself. From the frenetic dream, and the wine they'd consumed. Not wanting to wake her lover, she silently glided off the sheets, her bare feet making no sound on the carpeted floor.

In the living room she stumbled off to the side to avoid stepping on the pants Aldiche had discarded; they were faintly visible in the dim light. As she did so, she glimpsed a patch of white outlined against the dark woolen fabric.

Her innate curiosity made her stop. Was that some kind of paper? Yes. She started to walk again, then stopped. Even in the dim light, the paper seemed odd. It was not a piece of newspaper, nor part of a blank sheet. It seemed like a kind of scribble.

Her character as a spy kicked in, her desire to *know*. She bent down to the ground. She thought of rummaging through the pants, as she had done with the admiral's sometimes.

'Wait!' she yelled to herself. 'What if Aldiche saw me?!'

She wondered why she felt afraid of how he would react to that, as opposed to her feeling no shame at going through the admiral's apparel.

Yet her curiosity deepened. She glanced at the bedroom door, and listened hard. She thought she could hear Aldiche breathing loudly. The sounds of someone sound asleep.

She got on her knees, and lowered her head close to the paper.

The scrawl had letters, and some numbers. Paragraphs worth. They looked like they'd come out of a machine. A typewriter? No, more like a teletype.

Her eyes were becoming accustomed to the dimness. She could make out that half of the script was in English, and the other half in an Asian language.

Chinese? Japanese? Korean? Something else?

She bent down her head some more, and squinted. The lines followed each other sequentially. First a line in the foreign tongue, then one in English. About the same length.

It was a translation.

But the light was too dim to make out the words.

Her curiosity seized her. She stood up, and remembered the penlight she kept in a kitchen drawer, and the spy camera in the drawer's false bottom.

Liz strode rapidly, but silently, to the kitchen, and toward the drawer. She banged a shin against the oven and winced in pain. 'Damn it!' she thought angrily. 'The clang might have woken Aldiche!' She peeked out toward the bedroom door, and didn't see him, or hear him call out.

Her hands found the light easily, but she fumbled with the drawer's false bottom before opening it, praying the noise made wasn't too loud, and grasped the Elgin camera.

Liz stepped silently back into the living room, and stooped over the trousers. She listened. She couldn't hear Aldiche's breathing. Had he awakened? Was he about to emerge and surprise her? How would he react?

She listened some more. Cupped her ears. She heard the breathing again. The telltale sound of sleep.

Liz scrutinized the script with the penlight.

Though masterful with Romance languages, Liz was ignorant of Asian ones. But she knew enough to distinguish Chinese script from Japanese. It was the latter.

The language of Britain's and America's enemy!

She read the English script. She felt butterflies in her stomach as she did so.

The message read:

"134 nautical miles, battleship, Palau destroyers three ; regiments five Imperial Marines ; 447 miles nautical carrier Hornet 48 planes ? torpedoes 17 dive bombers; 612 miles nautical XXX coast watcher 2 subs; XX 1 sub tender…"

It was a translation of Japanese into English. Of Navy information.

Top-secret information! Was her lover a spy?

And for the other side!?

She clicked off the light, and thought. And listened. Had Aldiche's heavy breathing paused again? She thought frenetically of what she would say if he appeared in the doorway.

'Oh, I just started to pick up your pants for you.' Pretty weak, but maybe he'd believe it. 'No, that's ridiculous, as he'd see the camera!'

She flicked the light back on with one hand, and held the camera over the paper with the other. It was difficult, holding the Elgin in the right position while maneuvering her index finger over the shutter. She pushed the shutter once, and then again as the camera almost slipped from her hand. She took a third picture, believing it and the first shot were adequate.

She pushed the paper back into the pants pocket, with some of it sticking out again. No sound from the bedroom. After hesitating, still curious, she pulled the paper out again.

A sound came from the bedroom. A rustling sound? Was he awakening? No, she heard nothing. She was safe. For now.

Nervous, she stared at the paper and memorized the paragraph of English script. Her visual memory was superb; she even managed to burn some of the Japanese characters into her mind. Hands shaking, she pushed the paper back into the pocket, its end sticking out. Close to where it had been when she first noticed it. Not that Aldiche should notice any difference. So she hoped. She flicked off the light.

'I must make it seem realistic!' her spy training told her. She nearly ran to the bathroom and, keeping the door open, flushed the toilet. She stuck the penlight and the camera behind the pipes of the wash basin.

It was well she had moved fast, for Aldiche had awakened. He heard the flush. He got up, and had reached the bedroom door when he spotted Liz walking past his pants, her eyes glancing at them, as he dimly made out the paper sticking out of them.

'*Maldita sea*!' he thought, cursing himself. That had been careless of him. 'She couldn't have noticed the decryption, could she?'

Liz saw him in the doorway and stopped, her bare feet next to the pants. She forced a smile. So did he. In the dimness, they could see each other's teeth gleaming against the gloom.

'How long has he been in the doorway?' thought Liz. Had he seen her walk to the bathroom? Did he notice her flushing the toilet just moments after entering the bathroom? The butterflies in her stomach came back.

'I'm overthinking this,' she told herself. But she knew that was the only way to survive in her work.

'I'm overthinking this,' thought Aldiche. 'Even if she saw the script, she wouldn't know what it was for.' But he possessed the outcome of the war in his hands, and even the smallest risk was great.

"It's very good to see you, *carita*," he said, tentatively.

"I am very glad you came here tonight," she answered, firmly.

She knew she had to contact someone at allied intelligence, and soon. But for now she was stuck. Liz walked to the bedroom door, and took Aldiche in her arms. They pressed their naked forms together, and went back to the bed.

Aldiche forgot any concerns while rolling in the arms of the beautiful woman.

Afterwards, he dozed off, while Liz feigned slumber. Her mind was racing. She forced herself to remain still.

She doubted it, but what if Aldiche knew that she knew?

'He could strangle me right here in this bed,' she fretted.

'No, he would have done that already if that was his intent.

'Or maybe not,' her restless, troubled mind went on. 'If he is a spy, a spy for the other side, maybe he's more like Matías than I thought. His love for me might be fake. Just using me. As I've used men, before discarding them without a second thought.'

She imagined him sleeping with her one more time before murdering her. Just for the "fun of it." After Matías, she saw men as capable of anything. Though not every man.

As she spent a restless, endless night, she decided her next move.

Assuming she lived.

Around dawn, Aldiche awoke. As he cuddled her, she half-expected him to break her neck. But he soon got up. With a great mental effort, she remained calm. To her relief, he dressed quickly, and said he had to leave for his embassy. As he reached the door, he called out to her as she stood in the bedroom threshold. "I can't be late for work today, *carita*. I promise I will call you soon!" As he closed the door, Liz caught a glimpse of him reaching into his pocket, and taking out the paper.

A Friend in Need

After double-locking the front door, Lizzy quickly dressed. She slipped on pants, a cotton blouse, and walking shoes. She waited a few more minutes to make sure Aldiche had departed her street. She peeked out the living room window from behind the curtain, and did not see him, or anyone looked like the FBI or other operatives.

She pulled open the front door. A trolley car was rattling up the cobbled street toward Georgetown University. Otherwise, O St. was empty. Liz hurried down the front steps and nearly ran to Wisconsin Avenue. She flagged a taxi, and went to a camera shop on M St. near Rock Creek. It was open, and she knew the manager, and knew he "admired" her. And knew he did work for MI-6. She had used his services before to quickly develop film for a mission. He immediately got to work on her photos.

After just 30 minutes, she had the prints. She taxied back to O St, and asked the driver to let her out near her home. She knew where she wanted to go, but wanted to think it over some. She'd walk over while doing so.

Liz stepped to the corner of 34th St. She looked at the worn brickwork of the Colonial Era home across the way.

Sometimes, late at night, or very early in the morning, she had spied its tall, slim occupant coming and going, in a cab, or in a government-issue limousine. Liz knew of the occupant, and his role, which was one of the most important in the world. The resident was Harry Hopkins, FDR's senior advisor. The President had entrusted Hopkins with control of the Lend-Lease program, to ply America's wartime allies, Britain, the Soviet Union, China, and others, with billions of dollars-worth of weapons, vehicles, airplanes, and food.

The program's name was misleading. Though supposedly the vital supplies were "lent" or "leased" out, many would never be paid back. It was how the Arsenal of Democracy kept its friends fighting.

When she occasionally spotted Hopkins, he seemed wan and strained. Not at all surprising, as he worked nearly around the clock on his daunting duties, supplying armies from Moscow to the interior of China. He hardly spent time in this place, in fact, and commuted from it to the White House, spending the bulk of his hours in the Executive Mansion, often staying the night at the White House.

The importance of this neighborhood, filled with ranking diplomats and powerful politicos, was indicated by the special telephone stand across from Hopkins' house. It was not a telephone booth, but a tall metal pole with a phone attached to it. From it, in the event of a fire nearby, or other emergency, a passerby could directly contact the nearest fire or police station.

As she headed up 34th St., Liz's head ached, from the liquor she'd shared with Aldiche, but much more from her discovery of the coded message. A few more flashbacks from Matías's assault also afflicted Thorne. But it was the Argentine she focused on.

'Has Aldiche played me?' she considered. Had he gulled a woman who had seen herself as a superb spy, a master of her craft? 'Was I seduced by an operative from the other side?' she agonized.

Thorne ran through the possibilities.

'Is Aldiche a foreign agent? Could he be an agent for *our side*?' She thought her contacts might be able to confirm this one way or the other. Her breathing became more labored from the steep incline, which ran up to the high heights of Georgetown.

'And is his affection for me fake?' she pondered. She had thought his love for her was real, but now she doubted it. 'But should I care about his affection? What kind of an agent am I after all?' Her emotions grew stronger. 'Still, I am a woman, with feelings like anyone else!'

'Is it possible I'm making the wrong conclusion?' Liz's train of thought went on. 'What if the paper I found wasn't what it seems. Could it have been a cutout from a book of some kind, a publicly available book? On the Japanese language perhaps? Even a children's book on simple codes?' She hurried up the hill. 'No! I know official documents when I see them. That was actual military code. Vital information about our own warships!

'And Aldiche claims to be a commercial attaché, and not a military man!'

She neared her destination, next to the Volta Place park. It was a locale suffused with ghosts of the past, and intrigue from the present.

An expanse of lawn stretched ahead. A full city block in extent, it had been, until the 1840s, the cemetery for Georgetown's elite. Then it became the "moveable graveyard." Because torrents of rainwater streaming down from the city heights had scoured the slants of its hillside, digging out coffins, and sending them floating down 33rd and 34th streets toward the Potomac. The cemetery was itself churned into a smelly, desecrated marsh. For years after, boys playing in the graveyard would find bones and skulls sticking out of the soil.

The city fathers were naturally disturbed. They determined to move the resting places to higher, dryer ground. Georgetown was a wealthy place, built on tobacco fortunes, and its affluent magistrates were able to hire America's most prominent designers, Andrew Jackson Downing and James Renwick, to lay out a new graveyard and to build it a fine chapel. Placed on a promontory just east of the Martha Washington family's old estate of Tudor Place. The graves at the future Volta Place park were disinterred and moved to their new, final, final resting place, dubbed Oak Hill Cemetery.

Volta Place was witness to drama in the present as well. In a narrow, darkened townhouse several doors over from the park lived a dark-haired, sallow-faced man Liz had occasionally glimpsed while walking in the neighborhood. He was unassuming in appearance, and was careful to keep a bland, expressionless face. As a good spy should. For that man was Alger Hiss, the person Liz had recognized at Cissy's soiree. A ranking officer in the U.S. State Department, and a mole working diligently for Moscow.

Yet on that morning, Liz hardly noticed Volta Place and its surroundings as she scurried up the sidewalk to a modest townhome on 34th St. She paused outside, and wondered if she should have contacted her handler first. 'Yes I should have,' she thought. But she felt unusually vulnerable, and needed to meet with someone she instinctively trusted.

Thorne pressed the door buzzer. It wasn't clear if it sounded within, so Lizzy began to knock. Softly at first, then hard, almost banging on the door. 'What is wrong with me?' she asked herself. Where was her normal self-possession? As she raised her fist to hit the door again, it swung open.

Ivar Bryce was there, a surprised look on his handsome face, making it seem more elfish than devilish. He had recently woken up, with a hangover, and had only a robe on. Still, his fine black hair was oiled and pushed back perfectly straight as at a dinner party.

Without asking about her evidently troubled state, he said helpfully, "Come on in, Elise."

Inside, it did not look like bachelors' digs. The sitting room was finely appointed, with William Morris window drapes of linen, an open-armed sofa of Danish design, and wing-backed, Chippendale easy chairs. Liz noticed that dark blackout curtains had been stashed away below the windows.

On the red, satin-covered couch was Dahl, his long legs and arms languidly extended, then becoming rigid with attention on her entrance. In front of him was a mahogany table with a notepad and pencil on which he had been doodling and sketching out story ideas.

A Crosley radio, encased in walnut paneling, took up a corner of the small but comfortable space. It was playing an English pop song, by Noel Coward. The lyrics were sad and soft:

"I'll see you again.

Whenever spring breaks through again;

Time may lie heavy between

But what has been

Is past forgetting…"

"How are you feeling today?" Dahl asked gently, with a gaze of concern. Liz didn't answer.

Ivar, thinking the words of the song might be too apropos, thought of lifting the needle from the record. He nervously stated: "We actually know Noel Coward. The playwright's visited here."

Liz seemed to hear him, to register this little fact, but stayed silent, and worried.

Ivar said, "We're friends of sorts." He didn't add that Coward, rather like Dahl, was in the U.S. to make nice with the Americans. A spy, to make the alliance stronger.

Roald Dahl repeated his query. "Liz, How are you doing?" He watched attentively for an answer.

Liz, taking quick glances at Dahl, opened and closed her mouth, but no words came out. Ivar sensed he was the third in a "three's a crowd."

"Well," he said, his handsome face looking distant, "I fancy I'll leave you tw—I have something to do, that can't wait." And he strode upstairs to a den.

Dahl got up and took a few brisk steps to Liz, as another Matías flashback gripped her mind. Without thinking, she found herself falling into Dahl's arms.

A couple of tears dripped from her eyes. She blinked them away. Dahl softly brushed her cheeks, stating in a low voice, "That's quite all right. Even for the bravest lady. Let it go." She broke out crying, then got a hold of herself. But for a minute, Liz let herself bury her face on his shoulders. Her head still ached, but her mind cleared.

In the background, Noel Coward's lyrics sounded:

"I'll see you again,

When ever spring breaks through again;

Time may lie heavy between,

But what has been

Can leave me never…"

Liz took a step back, and Dahl took her over to the sofa. They sat together, and she took the blue handkerchief he offered.

She started to speak, but the words came out like warbles, like a swimmer speaking underwater. She coughed hard, clearing her throat.

The perceptive Dahl said to her, "You're not reliving that terrible incident, are you?"

"It's not the beating I took that's important," she replied, her words quickly becoming clear, her strength and determination returning.

"Or the beating I gave him?" asked Dahl wryly, eyeing Liz closely, surprised at her sudden shift in mood. He glanced at his knuckles, as if they were still rubbed raw.

Liz smiled a bit. "I'm, I'm okay. And him, I don't care what happened with him. Hopefully something bad."

"You could show some concern for me," Dahl said airily. "That lout might still sue me for assault." He winked to show he wasn't serious.

The humor made Liz feel better. And she admired how he could joke at such a thing.

"It's about not *that* character." She paused. "I guess you don't know his name. Matías. He's Spanish. A Spanish—*diplomat*." She pronounced the last word acidly. "But he little matters.

The Noel Coward tune had ended, and they heard the needle of the record player start to scratch repetitively. Dahl got up to turn it off, and came back to Liz.

Wondering about her physical and mental health, he quietly asked, "Have you seen a doctor?"

Liz turned her head dismissively, as if that was a trivial question.

"What I need to say, what is really important," she looked at him fixedly. "My health is not important, not the issue. What I need to tell…" Her voice fell off, but she kept looking at him, as if sizing him up. Dahl for his part looked back in complete honesty, without the usual spy's façade. He felt no façade was necessary with her.

"I had to come here. To tell you, but…" She stopped, hesitant, worried about breaking the rules of the spy trade. Then suddenly, with confidence, she said, "You, and Ivar: you both work for British intelligence, right?"

Dahl smiled weakly. He thought of the espionage work Ivar had done. His housemate was indeed a spy, who had helped tug a then-neutral U.S. over to the side of Britain. In the fall of the previous year, Ivar had created a phony map that purported to show Nazi designs on South America. The chart showed the continent carved up into five German-dominated countries. It was published in newspapers throughout America and, in an October 1941 speech, President Roosevelt had referenced it in warning of German designs on the Western Hemisphere. But the map was a fabrication. Of which its creator, Ivar Bryce, as an ardent British patriot, was very proud.

Roald Dahl had learned that Liz worked for his and Ivar's organization, MI-6, and for the Americans now as well. But admitting this to another, fellow agent, without official sanction, broke the rules of espionage.

"You know that, even if I were an agent," he said lightly, with a charming smile, "and I'm not, that I couldn't tell you."

"And I couldn't tell you either," said Liz directly, "but I will."

She shifted nervously on the sofa, her face three feet from his.

In a louder and dead-serious voice, she added, "I have to.

"I found something last night. Among the effects of an Argentine, friend. His name is Aldiche Engardio. Also an embassy official. I found something that I have to share with our intelligence. British and American intelligence.

"Yes," Thorne went on, nodding her head for emphasis, "I am an agent. I'm working with MI-6. And, and with OCI now." Dahl stared at her, trying to keep a blank face. He wasn't surprised at her revelation, but at her direct approach.

"I found something last night that, that may be of the most vital importance to the war." She gripped Dahl's arm. "I'll tell my handler, of course. And I'll tell," she paused, to watch Dahl's reaction, "I'll tell, *Intrepid*."

Dahl couldn't hide his reaction to that term. And Liz now knew for sure, though she hadn't doubted it, that Dahl was indeed a spy. And on the same team.

Roald Dahl thought of denying it all, and ending the conversation. For just a moment. But he decided to hear her out.

Lizzy plowed ahead. "You wouldn't know any Japanese, would you?" And she told him of the paper with the Japanese characters, and their evident English translation, spelling out the entire message.

Dahl took this in with great interest, and complete belief in her story. And admiration. 'This woman has her vulnerabilities, sure, but she also has such nerve and courage!'

When she had finished, he sat thinking for some moments. At length he asked, "You don't know Japanese, I suppose. So I suppose you don't know any of those Japanese characters."

"I don't know them, but I have them with me."

"What do you mean?" he asked.

Dramatically, she pulled two photographs out of her purse, and placed them on the dining table. With pursed lips, Dahl looked them over for several minutes. Finally, he remarked, "You appear to have a photographic memory."

"I do," she answered.

Dahl looked up with a faraway expression. He felt a thrill of fear. This could greatly affect the war.

He felt excited. At being back in the game. In a real fight.

He rose, and walked over to a telephone on a nightstand. He turned to her. "I trust you. Implicitly. As you obviously do me." He grinned, winningly. His tall figure seemed gigantic to her. "I'm going to make a call, to help check out your information."

Within 20 minutes, they heard a taxi door closing outside. Stepping up to the front door was a skinny, scholarly-looking man in a checkered Highlander jacket and ill-fitting, herringbone tweed trousers. Dahl ushered him inside, and sat him on the couch next to himself. Liz got up and stood by the record player, and observed both men.

"Let's just call him 'Harry'," he told Liz, as he winked at the newcomer. "There's no need to give away any more secrets than we have already." 'Harry' seemed nonplused at the ruse. He also seemed uninterested in Liz, which was highly unusual in any man. Dahl gave him the photos, and told him to ignore the English script, and to translate the Japanese.

"Is this it?" asked Harry, sounding disappointed at finding so little text. His accent was flat, as if mastering many languages had stripped away his native Scottish accent. Which was the case.

"It shouldn't take long," he said, taking out reading glasses from a case in his shirt pocket. "The characters are small, but I can make them out, I suppose," he murmured in disapproval.

"And there are gaps in the message. But no matter, I can make sense of them."

After a few seconds he looked up and nodded at Dahl.

"You're finished?" the latter asked. Harry nodded again.

185

"What does it say?"

Looking up at the ceiling, Harry recited, "130 or so miles, nautical miles, one supposes; battleship or cruiser; Palau, an island in the Pacific; three ships, warships; regiments, Imperial Marines, unknown number; gibberish; 400 or so miles nautical; Lexington, a question mark, carrier, aircraft carrier I think; more gibberish; 48 planes torpedoes, a blank space, 17 bombers?, I'm not sure of the number or the type; 612 miles nautical, very exact that; coast watchers subs, two of them?; blanks; 1 underwater, a submarine perhaps?.."

He stopped, and with a bored air looked at Dahl. "That's it."

Liz happily clenched her fists. The translation more or less matched the English text.

"You have a good memory," Dahl told Harry.

"I would say so," Harry replied without braggadocio.

Dahl took him to the door. As he left, he whispered something conspiratorially to the linguist. Liz couldn't see their lips, but her hearing was keen. She heard him something like, "I stress the importance of saying nothing about this to any other person."

Back on the sofa, Dahl and Liz agreed that Aldiche had, or was close to having, a secret of great consequence. Someone had knowledge of the exact makeup and locations of the Japanese fleets and troops, and a knowledge of the American ones too. She filled him in on the comings and goings of the Argentine, as far as she knew them. Including how he loved to go for lunch every working day, and often at Martin's Tavern.

When she had finished, Liz asked, "Won't our bosses be crazy-mad at us, for breaking protocol?"

Dahl grinned. "I think it more likely we'll get medals. This could be the biggest story of the war." His expression turned serious. "We can't lose a minute. I'll get ahold of my handler now. Why don't you do the same with yours?"

"I'll go one better," Liz said. "I'll contact Intrepid as well."

Dahl looked at her with disbelief, then belief and admiration.

He stood up suddenly. "Yes, we may not have a moment to lose." He looked determined, and excited.

"Along with informing our superiors, I'm going to start tracking our Argentine friend. Immediately." He looked at his watch. "I'll be able to get to the Argentine embassy before lunchtime."

Tunneling into a Secret Past

Roald Dahl moved as fast as one of the Hurricane fighters he had flown. He phoned his handler. His MI-6 contact connected him to a ranking MI-6 officer, who assured him the organization could have the Argentine Embassy under watch by the following afternoon. That wasn't fast enough for the kinetic ex-pilot. He immediately rushed over from Volta Place to begin surveillance of the Argentine Embassy, across Q St. from the lobby of an apartment building. Luck was with Dahl, as he spotted his prey a little before noon. Aldiche appeared wearing a black silk suit with blue tie, and had a diplomat's mail pouch slung over his shoulder. Dahl watched him stop at a mailbox, place his jacket atop it, tie the pouch onto his shoulder, and cover it with the jacket like a cape.

Dahl tracked the suspect several blocks down to Dupont Circle. The Argentine did not go into one of the many luncheonettes and restaurants there. He furtively watched him pass the People's Drug Store, and approach the glorious portico of the Blaine mansion. Would he enter the Red Cross quarters there, where First Lady Eleanor Roosevelt and Mayor LaGuardia, the civil defense chief, were known to visit? It seemed a promising haunt for a spy. But Aldiche kept walking quickly on, passing the grandiose Larz Anderson mansion, turned two years prior in a museum of the Society of the Cincinnati, devoted to the descendants of officers of the American Revolution.

Dahl noted the irony of that structure, given his British ties. "Once enemies, the English and the Americans are now close allies,' he reflected. 'With mine and Ivar's job to make them closer still!' He corrected himself. 'Just *one* of my jobs—now I have a more important one.'

He hustled to keep up with the energetic Argentine. He felt the angst known by anyone tailing someone: the fear of losing contact. And concern about being spotted. After passing the Blaine and Anderson properties, the number of pedestrians dwindled to a few. Dahl scooted over to the north side of Massachusetts Avenue, and took cover behind a Magruder's Grocery delivery truck. Aldiche paused at the traffic intersection ahead.

Dahl knew enough about the neighborhood that the Phillips Collection museum was up the hill to his right, and many embassies and imposing townhomes were scattered down the boulevard ahead. Including the Japanese embassy, but that had been emptied of Nipponese in the days after Pearl Harbor. Dahl was unaware of the Spanish spies at that property. Up the hill was land the

German embassy had acquired, but it of course was closed as well, its diplomats placed under house arrest in West Virginia.

The traffic light changed, and thick exhaust from a few cars rose up, but Aldiche remained standing at the corner. He seemed to be making up his mind about something. The figure in the silk suit turned suddenly left, and went down 21st St. Roald Dahl was puzzled at this, for this block contained no embassies, and some homes of lesser importance leading to an impoverished neighborhood near Rock Creek.

Aldiche crossed over to the other side of the street, and Dahl followed, walking in the road behind parked cars and trucks. He gazed over his shoulder at a red Chevrolet Town Sedan slowly approaching him. When he looked back again, Aldiche had disappeared!

No, he caught a glimpse of him heading into an alley, and quickly passing out of view. Dahl rushed down to the alleyway's end, and stuck his head around the corner of an apartment building. The Argentine was striding down another lane toward a small courtyard. Further down the narrow back alley was an old carriage house, attached to which was a small shed, one of the alley dwellings in which the indigent lived.

Aldiche glanced over his left shoulder, and Dahl stopped cold. He didn't think Aldiche had seen him. But had he spotted him on the walk over from Dupont? Was that why he had been walking so fast?

Dahl ducked back behind the building. He silently cursed. His prey, or predator, was much more likely to spot him in these narrow passages. He slowly stuck one eye of his head around the corner.

Aldiche had disappeared! Completely this time.

Dahl stepped into the courtyard. The narrow alley stretched ahead for 70 yards. Aldiche wasn't in it.

'There's no way,' Dahl thought, 'he could have made it down that far in that amount of time, even by sprinting!' He had simply vanished.

Dahl saw the shed 20 yards down the lane on the right, and a back door to a tenement another 10 yeads down on the left. He hadn't heard a door shut, but he had no other places else to try.

He tried the shed first. Its boards were loose, letting him peer inside. It smelled of liquor and urine. Dahl was worried about Aldiche possibly springing out onto him. But he wasn't there: the structure was very small, no more than five feet in width, and Dahl could see it ended against a brick wall, devoid of human presence.

He tried the back door next. Its knob was rusted like it hadn't been turned in ages. Still, Dahl imagined Aldiche suddenly opening the door and jumping out. Gingerly he turned the knob. It was stuck. He tried it with all this strength. "No," he muttered, "it hasn't been opened recently."

"I lost him!" he said, more loudly, and walked slowly back to the courtyard. He was puzzled, disappointed. As he was turning onto the lane back to 21st St., his keen pilot's eyes caught sight of a band of metal on the ground. He walked over to it and bent down. The metal looked like some kind of handle. He brushed off some dirt, and a handle a foot in length appeared, attached to a circular lid. It was the aperture to something, but it didn't look like a manhole cover.

He squatted down, and pulled lightly on the handle. It gave a little; it seemed it had been used recently. He looked around the ground, and saw traces of footsteps on the dirt. The outline of dress shoes. The footwear of a commercial attaché?

Then he heard a patter below. Footsteps? The low rumble got louder.

"Damn it!" Dahl exclaimed. Could he get to the lane around the corner in time to hide? Probably not, but—

—In a flash he was sprinting to the shed. He pushed aside the rotting boards and twisted himself inside, and went flat onto his stomach, his head facing the courtyard. Shallow pools of piss and liquor soaked into his clothes. He turned his head to glimpse through the boards toward the courtyard.

Nothing. But after a couple of minutes, when he began to consider getting out, he saw the lid lift up. A figure in a fine yet dusty silk suit emerged. It was Aldiche.

The Argentine looked about. He didn't spot Dahl in the hiding place. Aldiche pulled himself out of the hole, and put back the lid. He looked around, while brushing himself off, and kicked dirt over the handle. He had the diplomatic pouch with him, and slung it around a shoulder. He took off his dirty jacket, fluffed out some grit, and flung it over his other shoulder. Then he walked purposefully down the lane leading to 21st St., and out of sight.

Dahl was seized with curiosity about where Aldiche had been, but was cautious. He went along the lane, and spotted Aldiche way up 21st St, evidently heading back to Dupont Circle, and to his embassy. If he came back later, Dahl figured he'd still have time to do some exploration.

He took out a book of matches, pulled on the handle, and peeped down into the hole. A wooden ladder led down to the ground seven feet below. He lit a match, gingerly went down the steps, and pulled the metal lid closed behind him. The match went out. As it was very hard to see, he very carefully stepped to the ground below. He lit another match, and spied a light switch on an electrical cable hanging down from above. He fumbled with it, and flicked the light on.

Before him emerged a subterranean passage of indeterminate length. It was about four feet wide, with a dirt floor, and side walls and ceilings of earth. Light bulbs dimly lit the way every 12 feet or so. The tunnel went in a straight line for roughly 20 yards, then veered to the right.

'Did Aldiche construct this?' Dahl wondered. Seemed unlikely. That would have taken weeks, perhaps months if the cavern was as big as it seemed. He began walking slowly ahead.

The smell of decayed—something—struck his nostrils. 'Animal matter? Plant matter? A dead human?' he asked himself.

Fear took hold of the former RAF pilot as he realized Aldiche might have accomplices, who might be lurking somewhere in this strange place. He felt queasy, but thought, 'Well, I'm certainly not going to back out now.' He told himself something he would say when flying combat missions: 'I may be scared, but the enemy should be much more scared of *me.*'

As he stepped along, he saw many dead insects—butterflies, wasps, moths, and other critters. Either on the ground, and on ridges in the walls. He turned where the tunnel went right, and literally froze with fear. On a wall above him was a giant spider, perhaps poisonous, seemingly poised to strike. Dahl instinctively ducked.

Nothing happened. The *Theraphosa blondi* just stood there suspended. A so-called Goliath bird eater, still retaining some of its yellowish color, and looking like a denizen of Hell.

Stricken, Dahl stared at it. Then realized there was glass in front of it. No, a glass box. This spider was dead, and had been placed in a container. An exhibit box.

When Dahl's heart calmed down, he continued walking down the tunnel. The air was close and clammy. Before him on either side were shelves, about waist-high, on which there were other glass boxes. Inside them were insects and creepers of various types, often exotic ones from distant shores. Spiders of all sizes, and clumps of dried-up worms. On one shelf was a collection of bee hives, fortunately no longer active.

Dahl was a brave man, but he did not like bugs, and did not like enclosed spaces. He much preferred the open air, a flyer's air high above the earth. 'This place gives me, as those American movies put it, 'the creeps.' From these creepers!'

The otherworldly passageway turned to the left. Here the collections were transformed. There were shelves again, but of steel or painted iron along the left side of the wall. On top were several safes, newer than the insect collections. At the bottom of the shelves were boxes, some with their lids off. Inside them were folders.

He tried the safes first. As expected, they were locked. He thought of the safecrackers MI-6 employed during break-ins of enemy installations, and wistfully wished one was with him.

He bent down and peered at the boxes. There were five of them, strung out along two shelves. The boxes had markings in ink pen scribbled on their sides. In the dim light he made out the scrawl: "US", "FA", "J", "DS/SD", "M/N".

The "US" seemed clear enough, but the box was double-sealed with electrical tape. Dahl made a mental note to try to find a knife, scissor or some sharp object to open it. 'Or should I?'' he asked himself. That would leave a telltale sign that an intruder had been here.

The "FA" box had a lid, but it was unsealed. Dahl opened it. He found a sheaf of articles on the new U.S. Army Air Force; several of them had newspaper clips about its new offices in Dupont Circle. 'That place is quite close to the Argentine Embassy,' Dahl realized. It was one of the armed service divisions MI-6 had suggested he contact, to chum up the American officers there. That made sense, given his own experience with aerial combat against the very same pilots the Yanks would face in North Africa.

Dahl had once taken a course in Spanish, and he figured the "FA" stood for "*Fuerza Aerea*" in Aldiche's native tongue.

He stepped over to the next box, marked "J". 'Did the Spanish word for Japan,' he thought, 'also start with a 'J'?' The word "*Japonesa*" flashed in his mind. But that box too was sealed. 'I'll save it for a later look.'

The lid was actually off the "SD/DS" box. As Dahl reached within it he wondered, 'Could 'DS' be the Spanish abbreviation for 'SD',' the feared Nazi secret police?

Within he found seven file folders. Each contained newspaper and magazine articles, from Spanish, English, German, and even Russian publications, on the U.S. State Department. '*Departamento de Estado*,' he realized.

One folder was dedicated to the Office of War Information, and another to the Bureau of Latin American affairs. Glancing through them, Dahl noticed that a reader, presumably Aldiche, or one of his colleagues, had underlined and circled much of the text and some of the photos. This folder was paper-clipped to another binder, marked 'SW'. Inside it were articles on the Assistant Secretary of State, Sumner Welles. Dahl knew the top foreign-policy advisor to FDR had been a specialist in Latin-American affairs. Oddly, this folder contained mostly gossip columns from the *Times-Herald* and other Washington and New York papers, many of them tabloids. Their subject was Welles. Some of the commentary was salacious.

Dahl and Ivar had once met Welles at a British Embassy reception, and there Bryce had told him, with a drunken wink, of the rumor the Assistant Secretary 'enjoyed being in the very middle of a rugby scrum, and played on both sides of a cricket match.' Dahl had met Welles's estimable wife, and doubted this innuendo. Still, he knew that even a false rumor of this type could wreck a diplomat's career, and could be used as blackmail.

As Roald Dahl reached for the final box, "M/N", he suddenly froze. A loud clicking noise came from the far end of the tunnel. It was answered from several loud clicks from the front of the tunnel. Then Dahl relaxed, and laughed. They were crickets, a natural part of this unnatural, subterranean menagerie of creatures, both living and dead.

"M/N" had been sealed, but its adhesive tape had loosened from the dampness of the cavern. Without breaking the tape, Dahl managed to slip off the lid.

It had two folders. One had a few general articles on the size and the ports of the U.S. Navy. 'Could 'N' mean 'Navy', and 'M' mean 'Mare' or some such?' he thought. The other folder was crammed with publications, and even two short books. The subject in question was abstruse, and relevant. It dealt with codes, both military and generic. One of the little books was on Morse code. And the other, and Dahl drew in his breath, almost whistling, was in Japanese. Possibly a Japanese code book from the look of it. Further, some of the articles outlined how the warring nations were encoding their communications, or attempting the decipher the codes of their adversaries. Most of them dealt with Japan, America, Britain, Italy, Germany. There were also articles about Spanish intelligence.

Attached by a paper clip to this thick folder was one of smaller width. Dahl opened it while ignoring the clicking of the crickets. Appearing on the first page of a feature article was a lovely young American woman. Many of its paragraphs were heavily underlined and circled in pencil.

The story was about the lady and her husband, who was an Annapolis grad, now working in—in Naval Intelligence. Dahl scanned down to the end of the article on a stapled second page, where underscored were the words, "ascertaining threats from the Jap war machine, and helping to secure the military communications of our nation…" 'The Callaways, eh?' mused Dahl. 'Richard and Adelia, Callaway.'

He began to stuff the article into his shirt, then stopped and memorized the date of publication. Better to leave everything as it was, so when Aldiche came back he'd have no suspicions. 'Besides,' Dahl thought, 'MI-6 and OCI will case this place soon enough!'

He walked further down the dimly lit cavern. 'Liz is really on to something!' he reflected. 'This Aldiche character is running a whole spy operation, including intel collection. And by himself! Well, maybe with others.'

A worry broke his train of thought. Had he heard a sound? Of crickets, or something else? 'Could that be Aldiche? With others?' But he heard no other sound.

He next came across evidence of antiquated weaponry. A rusted hand grenade. Some bullets, from a P08 Luger pistol. A dirt-encrusted cannon shell, its point sticking out from the loose dirt below a wall. From its shape, Dahl, who was knowledgeable about ordinance, estimated it to be a poison-gas cannister. He stepped carefully past it.

He came to an odd-seeming display. In the exact middle of the path was a tall rectangular box, with a shiny, long-muzzled gun atop it. The box looked new, and the weapon, which Dahl didn't recognize, even newer. It seemed inviting, practically begging to be touched, but very out-of-place with the rest of the passage, a tunnel crammed with dusty artifacts, desiccated insects, and rusty containers.

Dahl turned suspicious. He recalled the traps Axis pilots had laid for his fellow RAF pilots over Libya. Pretending to have engine trouble, for instance, then suddenly spiraling into an attack.

He stopped a few feet from the box, and at an angle away from the muzzle. He reached out his left arm, and gave the weapon a shove, jumping backward as he did.

Dahl heard an explosive blast, and the noise of impacts a fraction of an instant later. When he had gotten over his surprise, he stepped over to a wall where he had heard an impact. At the level of the middle of the box, he found an indentation. In it was a dart. Carefully walking around the box, he found an identical indentation, and dart, on the other side of the passage. He next examined the container, which had dart guns on either side.

'Poisons, probably,' he reflected. 'No doubt meant for an intruder. And maybe an exotic poison from the land of these insects.' Someone wanted an intruder to pay a terrible price. He concluded: 'Aldiche will know someone was here now!'

The next part of the tunnel had no shelving, but it did have insect specimens, in glass boxes, some of which were cracked or broken. Dahl had visited a butterfly collection at the Smithsonian's Arts and Industries Building, and spider collections at London's British Museum. He wondered if this weird space had been some kind of storage site for such creatures.

In fact, the tunnel had been the creation, decades before, of an eccentric Smithsonian entomologist, a specialist in insects, one Harrison Dyar. He created the tunnels below his Dupont Circle townhome as a place of play for his children, so he said, as well as a depository for some of his specimens. That was likely a half-truth. For he had been carrying on a secret, second marriage, and the cavern may have been a place of romantic rendezvouses with his other spouse. Moreover, and Dyar never knew of this, but after he moved out of his home, leaving the undiscovered tunnel intact, spies working out of the German consulate had evidently used it as a safe house for themselves and their collaborators. And even after the FBI had shuttered the German Embassy, after Hitler's December 1941 declaration of war, the Führer's spymasters had gotten the word out to allied operatives like Aldiche to use the hidden lair for their own ends. Stepping along cautiously, on the watch for folders that had been dropped on the earthen floor, as well as for other mantraps, Dahl reached the tunnel's terminus.

He looked up and around meticulously, but could find no aperture, no ladder. He listened hard, and heard, not crickets, but music, and the sound of a sonorous voice. A radio music show. Dahl couldn't make out the words to the song, but the vocalist had a tone similar to Bing Crosby. 'Coming from an apartment above this tunnel,' he estimated. But there was no discernible way up to it.

Roald Dahl judged it opportune to leave, before Aldiche showed up again. He realized with some concern that, if the Argentine or his henchmen did arrive from the other end, there were no niches in the walls in which to hide. He determined that, if he spotted someone, he'd crouch down, use some shelving to screen himself, then make a bull rush. If the intruder didn't have a gun, he might be able to overcome him. If he did have a gun, well, surprising him might make him miss. If there were several men, armed, and ready for action, 'Well,' he realized, 'this would be a horrible place to die.'

Dahl passed the shelves with the safes and the boxes, thought again of taking some of the papers, and kept going. He quickened his pace. 'Aldiche, and some of his thugs, might come back at any moment,' he worried. At length, he reached the entrance end of the tunnel. Dahl looked the ladder over, switched the light off, and slowly climbed the rungs.

With two rungs to go, he heard noises in the courtyard outside. He stopped, and amid the darkness broke into a sweat. Was it Aldiche? 'Will he trap me inside this awful place?!'

He waited a minute, and heard no other sounds. He stepped up and pushed on the iron lid. It didn't move. He paused, wondering if Aldiche would pull the lid open, and blow away his brains with a Luger. He heard a soft scraping sound, like footsteps. He paused again, his nerves on edge in the blackness. Then, on an impulse, he pushed up, harder this time, the lid giving way a bit, and prepared to rush up the ladder as best he could.

Suddenly the lid opened wide from above.

His eyes were blinded by the exterior light. He saw a figure, a human figure, like a ghost, or an angel, with a bright light surrounding it. He tried to climb up, but his feet slipped. He managed to catch the rungs again.

"Oh sorry, mister," said the figure, in a slurred voice. "Ah didn't know there was somethin' down there!"

Dahl pulled himself up into the light and a vagrant, a black man in dirty overalls, stood blinking before him. His breath reeked of hootch.

"Ah guess ah was standin' on top of it!"

Dahl forced a smile, saying, "That's all right—mister. I'm sorry, sorry to scare you." And he bent down and put the lid firmly back in place.

He looked past the vagrant toward the alley dwelling. 'Was it this man's hovel that I was sheltering in?' he wondered, kicking dirt over the lid handle.

The bum pulled a dusty pint of Four Roses bourbon from a back pocket, and took a swig. Swaying on his feet, he offered it to Dahl. Relieved at the surprising end of his underground adventure, he accepted the offer. As he handed the bottle back, Dahl was about to swear the man to secrecy about their meeting. But he judged the fellow so inebriated he'd probably forget the encounter, or wouldn't be believed if he told someone about it.

After urging the man to take another deep drink, Dahl walked quickly down the lane back to 21st St. Aldiche was nowhere in sight.

Dahl sprinted back toward Dupont Circle.

A Council of War

From a pay phone near the Blaine mansion, Roald Dahl phoned Liz, and then Ivar, who were waiting expectantly back at their residences. He knew the FBI, or anyone else, could not listen in on a paid call, and he spoke freely of what he had found. They arranged to meet at Ivar's in an hour.

Famished from his expedition, Dahl stopped briefly at the Peoples Drug Store on Dupont Circle. He found it odd, if convenient, that the Americans often stuck a small restaurant in their pharmacies, dubbed a "soda fountain," where they made the quintessentially American beverage of a milk shake, and its New York version, a "malted milk." Dahl found them not at all as disgusting as he expected, so he called for one, along with other "common man's" fare. Including the oddly named hamburger—ground beef from the Midwest named for a Nazi seaport—and "French fries." He was disappointed in the latter, which were soggy and lacking the unique taste of British "chips". After tossing a tip, another unusual American practice, onto the counter to the twenty-something "soda jerk," who told him he was volunteering for the U.S. Marines, Dahl grabbed the food to go and hailed a cab. The heavy downtown traffic slowed him from getting back quickly. He got out near the Tudor Place estate, once the home of Martha Washington's descendants, and jogged the mile back, his stomach rumbling, stretching out his long legs down the Wisconsin Avenue hill.

When he entered the snug townhouse at 1610 33th St., he saw Ivar standing by the record player, and Lizzy on the living room couch. They were eager for his arrival. So were two middle-aged men, one British, the other American, both standing next to a window.

Lizzy had seen the Brit at Martin's backroom, and she and Dahl had heard him speak at Cissy's soiree. He was thirty-three years of age, black hair carefully combed back, tall, with an eagle-like nose on a finely featured face. He was holding his large, carpenter-like hands on his hips. Pulsing with suppressed energy, he glanced back and forth around the room at everyone else.

He was Ian Fleming. And he was the aide de camp to Britain's head of naval intelligence, and a key liaison to MI-6. His assignment in America had been to "tutor" the Americans, to help them set up their own covert intelligence agency, OCI, along the lines of Britain's MI-6. He was in town on one of his periodic visits to see how the new spy shop was doing.

Dahl and Thorne also knew who the Yank was. He had been featured in some print and radio news pieces. He had a direct yet mild gaze, and a heavyset build that, as he approached the age of 60, was getting the better of his former athleticism. He was the man President Roosevelt had appointed to head the OCI the previous summer.

He was William "Wild Bill" Donovan, a Medal of Honor winner in the prior world war and more recently a highly successful Wall Street lawyer. Called "Wild" due to his reckless courage in the Great War, and his kinetic energy to try new ideas in the current conflict. From his body posture, Dahl thought Donovan, however "wild," seemed deferential to the younger man.

Indeed Fleming spoke up, while Donovan and the others listened with keen interest.

"I've been informed," he said, in a voice of careful consideration, and staring at Dahl, "that you were on something of a secret mission today."

The former fighter pilot reddened. He had broken the rules by acting alone without planning his moves with his superiors. He wondered how Fleming would react. He listened with concern as the Englishman continued.

"You showed excellent initiative—exactly how we would like agents to be," said Fleming, nodding sharply. "Congratulations. You've uncovered valuable information, that goes along nicely with things we already know. Largely," he added, gesturing at Liz, "through the fine work of this lady here."

Dahl was relieved and pleased, as was Liz.

"Take a seat," Fleming instructed him, waving to a large, orange-colored ottoman next to the couch. "Would you like a refreshment" he asked in his cultivated Eton voice, while ignoring the dirt stains on Dahl's clothing, and the smells wafting off of it. He looked over at Ivar. "I've heard that Mr. Bryce keeps a well-stocked bar." Ivar went over to the liquor cabinet to make some drinks, grateful for the extra ration cards and supplies of gin and Scotch that MI-6 had supplied him.

"Now," said the master spy, "if you could tell us in detail what you saw today."

And Dahl outlined his excursion through the tunnel."

Donovan broke into a hearty laugh when the menagerie was described.

"As a newcomer to this city, and country, Mr. Dahl," he said in halting voice, similar to that of his friend, President Roosevelt, "you are obviously not familiar, with a Mr. Harrison Dyar."

Dahl looked at him quizzically.

"In fact, few Washingtonians know of him. But perhaps, perhaps," and Wild Bill himself took on a questioning, if ironic, look, "perhaps the Germans do!

"Dyar was a scientist, at the Smithsonian. An eccentric one, as those scientists often are. His own studies were rather—off base. His specialty was in insects, especially butterflies.

"But he wasn't content, with keeping his many specimens at the museum. He dug out his own Smithsonian—in the basement of his house! That was the tunnel you went through."

Dahl's hazel-tinted eyes glittered. "So that explains those giant bugs. They scared me more," and Dahl's voice trailed off as he recalled his RAF service, "more than a Messerschmidt 109 coming at me out of an African sun…"

Remembering who he was with, he snapped back to the present. "But, is there a connection then, between this Dyar, and the espionage files?"

Donovan looked at Fleming, who looked back, and Wild Bill, shaking his head, continued.

"That's unlikely," he smiled, "as Ayers died back before the Depression." His smile turned into a grimace.

"But the Huns," and Donovan uttered an expression common during his Medal of Honor service, "those Huns used the tunnel, some say, as part of their sabotage in America, during, well, during what folks are starting to call World War 'One'." A glum expression came over him. "We're certainly in another."

"Maybe the Jerries," Fleming broke in, "had stopped using the tunnels years ago."

"But," said Donovan rapidly, "now we know they're definitely using them again! Or their agents, or both. We know now—thanks to your detective work!"

Dahl and Liz shook their heads in amazement at the tunnel's weird history.

Thorne began to speak.

"So the question is—"

"—What do we do now?" interrupted Fleming suddenly.

"We act!" he shouted.

"Air squadron Leader Dahl isn't the only man working today," he noted, his voice returning to its normal, cautious register.

"Several of our agents," and he nodded at Donovan, "an Anglo-American team, you might say, spotted Aldiche heading back into the Argentine Embassy. We've been keeping that place, under watch, for quite some time.

"And now we'll be keeping it and the tunnel under surveillance, every minute of the day and night.

"And, based on what our favorite spy has told us," and Fleming winked at Liz, "as well as Mr. Dahl, and based on what certain sources with knowledge of the Argentine delegation have told us as well, Aldiche's latest, most vital intelligence is kept at his embassy. So that he can transfer it quickly to the Axis. That includes material on the Japanese codes."

He paused for emphasis, then added: "We have to make sure of two things. That those codes don't go anywhere else. And that we get our hands on them!"

The others pondered this for a moment.

Fleming saw their hesitation, and stated, "The question is: how?

Donovan gazed at Thorne and Dahl, and said: "We can't tell you much more, but I doubt we have to. You can well imagine how vital that knowledge is to the coding operations of America and Japan."

Liz murmured something.

"What was that?" asked Fleming.

"Enigma." She saw the startled expression in Fleming's eyes.

It was the ultimate secret. It was something that should never be mentioned in company.

Liz went ahead anyway. "What we're talking about is the American version of the Enigma decoding. Deciphering the enemy's main way of communicating." Dahl didn't catch the reference to the ultra-secret British program, but Fleming knew, and Donovan had also learned about it. They were astonished that a relatively "low-level operative" like Thorne knew. But they didn't know she'd been involved in getting hold of a prototype Enigma machine.

Lizzy's emerald eyes glanced at everyone in the room. "The war could turn on this. And our own lives. The destinies of our nations."

Ian Fleming wiped a meaty hand across his face. "Well, enough of that." He was displeased at Liz's remark, and at the mention of the war's greatest secret in the presence of Dahl, or anyone else not cleared to know about it. "We have to focus on the here and now.

"Namely, how do we get our hands on Aldiche's intel?"

The others pondered again, embarrassed they didn't have an answer. Except Liz.

"I know. I know how. I can get it. And soon."

Wild Bill laughed skeptically. "Well, young lady, I'd at least give yourself some leeway, and some time to pull it off."

She looked at him, and at Fleming, in a deadly serious way.

"I'm not kidding," she answered in a knowing voice. "And I already have much of it arranged."

There was dead silence. She had everyone's attention.

She lowered her voice conspiratorially.

"Aldiche and I have been, seeing each other. For about a month now."

"And some of our, meetings, have been at his embassy."

"So you're the woman!" exclaimed Fleming.

Seeing everyone was dumbfounded, he quickly explained.

"Yes, we do have sources within the embassy. One contact informed us that an official there is, at times, rendezvousing, with his lover inside the diplomatic compound.

"The unverified source," he added dryly, "is now verified."

The others turned their heads in astonishment toward Liz, and waited for more.

"Well," she said, "as you know, hotel space, living space, is at a premium in town. So Aldiche likes to take his, girlfriends, to a special room at the embassy. A boudoir."

She looked at her listeners. She wasn't embarrassed, nor was Fleming. Donovan and Dahl were stunned.

"It is very well appointed. In an adjoining space is a bathroom with gold-plated faucets. It has an antique bed, from one of the Spanish monarchs, fit for a king, and queen. It's used for dignitaries from Argentina when they visit Washington. Or, for other special guests of the embassy."

Fleming stared at Liz. "So you're proposing to arrange a"—he almost said "tryst"—"arrange a 'rendezvous' with him at the embassy. A liaison. And—"

"—Not proposing," Liz broke in. "It's already arranged."

Wild Bill scoffed. "What!? How in Heaven's name!?"

Liz went on calmly. If there was one thing she knew, it was the craft of a spy. That, and her power over men.

"Our 'anniversary' is this week. A whole month together. We've arranged to celebrate it at the Argentine Embassy. And to spend the night at, in, the 'Queen's Bed', as we call it.

Donovan's scowl turned to thoughtful consideration. "So we'd have our agent, you, inside the place. But how could we get help to you—"

Fleming waved him silent. There was something more immediate.

"What day this week is this, this liaison?"

Liz paused a beat. Then answered. "It's tonight."

"Tonight!" shouted all the men at once.

"But surely that doesn't give us enough time, time to plan an operation," pleaded Wild Bill.

Dahl was stunned silent, but Fleming remarked smoothly, "It might in fact be better to pull off such a thing off right away. Certainly time is critical; we must stop the Japanese from getting proof of the decoding, and now!"

After recovering from his surprise, Dahl's war-time love of adventure began to come back to him. "How might we pull off this off, on such short notice," he said, "if we were in fact serious about it?"

Fleming moved over to the couch and sat down at its end. He addressed Liz, "So give us the details, of what you and Aldiche have planned for tonight. And then we'll see how we might build on it."

She replied flatly, "Well, we're to go to his embassy."

"Go?" asked Fleming.

"To, stay the night," Liz answered, with a slight hesitation, and slighter embarrassment. She added quickly, "Or a good portion of the night. Most of it. If it's like the other times."

"This is surely fortuitous timing," remarked Dahl, with concern and a trace of suppressed jealousy.

Liz turned to the practicalities. "I know he keeps his most critical papers in the embassy safe. The safe where I'm sure he keeps the coded information. It's just one floor from the 'Queen's Room' bedroom, one floor up from it."

Dahl laughed softly, skeptically. "But how would you, or someone, get into the safe?"

"I'm worried more about the diplomatic angle," said Fleming matter-of-factly. "If one of our agents got caught in a foreign embassy, the embassy of a neutral power—"

"—It would cause a stink to high heaven!" Wild Bill shouted. "And just imagine how Director Hoover would react!"

The Royal Navy operative smiled. Fleming had had run-ins with Hoover, even after their countries had become formally allied.

"It would certainly complicate matters between our two nations," he allowed. "To be avoided if at possible. But if this intelligence is what we think it is, and it surely is, the 'complications' resulting from *it* would be far worse." His face darkened.

"Like losing the war in the Pacific."

"The Japanese invading India," remarked Dahl glumly.

"Their fleet taking Hawaii," said Lizzy. "And even moving in on our West Coast."

"Or us losing the war outright," muttered Fleming.

The two Americans, Thorne and Donovan, thought of the recent "Bataan Death March" in the Philippines. The news had spread on how thousands of Yanks and Filipinos had suffered and died horribly under the Imperial Japanese boot. The Brits, Fleming and Dahl, thought of the loss of Singapore earlier in the year, with 80,000 men felling into horrifying captivity.

Silence filled the living room.

Then Wild Bill startled everyone. He stated firmly: "I can get you into the safe."

With all eyes on him, he turned to Fleming. "On your advice and counsel, Commander, we have been training squads of specialists for work behind enemy lines. Along the lines of your commandos, in the MI-6."

Fleming said, "And among—"

Donovan finished the thought: "—And among the specialists are safe crackers.

"And explosive experts." He grinned the wicked grin that his men in the trenches of the Great War had seen. "But this would be a more, subtle, operation. Which needs a lighter touch.

"And in fact, we have a cracker right here in town, in east Georgetown. A fellow, a felon, from Georgia."

When this had sunk in, Liz asked, "So you hired a thief?"

Wild Bill's grin transformed into an understanding smile. "Well, all of us here have been bending, or breaking, the law. It's not unusual what we've done: Offered the fellow a commutation of his, prison term, in return for patriotic service. His name is Travis Lee by the way."

Fleming stated: "Well, we can worry later about getting this Travis to the safe. But Elise," he continued, "how would you propose to handle Aldiche?"

Liz looked down at her knees, then at Fleming. "The timing is too good not to try it. The 'anniversary' of our, friendship, is tonight. There are no receptions at the embassy this evening.

It will be just us two." She warmed to her own idea. "We've already planned to bring food and wine to the embassy. I'm sure I could doctor Aldiche's drink." She nodded firmly. "Make him pass out."

"Perhaps," said Fleming slowly. "Although he's a big man, he would need a larger portion of the drug," he figured, thinking of chloral hydrate, or knockout drops. "We could put some in a legitimate bottle of liquor."

Dahl, a veteran of carefully planned aerial operations that had gone horribly amiss, thought the thing far too simplistic. He worried about Liz exposing herself to so much danger. He asked doubtfully, "Isn't there security in the embassy at night?"

Liz smiled faintly. "There is. A big lug from the slums of Buenos Aires." Her smile left her. "And an Alsatian almost as big.

The men stared at her.

"But Mache, the lug, knows about the, affair, between Aldiche and me. He thinks it's amusing. Aldiche has made an arrangement with him to turn a blind eye whenever we use the Queen's Room.

"A 'gentlemen's agreement,' among men who are not gentlemen. And Mache knows we're coming there tonight."

Lizzy licked her lips. She was resolute whenever an exploit took form. "I'll invite him to have a drink with us. He's already shared a sip or two with us before."

"And what about the German Shepherd?" asked Donovan, using the American term for an Alsatian.

"Brutus, that's his name. He likes anyone who Mache introduces as a friend. And he likes me a lot.

"Besides, the guard keeps a pan of water for Brutus. I can doctor that too.

"By the time Aldiche and Mache, and Brutus, rouse themselves, I'll be long gone with the codes. Travis too."

Dahl remained worried, while Donovan and Fleming were lost in thought considering how to effectively put such a daring operation in play.

Finally Fleming said, "We have to stop Aldiche. Before he gets proof of the decryption operation into the wrong hands. We *must* stop him, as soon as we can. Which means tonight."

Then Dahl remarked, "Aren't we forgetting something?"

They all looked at him.

"The tunnel. What if Aldiche kept the critical information in his secret tunnel, instead of transferring it to the safe, like Liz thinks."

Donovan's face fell. But Fleming retained his confident look. He looked at Dahl, then at Liz.

"I trust this lady's instincts, and our sources. But you have a point. Bill and I will have our teams case the tunnel within the next two hours. If they don't find the material there, then Liz's mission gets the green light."

The foursome spent the next hour and a half sketching out the scheme. Donovan would get the safecracker ready, and obtain the knockout potion for Liz. And after she grabbed the documents, a car would be waiting outside the embassy, to speed her and her precious stash away, to a safe house on Embassy Row.

Near the end of this session, a look of concern came over the intrepid femme fatale. Eyeing Fleming and Donovan, she stated, "There's one thing that maybe you two don't know about. Or maybe you do." She paused, and asked sharply, "Are you tailing me?"

Surprised, both men flatly stated, "No." Liz believed them.

She explained: "Two men have been tailing me for weeks. I assume they are Hoover's men. Or maybe Franco's or Mussolini's.

She went on, "What if they follow me to the embassy? Couldn't that cause, 'diplomatic complications'?"

Wild Bill was firm. "You're one of our best agents, Liz. Before meeting Aldiche, take the standard measures, to shake a tail. And then some. Lose 'em."

Fleming added, "And if they do show up at the embassy, we'll have the manpower to handle them." Then his normal confidence weakened.

"Of course, if they are FBI men, they could complicate things."

"I think it's past time," said Donovan, "that I had a talk with Mr. Hoover, about calling off his dogs, if they are his. And stress to him that Lizzy here is now on our side, after all." He concluded: "Even if Hoover keeps her tailed, he'll be forewarned. Which might ease things, if there's, friction, outside the embassy." He didn't look confident about that.

SECTION 3

DENOUEMENT

A Night at the Embassy

By 9 p.m., everything was as ready as possible. Well, many things were. Donovan and Fleming had placed teams of armed operatives outside the Argentine Embassy. These men were in plainclothes, their weapons holstered; most were in cars parked a half-a-block away. Several were already training high-resolution cameras on the windows closest to the Queen's Bedroom. Donovan and Fleming, the latter officially an "observer," were in a center of command, an OCI safe house in the basement of the Cissy Patterson mansion. Cissy, eager to reprove her patriotism, had turned it over for the "temporary use of war-related work," no questions asked. It contained stands of high-intensity lights, tables with cameras, and a gaggle of document reproduction specialists. In the event Liz had time to make copies of the codes, instead of simply stealing the documents. The less the Argentines knew about what OCI knew, it was thought, the better.

Wild Bill had argued ferociously against using the Patterson manse, as Cissy was a notorious critic of the President and, if the operation failed, and OCI involvement became known, FDR would likely be furious with the agency, perhaps enough to shut it down. But Fleming, the more experienced spy, countered that the copying of the documents, if it took place, had to be very close to the Argentine Embassy to save time. "And as you know," he pointed out to Donovan, "we've been unable, under this extreme time pressure, to find an alternative."

At 9 o'clock, Lizzy and Aldiche were already dining at Martin's, their favorite bistro. The Argentine had begun to consider the place somewhat déclassé, but he knew Liz loved the restaurant and he was happy to indulge her.

Indeed, he had found himself increasingly in love with the woman. He had rarely met anyone, of either sex, so high-spirited and intelligent. And the inescapable fact that she was jaw-droppingly beautiful, and a tigress behind the bedroom door, only heightened his affection.

Donovan had met with the owner to elicit his help in the upcoming exploit. The two already knew each other. As a patriot with a son joining the Navy, the Martin's owner was eager to help out with the war effort. In fact, in the little backroom of the Tavern, Donovan, with advice from MI-6 executive Fleming, had been transforming his fledgling, pre-war OCI group into a daring, wartime outfit.

His organization, small but expanding greatly, was administered by his boyish-looking, bespectacled chief-of-staff, Duncan Chaplin Lee. Yet this 28-year-old had the tell-tale signs of a security risk. He was exceedingly nervous, largely for fear of being found out. For he cheated on his wife. And he drank a lot. The only thing missing from the classic turncoat profile was financial distress.

Remarkably, Duncan Lee was descended from the family of Robert E. Lee. True, most people across the Potomac considered General Lee a hero. But many north of the Mason-Dixon Line viewed him as a traitor. Certainly Duncan was, as he was in fact at this very time working for Moscow's foreign intelligence agency. And so, from the very start of the OCI, and its successor agency the OSS, which were to morph into the CIA, the American spy agencies were penetrated by a high-level Soviet mole.

Lizzy was unaware of all this. The Russians were allies, for now at least, though she did harbor qualms about the ruthlessness and double-dealing of Stalin's minions from her experiences in the Spanish Civil War, in which the Soviets had heavily intervened. But she had had no contact with anyone who was a known Soviet operative. Besides, her focus, as with Donovan, was on thwarting Axis subversion.

On the day of the Aldiche operation, Donovan had arranged with Martin's owner to switch Aldiche's drink. He usually ordered a bottle of Armagnac brandy, which Liz offered to buy for him for their "special occasion." Beforehand, a trusted waiter had switched it for another wine of much stronger vintage. Liz thus hoped her paramour would be rendered sleepy even before doctoring his drink at the embassy.

Things went well at the restaurant. Plied with cocktails—strong martinis that came on Liz's expert recommendation—Aldiche didn't notice the stronger wine served with dinner. His attention was fixed on Liz. She wore a beige, closely fitted, slit-cape dress with a low neckline and a hem cut daringly above her knees. She was also garnished with a silver necklace, and Tahitian pearl earrings that her father had brought back from his service in the Pacific.

Like Thorne a lover of the outdoors, Aldiche, despite a woozy head, preferred to walk, in the springtime weather, the mile-and-a-quarter to the embassy. And normally Liz would have desired the same. But eager to save as much time as possible for the coming exploit, she feigned a slight ankle sprain, and convinced her paramour to take a taxi. Its driver was an OCI man, ready to radio the safe house in case of trouble.

At the embassy's Q St. entrance, a tipsy Aldiche pulled out a key ring with many keys. Eyeing this, Liz figured one likely contained the key to the room with the embassy safe.

Teetering from the alcohol, Aldiche pulled open the heavy metal door, and they entered the spacious, Beaux Arts vestibule. Liz swept her keen eyes up and down the adjacent halls, and listened closely for human voices. There were none. 'Good,' she thought, 'all the everyday workers must have left hours ago.'

As Aldiche pushed shut the door, however, she heard the sound of heavy footsteps, as well as a somewhat lighter patter, from around a corner of the hall.

It was Mache the security guard, and his Alsatian. Lizzy noted again how Mache, both in height and girth, outmatched Aldiche, who himself was tall and strongly muscled. She eyed the giant canine, who trotted over and began licking her on the knees. The dog suddenly turned, and growled menacingly at Aldiche. But after Liz bent down and stroked his back, he quieted, and happily stuck out his tongue.

The guard and Aldiche laughed. "He usually acts aggressively," said the latter, "and never this affectionately." Mache remarked that no other visitor, nor any embassy hire, had been able to so charm the animal. Aldiche nodded, and Liz watched him hand the keys to the guard.

Brutus lay down beside Liz, and his brown eyes seemed to soften to an ochre tint. Thorne reflected, 'Indeed. No male, human or not, seems able to resist me.'

Despite the friendly welcome, Liz felt a dread slip over her. She was not in her element: her home, her bedroom. She was in the foreign embassy of an enemy agent, a strong strapping man, of strong emotions, with a guard even stronger and no doubt more prone to violence. And with a giant hound that could be ordered to turn on her in an instant. With men, she was almost always in complete control. She had to wonder if she would be there.

Aldiche took her into the grand ballroom. Liz was impressed by this setting more than ever. She almost wished they were there to simply dance again, and then make love. But her professionalism returned. And her fear. The fate of the war, of the world, might turn on what happened that night. She kept a placid face, and then a fake, but convincingly loving one, as Aldiche playfully took her around the dance floor. And she was careful to feint a slight discomfort with her supposedly injured ankle.

Mache had turned on a tango from a record player set up near a French window. "Just a little more dance, *carita*," Aldiche cooed, and he skillfully glided her about the light-brown parquet, bracketed by the rectangular panels of freshly painted white walls.

After two dances Liz was sweating, from the exertion—Aldiche was especially active in his dance steps—and from her fear. She was glad when her lover, after clasping her hard about the waist, whispered, "Oh, let us not hurt your leg too much. Is it now time for a further repast, Elise?"

The guard had set up one of the ballroom tables for them, next to another of the French windows. Aldiche closed its shutters so that Liz would have only have him for her attention. But Liz found her eyes glancing at the ballroom. The dozens of empty tables made the vast dance floor seem barren and forbidding and, with the end of the tango, more silent than silence itself.

But, as a consummate actress, she feigned delight in the impressive table he and Mache had set. On a chilled silver tray were chocolates with orange filling, crème caramel, chocotortas, and sweet Malbec wine. While smiling at these treats, she took out from her large alligator purse a bottle of champagne, with a fake Jouet Belle Epoque label. With a coquettish wink, she dramatically held it in the air, before placing it with a flourish on the table. It was the kind of dramatic gesture Aldiche would make, and he laughed appreciatively, unaware that the sparkling wine had been doctored.

Though her stomach was roiling, Liz forced herself to munch on some of the sweets. It was then time to open the champagne, one of the critical moments of the exploit. "You know, darling," she breathed, holding a chunk for crème caramel on a gold-plated fork, "Mache has been such a darling himself. So understanding of our special relationship. Shouldn't we let him share some of our celebratory champagne?" Seeing some hesitation on his face—was it jealousy or his growing lust?—she added, "Before sending him off to make his rounds."

"Well, that's very kind of you," Aldiche answered, persuaded. "He has been very kind to me, to us." And he was truly appreciative of Mache's help with their tête-à-têtes.

"I agree," he said, and drank deeply from the champagne Liz poured him. Then he pushed back his gold Chiavari chair and stood up, and swayed from getting up quickly, and from the drinks. Liz took this as a good sign. 'He's ready for the fall, and for the champagne,' she thought.

Still, he strode across the parquet with a certain grace. As he did, he imagined he was skiing in Patagonia, fantasizing Liz was at his side, gliding alongside him. He reached the stairwell and called out, "*Machito, si vous plait! Si quiere, yo, yo y mi mujer tienen un 'dulce' para usted!* (My little Macho, if you please! If you may, my, my lady and I have a 'treat' for you!")

In a minute or so Mache came lumbering across the waxed floor.

The diplomat motioned him into a chair, and stated rather formally in Spanish, "*Elisa y yo nunca deseamos que usted piensa, como los engleses—?como los americanos lo dicen?—que 'tres es una multitud.*" "(Elise and I never want you to think, as the English, the Americans maybe, say, that 'three's a crowd'.) *"!Así, por favor, probarele algún de esta 'aqua mineral' con nosotros!* ("Please, share, briefly, some of this 'sparkling water' with us!")

Mache grinned, and sat down, and was taken again by Liz's entrancing countenance and goddess-like form. He drained the glass of bubbly offered and, despite himself, knowing he should be going, poured himself another, really to just take in the sight of Thorne. She smiled sweetly at him, while Aldiche, wishing him to go, made a show of tolerating his presence.

A thought occurred to Liz as she saw through Aldiche's facade. Would her suggestion seem too ridiculous, and its intent too obvious? And would Mache fall for it? 'Well!' she decided. 'It's too good an idea not to suggest!'

"Mache, Machito," she said with warmth, and reaching for the bottle, "would you take something back for Brutus? *Un regalo poco por Brutus, este.*" ("This little gift for Brutus.") And she filled up a metal container with the champagne. She laughed skittishly, pretending drunkenness, and carelessness. "Shouldn't our Alsatian friend be in on the celebration too?" she said in English, then added quickly in Spanish, *"?Unirse nuestro perro en la fiesta, no?* ("Have our pet join in the party?)

She was pleased to see that Aldiche, quite drunk by now, just smiled happily at this suggestion, to which Mache quickly agreed.

Mache rose, drank heartily from his glass, and Liz jumped up to refill it. He stepped back, spilling a bit of the bubbly. He steadied it in one hand and, grasping the container with the other, walked with a deliberate gait across the parquet. He gripped the flat-bottom glass in his palm like a waiter carrying a small drink tray. Liz couldn't tell if he was doing this for comic effect or if he was already filling the effects of the drink, or both. Aldiche's gaze, filling with desire, had returned to her, so he didn't notice.

He was obviously ready for the Queen's Bedroom, but Liz lingered. She poured more of the potable into his champagne glass, saying, "For 'our anniversary', my love. May it be the first of many."

Not for the first time, Aldiche wondered if it would be possible to marry this foreign beauty. What would the embassy think? Should he care? He didn't notice that Liz only took sips of her champagne, which she actually let drip from her mouth back into her glass before placing it back on the table.

Aldiche was clearly woozy now. Liz wanted him to pass out in bed, and not in the ballroom for Mache and Brutus to discover. She reached across the table and took his right hand hers. "My darling, *mi carito*," she said, emphasizing the masculine "o," "I think it is time that I felt like a Queen. In the company of my *King*. And in their very own boudoir."

They got up, with Liz taking the bottle of champagne and the two glasses, and walked slowly, his hand around her waist, across the parquet, their footsteps echoing in the empty ballroom. Though about to sleep with a man, Lizzy felt weirdly alone. However, she also felt she was once again in control of a situation.

That would change.

The Queen's boudoir was down a plushy carpeted hall.

The door to it was open; the two paused at the threshold. Liz had been carried into the room the previous times, but now Aldiche was inebriated and passive. Arm in arm, they swayed as Liz took in the scene. She could see the place had been nicely prepared.

Golden-colored drapes hung from the rosewood posts of the monarchial bed. Scarlet silk sheets were pulled out from the twin pillows, inviting the two lovers to slide right in.

Lizzy was surprised to find one of her own tricks in play. On settees and tables about the bed, candles with the aroma of pomegranate ginger were lit, suggesting the ring of fire to come for the lovers. It was a feminine thing to do, surprising for a macho fellow like the Argentine. Liz wondered if he had arranged and lit the candles, or got someone else to do it, probably Mache, who seemed to have a surprising romantic streak.

Whoever it was, he had forgotten to close the window drapes. One could peek out the panes to Q St., where OCI and MI-6 agents lay in wait watching.

'An amateurish 'security lapse,'' thought Liz, who expected Aldiche to walk over to close the curtains. But from his glassy eyes it was clear he hadn't noticed. Instead, he lowered his chin onto Liz's neck, and slurred, "My love for you, *carissima*, has never been greater." He drooled a little on her soft skin.

Lizzy figured the time was as good as any. She nudged him toward the bed. They sat down together, but Aldiche immediately fell onto his back.

'Now *is* a good time!' concluded Liz. She straddled him, her rear against his thighs, and hitched up her beige-colored dress. She twisted around, and bent her face over his, letting him smell the fragrance of her Quelques Fleurs perfume. Grasping the champagne bottle, she tempted, "For our anniversary, my love—let us sip, and celebrate, a bit more." She reached for a glass, but decided the bottle would do, and held it at an angle to his lips. Aldiche lazily sipped, then gasped, coughing up some of the drink.

'This won't do!" thought Liz. 'I don't want him to choke!' She dabbed the dribbles of champagne coming down his chin with the sleeve of her dress. She lowered the bottle back to him, and he sipped, more carefully this time, and swallowed. And stretched out fully on the bed.

'This is going well, almost too easy,' reflected Liz. The man who had at times dominated her was now putty in her hands. 'Now the next move,' she thought again. After breathing some words of affection into his mostly inert ears, she reached down and unzipped his pants. A low moan resulted, but not much evidence of arousal. 'Is the 'Bull of the Pampas' having a bad night,' she thought naughtily. She unhooked his belt, and slid it from the pants. Liz eased down to the foot of the mattress, and firmly pulled off the trousers. Then she climbed back to his hips, pushed down her panties, and straddled his manhood, which was still quiescent. 'Am I losing my charm?' Liz chuckled to herself.

"Oh Aldiche, dear," she intoned, "just one more drink. For us," and reached for the bottle, tilting it carefully so it wouldn't spill on the sheets.

And heard snoring. Soft, then loud, and regular.

Her lover was out cold.

Lizzy didn't celebrate. Time was critical. She had to check on Mache, and deal with Brutus. And welcome Cracker into the building. And get the codes out. And copied. And get them back, if there was time. 'Not enough time!' she worried. The timetable was very tight, too tight.

She forced herself to focus on the immediate. 'Just the next step for now, forget about the clock!' Each part of the plan was hard enough, she knew, and needed her full attention.

She grabbed the bottle and got off the bed. She pulled the silken sheet over Aldiche's naked form, but not before taking an admiring glance at his Adonis-like physique. She had actually liked him, but now he was an adversary, an obstacle to the success of her mission.

As she stepped to the door, Liz stopped, and went over to the window. She looked outside onto the streetlamps dimly illuminating Q St. Would she be able to spot some of her fellow agents in wait, watching over her?

What she saw came as a shock.

Two groups of men were on the far side of the street, near the intersection with New Hampshire Avenue. Liz looked over her shoulder at Aldiche, who was snoring loudly, and opened the window a tad. She could hear voices, low voices from her vantage point, but loud enough to make out that the men were arguing. One group was a bit further up the block and a half dozen in number, and the other group had four men or so and was a little closer to the embassy. An alley was alongside them. The two groups came closer together, appearing to Liz like two rugby teams in scrum. Both groups became louder, and jostled each other.

Brothers in Harms

Roald Dahl had been watching for an hour in the dark, sitting in the shotgun seat next to the driver, a man named Jimmy. He had been a scuba diver, of all things, who had just joined OCI. Another agent, an ex-cop and ex-infantryman named Al, was in the back. A bit of light from a streetlamp filtered through the car windows. They had absolutely nothing to report. No sounds or movement from the embassy.

Against Wild Bill's strong objection, but at Ian Fleming's urging—based on his knowledge of Dahl, the combat medals he won in North Africa, and his service in Washington—Dahl had been stationed with the watch team. He and the two armed OCI men were in the four-door Chevrolet Master Deluxe sedan, two cars behind several others in a Ford, also brand-named Deluxe. They were training their Taylor-Hobson binoculars on the embassy entrance and windows, and thus far had seen nothing.

'That might be good,' Dahl figured. 'Liz's operation could be going smoothly.' He felt a wince of jealousy knowing success meant she and Aldiche would get into bed together. 'Ridiculous to think of such things,' he chided himself, 'when on a perilous mission.' But he couldn't help himself. He liked the woman. 'Or is it more than 'like'?' he wondered. 'Still, isn't all fair in love and war?' He grinned at that thought.

This operation had parallels to his slowly developing night missions over Tripoli. A lot of waiting, of staring at instruments or the clock, and then, perhaps, sudden action. He waited with the others, glancing at his chronograph wristwatch, the luminous dials dimly visible. Looking at them just made the time go slower.

Suddenly, he saw the sidewalk side of the car ahead swing open. And two men, not with his team, were standing outside the auto. They had on business suits, and fedoras. And they were pointing revolvers at the OCI men inside the car!

'D.C. police? Undercover?' Dahl thought frantically. 'Argentine security?'

An international incident putting at risk the war's most important alliance, and espionage secret, seemed ready to explode.

The driver of Dahl's car was in charge of their team, but Jimmy just sat there. The agent in the back, Al, was jostling about trying to get a better look. He said, "What is happeni—who the hell are they?!"

The driver was stunned into indecision, Dahl saw. And he knew one thing. They couldn't just sit there while their comrades were in peril. He steadily swung the door open. He got out slowly, cautiously, while patting the .38-caliber Enfield pistol in his jacket holster. In response, Jimmy swung open his door, and Al did likewise. Dahl waited for the two to join him. They hesitated. 'I guess I'm in charge,' he thought. He walked up the sidewalk. The other two followed, nervously patting their own hidden guns.

The gunman closest to Dahl's group saw them coming. He was a stocky, grim-faced man named Ray. He turned toward them, his pistol raised. "Don't come a step closer!" he barked. Dahl and his group stopped 20 feet away. The other gunman, a tall figure named Will, stiffened his arm, his revolver pointing inside the other car. He said angrily to the men within: "How am I supposed to believe you're on our side?!"

He grimaced, and continued speaking. "We track this Elizabeth or Elisa or Thorne or whatever this dame is down to this spot. We know she's gone into the embassies of enemy countries. Now this 'neutral' one, one with lots who love the Nazis!"

'They're G-men!,' Dahl figured. 'On our side!' Maybe.

Will's gun wavered. In the gloom, Dahl was unclear whether his hand was shaking from nerves, or from simply waving the gun around.

"Then we run into these guys," Ray responded to Will, while staring at Dahl's group. "An armed party from the looks of it." He was looking at Dahl's chest.

Could he see the bulge from the Enfield? Meanwhile, Will's gun hand seemed to stiffen.

Will stared into the OCI car, and said, "You're to come out with any guns up, up in the air, and place them on the sidewalk!"

There was silence from the auto. Deadly silence in the night. The duo making the challenge fingered their gun triggers.

Dahl thought fast. A natural with language, he had quickly picked up on how the locals spoke. He employed an American accent.

"You're making a terrible mistake," he earnestly. "We're on your side."

"That so?" said Will, all of six-feet-three, in a flat, Midwestern voice. "And who are you?"

Dahl was even-voiced. "A friend. An ally." He studied the man's face. His grim expression was touched by puzzlement.

Roald Dahl had seen enough of them to know. And they usually worked in pairs. 'Yes, FBI, for sure,' he concluded.

"FBI, *and* the *OCI*, a team: We're all on the same side!"

Ray stood unflinching by the other car, his revolver pointed steadily at the door of the shotgun seat, a nervous OCI man on the other side of the door. Dahl dimly saw the agent in the rear seat looking back toward him through the window.

It was hardly a Mexican standoff, as one side was brandishing all the guns. Holding all the advantages. For now. Unless Dahl and the others pulled their guns. If they got the chance. If that was the right choice.

'Time to make a move, break the stalemate,' thought Dahl. 'A diplomatic move.'

He slowly raised both hands in the cool night air, the sleeves of his suit jacket sliding down his wrists.

"I'm going to do something, very careful-like," he stated quietly. "I'm going to reach in, my jacket, for my ID. And no, not for a weapon."

Will seemed to hesitate. Jimmy, Dahl's OCI colleague, flinched.

Keeping his left arm high, Dahl tentatively reached with his right hand into his jacket. His fingers felt the document as his arm brushed against the revolver in the left shoulder holster. That might come into play yet. 'God, I hope not!'

He very slowly took out his ID and, bending his knees some, in a kind of supplication, he held it out. The gunman stared for a moment, then snatched it.

In the dim light, Ray held the document out from his chest, and made out the most famous identifying document in the world, with the lion and unicorn on a blue cover. A British passport. The FBI man flicked it open, and in the dimness, nervously looking to and from, tried to match the photo with this strange man in front of him. The image seemed close, but he needed better light to make a match.

He said, "English? You sound American to me."

"American mom," Dahl lied quickly. "Working with the British, against the Nazis. Working with you Americans. Us Americans." He gestured his head toward the OCI car, where all was silence. "All of us are." He hesitated, then decided to reveal some of what his team was up to.

"We're undercover, part of the new intelligence team, and working with the MI-6."

Mistake. Will was suddenly furious.

"Oh, the ones stomping on our turf, here in America. And right here, on our assignment!

"If you are limeys, and not Jerries!" And he shook his gun angrily.

Dahl made a worse move. Surprised at Will's words, he reflexively snatched back the passport, and pulled it back toward his own chest. Back to where he had his gun, where any agent would have a pistol.

The G-man acted reflexively. He probably would have shot Dahl, if he hadn't seen the passport. Instead he took a step forward, and hit Dahl with a strong right cross. His fingers were gripped around the revolver, so the blow had the effect of getting smacked with big brass knuckles. From a powerfully built man.

Dahl saw flashes of light, like the ones when he crashed in the African desert. He didn't fall, but was bent over by the blow as by a hurricane gust.

At this, doors to the other car flew open. The other OCI agents piled out. Will pointed his revolver at the man rushing toward him from the shotgun seat. It may have been the darkness. He was about to shoot, but didn't see the man's own right cross. Which hit him, not in the jaw, but in his right hand, causing the gun to clatter to the sidewalk.

The two men bent over, both muscle-bound, both banging into each other, both sets of hands reaching for, then both clasping, the pistol. They lurched over to the alley. Ray, holding his weapon high, ran over to them, and a bleeding Dahl followed with the other OCI men. In moments they were all in the alley, shoving and pushing, the gun on the ground kicked into the darkness, while Ray wildly pointed his gun from one man to another.

It seemed inevitable he would shoot. Dahl, feeling pain in his jaw, looked around desperately. Did any of his men have their guns out? It was too dark to tell for certain. They were on the knife edge of a pitched battle, an "international incident." And death.

Ray shoved Dahl hard on his chest. One OCI man was on the ground, holding onto the legs of Will, while another tried to pin his arms. He failed, and Ray waved his gun wildly again, finger on the trigger.

Dahl's teeth ached horribly from the punch. He thought furiously what to do. He got an inspiration.

He screamed, "J. Edgar Hoover sent us!"

The G-men froze. The OCI agents scrummed some more, then stopped.

"Mr. Hoover, the Director," Dahl stated in a firm, loud voice. "He sent us on this mission. An American, a British—a joint mission." He paused in his lie, and gazed skyward, reaching up his hands in as if in prayer.

"What, he didn't tell you?! His aides didn't?"

With a mix of anger and regret, he shouted, "What a screwup!"

The deceit got their attention. It broke the worst of the tension.

Dahl rapidly explained that the OCI and MI-6 were on a mission tracking a woman suspected of spying for the other side.

"A woman named Elise Thorne."

The G-Men still hesitated, but were warming to his plea. It was a way out of a bloody mess. Dahl took advantage of this, and turned to his colleagues. "Everyone!" he almost shouted, while trying to keep his voice low. "Show these gentlemen from the FBI your IDs!" Now the OCI agents hesitated. Dahl repeated, "Show them you IDs! Hand over your wallets—carefully!"

They also hesitated, but after a few moments they did so. In the darkness, the G-men nervously looked over their papers as best they could.

The FBI man who had hit Dahl started to feel embarrassed. And wondered what might happen to him for punching someone on his side.

"All right, all right," Ray called out to his fellows. He handed back a wallet. "They're okay. Let them be."

And, after several more minutes of hesitation, the two groups went back to their lookup stations. The FBI agents began to feel ridiculous about their intervention. But also relieved.

Dahl even more so.

Guards and Crackers

Lizzy was worried about the turmoil outside. She knew it had to involve the agents watching for her. Her concern was who were they fighting with. If with operatives connected to the Axis powers, or with Argentina, then her mission might soon be over. And possibly her life.

The other worry was Cracker. If there was a full-blown fracas outside, she couldn't imagine him trying to get into the embassy.

The thought of her aborting the exploit was never a consideration, however. She had accomplished a key part already: drugging Aldiche. She couldn't let that effort go to waste.

Liz moved away from the window, and made sure her Romeo was sleeping soundly. With champagne bottle in hand, she was about to open the bedroom door when she heard a loud knocking outside it.

"*!Señor Aldiche!*" came a voice. "*!Hay un problema largo fuera! !Mirelo, por favor!*" ("Mister Aldiche! There's big trouble outside. Please take a look!)

It was Mache. He hadn't been knocked out by the drink! And he had noticed the commotion in the street.

Liz glanced quickly at Aldiche, who hadn't awoken. She hissed at the door: "*!Uno moment! !Silencio, Por favor! Silencio*" ("One moment! Silence, please! Silence!")

Liz strode to the window and glanced down at the alley. The two groups were no longer scrumming, but seemed to be talking. Maybe things had settled down.

Another knock came, a bit softer. And a voice, less loud, but more insistent.

"*!Señor, señorita! !Debo hablar con ustedes!* (Mister, Miss! I must speak to you!)"

Liz walked over, thinking what to do. She couldn't let him try to awaken Aldiche. She had make up some kind of excuse. She couldn't think of a good one.

Then she did.

She reached behind for the fastener of her dress.

Moments later, Mache watched as the door pulled open.

Filling the doorway was a vision from Heaven.

It was Liz, stark naked except for her silk stockings.

Her dress, her panties, and her brassiere lay dumped on the carpet.

She completely blocked his view of the bed, and Aldiche. Not that Mache minded. He had never seen a woman so perfectly formed, and with a face so beguiling.

Even as he tried to speak, he knew no words would come from his mouth. He was thunderstruck, stunned into silence.

It was Liz who spoke.

"Oh, Machito, I hope I'm not embarrassing you," she said softly, seductively. "Aldiche, we," she half-looked over her shoulder, "were, in the middle of something."

Mache's jaw nearly hit the floor. No words came from his open mouth. He knew enough English to understand, but it wasn't the words that impressed him.

"And we noticed that commotion outside," added Liz. "I just looked out the window. It's calm again." Liz couldn't help herself. She placed her hands on the sides of her breasts and arched her back, elongating her form, which was already vast in Mache's estimation.

"Probably some common criminals. *Tranquilo ahora. No problema.* (It's quiet now. No worries.) Maybe breaking into a car. All gone now, *tranquilo*, into the night."

Heart pounding, Mache started to back away.

Liz ended the conversation. "And by the way, *Señor* Aldiche requests, insists, that we be *left alone. Déjanos en paz. Y silencio, por favor!*"

She dropped her hands, revealing herself fully again, and went tippytoe on her feet, and bounced up and down. Mache almost fainted.

"We're sure you will understand. *¿Comprendes?*"

Mache escaped to his small office on the floor above and, hands shaking, fell into a swivel chair. His mind in a daze, he gulped down the doctored drink Liz had given him.

The Key to It All

'Timing is everything,' thought Lizzy, 'and the time is ripe for our Cracker.'

But first she had to get Mache and the hound out of the way. After quickly dressing, she grabbed the champagne. "Somehow, I have to convince that lug to drink it.' She thought she could.

After making sure Aldiche was still out for the count, she walked barefoot and silent up to the third-floor, where she knew Mache had his small office. With most of the embassy lights turned off, the stairway was dim, and she stepped along with care.

Mache's space was two-thirds down a bare corridor of pine-wood flooring. His door was cracked open. Thorne cautiously pushed it open completely.

Lizzy almost laughed aloud at the sight. The hulking guard, shirt tail out and shirt unbuttoned, sat slumped on a chair pushed back from a small, battered desk. There was a bottle of whiskey, half drained, Mache's private hootch, on his desk. Probably taken from an embassy party. The container of champagne sat half-empty in the middle of the bureau. He had continued the lovers' celebration on his own, at least to some extent, and had imbibed even more after the sight of Liz. His right leg was propped up on the desk's side, his foot dangling and threatening to fall to the floor. Mache was mumbling incoherently; his eyelids were closed. He seemed unconscious.

Lizzy stepped into the little room, and got a shock, and then a pleasant surprise. Brutus was sitting by the wall, next to his water pail, and staring at her. Her legs reflexively jumped backward, and her stomach turned inside out. But she relaxed, on seeing the dog's placid, even friendly, expression. "Such a good boy," she cooed to him, "my big bad boy." She bent down to pet him. He flicked his giant, spongy tongue appreciatively.

Then Mache's foot twitched, the shoe leather making a squeaking sound on the desk. The guard, who continued to murmur, came within an inch of knocking over the whiskey bottle. Liz stood up to grab it, and got an idea. She poured some of the remaining champagne into the pail. Then stepped back to watch Brutus lap it up, his thick dark coat shivering with pleasure. Next, she placed the whiskey square in the middle of the desk, where Mache couldn't miss it if he awoke.

Lizzy cocked an ear, and made out some of the guard's muttering. "*Amate, señorita, Thorne, desolate sin te. Thorne, una espina in mi corazón. Oh señor, Rita-, Thorne, oh, ama, besa...*" ("I love you, Miss Thorne, I am so alone without you, Thorne, a 'thorn' in my heart, Mi--, Miss,

Thorne, oh, love, kiss…") Liz smiled at the evidence of her unmatched charm. She figured the dog would soon fall asleep, and the guard couldn't resist another soporific drink if he awakened. 'Three down!' she thought triumphantly. Then Liz became anxious. She didn't like the method of Cracker's entrance, something for which he hadn't trained. She knew it was a big risk to introduce an unknown variable into a complex mission.

The plan was for her to signal the team in the street outside to send in the safecracker. An OCI technician had placed a tiny but powerful flashlight into the sole of one of her shoes. She took it out, and stepped lightly but quickly back to the Queen's Bedroom, to signal her colleagues from the window.

As Liz parted the curtain, she got another shock.

She heard the rustling of sheets, and turned to see Aldiche sitting up in bed!

'What should I do or say?!' she wondered in horror.

Liz waited for him to glare at her, and demand what had happened. But he said nothing. Eyes open, he strangely raised his arms forward, straight out, and fluttered them. He mumbled something. Something about his love for Liz, in words not unlike those Mache had uttered.

His upper body swayed. Then his arms came back down, and he fell back down onto the sheets. Both his eyes and his mouth shut.

Lizzy realized he had been, well, not sleepwalking, but sleep-bedding, if that was the word for it. 'Must be the doctored alcohol,' she figured. She didn't like this. She knew from relatives of hers that sleepwalkers often did unpredictable things. Other than the sleepwalking itself! She wanted Aldiche out cold. His bizarre behavior might reoccur. He might get out of bed, and start sleepwalking through the embassy, and awaken at a critical moment!

She thought about trying to slip some more of the liquor down his throat, but realized he'd likely gag, and wake up. She regretted not following up on a suggestion of Wild Bill's, during their rushed strategy session, that she take a hypodermic needle and vials of sedatives with her. But the idea had been sidetracked during an argument over Cracker's mode of entry.

Speaking of which, it was time for the Georgian thief's arrival. The OCI team, on getting her signal, was supposed to send Cracker off toward his entry point to the embassy: the back alley of the building. Liz was worried this component of the operation had been blown from the near riot outside.

She pulled wide the window curtain, and flicked on the flashlight. She flashed it four times, paused five seconds, then flashed it four times again. She did this again without any response. Liz scanned the street. She stared at the cars where the agents had been sitting before the altercation, but couldn't make out any movement within them. But it was so dark along the curb that it was hard to tell if the vehicles were occupied.

She started to repeat the flashes. On the third iteration, she saw blinking lights near the alleyway. They had seen her, and were returning the signal! She stared down at the darkened alley, trying to discern the agents that had been slated for support. There seemed to be more men than expected there. How Fleming and Donovan sent reinforcements? Or was it some other persons? Those from the fracas?

They flashed five times, then a pause, followed by three flashes. The signal was repeated. That was it! The sign that they understood, and were sending Cracker off to her. She rushed out of the bedroom, feeling relieved.

In the planning session, Liz had argued for having Cracker enter the embassy through the front door. She reasoned that if Aldiche, Mache, and Brutus were the only ones in the building, and were indisposed, the front entrance was the simplest and most direct approach. Fleming agreed, but Wild Bill, anxious to keep an illegal entry as surreptitious as possible, demanded a trickier entrance: via a second-floor window in the embassy's rear alley.

So Liz, wiping sweat from her brow, made her way down a hall to the north side of the embassy that faced the alley. She approached a room where office supplies like writing paper and ink pens were kept. Her team had learned from a source in the embassy that the storage place of such inconsequential items was kept unlocked. She glanced at her watch. With luck, Cracker should arrive within 10 minutes. She turned the doorknob.

The door was locked!

She let a pang of fear roll over her. She imagined Cracker on a ladder outside the window, unable to open it, and panicking. What if a passerby, a vagrant say, came by and saw him? And started a ruckus?

Liz turned the knob hard and pushed in on the door. Nothing.

Thorne took a step back. 'OK,' she told herself. 'What are the alternatives?'

Her gleaming eyes scanned the corridor for another door, while knowing she would find none. She had looked over the schematics of the embassy in preparation for the exploit, and knew there were no other rooms in that section of the hall.

'Tools!' she figured. 'I need something to jimmy the door.' But despite wracking her brain, she couldn't remember seeing a maintenance man's room in the diagrams.

'Damn it!' she fumed. 'I secure a relationship with Aldiche, drug him, put the security man asleep, lull the hound, arrange for a safecracker—and then this happens!'

But the professional calmed down again. Like a veteran soldier, she knew most plans of battle got tossed as soon as the fighting started.

Yet she stiffened again on hearing a noise. A human voice? No, it sounded like an animal. Had that been Brutus barking? Maybe he hadn't taken the bait, hadn't lapped up the sleep-inducing drink. And his barking could wake Mache!

She listened, and heard nothing else. If it had been Brutus, maybe he had gone back to sleep. If he had been sleeping. Maybe he had left his snoozing master, and was now prowling the embassy! Assuming his master was still asleep. And Aldiche too!

Liz was surprised at herself. A wave of fear kept hitting her, before a period of calm returned. Normally during a mission she was nervous, but steadily so, a useful alertness, but not this time. There were too many uncertainties. On ground not of her choosing.

'Mache, Mache', she reflected. Maybe there was a solution with him. After making up her mind, she strode rapidly along the darkened hall and down the stairs back to the guard's office.

She slowed as she neared the door. She tilted her head so only one eye appeared around the doorframe, and peered in.

Mache was asleep still, and snoring. Brutus was awake, but placid, his gigantic form lolling on all fours.

She wondered how it would feel to be bitten by a giant Alsatian. She figured she knew. She wondered if she would scream. She figured she would.

'Hesitating won't help,' she thought. She stepped inside, over to the dog, and tried patting him, saying, "Such a good boy, my boy." To her relief, instead of biting her hand, Brutus stuck out his tongue happily.

'My charm over any kind of male is holding up,' she surmised, forcing a crooked smile.

Liz looked down on Mache. Feet up on the desk, he was leaning back, almost flat on his back, his chair almost tipping over. Though he was a strapping, muscled man, from this angle she could make out a paunch.

'The key ring,' Liz told herself. 'Aldiche gave him the keys, when we entered the embassy.' She stepped softly beside Mache. There it was, attached to his pants belt! A key ring, including, she suspected, a master key that could open the door to Cracker's entry room.

She fervently hoped the whole ring could be taken off, instead of each key individually. She peered down, as Brutus huffed happily in the background. The ring had a fastener!

She reached down to touch it, and inadvertently her hand brushed against Mache's waist.

He began murmuring, "*Señor, Ita, Thorne, no dura spina, pe—ro, algo dulce, lo espero, por mi, solamente mi…*" ("Mister, --iss Thorne, not a hard thorn, bb—but something sweet, I hope so, for me, only me…")

Liz thought, 'Please Machito, control yourself. Go back into your dream world.' She could only imagine what that dream might be. No doubt with her in the starring role.

The ring of keys came off. She stood up and stepped to Brutus, ran her soft fingers along his spine. She moved the pail closer to the brute. "My nice big boy, drink up, a reward for my nice boy."

Brutus merely breathed hard, ignoring the liquor, his glistening eyes staring at Liz. He started to sit up.

"No, no," she said softly. "Sit. Stay here. Sit. Drink. And I'll come back for you later."

He sat down, looking disappointed.

Cracking Windows and Safes

Liz stepped back into the hall, her head aching with the thought of entering that room again to return the key ring. Maybe she wouldn't have to. 'The way this operation is going, I may have to make a quick exit, with a messy ending.'

She rushed back down the stairs, wondering if Cracker was already waiting anxiously for her. And wondering if Aldiche would meet her on the way.

When Lizzy got back to the storeroom door, she heard nothing within. Moments later, as she examined the keyhole, she heard a rapping on the window inside.

'Damn, I hope this works,' she thought, looking closely at the ring. 'There must be 20 keys on it, of different sizes. And maybe none for this door!'

But she reasoned the door, for an inconsequential room, would have a master key, not a specialized one. She looked over the set for one that looked more generic than the others. Three seemed to fit that bill.

She tried the first. It didn't fit. She tried the second. No luck.

She heard a rapping sound within, and maybe a voice. She wondered what Cracker's nerves were like. Probably pretty good, as a professional thief. 'But he's never been on a mission like this,' Liz thought. 'He might be thinking his handlers considered him expendable. And he's alone outside a window high above the ground!'

She tried the third key. It almost got jammed inside the lock, and Liz had to jiggle it hard to get it out.

'All right, let's do the methodical approach.' She started from one end of the ring to the other, skipping the master keys she had tried. She heard more rapping, and the voice sound again. Same volume, it seemed. Maybe Cracker wasn't panicking yet.

The 11th key fit in securely. But it wouldn't turn! She examined it. It looked just like the 13th key. She tried that, but it didn't fit as snugly. She tried turning it anyway.

It turned!

She pushed the door in, flicked on a light, and stared at the window of the far wall. Liz saw the dim shape of a man outside the window shade. In her excitement of rushing over to Cracker she left the door ajar.

Outside in the dark, the heavy figure of the safecracker looked like a large hungry seal stuck on a slippery iceberg. He was standing on the rungs of an extendable metal ladder, which was teetering.

Liz pulled up on the window. The pane was filthy; it hadn't been opened for months. After moving one foot up, the window stuck. 'Damn this damnable mission!,' thought Thorne. She pulled harder. It wouldn't budge.

She called out softly, "Hello, Cracker, hello. It's your contact. I'll get this open! Hold on." He heard her.

Cracker tried to help Liz. He reached out to pull up the outside of the window frame. As he did so he teetered on the ladder even more. Liz figured that if he fell from that height he would probably break his back.

She cried out in a low hiss, "Be careful! And let's pull together. One, two, and then three. Ready?! One, two—" But before she got to three, Cracker pulled, and almost fell off the ladder. "On *three*," hissed Liz. "Do it on the count of three!"

They tried it, and the windowsill budged a couple of inches. Then Liz tried it again herself, and the windows went up significantly, about two and a half feet.

"Can you get in?" she asked, while wondering how much time had elapsed.

"Ah can't tell," replied Cracker, in a nervous Southern accent. "Ah'm afeared ah'll fall."

He was indeed a heavy man, and Liz doubted he would fit through. She tried pulling on the frame again, but it was stuck again. Then they tried together again, and it wouldn't move.

"I guess I can try to break the window!" half-shouted Liz, wondering if she could find something in the room for that purpose.

"Oh don't," answered Cracker. "Ah think ah might fit. Lemme see."

To Liz's shock, he rolled himself onto the ledge. As he shimmied, his legs hit the ladder, which went crashing down into the alley.

'Now we're stuck with this option!' realized Liz. No way for Cracker to get down. The mission might be over.

Cracker lay on his ample belly, his left shoulder to the window, his shirt poking through. "This doesn't feel right, Missa," he said. And he rolled over onto his stomach, almost falling off the narrow ledge, his shirt and pants smearing with dirt. His shoulder and hip poked through the window, along with part of a pouch strapped to his torso that contained safecracking tools. "Uh, now that's better," he stated.

Liz couldn't see much difference, but thought, 'I'm getting him in here even if it kills him!' She pulled up hard on the frame, and Cracker did so weakly, using one arm while lying prone. The window didn't move.

"I'll just shatter the glass," stated Liz.

'Although the noise,' she thought, 'might wake Mache, and Aldiche.'

"Let me try gettin' through first," pleaded Cracker. And he wallowed his pudgy form into the opening some more.

And got stuck, like a pig in fence rails. He pushed from the ledge from one arm, and Liz pulled with both of hers, but he stayed in no man's land, in limbo.

"Ah scraped my arm, and my hip," he said sadly. "Ah think I was better off out on the ledge."

Liz awkwardly reached around him to tug at the frame. It made a scraping sound.

"That's promising," she noted, and began to tug again, then she stopped.

There was a noise. A bark. The hound? 'He's far away, probably still a floor below,' she estimated. 'But he's got a dog's hearing. And we're making a racket.'

She turned about, and scoured the storeroom for something to break the glass. She opened drawers to some desks, at first quickly, then slowly when she realized the noise she was making. She found a recently invented adhesive, Scotch tape. Worthless. Next, a box of newfangled ballpoint pens. No good either. Some twine. Nope. Wait!

'I'll tie this around his thighs,' she figured, 'and pull hard!'

Liz turned toward the window, and was surprised and elated to see Cracker sitting inside, on the interior of the sill. He was red-faced and sweating, but smiling.

"Ah wiggled through, ma'am. Ah thought I could fit." He added, with a wink, "Now ya know why ah decided long ago not to become a cat burglar."

Liz couldn't help laughing. She stood him up on unsteady legs, and brushed some of the filth off him. Liz noticed how much taller she was than he, who was barely 5-foot, 3-inches, a five-inch difference. The differential seemed greater due to their body shapes: Cracker was rotund, while she was taut, albeit curvaceous.

Lizzy examined his right elbow, which was cut slightly. "We'll fix you up later," she assured. "We got to get going!" Cracker nodded with a stalwart expression, and patted his safecracker pouch.

They rushed to Aldiche's room. With trepidation, Liz looked in on him. With relief, she saw he was breathing loudly, still asleep.

'He never snored when sleeping with me,' she recalled. 'He was always game for more lovemaking.'

They hurried over to the room containing the safe. Liz tiptoed, while Cracker tread heavily until Liz admonished him. At the threshold, Thorne thought, 'OK, another locked door. Here goes.' But the fourth key from Aldiche's ring fit snugly, and the door opened easily.

It was a modest-sized space, 15 by 25 feet. It had no windows. They could make out three large work desks with chairs arrayed around the far wall. Liz switched on a standing lamp, and pulled the chains on two yellow-shaded banker's lamps. The light illuminated four wall paintings, two of gauchos on the Pampas, and two of Argentine coastal scenes by the artist Ballerini.

"No safe in sight," mumbled Liz.

"That's not surprising," answered Cracker calmly. "They rarely make it obvious, ma'am."

He put his shoes back on and stated, "Let's check the obvious." He sounded confident in his expertise. Liz was pleased at his change in mood. She felt she had now a real colleague at her side, a man of temperament and skill.

"Ah'll take these two," he ordered, gesturing at the Pampas sketches on his left, and you take those," he added, gesturing to the shoreline depictions.

"Actually, wait!" he called out, and Liz froze in her tracks. "Let me do it with you," he added. "First, mine."

He approached the picture of a gaucho galloping toward a rancher, and carefully peered at its back. "Ah don't think there's an alarm," he stated, "but ya never know for sure." Liz imagined a loud alarm going off, and Aldiche and Mache appearing at the door, with pistols, and with Brutus, barking and ready to pounce. 'I don't mind dying for our cause,' she reflected, 'but not if this mission fails!'

The safecracker examined the back of the picture, and then the second one, an even more rustic scene of cowboys and peons.

He shook his head negatively, and came over to Liz's side of the room. A brief inspection of those paintings yielded no sign of alarms.

"We can take them pictures off the wall," he announced, "but first we'll check the rest of the room. Less risk that way." He told Liz, "Let's start opening up them desk files.

"And real careful-like!" he inveighed, though the words came out soft and Southern-like.

Liz hit paydirt with the second desk, a tall, rollup type. It consisted of 12 drawers. When she pulled on two of the handles, real careful-like, they all pulled out—and revealed a safe.

"That's darn good, missy!" cried Cracker. He got down on his knees in front of it and appraised it carefully.

"This is a Diebold. 1935, fireproof. Manganese? Not that that matters with the lock. Have cracked them before." He jutted out his jaw in thought. "Kinda unusual for an embassy. Pretty common safe."

"Well," said Liz, "they aren't at war." 'Though they do,' she said to herself, 'have the fate of the war in their hands.'

Cracker took out a stethoscope from his pouch. He attached the earpieces to his jug-like ears, and tried kneeling in front of the safe. This didn't work as the safe was high, its dial too far off the ground for the diminutive Southerner. So he stood up and crouched awkwardly by the combination lock. He took out a small piece of paper and a stubby pencil, and stuck them in his right pants pocket. He pressed the stethoscope to the safe. He cocked his head and drawled, "Kindly be quiet, missy." He began to slowly turn the dial, listening intently. To Liz, it was just like a scene from a gangster movie with Jimmy Cagney or Edward G. Robinson.

She backed off to the door, and listened intently for any noises coming from the hallway, while keeping her gaze fixed on the safecracker.

"This is goin' better than ah hoped," he called out, as his fingers stopped moving the dial. He reached for the pencil and paper, and wrote down a number. "Five." He started again, and said, "If I remember rightly, this safe has a four-number combo. Funny it doesn't have more, being an embassy and all."

But it was tedious work, and another 12 minutes had passed before he heard the very faint click of the tumbler that signaled the correct number. "Thirteen," he called out, this time rather weakly, as if he was talking to himself.

Liz listened intently, the only sound the breathing of Cracker, which had become noticeably louder, almost hyperventilating. That was odd, as he was obviously in his element, and had seemed very calm just moments before. He was hunched along the safe, his face hidden by his broad, drooping shoulders.

'We don't even know for sure the information we want is in this safe,' she worried. 'But don't let your mind wander!" she reminded herself. She was on guard duty, and had to focus on her task. Liz listened harder to the silence in the corridor, but heard nothing.

"Tonta, seven," said Cracker, softly.

'Did he slur his words?' thought Liz vaguely. 'Or was that his accent? He said, 'twenty seven,' I'm pretty sure."

'Focus on the hallway!' she again urged herself. Again, she heard nothing.

Cracker's arms flopped about and dropped to his side. He waved his hands about, then slowly lifted them back to the safe.

"I suppose," Liz called out in a low voice, "your arms can get numb with a job like this." Cracker said nothing.

'He's got a stethoscope on,' she reminded herself. 'Be quiet, and patient.'

But it was hard to stay still. 20 minutes must have passed by. Cracker seemed to be turning the dials more slowly. His breathing got louder, then couldn't be heard at all. Liz thought she heard barking from downstairs.

Finally her colleague said softly, almost inaudibly, "Fo'."

'That must have been 'Southern' for four,' thought Liz, suddenly excited. If so, he had the four digits. She thought she heard the dial turn.

She looked to see if his arms were still moving. They weren't.

Cracker had collapsed to the floor!

It had happened so suddenly that a shocked Thorne wondered if he had been shot. 'Could it have been a silencer?' she thought confusedly.

Lizzy glanced about the small room. There was no one else there, no hiding place, no place to shoot from.

She rushed over. Cracker was lying on his left side. His face had turned a sickening blue. Drool dripped from his thick lips.

'A stroke?! A heart attack?!' Liz wondered in horror. She reached down and felt his right wrist. She didn't feel any pulse. She pressed a hand to his carotid artery. She felt a pulse. Intermittent. Weak.

'What do I do?!" she screamed to herself. She had learned basic medical treatments during her MI-6 training, and she ran through some of the options. 'Mouth-to-mouth? Not sure: He still has a pulse, he's still breathing. Drugs?: I have none to administer. Massage his chest? Not sure. Does this even have to do with his heart?!'

She unbuttoned his cotton shirt, and saw that the thick gray hair on his chest was matted with sweat. She pressed her hand on his heart. Weak, but the pulse was more regular.

Then, with a gasp, and spitting out drool, Cracker turned over on his back at the side of the safe, his belly jiggling.

Liz smelled shit and piss; he had lost control of his bowels. She blocked out the stench, and pressed open his eyelids. His eyes were fluttering, unseeing.

Then they became almost normal, if bloodshot. He raised, and lowered, his right arm, and said, "Fo'. Fo'."

'That was no accent,' she realized, 'but a number.'

He then closed his eyes and went limp. 'Has he died?!' Liz asked herself in terror.

Liz shook him lightly. Nothing. Shook him harder. Nothing. She was very scared. She felt his carotid artery again. Barely registering, very intermittent.

Was he dying?!

He might be, she knew, but at least he had opened the safe.

Hadn't he? She pulled on the safe's lever, and it didn't move. She tried again, nothing. Was it stuck?

Then she saw to her horror that the dial was not on the number four, but on thirteen.

'How in hell?!'

'My God!: Did his hand brush against the dial, changing the number, when he fell?'

Liz turned the dial back to four, and pulled the lever. The safe didn't open.

She would have to enter the right combination herself!

She was certain "fo'" mean four. But what were the other numbers?!

For an instant of panic, Liz thought they hadn't registered in her mind. But there had been long pauses between Cracker calling out each one, and she had repeated the array many times in her mind.

'5. 13. 27, and 'Fo'!,' she remembered. But was that sequence correct?

She tapped herself hard on the head in disgust. 'Of course: the paper!' She rifled through his pockets, and found it. He had scrawled, '5. 13. 27.' No number 4, but she had heard it. And she had heard him say it was a four-digit safe. Unless she had misheard the 'Fo'!

But, considering the overall situation, she felt confident. 'A piece of cake, a corn of corn,' she told herself, recalling pat phrases from childhood.

She kneeled at the safe, her left leg against Cracker's paunch and, with her right arm raised, turned the dial in sequence clockwise and counterclockwise.

'5 13 27 4.'

The safe stayed locked.

She tried again, making doubly sure of placing the dial at the right numbers.

Still locked.

Liz had assumed she had to make two backward revolutions of the dials before "13" and "4", which she thought to be standard practice. She tried the opposite way, making two forward revolutions for those two digits.

Still locked.

She broke out into a sweat. She quelled incipient panic. She tried the combination without any extra revolutions. Didn't work.

Liz tried to estimate the number of possible sequences. Was it 16? Was it four to the fourth power? She frowned. This could take far too long. And they had been in the room for some time. And she had to get Cracker medical help. Soon.

Should she just call off the operation? 'But it's so important!' she anguished.

Rush outside to the OCI agents? They could rush inside, she supposed, and help Cracker, but they wouldn't be any help with the safe. And they might alert Mache and Aldiche, and certainly the hound.

Liz wracked her mind. During prior problems, she had called Intrepid, or one of her handlers. Sometimes Intrepid could be had almost immediately. 'But how could he help me with this!?'

She heard silence. Cracker had stopped breathing! She peered down at him: he started breathing again. More drool came down his double chin.

She wished Dahl was with her. He might think of something. To have him by her side! He was outside watching, she knew. Should she race outside, and bring him in? But her training—to stay with the operation, to keep with the plan—made her hesitate.

The silence was broken by a sound within the embassy. It was the dog, unmistakably so this time. Had he come closer? Liz couldn't tell. But the bark was definitely louder. The chances of Mache and Aldiche waking up was growing.

'Maybe they are already on the way here!'

She checked Cracker's breathing again, saw the sweat-drenched gray hair on Cracker's head. Something seemed to be missing.

The stethoscope: it had fallen off his ears when he'd dropped to the ground. She reached under his head, and found it.

'Of course!' How had she been so ignorant? Cracker had worn a stethoscope for a reason: to *listen* to the sound of the tumblers clicking, as well as the feel of it. She recalled an odd remark of his that opening a safe was like caressing the bottom of a newborn baby. Meaning the sound of a tumbler was subtle.

She lifted his head up slowly, grabbed the scope, and delicately put his head back down. He was breathing, shallowly.

Liz put on the stethoscope and gave it a try.

On dialing to "5", she heard nothing. She tried again; nothing.

'Concentrate!' she urged herself. 'Relax, and listen for the faintest noise.'

She turned the dial around to 5. Nothing.

Feeling desperate, perspiring in the still room, she tried again. And heard, not a click, but a faint blur of sound.

Was that it? She tried again, first to 5, heard something, then did a reverse revolution to 13. She wasn't sure if she heard something. She tried again.

5, then a backwards turn to 13.

She heard a barely discernible pin prick of sound.

Next she tried 5, 13, then a clockwise revolution to 27. Nothing.

'Keep going!' she urged herself, her forehead covered in sweat.

Another attempt. With a clockwise revolution, 27 sounded faintly.

Then again a very faint noise, when she turned counterclockwise again, to 4.

Her heart seemed to have stopped beating when she tried the handle.

It didn't budge.

Despondent, she tried again.

It opened!

She pulled on the handle. It got stuck a quarter of the way out!

No, it was just that it was a heavy door. With both hands Liz pulled it open wide.

Inside were five file folders jammed with documents, and a very thick book. She scanned the latter: it was a Japanese Navy code book. Two of the folders had labels having to do with codes, her knowledge of Spanish informed her. She reached down to the pouch that Cracker had draped around his shoulder and back. With difficulty, but without disturbing him too much, she pulled it off his heavy physique.

With a start, she thought he had stopped breathing again. No, she was wrong. He was taking somewhat deeper breaths.

Liz was about to put away the documents when the mission's instructions came back to her. As best as possible, she tried to recall where each document had been, if she had time later to put them back in place. Then she stuffed the code book and the two code folders into the bag. Would they have time to copy them, and return them? She doubted this. Could Aldiche and Mache stay asleep much longer? Doubtful. And the hound was awake.

She sat down on the floor and peered inside the safe again. There were other documents. As she scanned them, it seemed they were unrelated to the codes. But should she take them too?

As she decided, her hand rustled over the bag, blocking the sound behind her. Then she heard. And looked behind her.

Lovers' Quarrel

At the threshold of the opened door stood Aldiche.

And Brutus. Who was no longer lapping his tongue. He stood on all fours, his tail out, his massive jaw set, his face impassive.

Aldiche had a stunned, almost blank expression at first. Bloodshot eyes. A facial expression that steadily reddened, then took on a furious expression.

He looked past Lizzy at the open safe. He glanced from it to Liz and back again.

He said, hesitantly, in a husky voice that almost sounded like someone who'd been crying:

"So this—this, is *you*."

Liz twisted her back toward her former lover, her mouth agape. She had thought about what to do, given such a turn of events, but her mind was blank.

Aldiche was silent. He tilted his pale yet handsome head to the side in thought. He stroked his left hand back up through his luxurious dark hair.

"Are you," he continued, growing firmer in voice, "working for the Axis? For yourself? Or for the Alli—"

"—Oh, Aldiche," Liz cut him off, as she got past her initial shock. "I meant to tell you, to ask you." She realized her argument was weak, but it seemed the only card to play.

"This information is so valuable. And I have contacts who would pay so much for it."

He started to cut her off, so she rushed her words.

"We could be lovers together, on missions together! Share the profits. A team—"

She gave him the gaze that had often kindled a ferocious passion in him. But his eyes turned metallic and cold as he answered:

"—Drugged, you drugged me! You betrayed me!

"*!Puta!* (Whore!) You've ruined my career!"

He stood rigidly, his tall frame seeming even larger than normal.

"You've taken me for a fool. *!Estas traitor! (You are a traitor!)*

"You mock my pride!"

He took a step forward, then stopped. The hound, his dark-brown eyes alert, his tongue wagging in anticipation, mimicked his movement.

Aldiche's head tilted again in thought.

Liz took the opportunity to slowly rise. If it came to a fight, with the odds deeply against her, it was better to be standing. The MI-6 training camp had given her a knowledge of martial arts, though she knew her skills had little chance against a big, strapping man. And hound. Still, as she rose, she grasped Cracker's pencil and hid it in her palm, hoping Aldiche didn't notice.

His gaze met hers, and he spoke again.

"A paltry weapon, my dear," he said mildly.

He looked away, became reflective, distant again. "This all could be cleaned up. I kill you, and explain it as an attempted robbery. Mache, to avoid embarrassment, to avoid a scandal, will back me up."

His eyes, chilly cold now, ruthless, met her green gaze, unmoved by its usual charm.

"And I'll move the codes very quickly to my buyers," he said absently. "Perhaps first to my tunnel, and then to them."

Liz, standing steady, ready to try to defend herself, attempted to take advantage of that admission.

"We know about the tunnel. We know everything about you."

He smiled grimly. "*?Nosotros?* We? So, you are working for someone. Probably the Limeys. Maybe the Yankees too."

"You have it wrong," Liz attempted, knowing it was a weak parry. Her heart was pounding with hammer blows.

Aldiche took two strides forward, halving the distance between them. He stopped and said, "I will make it quick." He reached out his two large hands, which seemed like giant mitts to Liz. "I will place these around your throat, *carita*. I will snap your neck.

"You probably won't feel any pain, before losing consciousness. Forever."

He strode forward again.

Liz quickly stepped over Cracker, and backed up to the far corner of the room.

'Change the scenario,' she urged herself. 'Do something to shake things up!'

She backed against a desk, pushed her right hand along the top. All it found was a 1942 calendar. Three-hole-punched. Maybe two pounds in weight.

She grabbed it and hurled it at Aldiche.

He ducked, as it glanced off his right shoulder. He laughed. Brutus barked angrily.

Aldiche said, "So you won't make it easy. Well, a few scratch marks will help back up my story."

Liz moved along the desk to a bricked-up window. No escape there. Her left hand, still on the desk, came upon a sheaf of looseleaf paper. In desperation, as Aldiche pounced, she flung it up in the air toward his face, which was coiled in rage and revenge.

As the Argentine flung out his arms toward her neck, he felt a shock, and agonizing pain, in his left biceps.

He pivoted, and found the giant hound upon him. Its mammoth physique fully stretched itself out. He savagely bit and clawed into Aldiche, from his face to his shins.

Liz slipped over to her left, away the brick window, just out of range.

Aldiche reflexively flung up his neck and head in alarm. This made it easy for Brutus.

The hound went straight for the jugular. He ripped the throat out of Liz's tormentor, piercing multiples veins and arteries in two slashing gulps.

He hurled Aldiche Engardio like a rag doll against the desk.

The Argentine smashed along it, then crumbled to the carpet.

Dead.

Liz's eyes were wide-open in wonderment. A crazy thought came to her. 'Should I pat my friend Brutus in thanks?' Her nerves felt pulverized with astonishment.

She shakily stepped over to Cracker and bent over him. He was still alive, it seemed.

Liz felt her heart hammering harder than ever. Yet she'd survived somehow. No thanks to herself. Well, not quite. 'Almost all males,' she thought blankly, 'and especially Brutus, have a special fondness for me.'

She stared at Aldiche's stricken form. Brutus paced up and down alongside him, his paws stained with blood.

She wondered if Mache had finally come to.

She decided to toss the plan once and for all.

And take direct action.

A Rapid Escape

Liz slipped out of the room, closed the door, and ran to the stairway.

She raced down directly to the grand vestibule, and the front door. The plan was for her to signal in the case of an emergency, or for calling off the operation. No time for that.

Thorne searched for a switch to turn on the exterior light. 'Where is it!?' she raged. 'Americans always put the switch right inside the entrance. These damn Argentines!'

She caught herself. It was common for a venerable mansion, this former American residence, to place the switches elsewhere. She thought for a moment, and remembered how on a previous visit Aldiche had asked Mache to turn on the lights, near a settee on the far side of the vestibule. She ran over, flicked various switches and, *Voila!,* the lights came on, outside the house, and throughout the first floor. If she needed to signal the OCI about a change in plans, it couldn't have been better.

With an effort Liz pushed open the heavy, metal door and stepped onto the threshold. Her slit-cape dress was gaudily illuminated amidst the gloom of Q St.

She stared at the cars across the way. Yes, there were men inside them! And on the sidewalk were other men, in hats. She waved her right arm frantically at them.

The OCI men stared, and tried to figure out her intent.

The FBI men too.

"This could be a trick," said Ray, the FBI squad's leader. "The Argentines could have put her up to this."

His colleague Will agreed. "If we go in there, we could be taken. That would be one hell of an int—an international incident!"

They all looked at Liz in astonishment. She was thrashing her arms about manically. She shouted: "Come here! Come this way! I need help! Now!"

The OCI men were silent. Dahl was not.

"I know that woman. She has character! She would never," he insisted, "lure her colleagues into a trap!"

Jimmy said, "I think you've fallen for her. Warping your good judgment."

Roald Dahl didn't answer, but simply opened the door to the curb side.

He jumped out, and told his two colleagues, "Fallen, no way! That's an agent of ours in danger. Abandon no one!"

And with that he began running across the street.

The OCI duo looked at each other, and felt ashamed. After a few seconds of hesitation, they jumped out of their car and ran toward the entrance.

As she watched the three men run up, Liz scolded herself for leaving, due to shock and relief at Aldiche's death, the bag of coded information back in the room. 'I should have brought it down and handed it right over!"

Breathlessly, she explained the situation. "I have the codes. Upstairs. Aldiche's dead." Her words poured out. "Cracker had a heart attack I think. I need your help to get him out of there." They entered, and trotted together rapidly up the stairway, Liz leading, followed by Dahl, the others close behind. The carpet muffled their sound. "The guard, Mache, may be awake," she hissed to them. "He may be trouble."

She stared at their coat jackets, looking for telltale bulges. "You're armed, right!?"

An OCI man nodded, "Yeah." At the top of the stairs, Liz halted them with a sharp gesture of her arm, and stated, "You might need those pistols. There's a guard dog too, a giant Alsatian. Still very much alive."

They hustled to the room with the safe.

Liz didn't have to tell the agents to take out their .38s. She then made a strange clucking sound, like someone would do to a child or a pet. And opened the door slowly.

The sight was—unusual.

Cracker lay face up on the worn linoleum in front of the desk safe. He looked dead.

Aldiche lay with his back and head against the rear desk. His face was frozen in a mask of agony and horror. His lower body lay atop a wide pool of blood. More blood was splattered on the desk. Liz thought his body's location differed from where she had left him. Had he awakened somehow from his wounds, then died after? Or had the hound thrown him there?

That was another unbelievable sight. Brutus was on all fours beside Aldiche, the blood on his mammoth jaws looking like a macabre overapplication of lipstick. Steam hissed from his maw. His dark eyes looked at the men accompanying Liz. He stroked his right front paw like a bull getting ready to charge.

Jimmy, the OCI lead, was stricken. He fingered his .38 nervously, pointing it somewhere in the direction of the dog.

Dahl took a step forward to put himself between Liz and the hound. But Thorne was too fast for him.

She strode right up to the dog, while making that strange clucking sound.

To the astonishment of the men, she bent over and began patting him!

"Good boy, so good. What a good job you did with that bad man, that bad, bad Aldiche." And she moved her hand from his back to his giant snout. "My best boy." The hound stopped mid-snarl, and lapped his tongue happily.

"I want you to stay here," she told the beast, "right here, for now. Understand? Stay. Sit. Good boy. I'll be back for you later." Liz actually felt a little guilty at the lie.

The stocky figure of Al moved over to Cracker. He bent over and felt his neck. "I think I feel a pulse," he muttered.

Dahl asked Liz, "Where's this Mache?"

"I left him in his office. Drugged. Maybe he's still there. Maybe awake. He could be dangerous."

Dahl turned to the others. "All right, let's carry Cracker out of here. And keep your guns ready. To deal with Mache." He looked toward Brutus. "Or this hound, if Miss Thorne's charms wear off." Liz smirked, shut the safe, and hoisted the bag of codes around a shoulder.

All four took an arm or leg of Cracker's, and awkwardly took the heavy, unconscious man down the stairs.

Grunting and sweating, they reached the entrance. There was no sign of Mache. Liz switched off the lights, and they staggered outside. Dahl expected to see half the city's police force outside. There were no cops at all.

The FBI men and some other OCI agents ran over, and they lifted Cracker into a sedan, which took him to the District of Columbia General Hospital.

They had hardly time to take a deep breath when a black Chevrolet Deluxe Sedan rolled up. In the back seat were Donovan and Fleming.

Fleming seemed calm, and smiled slightly. Wild Bill's face was flushed. He told Liz, "I guess you have quite a tale to tell us. You and Dahl get inside. Elise, you can begin your report."

242

A Fortuitous Aftermath

Two days later, the principals met at Ivar and Roald's place. The Volta Place neighborhood was quiet that humid spring day, except for a half dozen boys having a baseball catch in the park. Ivar had arranged for Martin's to deliver a lunch for four people, complete with wine and with Senate-label beer from the Heurich Brewery.

He laid the meal out on settees fronting the living room sofa. He had some of the beer placed in ice, and some kept at room-temperature, British-style. Coffee for the Americans and Twinning's tea for the Brits was also provided.

He greeted his arrivals, with Dahl and Liz coming to the door first, and almost at the same time. Ivar wondered if Liz and his housemate, who hadn't come home the previous evening, had spent the night together. He wouldn't have been shocked: they were two very attractive people who obviously enjoyed each other. Ivar pushed away the trace of jealousy he felt about that. 'There are countless attractive women in this war-time town,' he justified. 'And a great many eligible men, like Roald and me!'

Dahl and Thorne were sitting on the couch when a Ford Deluxe engine roared outside. The bell rang, and Ivar opened the door for his two other arrivals.

Fleming and Donovan shook his hand and, after greeting the other two, sat down in facing chairs. Liz noticed that both men, as the springtime weather had warmed, had switched to humid Washington's survival gear: custom-made linen suits. Ivar Bryce excused himself to the upstairs den. He was definitely a member of the team, but was not privy to some of the more sensitive intel, especially intel this sensitive.

"I hope that friend of yours isn't a Nazi spy," Wild Bill joked in introduction. "It would be a pity if this living room were wiretapped."

"Given Ivar's Russian roots, sir," answered Dahl with a mild smile, "that may be. Those Slavs are conspiratorial sorts. But given the recent news, probably not." The German spring offensive in southern Russia was in all the papers. Hitler's minions, seemingly in full recovery from their horrific winter outside Moscow, were once again advancing fast.

Both of the older men took in Lizzy. She was garbed informally in dark slacks and a white cotton blouse without embroidery, her feet clad in brown Oxfords. To Fleming, she looked like someone who would head out that afternoon for a horseback ride or a round at a golf course.

Perhaps she would, and perhaps with Dahl. 'Her demeanor reminds me,' the Englishman thought, 'of Kate Hepburn! Yes, Katherine Hepburn, but prettier.'

Fleming, sitting up straight, hands on his thighs, got to the point. "We knew you would want to be filled in on what's happened at the embassy.

"According to our sources there," and he looked away mysteriously toward a window, "we seem to have little to fear. The Argentines were shocked, and greatly embarrassed, at the murder, the death, of *Señor* Aldiche. And they have no desire that such an affair be publicized."

"That's right," chimed in Wild Bill. "They haven't even called in the police on the matter."

Fleming continued. "Naturally, they interrogated Mache, and checked the contents of the safe. They don't think anything's missing, as they don't know about the codes, and the associated files. Aldiche kept that to himself. At first, they suspected the guard of the murder, with the help of his hound. But he was able to convince them of the culpability of 'a female visitor.' Bloody footprints of a lady's shoes were found near the corpse."

Donovan stated, "I would suggest, Elise, that you incinerate those shoes." Liz, transfixed like Dahl by the visitors' revelations, nodded.

"It seems Aldiche," Ian Fleming went on, "has quite the reputation among the embassy staff, especially among the ladies. A Lothario. A reputation that Thorne's work has surely born out. It seems the Ambassador believes the killing was the result of a love affair gone bad, a jealous woman perhaps, of which Aldiche had many.

"For his part," the MI-6 man went on, "Mache has been anxious to cover up his role in assisting the late-night encounters between Aldiche and Liz. His story is he only saw the two of you for the first time that night, and that he objected to Liz coming into the embassy. He claims he intended to report this flouting of the security protocols the next day.

"He is the only other person in the embassy at nighttime, so there's no one else there to contradict his story. Obviously he wants the incident kept under wraps. Everyone there does."

"And that," interjected Donovan, "is just fine with us."

Wild Bill winked at Liz. "The Argentines *are* still puzzled at why the hound acted the why he did."

Liz smiled a bit.

Dahl looked worried. "But as for the coded…"

"…So far, we haven't identified," remarked Donovan, "anyone with whom Aldiche shared his knowledge, of the Japanese ciphers. We think he intended to soon meet with Axis agents with the proof, with the coded information. *After* he had obtained ironclad proof, of the kind Liz discovered that night at her apartment.

"Both Mr. Fleming and I are convinced his secret died with him."

"Thanks to you, Elise Thorne," added Fleming.

"Of course," he noted, "if our intel about the Japanese Navy goes cold, our suppositions might be wrong. Or our Nipponese friends might find out about the codebreaking in some other way. In either event, we'll find out sooner or later. Hopefully much later, until it's too late for them!'"

Lizzy thought of a colleague for whom she had grown rather fond.

"How is Cracker?" she queried.

Wild Bill's eyes twinkled. "He's doing all right: The doctors say he's out of danger. His heart is not strong, however. They want him to lose some weight. Perhaps by cutting back on that Southern fried food of his."

Liz grinned. But she remembered, with a shudder, the men who'd been stationed outside her home, obviously keeping a watch on her.

"What about the FBI?" she asked suddenly. "Surely they're upset about the fracas."

Wild Bill pursed his lips. "That, is a very good point. I did finally have that talk with Mr. Hoover. In his rather formal office. With him sitting on a chair propped up high over his desk, looking down at me.

"Mr. Hoover had been as hot as a fireplace poker about the, fracas, outside the embassy. And about us stepping on 'his turf.' Well, it is his turf," he noted wryly, "except when we have a pressing need, a need to step on his turf ourselves.

"During our conversation, I praised his service in the Great War, his domestic 'police work,' while mentioning obliquely my military service, my frontline service, in the trenches of France. I hoped that the comparison sunk in."

Fleming thought that Donovan was speaking too freely about Hoover, but remained silent.

Wild Bill waved a hand in the air for emphasis. "Then I lauded his crime-fighting organization as 'the best in the world,' and praised his anti-sabotage efforts, in breaking up the Duquesne spy ring, as a 'textbook case' for foiling Nazi agents.

"I got to the point," Donovan intoned. "I stressed how it was in the interest of both his FBI and my OCI to avoid a public spat. After noting that I had the full backing of his boss, the President." Wild Bill crossed his arms in a gesture of satisfaction.

"Mr. Hoover wasn't overjoyed. But he pledged to keep his whole organization quiet, about that street scuffle with our men. And he vaguely promised to cooperate with us, 'when it is feasible.'"

"And that," remarked Fleming, "is about a good a deal as we can get for now."

Donovan leaned toward Liz.

"I also made your role clear. That you're on our side. A vital asset. As if the embassy escapade hadn't made that clear.

"There'll be no more FBI men stationed outside your house."

Fleming loudly cleared his throat. Then Donovan said that they had an exceedingly busy schedule that day, and both men rose to leave.

As they went through the door to the waiting sedan, Liz and Dahl exchanged pleasantries. She was taken in again by the former pilot's easy charm and smashing good looks.

'Oh the hell with it,' she thought. 'How does that song go, 'The Lady Is a Tramp.' But I'm no 'lady'.'

So she asked Dahl what he was doing that evening.

"Would you like to have dinner, Roald? Perhaps to, compare notes?"

Dahl shot out his winning grin. "I would love to, Liz. But tonight, well, I'm previously engaged. I have a," and he stopped, having almost used that awfully informal American term, "a date."

"I have a dinner rendezvous with a prominent lady." His auburn eyes twinkled. "Though not as prominent as you, given your crucial labors of recent days."

"And who might that be?" asked Liz, with some jealousy and a surfeit of genuine curiosity.

Dah answered, "A woman named…" and he mentioned the wife of America's most powerful magazine publisher, Henry Luce of *Time* and *Life* magazines.

Liz understood. What better way to strengthen ties between Britain and the U.S. then though an affair with Mrs. Clare Booth Luce? It was well-known the Luces had an "open marriage."

"Well," Liz stated, "I'm sure she's a delightful, lady." She stood up from the sofa, and asked offhandedly, "Perhaps another time?"

"Absolutely!" came the instant response. And a dazzling look from his eyes.

EPILOGUE

High-Level Admiration

Some weeks later, Donovan briefly stopped by O St. to give Lizzy a special invitation.
Of course she couldn't refuse; it was more of an order than a request.

Two days later, Liz arrived at the security gate on the southwest side of the White House
complex. She had dressed properly for such an occasion, so she thought. But her red, polka-dot
belted dress drew a lot of attention to herself, as she approached the southwest end of the
government complex. On Pennsylvania Avenue, several of the servicemen she passed by
whistled in admiration.

Ahead of her loomed the massive, French Empire-style War, Navy, and State Department
Building. It still retained some of the offices that hadn't yet been moved to the new Pentagon, or
to the Navy and Munitions Barracks a few blocks south, which had so intrigued Aldiche. Two
M3 Scout Cars, their weird rollers attached to the front chassis to maneuver over ditches, were
parked at a side entrance. Three Army corporals and a sergeant were carrying sealed boxes into
the vehicles, for transport to the Pentagon.

Liz thought she saw an anti-aircraft gun on the building's roof, though there had been no threat
of an enemy air raid. A Secret Service agent checked her in, carefully examining her driver's
license and the passport she had brought along. He seemed to look at her longer than was
sufficient to verify her identity. Liz was herself unaccustomed to using her actual identity papers,
instead of the many phony IDs she employed.

She walked along a gravel path for 80 yards to a well-manicured lawn alongside a squat, light-
painted structure, about 60 feet across. At its entrance, a faultlessly dressed Marine Corps
sergeant, his left chest bedecked with ribbons and his shoes polished to a glare, checked her IDs
again. He was all-business, and didn't seem to appreciate her good looks. 'That's just as well,'
Liz smiled to herself. 'Marines remind me of my father, and it wouldn't do to have that kind of
gaze from one of the Corps!'

Stepping inside, she felt a wash of cold air from the air-conditioning. She was used to
Washington's subtropical clime, and didn't know yet whether she liked this innovation. It
seemed fake, like an enemy spy trying to pull one over on her. Once again, she had the
butterflies in her belly that she'd experience at the start of a spy operation. She had little idea of

what to say or how to act. This figured to be a very formal occasion, of the type where she felt ill at ease, because she'd have to restrain her naturally impetuous spirit.

A 32-year-old staffer in a lumpy brown suit—giving her that once-over again—took her down narrow corridors with crowded, noisy offices. Liz was struck at the jammed, ramshackle conditions, which contrasted with the airy elegance of the White House residence.

The aide brought her into a room without air-conditioning, and directed she sit down at the edge of a row of chairs. There was a pair of doors in the ancient, but freshly painted, wall in front of her. The wall, she noted nervously, had a marked curvature to it. "You'll be shown in soon," the aide stated, and withdrew.

Liz waited for 35 minutes. She fidgeted. She was uncomfortably warm, and wondered if the meeting had been canceled. There were certainly more important things going on in the world than meeting her. A major German offensive in the Crimea, for instance, and Japanese landings on a little-known island called Guadalcanal.

The door cracked open a bit, then swung wide. Another aide, also in a rumpled suit, in his mid-40s it seemed, appeared in the threshold. He stepped out and said, "Elise Amelia Thorne, I assume?"

Liz jumped up, and almost ran to the door. The aide stood aside and pointed her to a desk, Lincoln's desk. It was in front of a window at the other end of the ovoid room. The large bureau with the maple veneer was piled with books, binders of collectible stamps, official documents, and statuettes. Also framed photographs of five young men, most of them in uniform, the sons of the user of the desk.

Next to the desk, to Liz's right, was a Chesterfield sofa. A wan-looking man of about 50, dressed in a rumpled suit two sizes too big, was slouched across it. Liz recognized him from the newspapers and news reels, and from his comings and goings from the house near her own. He was Harry Hopkins, the President's advisor.

She walked up to stand on a brightly colored carpet emblazoned with the symbol of the United States. An eagle with brown wings clasped laurel leaves of peace in one claw, and arrows of war in the other.

The man behind the desk, 60 years of age and looking older than that but a little less worn than in recent newsreels, motioned for Liz to step forward and take a plush chair in front of the desk.

"Well, well," he said in the resonant, halting voice of an American aristocrat. "This must be the notorious Elise Thorne.

"Notorious, but not that famous, for we must keep her work secret from the public."

He held the holder of his lit Camel cigarette to his lips, blew out smoke, and winked at her from behind his pince-nez.

The man on the sofa, continuing to slouch, but with alert eyes, spoke up. "The President has been following your missions carefully. He wanted to personally thank you for your work—in Poland, with the Spanish admiral, and, and with the Argentine."

Liz held her hands together in silence. Normally witty and loquacious, she couldn't get her lips to move.

"Oh please relax, Elise," said the President. He pointed to a small settee next to her chair.

"Would you share a drink with us?" And Liz noticed the cocktail glass on the settee. And that Franklin Roosevelt was himself drinking a martini.

"I understand that you make a mean martini, and it is my hope that our kitchen staff approaches your own high standards."

Liz was able to smile. She reached for the glass.

"Mr., sir, Mr. President," she said. "It seems you know a lot about me."

Roosevelt flicked his cigarette holder. "We follow your work with the keenest interest."

The President placed the cigarette on a large ash tray. The smile vanished from the light-gray of his worn face, marked by large, dark circles around the eyes.

"In all seriousness," and he nodded toward the man on the couch, "Harry and I wanted to thank you in person and, I must say, to meet you. To meet the legend—one of our best, if not the best, 'intelligence operative'." He winked again. "That's a fancy way to say a spy."

Lizzy returned Roosevelt's words with a forced smile. She took a long sip from the cocktail glass. "I, I thank you, sir, Mr. President. I do not deserve such a compliment."

FDR shook his head vigorously. The thick flesh hanging from his neck jiggled.

"No, no. My dear, no false modesty!" He placed mottled hands on the big desk and leaned forward. He lowered his voice in a conspiratorial manner.

"I cannot say much. And things said during this gathering should not leave this room. But I can tell you that your work, from Poland to Dupont Circle, has greatly aided our efforts in the North Atlantic, and in the Mediterranean." He pointed to the model of a Great War destroyer on the desk. "As an old salt, I appreciate that more than most," said the former Acting Secretary of the Navy, and now Commander-in-Chief. He leaned back in his chair. "Because of you, the Mediterranean is now a British, and an American, lake. And the Pacific Ocean is becoming one. "Someday, though perhaps not for some time, the nation will learn of your endeavors."

As Liz drank the martini, Hopkins looked at his watch and rose suddenly from the couch. He winced, grabbing his stomach in pain. FDR glanced at him, and seemed to think of a subject unrelated to Thorne. Probably news from the Southwest Pacific. Or perhaps the terrible cancer from which his assistant suffered.

"Well my dear, our meeting must be brief, however cordial. Mr. Hopkins and I have some important, some other important, matters to attend to. After he has his doctor's appointment. So kindly finish your, well-deserved, drink, and bid us adieu."

Liz did so. She got up and walked quickly to the door, and felt lightheaded. And not so much from the martini, she knew. It was indeed a dizzying experience to meet the head of the vast war effort to which she had dedicated and risked her life.

The door opened before her, as if by magic. The older aide was there to shepherd her outside.

At the threshold, she heard that voice again, familiar to all Americans.

"One last thing, Miss Thorne. Or is it Mrs.?" Liz stopped and turned around.

"Those action reports of yours. They have been forwarded to me, by Mr. Donovan, and some others.

"I must say this: They make the best *bedtime* reading I've ever had."

As President Roosevelt flickered his cigarette holder, and smiled, Liz broke into a hearty laugh. She began to salute, then made an awkward bow, then walked grinning away from the Oval Office.

Outside in the springtime air, she became serious again.

And wondered what her next assignment would be.

www.ingramcontent.com/pod-product-compliance
Lightning Source LLC
Chambersburg PA
CBHW051636260626
47170CB00004B/1197